Eddy Shah started out as a writer but was side-tracked into various business enterprises. As the founder of a group of provincial newspapers, he rapidly became one of Britain's most successful entrepreneurs. He founded *Today*, Britain's first all-colour daily paper, but sold his interest in newspapers in order to return to writing. He was the first person to fly an executive jet into the USSR without a Russian navigator, and this novel draws on his extensive experience as a pilot. He has completed his second thriller, *The Lucy Ghosts*, and is at work on a third.

'The well-above average book of its kind. He has a good sense of dramatic pace. The story moves confidently between the melancholic emptiness of the countryside and the claustrophobia of Kremlin conspiracies . . . The action sequences lean heavily on Shah's own experiences as a pilot . . . He deserves being labelled a writer, not just a celebrity who has written a book.'
Marcel Berlins, Sunday Times

Author photograph by Jane Bown

D1136202

RING OF RED ROSES

Eddy Shah

CORGI BOOKS

RING OF RED ROSES
A CORGI BOOK 0 552 13771 5

Originally published in Great Britain by Doubleday,
a division of Transworld Publishers Ltd

PRINTING HISTORY
Doubleday edition published 1991
Corgi edition published 1992

This book was set in 10/11pt Times by
County Typesetters, Margate, Kent.

Corgi Books are published by Transworld Publishers Ltd,
61–63 Uxbridge Road, Ealing, London W5 5SA, in Australia
by Transworld Publishers (Australia) Pty Ltd, 15–23 Helles
Avenue, Moorebank, NSW 2170, and in New Zealand by
Transworld Publishers (NZ) Ltd, Cnr Moselle and
Waipareira Avenues, Henderson, Auckland.

Made and printed in Great Britain by
Cox & Wyman, Reading, Berks.

to 'J'

who has seen the best in me, and the worst,
and somehow managed to stay constant
and loving throughout it all.

To you and to the three young Shahs.

I love you.

'S'

1

BEFORE OUR TIME

Ekaterinberg
The Urals
Russia
16 July 1918

Yurovsky, the Siberian Jew, was late.

The small group of men waited for him in the evening shadows, by the four lonely trees in the Koptiaki Forest that were known as the Four Brothers. There were nearly twenty of them and they stayed hidden, not smoking or talking, not wanting the villagers to know of their meeting-place. It was the third time they had visited the location in the last two weeks. It had started to drizzle, and some of the men were more restless than normal. But nobody complained. In those days nobody dared complain. It was unwise to stand out from the herd.

One of the men heard someone approaching and signalled the others to watch out. They took cover, hunched low in the bracken, until they saw a tall wide-shouldered shape in the distance, hurrying down the slope towards them. As it got closer, they recognized their leader, Yankel Yurovsky. He came through the thin mist of rain and into the semi-shelter of the trees.

The others moved towards him. You could tell by their stance that they were afraid of him – a dangerous man who could turn on any one of them for no reason. None of them had known him before he arrived, a month earlier, to replace Avdeyev as commandant of Ekaterinberg. They didn't trust him anyway, once they had found out he was a Jew.

'Did any of the villagers see you?' he asked.

The men shook their heads, looking at each other, not wanting to be the one who had given the secret game away. Yurovsky knew at least one of them was lying.

'I saw villagers,' he went on. 'Two of them, looking in this direction. They knew something was up. I threatened them, sent them away, told them not to look back.' He paused. His grizzled eyes, hard black behind his wool-bearded face, searched each man in turn, looking for the fear that he knew was there. 'Tonight is the most important night of the revolution. I hope you're all up to the great task we have before us. If not, you'll answer to me. One by one. Now, let's check the mine.'

Yurovsky pushed through the men and led them towards the nearby deserted mine-shaft. It was a deep shaft, about seven feet across, that disappeared steeply into a black hole in the ground.

'Where is the benzine and the vitriol?' asked Yurovsky.

'Farther along, up the hill,' answered Voikov. He was one of only four Russians in the party, and a member of the local Ural Soviet. The rest were all Austro-Germans. 'It's still in the carts.'

'Unload it now. All of you help. Store it here and then bring the carts back to the house. We will need them. Five of you must remain behind to guard this place. Make sure no one comes here. Be back at the house in two hours.'

'Where is it to be done? Here?' asked one of the men.

'That's not your concern. Just do as you're told. Such decisions are not for the rank and file.'

With that, Yurovsky turned and left the men to their task. They stood there, uncertain and nervous.

'So it really is going to happen,' one of the men said to no one in particular.

'What did you expect? A game we were playing?' answered Voikov.

'No. *Talking about* – that's one thing. But to . . .' His voice trailed off into silence.

'I thought we were to do it here,' said the one who had spoken to Yurovsky, his tone angry. 'That's what we were told. It was to be here.'

'Afraid of missing the fun, eh?' jeered someone else.

'Watch your mouth. Or do you think you won't be involved if they do it there? Eh, is that it? Some chance. Wherever they do it, you'll be involved. Wherever. So they may as well do it here as anywhere else.'

'Enough. If the commander wants it done here, then he'll let us know. But mark my words: whether here or at the house, it will be done.' Voikov looked round at the others as he spoke. 'Anybody want to change his mind?' he asked threateningly.

The others looked at each other. Deep down they knew there was no other way.

One of them laughed. 'You can either face Yurovsky or do it. And I know which one I'd rather do.'

Some of the others joined in the laughter with him.

'Come on,' said Voikov, 'let's get started. It's going to be a long night.'

Although summer was settled in, some of the streams were still frozen over. Frost lay deep in the gullies and hollows of the countryside as Yurovsky rode back the fourteen miles towards Ekaterinberg and the house which they now called the House of Special Purpose.

It was a pretty house, graceful in its older design. Known locally as the House of Ipatyev, it sat on a slope that ran down towards the town. It was a house of history, for five years earlier, celebrating the tercentenary of their dynasty, Tsar Nicholas and Empress Alexandra had visited the Ipatyevsky Monastery nearby. It was here that the first Romanov, the young Mikhail, had accepted the throne to which the old Assemblies of the Land had elected him.

But Yurovsky was not a man of history or sentiment. His world was now, his purpose the future. Which is why he had been specially chosen to go to the House of Ipatyev, the house he himself had renamed the House of Special Purpose.

He climbed the hill towards the house, its appearance made sinister by the whitewashed windows on the lower floor that stopped outsiders from looking in. A high wooden palisade had also been built around the house. As he got closer, he realized that the outer guard still consisted of Russians. That made him angry, and he swore in frustration. They should have been replaced by Letts (Bolsheviks) before he got back. The uniformed guards watched him pass them and go into the yard. Pavel Medvedev was there, in front of a camp-fire with more of his Russian troops.

Yurovsky stopped short of the second group and dismounted, tying the horse to a post. 'I want a word with you,' he shouted to Medvedev.

As chief of the Russian troops, Medvedev was irritated by Yurovsky's manner. He was not accustomed to being treated like that, especially in front of his own soldiers. But he knew that the Jew was in charge. He finished talking to one of his men, but it was a weak act of defiance. He turned and went over to Yurovsky.

'Why are your guards still here?'

'I kept them on in case there was a change of plan.'

'No change. The die is cast. Where are the Letts?'

'At the back of the house.'

'And the lorry?'

'Also there.'

'Change the guard now. Order your men into Ekaterinberg. And make them understand that no soldier is to return here again. And bring the twelve Nagan revolvers which your soldiers have.'

Medvedev didn't answer; he stared unbelievingly at Yurovsky.

'Well?' Yurovsky's eyes derided the old soldier. He knew the man had no choice. 'Do it.'

Medvedev finally realized that now there could be no reprieve.

'I'll take my men into the town.'

'No. You will stay here and take charge of the Letts. You must do it with us.'

'No!' The old man's cry startled the nearby soldiers at the camp-fire. He moved closer to Yurovsky, so as not to be heard. 'I cannot.'

'Then, you can join them and share the same fate. Or does your passion not run that deep?' Yurovsky walked away from Medvedev, speaking loudly so that the soldiers heard and would know who was really in charge. 'It is all over now. You're too old to fight a new battle. Do as I tell you. Change the guards.'

And Yurovsky left the old man with his broken past and went into the cellars where the cook Sednev waited for him.

Beside the cellars there was a half-basement. Three chairs were placed side by side in the middle of this room.

'Why are the chairs here?'

'They asked for them.' Sednev shrugged as he spoke. 'I saw no harm. The boy is very ill, and his father will carry him down.'

Yurovsky nodded. 'You told them they were to be moved to another house? A safe house.'

11

'I did. They have packed and know that they will be transported in the middle of the night. Shall I feed them?'

'Very little. Food is still short, and I don't want any wasted. When you've fed them, bring them down here. By then my men will be back. Inform me when they are all here.'

Yurovsky left the half-basement and walked back into the yard. He saw that the guard was already changed. The Letts now stood around the camp-fire and watched the Russians gather up their belongings ready to leave the yard.

As Yurovsky turned back towards the house, he saw the familiar bearded face looking over the balcony at him, brightly lit by the roaring fire in the yard below him. The man stood with his fourteen-year-old son, a weak-looking boy. The father had his arm protectively around the boy's shoulders. From behind them, from the dimly lit room, Yurovsky heard the chatter of young girls, heard one of them start to sing a song.

> Ring-a-ring o'.roses,
> A pocket full of posies,
> A-tishoo! A-tishoo!
> We all fall down.

He recognized the old English nursery rhyme. It was one they had sung many times before. He remembered one of the girls telling him that their mother had learnt it in England when she had visited their great-grandmother, Victoria. He wondered if they knew what it meant, that it was sung by children during the Black Death. He shook his head; they didn't know how the English had turned against them, ignored them in their moment of peril. It was too late now; no one could help them since the telegram from Moscow had arrived.

Yurovsky turned away and went into the house.

In silence, the man and boy on the balcony watched the troops march down into the town.

It was already late evening, and the Russian summer night was chilly and damp. The boy coughed and his father hurriedly took him back into the warmth and song of the House of Special Purpose.

The Letts at the outer gate looked up as they heard the clatter of the carts on the rutted and hard-frozen road. They took their pistols and rifles and spread out. It was their instinct to be watchful. After all, there were still troops who felt loyalty to the monarchy.

But it was only the men returning from the mine. Voikov hailed them from the road, and some of the guards waved back.

Medvedev came out from the cellars and up to Yurovsky at the camp-fire.

'They're down there,' he reported to Yurovsky. 'I told them that we would be moving very soon, that there was unrest in the town and it was for their security. The family is now waiting there.'

'They made no comment?'

'Nothing. They suspect nothing.'

Yurovsky turned away from the old man and watched Voikov lead the men and carts through the gate towards the camp-fire. The outer guards followed the men into the courtyard. No one spoke, no sound, just the flat clatter of the cart-wheels against the deadened night.

Voikov stopped in front of Yurovsky.

'Everything is ready at the mine.'

All eyes were on the big Jew. They knew the momentous time had arrived. History was theirs to write.

Yurovsky turned and walked into the cellars. Medvedev, Voikov and five of the men followed him into the dimly lit half-basement.

As the small band entered the house, the lorry which

was parked in the courtyard was started. The driver was under instructions to keep the engine running while the men were in the cellars. Yurovsky did not want those outside the house and courtyards to know what was to take place.

The driver gunned the engine loudly.

In the half-basement, the father sat on one of the chairs. His wife sat to his right, his sickly son on his left. The imperial family, including the young princesses and some retainers, stood behind them in what was to become a deadly tableau. As the door opened, the father put his arm protectively around the coughing boy.

'It will soon be time to move to our new home,' the father told his family. Behind him, his youngest daughter, Anastasia, giggled nervously, her hands flying dexterously over the two wooden needles that knitted yet another shawl. Anastasia always knitted shawls and scarves. It was her passion, her pleasure.

Yurovsky entered with his small band. Medvedev could not look at the father and stared firmly at the little window at the side of the room.

When the door was closed, Yurovsky took a folded piece of paper from his inner pocket and held it up to read from it.

'There are rumours that the town may be taken by counter-revolutionary troops who are on their way here to rescue you. Therefore, to avoid further bloodshed between our peoples, and in accordance with the order of the Soviet of Ekaterinberg, we are here to carry out the sentence passed on you and your family. For the crime of treason against the Russian people you are sentenced to death. We are here to execute that sentence.'

The father half-rose in an expression of surprise. He started to speak.

Yurovsky carried two Nagan pistols. He took them out and shot Tsar Nicholas at point-blank range in the head. He then turned and shot the boy Alexis. The child was not killed, and cried out in pain. Yurovsky pumped the rest of the bullets from both guns into the boy.

The empress and her daughters fell to the ground, their arms up to shield themselves from what was to come. As Yurovsky stepped back, the rest opened fire with revolvers and rifles on the defenceless family. The fusillade of shots tore into the frail bodies. With the exception of Anastasia, who lay wounded under her mother, they were all killed. One of the men then bayoneted her several times.

A faithful doctor, a manservant and a maid were also despatched by the assassins. Afterwards, during the inquiry, Medvedev was to describe the flowing blood as 'thick, like liver'.

When the shots were over, and death's silence filled the basement, only the children's spaniel, Jimmy, was left alive. He whined in a corner, shaking in a pool of his own urine. One of the men went over and smashed the little dog's head with the butt of his rifle.

Yurovsky and Voikov then cleared the room of the assassins. They were told to wait outside. Yurovsky and Voikov, after checking that the family and their attendants were dead, then dragged each body, now shrouded in bedsheets, out of the room and into the narrow corridor. The assassins were then instructed to carry the shrouded bodies out of the building.

Outside, in the courtyard, the lorry engine raced loudly as the driver kept his foot on the accelerator. Those who heard the shots, muffled, but terrible in their import, looked unbelievingly at one another. For some of them, part of the soul of Mother Russia was being brutally murdered in that small bloody cellar. For others it was the birth of a new age, of a new country, of a new freedom.

Yurovsky and his men dragged the bodies into the courtyard and threw them on to the truck.

They drove to the mine where they piled the bodies into a pyre and set fire to them with the benzine. When the charred remains had cooled, they poured the vitriol over the family and then threw the mutilated bodies down the disused mine-shaft.

Some of the men burnt their hands with the acid vitriol. They washed in standing pools of water, but the burns deepened. Yurovsky cursed them for their carelessness.

'Why didn't we just bury them in a deep hole?' one of the men grumbled.

'And let the wolves or the village dogs dig up the bones? Don't be stupid. The world must never know what happened here,' Yurovsky replied.

The men then covered up the mine-entrance and returned to the house. Yurovsky waited behind and spent the night in front of the now hidden shaft-opening.

When he saw the last of the men leave, only then did he let his true emotions show. His sinister face softened, was covered by tears. He sobbed in the dark, afraid of what he had done.

He stayed the night, because his grandmother had taught him that no one should spend his first night of death alone. It was the Jewish way, and Yankel Yurovsky waited till the first rays of early-morning light streaked the sky before returning to Ekaterinberg to make his final report on the incident.

Two days later the Central Executive Committee in Moscow met to discuss a report by the new Commissar of Health, Semashko. It was a detailed study and would occupy the Committee for the rest of the sitting. There were reports of typhoid in Omsk and Petrograd. The situation needed dealing with before it became a major crisis.

The six-year-old boy, Grigory, sat on his father's lap. Mikhail Marshka was a member of the Central Executive and, since his wife Anna's death two years earlier, was committed to bringing up his son in as responsible a manner as he saw fit. The boy went everywhere with him. In this way, Mikhail believed that Grigory would absorb all that passed around him so that one day he could follow in his father's steps and play an important role in the development of Mother Russia.

The boy drew on a sheet of paper his father had given him to play with. The boy leant forward and kept his head down as he concentrated on his task.

Semashko's voice droned on, reading from the report. Suddenly there was a buzz in the large hall, and the boy looked up.

A man had entered from a side-door and now walked towards the main rostrum. All eyes were on him, this small man with a purposeful stride. In the background Semashko's voice floated into silence.

Mikhail leant over to his son and whispered in his ear.

'It's Lenin.'

Grigory watched Vladimir Ilyich Lenin mount the rostrum and stand alongside Semashko. Without understanding, he felt the man's power reach every corner of the room, touch every person who looked on.

'I am sorry to interrupt, Comrade Semashko,' said Lenin, 'but I have to make an important announcement to the Committee.'

Semashko moved away and returned to his seat behind the speaker's rostrum.

Lenin looked round the packed room. He waited, as others, who had not been present, scurried in and back to their places. When it was quiet, when the last door was closed, he spoke. It was a soft voice, but one that could be heard in the farthest part of the room as though the man was sitting next to you.

'I have just received a communication from our comrades in Ekaterinberg. They inform me that the Soviet of their town passed a sentence of death on Tsar Nicholas. They inform us that the order of sentence was

17

executed last night.' He waited as the words took hold. Nobody looked away from him; for many it was expected. 'The rest of the family have been removed to a safe place. As we get more information we will let you know.' He turned to Semashko. 'Comrade, you may continue.'

The boy watched Lenin leave the hall. Although he didn't fully understand the words, he knew when his father's body had stiffened as Lenin spoke that something was wrong.

Mikhail put his arms around his son as Semashko started to speak again. He squeezed him and held him close. Grigory felt his father's tears on the back of his neck.

'Now Mother Russia is broken,' he heard his father whisper. 'There was no need. A democracy and a monarchy. We needed both. From now there can only be more death before it can get better. There was no need.'

At the back of the hall a young Georgian, one of the leaders of the revolution, stood up to ask a question of Semashko.

'Yes, Comrade Stalin,' replied Semashko.

Sixteen days later there was another official announcement. The Soviet government admitted that the whole family had been killed in the Urals. This time there was some satisfaction with the statement. Nevertheless, an inquiry was held into the cause and effect of the deaths.

It was two years before the acid-burnt corpses were discovered. They were only positively identified when the carcass of the little spaniel, Jimmy, was found with the rest of the family in that deepened and dark mineshaft. Further examination revealed the tsar's belt-buckle, a portable frame containing the empress's picture (which the tsar always carried on him), and over a hundred other small articles which were traced as buckles or ear-rings or other personal belongings of the tsarevich or his sisters.

In September 1919 five Socialist Revolutionaries who were connected with the murders were executed for their part in it. Pavel Medvedev, a key witness in the inquiry, died a month later, in Ekaterinberg, of exanthematic typhus. He claimed to have been present but denied shooting at the family. Voikov, the chief of the Ural Soviet, went on to become ambassador to Poland, where he was eventually assassinated by revolutionaries.

Yurovsky, the watchmaker turned High Executioner, after remaining as Commissar for Ekaterinberg, was eventually prejudicially treated as a Jew and moved to Tobolsk, where he married and had one daughter.

In that time, and for many years after, the boy Grigory was never allowed to forget what Russia had been, where it was going, and how tortuous and blood-stained that path would become.

And, whenever his passion dimmed or he was diverted from the dream that was his father's, Mikhail Marshka was never slow to remind the boy Grigory that one day Mother Russia would be whole again.

2

AUTUMN DAYS

England
Summer
14 July, early 1990s
3.30 p.m.

Mark Duncan waited on the Gloucestershire hill by the red Wessex helicopter. He watched the oncoming dark clouds to the west, their cargo of rain a hazard to his journey home. A soft rumble of thunder reverberated far away in the billowing darkness.

Two hundred yards away, below him, Victor Oldenburg watched his wife Anna dancing in a circle with their two daughters, holding hands as they circled. Victor held the third, Alex, an eight-month-old son, in his arms.

> Ring-a-ring o' roses,
> A pocket full of posies,
> A-tishoo! A-tishoo!
> We all fall down.

Their singing carried up on the wind to Duncan, a distant chant of remembered childhood. He saw the children all fall down and collapse into shrieks of laughter and playfulness as their parents applauded them. Duncan smiled and remembered when he and Victor had flown into Port Stanley during the Falklands campaign. The children had been singing the same song when they had landed near the local school. He wondered if Victor remembered.

At thirty-eight, Duncan was a Falklands veteran who had gone on to be recruited into the SAS. Now, as a helicopter scout pilot with the Hereford unit and promoted to captain, Duncan had spent the last two years as a member of the 14th INT, the secretive intelligence arm of the SAS. Unmarried, a loner by instinct and profession, he often flew the red Wessex helicopters which the British royal family used when they visited Northern Ireland. The rule was that an active SAS pilot operated the trip over what was, in truth, a war zone. With a royal trip imminent, Duncan was taking a refresher course on the Wessex.

The coming trip was with one of the British royal princes, the same young officer with whom they had shared danger in the Falklands. Because of their special relationship, and because Victor was an officer on the royal staff, they had managed to talk the ops officer into letting them use the Wessex on this 'jolly'.

He saw Victor turn and wave, then start running up the hill towards him, the child Alex carried gently under his arm. Behind him, Anna and the girls were gathering up the remains of the picnic that they had all shared on that brilliant English summer day.

'Why aren't you helping them?' he shouted down the hill to Victor.

'Women's work. Not for the likes of us.'

Duncan laughed and waited for his friend to reach him. He shook his head at Victor's breathlessness, at his sweat and red cheeks.

'Soft life's getting to you.'

'The good life. The only way to live. Here, do something useful and hold your godson.' Victor held out the child, and Duncan took him, clumsy yet sure in his grasp.

'You always were a lazy sod,' he replied, his eyes fixed on the child that he now held. 'When you're older, Alex, I'll tell you about your father, the real Victor Oldenburg.'

'He'd enjoy that. Listening to you and your memories in some old soldier's home. I can just picture you in a Chelsea pensioner's uniform.'

'Dammit!'

'What?'

'He's wet himself.' Duncan held the child away from him as Victor burst out laughing. 'Very funny. Your usual good timing, you lucky bastard. Always pass the problem on before it dumps on you.'

'Stop moaning,' Victor replied. 'It's just like water at that age. It'll evaporate in minutes in this heat.' He reached forward to take the child, but Duncan stepped back.

'Keep your hands off my godson.'

'You going to change the nappy, too?'

'Let's not get carried away,' answered Duncan, handing the child over to his friend.

Victor put Alex on the floor of the helicopter and took a fresh paper nappy from the box at the back. Duncan leant against the aircraft fuselage and watched him expertly change the baby.

'Tell me, if he'd been a daughter, would you have tried again?'

'Probably.'

'I never asked you before. Why this desperate need for a son?'

Victor stood up, his task now complete. He turned to Duncan, looked into his friend's face for a long moment before answering.

'No family should die out, Mark. I know you've never

22

cared about your lot, that you've always gone your own way. But it's important that things continue, that the name goes forward.'

'Why?'

'Because that's how it is. Tradition, values, honouring your parents, honouring their parents, remembering the past, all that got you where you are today. All those generations of hardship, suffering, happiness, the whole business of living. Kill the line and you kill all that they went through.'

'But they went through that to survive, not to be remembered by someone a hundred years on.'

'No. Believe that and you don't believe in family. Family is life, Mark.' He put his arm around Duncan's shoulders and hugged his friend; they had always been as close as brothers, ever since the first days at school when Duncan had fought off the bullies he had seen picking on the young Victor.

'You're too long in the field, Mark,' Victor said, stepping away from Duncan. 'What you do, what happened to us in the Falklands, that isn't reality. It's a dark side that most of us don't even know exists. We read about it in the papers, we even see it on television. But it's not real, Mark. It's not normal.'

'Still got to be done. Somebody's got to take on the bastards.' It was a defensive statement. Duncan surprised himself with the naïvety and ferocity of his reply.

'Why you?'

'It's all I know.'

'That's a shame. There's more to life than just hiding in some Irish bog trying to find a fucking terrorist. It's time you got out. Leave it to the younger ones. Let someone else have a bash.'

'And what would I do? I don't know anything, Victor. Except how to fly aircraft – and hide in an Irish bog.'

'Did I hear a light-hearted quip there? Well, flush my mouth.'

23

They both laughed at the pun as the first raindrops started to fall.

'I have to say' – Victor was suddenly serious, his thoughts triggered by Duncan's commitment – 'there are times when . . .' His words trailed off into silence.

'Times when what?'

'When one looks beyond . . . where one is. Times when the meaning should be more obvious, purpose more defined. It's all right for Anna. Kids, they're part of most women's existence. Men need more.'

'The services are the only way. Unless you want to be a mercenary, or do something crooked. Can't see you robbing banks.'

'You're wrong. There's much more than that. You've been in the Army too long; you can only think in terms of a uniform, of something physical. That is the Army. But there're different responsibilities, different ways of getting that excitement.'

'Like what?'

'Like . . . You're my dearest friend, Mark. You're family to us, to Anna and me.' Victor paused, suddenly leant forward, as if to confide to Duncan. 'It's time for change. Things are happening, events which will change all our—'

'Give us a hand, you lazy devils,' Anna shouted from the bottom of the hill, breaking the moment. She and the girls came towards the helicopter with the packed debris of the picnic lunch.

'You wind her up,' said Victor, stepping away from Duncan. 'I'll help them.'

Duncan climbed into the helicopter and flicked on the fuel-cock. He pressed the starter button, and the rotor started to turn slowly. As he waited for the first of two Rolls-Royce Gnome engines to build up speed he wondered what it was that Victor was about to tell him. As he thought, he instinctively switched on the avionics master switch and pressed the transmit button on the handle.

24

'Staverton, this is Kittyhawk Five.' He spoke into the hand-mike, using the call-sign that was accorded all royal flights.

'Kittyhawk Five, Staverton Tower,' came the crackled answer. They'd been waiting for him. It wasn't every day they spoke to a royal flight. Duncan grinned; he wasn't going to spoil their fun by telling the controllers it wasn't a true royal trip.

'Kittyhawk Five is ready for return to London. We hope to lift off within the next three minutes.'

'Roger. London Military will handle the flight. Their frequency is one thirty-four, decimal six two. Local QNH is niner niner six.'

'Niner niner six. Ready to copy the local and *en route* weather if you've got it.'

'Rog,' came the reply.

As Duncan copied the latest weather report on to his lap-pad, Victor and the rest of the family reached the helicopter. Victor helped them all into the Wessex, then handed the baby to Anna before climbing in and closing the door.

The turbine temperature-gauges hit their green marks, and Duncan turned up the throttle. Overhead the rotors picked up speed, and the aircraft started to shake, impatient to leave the ground.

'Have we got our clearance?' said Victor, climbing into the co-pilot's seat and strapping himself in.

'Yes. We'll have to keep it below one thousand feet. Low cloud all the way from here to London with the base between eight hundred and one thousand. We've been purpled between eight hundred and fifteen hundred feet.' Duncan was referring to the purple airways which were allocated to royal flights and kept other aircraft clear. Duncan turned to Oldenburg. 'OK?'

The co-pilot nodded his head. 'Weather's quite nasty in London. Low cloud, a bit of rain and some lightning thrown in for good measure.'

'Didn't worry you in the Falklands,' Duncan retorted good-humouredly.

'We were a lot younger then.'

'Age is a state of mind. Isn't that what they say?' Before Victor could answer, Duncan triggered the microphone switch with his finger. 'Staverton, Kittyhawk Five lifting off.'

'Roger. No known conflicting traffic. Have a nice trip home, sir.' The air-traffic controller thought he was speaking to the prince, who often piloted the helicopter himself. Duncan smiled as he pictured the scene at home later on: 'Guess who I spoke to today.'

Duncan pulled the collective lever up, and the Wessex lifted from the ground, its harsh downblast from the powerful turbine-driven rotor-blades flattening the Gloucestershire grass below it.

'Thank you, Staverton. Calling London Military on one thirty-four, decimal six two.'

As Victor tuned the radio to its new frequency, Duncan monitored the instruments. He looked across at his flying partner who was now talking to the military controllers on the new frequency.

The Wessex climbed to eight hundred feet and sat just under the bulbous cloud-layer as it flew eastwards, towards London.

The military controller was waiting for them; a young corporal sat next to a civilian controller over the radar screen at West Drayton, near Heathrow.

As soon as he was contacted by the Wessex, he passed his message on. It was a priority signal, and he was impatient to relieve himself of his responsibility.

'Kittyhawk Five, this is London Military. We have a message for one of your passengers, Mr Oldenburg.'

'Go ahead, London,' replied Duncan, looking across at Victor. 'Mr Oldenburg is listening out.'

'Mr Oldenburg is to return immediately to Head Office. He is to take his passengers with him.'

'Wilco,' replied Duncan. 'Head Office' was the code used for Buckingham Palace. 'Have you my clearance?'

'Yes, sir. You're cleared direct from your present position to destination. Not above four thousand feet on the London QNH, niner niner eight.'

'Roger.' Duncan knew he wouldn't climb to that altitude in the rough weather ahead. 'Hold her on course while I sort out the route,' he said to Victor.

He reached in the back and took out the London-area half-million-scale map. Within a minute he had calculated the change in track.

'Heading of due east will get us there,' he said.

'Can you take it alone?' Victor asked suddenly.

'I have control,' replied Duncan, taking the control-yoke in his right hand.

He was surprised. Since they had learnt to fly together at Portsmouth, he had never known his friend refuse the opportunity of hand-flying the aircraft. Even at the height of the Falklands campaign, when the only sleep you got was of the permanent kind, Victor Oldenburg was always one of the first to fly. He was even more surprised when Victor unclasped his seatbelt and climbed into the rear, seating himself next to his wife.

As the Wessex settled into its cruise speed of ninety knots, Duncan turned and looked at his two friends in the back. They were huddled together, conspiratorial in their manner as Victor spoke intently, with Anna occasionally nodding in agreement. Duncan was disconcerted; this was the first time in all their years together he had felt deliberately isolated from a conversation.

But, as well as being a friend, Duncan was also a serving officer in the SAS. His was not to question, but to obey.

He concentrated on his duties, checked his instruments as he hand-flew the helicopter. The pulsating *woosh-woosh* of the rotors swinging over his head rattled and twisted in the turbulent weather as the helicopter slowly progressed towards London. Hand-flying helped Duncan concentrate his attention on the flight home and to safety away from the scud of low passing clouds. London was over an hour away, and the trip would need all his experience and expertise.

In the back, the couple continued the conversation, never looking up, never being distracted from their secret intent. Their daughters giggled nervously in the turbulent conditions, their anxious faces looking out at the ground slowly passing by underneath.

Alex, the baby, strapped in tightly in the seat next to Anna Oldenburg, slept peacefully through all that went on around him.

Forty miles up, a Soviet satellite tracked the movement of the helicopter. It transmitted the picture to a relay station in the Ural Mountains and then, via a landline, to a technician's monitor in Moscow. The technician was one of a small and secret team who had been monitoring the prince's movements for three months. He reached for a phone to pass his report on.

The Kremlin
Moscow
14 July
4 p.m.

The man the report was intended for looked out of his window in the Kremlin some fifteen hundred miles to the east of London.

The president of the Soviet Socialist Republics, that which is more commonly referred to as Russia, looked down on the Taman guard changing their watch, down from his office on the fourth floor of the Council of Ministers. It was an exciting but intimidating spectacle, dramatized by the harsh crunch of the soldiers' boots that marched, in slow step, in a deadly unison. He smiled to himself, imagining those same soldiers marching him under guard towards prison, obscurity and even death in front of a firing squad.

He knew that that was the price he would pay if his plans were to falter now.

In the short time since he had come to power he had trodden a razor-sharp line. The days after Mikhail Gorbachev, the days when all the various political factions had bargained and jostled for power, had left him as the one man who was acceptable to all parties. They saw he was the safe choice, the man who could be counted on to do nothing but keep the peace.

But to him it was different. He knew it was his destiny and duty to continue the policies which were changing the face of the Soviet Union. He knew there were those of the old school who wanted him to fail – to fail in such a manner that the public humiliation and ridicule he would face would ensure that the old ways would return.

He remembered the early days of 'the new revolution', those first faltering steps of *perestroika* which had caught the imagination of the people. He remembered the flames of excitement of those days, his own belief in the future as he listened to Gorbachev in the Praesidium in 1985. But that was before the people realized that *perestroika* and the new order meant only a harder struggle and longer queues before Mother Russia could move into the modern era.

Then there had been the nationalistic struggles of the Balkan States, the civil war in Armenia and Azerbaijan, the break for freedom by the Eastern Bloc countries, the loss of power by the communists as new democratic parties insisted on having a say in running their country. The political map of Europe was redrawn; communism lay like a dying ember.

And he became president, elected to fill the gap when no one knew what to do, where to go. He was the popular choice, the man from nowhere whom the people trusted and no party feared.

He was the safe bet.

Now he had to do something to show that he was a great leader. They looked to him to shorten the queues and fill their shopping-bags. And the politicians waited for him to fail, waited to take over the mantle which they had put over his shoulders.

Each day the papers were full of the latest strikes, of rising crime, of drug abuse and kidnappings, of religious persecution and outbreaks of nationalistic fervour. Even the acceptance of separatist governments and devolution from Moscow had done little to slow down the chaos that the Soviet Union seemed to be sliding into.

It was time for radical action. Time for the new order to be anchored into the future, the past finally swept away.

He shuddered as he felt the cold of fear run through him. But it was not fear for himself, but for his Mother Russia. If he had feared for himself, he would never have started on the course he had now taken.

The door opened as Danilov, his private secretary, came in. The president moved away from the window.

'The helicopter is approaching London,' Danilov reported.

'Nothing else?'

'Nothing,' replied his assistant. 'The Secretary for Industry would like to speak to you.'

'How important?'

'A minor problem.'

'I don't want to speak to anyone. Not until I have heard from London.'

'Yes sir.'

Danilov withdrew from the room as his superior returned to his desk. He looked at the folder marked 'Confidential' in front of him. He leant forward and took out the contents, a thick sheaf of typewritten papers.

30

It was a private report which had been prepared exclusively for him. Although it had been completed some two months earlier, he had reread the dossier many times. He leafed through the pages, then turned to the final section. He started to read the conclusion of the document once again.

CONCLUSION
The New Age is now in danger of failing.

In the last ten years, the movement to liberalism and freedom for the individual, which was first welcomed by the people, is now seen by many as a divisive element which has led to revolution and bloodshed between the peoples of the USSR.

The prime reason for this discord is the speed at which events have moved. After seventy years of repression and state control, those who want freedom still do not yet know how to handle it. There is now a real danger that if change continues at its present pace, then the economic and social fallout will be so great that Russia, as well as the other republics which constitute the new Soviet State, will be in no position to go forward into the next century. This breakdown of the social and economic structure will result in a collapse of agricultural supplies, industrial output, military power and political direction. In truth, Russia will become either a secondary world power (after the United States, Japan and the European Community) or once again find itself in the iron grip of a leader who will follow the same policies as those used by Stalin.

To pursue *perestroika* and the New Age under its existing structure can only lead to such a situation.

The main causes of concern have been spelt out in detail earlier in this document.

The Russian people are committed to wiping out the memories and records of the last seventy years.

There have even been moves to exhume the bodies of the last Tsar and his family. Any such action could only lead to a revival of a monarchist movement, where the bodies of the royal family would be a symbol for a new era. There are many 'pretenders' of Russian royal descent who would lay claim to the throne. The legal actions subsequently unleashed with regard to property and land would be calamitous.

All this points to a rejection of republican values. The State needs reunification with the people. Since the demise of communism, there is no bridge to unite the proletariat and the government.

He smiled at the writer's instinctive link with the past. There were no proletariat now, only people. He read on.

With all this, and a struggling economy as we find our way in a new world, the majority of the republics want to see your policies work. But they, because of the last seventy years, still don't know how to take responsibility for their own future. They still expect the State to have all the answers, to look after them from the cradle to the grave. The Yeltsin factor has worn thin, people need results, not just words of encouragement.

The danger is in the fact that some factions want change immediately, others want to slow it down. If we are not careful, then we could face the same situation as China, and end up with no alternative but to send in the guns and the troops. The consequences for us, in our trade and relationship with the rest of the world would be catastrophic, as has happened to China. Only this time it would not be a failed, half-hearted coup as in 1991, but a more determined effort with the people's support. A return to 'cold war' hostilities, which would be inevitable, could only lead to more rearmament and possible global aggression.

It took the Falklands campaign to unite Britain under Margaret Thatcher. The 1991 coup helped us unite behind Gorbachev and Yeltsin. After the shame of Vietnam, it was the Iranian hostages who helped make America a country with one common cause again. Afghanistan and the demise of communism helped destroy Soviet unity.

We now need our 'Falklands' factor.

Mihail Gorbachev said that the Soviet republics have a single destiny. Events are starting to disprove this. If you cannot unite them in that single destiny, then all that has been fought for, all those millions who died under Beria during the Stalin purges, all the pain of the revolution and beyond, will have been nothing more than wasted breath, a passing sigh in our great history.

We look to you, comrade, for our destiny. We look to you to give us that which will finally unite us as one great nation. It is time to wipe the slate clean, to atone for the last seventy years. This report is simply to inform you that time is running out.

Outside Moscow
14 July
4.15 p.m.

The old man in the wheelchair put down the report that he had been reading. 'We look to you, comrade, for our destiny. We look to you to give us that which will finally unite us as one great nation. It is time to wipe the slate clean, to atone for the last seventy years. This report is simply to inform you that time is running out.'

He smiled. The problem with confidential reports was that they were printed on paper. Once something was

33

written down, it could become anyone's property. The only confidence was one that couldn't be shared, one that stayed locked up in your own mind. Even then, with torture and other methods, even then there were ways of unlocking and sharing secrets.

He put the report down and rang the small handbell he always kept close to him.

As he wheeled himself towards the door, it opened and a manservant appeared.

'Bring the car to the front. I need to go to KGB headquarters. And tell General Vashinov to meet me there.'

'Yes, comrade.'

The manservant withdrew, and the old man wheeled himself through the open door and into the hall. By the time he had reached the front door, another servant had come through and draped a coat over his shoulders. He then handed the old man his scarf and hat, and placed a rug over his legs.

The servant opened the door and pushed the man in the wheelchair out of the door, under the porch.

The black official Zil limousine was already there, the chauffeur coming round the bonnet to open the rear door and help his passenger in. The old man smiled to himself. In all the years since he had been crippled, he had never once got to the porch without the Zil being ready. It was like a game between him and his staff – a game he would never win.

They helped him into the car. A space had been designed in the rear where the wheelchair fitted. Once, a long time ago, he had faced the ignominy and shame of being carried to a Politburo session by two hefty guards. He had felt like a sack of potatoes, useless and dead. He had remembered the look of pity from the others in the meeting. And then he'd been carried back to his wheelchair from the central committee room. Since that day he had made sure that he never left his wheelchair in public. His staff ensured that that would never happen; it

34

was their one objective. And, with his position of power, it was not a responsibility they took lightly.

The Zil pulled away from the dacha and sped into the centre of Moscow, along the central lane which is reserved for official cars only.

The old man watched the passing world through the darkened windows of the car. Traffic was heavy as commuters returned home. The new society wanted cars, and the roads were not built for the sharp increase in traffic that had resulted. There were traffic jams on most corners. The consumer society was taking off and could be seen in the increase of Ladas, Skodas and Moskviches that scuttled round. Even Japanese cars were being imported now. And the Russians preferred them to their own home-built cars. Just as the Americans and Europeans had done.

As they approached the centre of Moscow he saw the queues forming outside the latest McDonald's hamburger restaurant. Some things never change; always the queues. Was that the real legacy of the revolution?

And Grigory Marshka remembered his father. Would he have been proud of his Russia now? Maybe it wasn't religion that was the opium of the masses, but a Big Mac and a chocolate milkshake. Was this, then, where the revolution was to end, in an endless queue in front of a McDonald's restaurant?

He shut his eyes and thought of his father, drew strength from his memory.

He would need all that strength. For now it started. The dream the father had given the six-year-old boy was about to become a reality.

Duncan brought the red Wessex over The Quadriga on Constitution Arch and on towards the palace gardens. The wind had built up, and it was turbulent.

He kept his altitude high until he was over the statue of Queen Boadicea before starting his descent. Victor had rejoined him in the cockpit: the flight over the capital legally required two pilots. Duncan completed a near-faultless landing in the grounds of the palace.

'Nice one,' Victor told the pilot.

'Got to be, with you watching.'

'Thanks for today. When're you going back?'

'Saturday.'

'Anything special?' Victor was concerned for his friend.

'Not really,' he lied. He had learnt that morning that he was returning to Northern Ireland for another tour of undercover duties.

'See you when you're back. And take care.'

The two men looked at each other, a closeness between them that only the heat of battle and shared danger could bring.

'Is everything all right with you?' asked Duncan.

He saw the sudden turmoil in Victor's eyes, saw the loneliness and glimpse of fear. Then he saw his friend steel himself.

'If you need anything . . .'

'You've always been there. I know that, Mark. Thank you.'

The door was opened and the family got out, the girls chattering excitedly amongst themselves.

'Say goodbye to Uncle Mark,' said Anna, admonishing her excited brood.

After the farewells, after Victor had unstrapped Alex

36

and carried him out after the children, Anna leant forward and kissed Duncan on the cheek.

'Thank you for a most lovely day,' she said. 'It's one we'll remember for a long time. Goodbye, darling Mark.'

He returned the kiss before replying: 'Is everything all right?'

She nodded. 'We'll be together again soon. We'll need your friendship and your love.'

After she had left the Wessex, Duncan saw an equerry approach Victor and talk to him. He heard the words 'The family is waiting, sir. The prime minister is expecting you to call by five o'clock.'

Victor nodded and walked away from the helicopter. He turned, once clear of the downwash, and waved goodbye to Duncan. Then he was gone towards the palace, and Duncan lifted the Wessex from the ground and took off into the dark of wet weather that brooded heavily over London and the Home Counties.

High above, the satellite camera continued to click away, the cloud no barrier to its secret task.

The Kremlin
Moscow
14 July
5.30 p.m.

Danilov came into the office.

'Your call, sir. From the British prime minister.'

'About time. Put it through.'

Danilov left the room, closing the door behind him. The president waited, impatient for the call and the decision that he now knew had been made. Would the British play ball, or would they, as so often, decide to—?

The phone jangled. He stopped his thoughts, collected himself. Never be too eager. He let it ring four times before answering.

37

'Hello.' His English, though heavy in accent, was good. He always spoke Russian in front of the cameras, but those who dealt with him knew that he had a good grasp of many languages. 'Thank you for calling, Prime Minister.'

'Mr President.' He recognized the authoritative tone, the voice of another leader who had faced his own problems and, like himself, taken over from a stronger leader and still stamped his own personality and authority on a confused nation. 'I have just had a communication from Her Majesty. We are prepared to proceed as suggested, although there are many problems that will have to be resolved before a final decision can be made.'

'I understand that, Prime Minister,' he replied. The excitement built within him. They were going along with the plan. 'We shall discuss all aspects of the matter when we meet in London next month. In the mean time I shall recall my ambassador to give him a full briefing. All matters must remain just between us. The ambassador will be the only one who knows of the plan, apart from myself and my private secretary. He will discuss the matter more fully on his return to London.'

'I shall look forward to meeting with him and to your visit. We must remember this is a most confidential matter, Mr President.'

His answer was pleasant but, although he had a close relationship and high regard for the British premier, he was often irritated by his occasional treatment of him as a errant schoolboy caught with a pocket full of hidden sweets. 'I shall make it my duty to remind all concerned of the need for secrecy and security,' he replied, full of charm and diplomacy.

'As I will. My regards to your family.'

'And to yours, Prime Minister.'

The phone clicked dead in his hand. He stared at it, then very slowly put it down. He swivelled round in his chair, then stood up and went to the window. He controlled the excitement inside him; it was a time for a clear mind, for clear thought.

Now, at last, the door for a new future was opening. It had to work. Otherwise all that he had planned, all that he wanted for his beloved Russia would be lost. He would give Russia her identity, her cause, her future.

The Oval Office in the White House
Washington, DC
14 July
5.40 p.m.

The American president put down the phone. He turned to Jake Donahue, his national security adviser.

'Well, looks like it's going ahead. The British are behind the plan.'

'He's taking a big chance, Mr President.'

'He is. And for that he needs all the support he can get. Make sure we back off any hint of confrontation. Give him the time he needs.'

'Not easy. Not with all the flak he's getting from the minority groups.'

'Ride it out. He's going to have enough enemies at home. Let's not stir up the situation any more. If we're going to piss in any pots, make sure it's not in his. OK?'

'Yes, Mr President,' replied his national security adviser. He just hoped that the armed forces chiefs saw it in the same light. Trouble was that they didn't know what was happening anyway.

'There's not a lot we can do. This is between Russia and Britain. If anything goes wrong, just make sure we're there to help if anyone hollers.'

KGB Headquarters
2 Dzerzhinsky Square
Moscow
14 July
5.45 p.m.

The old man watched General Dmitry Vashinov in the darkened room.

The general was young, at forty-six the youngest general ever to head the KGB. He had campaigned in Afghanistan and been one of the few military leaders to succeed against the rebel *mujahedin*, having led an anti-terrorist wing for the KGB in that area. On his return to Moscow, the president had taken him under his wing and ensured a rapid rise in promotion. He had put him in charge of the KGB two years earlier. For that promotion, the president had expected total loyalty from his young protégé.

'So he is to proceed with his plan.' Vashinov spoke with the finality of a man whose decisions have already been taken for him. He pushed away the headset that lay in front of him. 'The British will, of course, report it to the Americans. But, then, maybe that is what he wants. If the Americans agree, they will ease the pressure on us internationally.'

'A most dangerous plan.' Grigory Marshka watched the young man closely. 'To most people it will appear to reverse everything the revolution stood for. There are those who will say that it will spell the death of communism in Russia.'

Vashinov stood up and pushed the report he had been reading back to Marshka.

'I shall do what is required of me, Comrade Marshka.'

'Your duty is all that is required of you, Comrade General.'

'What is our next move?'

'To wait. The pressure is on him to make things

happen, to make events take place.'

'Then, that is what I shall do, comrade. Wait. And watch.'

'Good. And remember, no member of the Politburo is aware of the situation. Keep me informed on a daily basis.'

As Marshka turned in his wheelchair, Vashinov rose from behind his desk and went to the door. He opened it for the old man, who wheeled himself out into the corridor. Marshka's chauffeur was waiting for him and he took the old man away. Vashinov closed the door.

It was difficult for him. Although his loyalty was ostensibly to the president, his responsibility rested with Marshka. In truth, Vashinov's loyalty was exclusively Vashinov's. Ambitious beyond reason, he knew he was a man of destiny, a leader who would guide Russia out of the turmoil it now floundered in.

But there was always Marshka. The old man, as one of the ruling Politburo, had been the most successful head of the KGB. A friend of Gromyko, Marshka had built an empire of fear and retribution that no Russian leader had ever dismantled. He was like the American FBI boss, J. Edgar Hoover. To many, he was bigger than the general secretary and president of the Soviet Union. After all, it was Grigory Marshka who had personally arrested Beria after the Stalin purges. The man had actually walked into a Politburo meeting and arrested Beria. At eighty-two, he was past the mandatory age of retirement. But no one had the nerve to tell him to go.

There were also the files.

Over the years the story was that Grigory Marshka had developed secret files on anyone who was anyone in the Soviet Union. The files, which had started as information on small bits of paper, had developed over the last sixty years to a major computerized database. Vashinov had seen some of the reports; they were part of the KGB archives. But certain files had been kept by Marshka. They were the ones that mattered, and no one knew where they were kept. Rumour was that he had even blackmailed Khrushchev and Brezhnev. That's why he had survived for so long, why his position of power was never even questioned.

Vashinov understood better than most that knowledge was all-powerful.

Vashinov wondered whether such a file existed on the president. Then he wondered what his own file would say. Like everyone, he had his own secrets, his own shabby world. He suddenly understood why the old man had been so open with him. Because the old man knew that he had nowhere to go, nowhere to hide. Vashinov, holder of the Order of Lenin and a people's hero, knew that he was trapped by his own weaknesses.

He sat back at his desk and picked up the report. He started to read it again.

And the more he read, the more he realized that Marshka was right, that the president of one of the two most powerful nations on earth could just be biting off more than he could chew. All was at risk. He knew he must support Marshka. The old man counted on that. Which is why he had come to him in the first place. Because he knew Vashinov had no choice but to do as Marshka said.

Ensor Mews
London
15 July
7.45 a.m.

The white and yellow Augusta 109 hovered at a safe distance from the house. At two hundred feet Duncan was low enough to be hidden by the hill, but in a position where he could see any movement in the house. In his downwind position, the clatter of his twin turbines could not be heard by his prey.

Behind, three miles to the east, he could see the convoy of white SAS Range Rovers speeding down the twisting country road. He knew that they would probably have left their police escort behind. It was always a cat-and-mouse game between the troopers and the boys in blue.

He turned his attention towards the house again. All was still quiet.

'Give me final positions, Pilot,' the SAS commander's voice crackled on the radio. 'Make sure you don't get spotted. I want to know if there's anyone outside, near the barn.'

Duncan turned the helicopter towards the house and brought her gently round the woods and skimmed closer to the ground. His co-pilot looked towards the barn, away from Duncan.

Suddenly it all went wrong. One of the kidnappers came rushing out of the building and saw the Augusta. He shouted back into the house, and two others came out.

They started blazing away with their automatics as Duncan swung the plane forward and raced towards the small group. Maybe, just maybe, he could scatter them, hold them off until the troopers arrived.

Then he saw one of the men had a small artillery rocket-launcher in his arms. He swung the launcher at the helicopter as Duncan yanked back on the cyclic handle and attempted to gain height away from the group. The downdraught from the vast rotors staggered the men on the ground, but the rocket-man kept his aim.

As he fired the rocket, Duncan's companion turned towards him. It was Victor Oldenburg, and he was smiling.

The rocket came up, slow-motioned as it gathered speed, and then through the perspex screen at the front of the Augusta. The screen didn't break, just stayed whole as the rocket passed through it and into Victor's face.

The face became a black hole, disintegrated into a thousand pieces of flesh.

Some of the flesh flew across the cockpit and stuck to Duncan's face, to his arms.

The flesh turned to pink worms and started to crawl and burrow into him, into his eyes and his nostrils, burning into his flesh. The aircraft, now out of control, turned on its back and plummeted towards the house. The turbines and rotors screamed as it exploded into the ground and tore the house into paper shreds.

Then he saw Victor's face, once again smiling at him, gently mocking him for his uselessness.

The nightmare died as suddenly as it had come. Duncan sat up in bed, his bedroom all quiet around him. Beside him, the alarm suddenly started to buzz. It was time to get up.

Duncan lay back against the pillows, his eyes staring up at the ceiling as he collected his thoughts. The nightmares didn't worry him any longer. He had become used to them over the years. They were part of his life, somehow necessary as an escape-valve in the pressure of what was not an ordinary everyday existence.

But the dreams had never been invaded by Victor before. Why was he in his nightmare?

The reminder alarm buzzed, and Duncan swung his legs over the side of the bed and switched it off. He stood up, stretching awake into the new day. He picked up his Lacoste bathrobe from the end of the bed, slipped it on and went down the stairs of the small mews house into the kitchen where he switched on the kettle. He put two slices of bread in the toaster and left the kitchen to go down the narrow staircase into the hall.

He opened the front door and went out into the small cobbled courtyard.

The blue 1935 3.5 Bentley was parked across his

garage entrance. It was his pride and joy; registered as AYN 1, it had originally been delivered as new to Sir Malcolm Campbell. Duncan had bought it at an auction five years earlier and had had the car totally rebuilt.

He went round and opened the boot. The milkman and paper-boy, as was their custom, had left their wares in there. For some reason the house had no letterbox, and it was a practice that had continued over the years. His mail was left at the local Post Office where he always picked it up. It was a simple system. If the car wasn't there, they knew not to deliver.

He returned to the kitchen, carrying the newspapers and milk. It was his last day of leave and last day of normality until the next tour of duty was over.

The toaster popped its contents as he walked in. He put the papers down, took out the toast and put the two slices on a plate. As he reached for the butter, he noticed the prince's face looking at him from the front of the newspaper. He stopped and picked up the paper.

'ROYAL TRIP TO RUSSIA,' blared the headline. And in smaller type underneath: 'Major visit by royalty to Russia planned.'

Duncan read the news story, then put down the paper.

So that was why Victor had been recalled to Buckingham Palace. With his Russian background, he would be in charge of most of the organization, but why had he kept it a secret? Over the years they had shared confidences more important than this.

Was there something about the trip the papers didn't know? What was it that had worried his friend?

And, as he thought, Duncan picked up the dish and started to butter the toast.

3

SPRINGING THE TRAP

**Northern Ireland
Summer, the following year
8 July**

It had started to drizzle, that misty garden-spray drizzle that comes regularly in Northern Ireland.

It had been raining for over three hours, and the hide Duncan lay in was filled with water. But he lay still, his eyes ever watchful on the white farmhouse that was at the bottom of the valley some two hundred yards away.

The men had arrived at the empty farmhouse fifteen hours earlier, just as dusk was falling. The first squad had drifted down the hill from the south, making sure that the coast was clear. The second group arrived in a banged-up old Ford Cortina, which was now hidden in the lean-to barn behind the house.

Duncan had seen nine in total, seven men and two women. The first he knew that something was up was when one of the first arrivals had suddenly tripped and fallen in the undergrowth, cursing softly as he did so, only a few yards from the hide. Duncan had already been there twelve hours, just due for a watch-change, when the IRA gang arrived.

The hide was twelve inches deep, both wide and long enough to fit one man and his equipment in. Covered with a tarpaulin and mud, supported by thin steel stresses, it could only be discovered by someone actually walking on it. But, when out in open ground, as Duncan was, the occupant had to lie absolutely still so as to avoid being seen.

The small radio strapped to his hip had an earpiece and small mouth-microphone with which Duncan communicated with his command. Once Duncan had managed to fire off a report and stop his watch-replacement from stumbling on the terrorists, he had settled down to keep an eye on the gang. Stiff, wet and hungry, Duncan had hardly moved since their arrival. All he could do was watch and report back.

Duncan was a member of the 14th INT, a small and select group of SAS members who were responsible for intelligence. Whereas there were nearly two thousand SAS and SBS members, the 14th INT had no more than a hundred, of which only thirty were field-operational. They were the ones who went in when all else had failed; they were the élite. Each member of the team had specific duties within that group, yet was still fully capable of fulfilling all the other roles within the team.

Duncan was number two in his group. Although his prime responsibility was transport, whether by air, road or sea, he still had to play his part as a full member of the team when it came to surveillance and attack. The team, five of them, had been watching this farmhouse for two months. They knew it was used as one of the staging-posts for the IRA, a safe hideaway from where they would launch an attack. But the team had been caught unawares, their information unreliable. They hadn't expected the terrorists to turn up for at least another two days.

'Clear call,' his team leader's voice came through the earpiece.

Duncan checked the area, his eyes sweeping the terrain without any movement of his head, his ears straining for any sounds from behind.

'Go,' he responded, satisfied that no terrorist was near enough to hear him.

'Change of plan. We have to get you out.'

'I'm OK. It'll be dark in six hours.' Duncan was puzzled; it wasn't like the SAS to worry about your comfort. 'Suggest wait till then.'

'Negative.' Team Leader wasn't in a discussion mood. 'Strike force is moving now. You are not to engage, I repeat, not to engage.'

Duncan lay silent; he was being ordered to keep out of the action.

'Is that order copied?' the voice asked again.

'Copied,' Duncan answered.

'Under any circumstances. I repeat, no action under any circumstances.'

'Understood.' He would follow orders, but he didn't understand.

'Position report.'

'One man at the front door, hidden in the porch. One in the bushes to the right, one under the cedar tree on the left. No known movements to the rear, but probably one or two in the garage. Women at top right window twenty minutes ago. Occasional movements in kitchen. Suggest this is the main area. All others expected in the house. No sight of weapons.' Duncan's report was comprehensive; even in his bewilderment his professionalism was total.

'Stand by for further. Report only major changes in status.' His earpiece went dead.

Six minutes later he saw a small movement on top of the hill opposite. He couldn't tell, but guessed it was one of the team.

Then he heard the helicopter. He could tell from the sound that it was an army Lynx, not one of the SAS Augustas. What was the Army doing there?

A few seconds later there were shouts from the hill opposite, from the top. He saw an army platoon setting up position and soldiers scattering along the undergrowth. Then, as the helicopter appeared from the left, swooping down on the farmhouse, a mortar exploded near the garage. Duncan lay still, confused and wondering why the Army had moved in from the south. The terrorists would break away, into the woods to the right, and escape back over the border. He heard single gunshots from the house, followed by the chatter of an automatic.

'Go now,' the voice commanded him over the earpiece. 'North, up the hill and away from the action.'

As Duncan scrambled from the hide, he saw that the helicopter was between him and the farmhouse. He realized it was shielding him, protecting him from the gunfire.

Duncan ran up the hill, keeping low. Two minutes later he was over the top and out of danger. He turned to look into the valley, saw the helicopter break its position and race away as soon as he was safe.

He ran down the hill, towards the small winding road. As he reached the road, he saw a Range Rover parked in the woods. It pulled out to meet him, and he climbed in. He saw that the team were all there.

'What the fuck's going on?' he asked his team leader, who was driving.

'I don't know,' he replied, gunning the Range Rover down the road.

'We had them cold. Sitting targets. With that lot in, screwing it up in their size twelves, they'll all get away.'

'Orders, Mark. I was told to get you out and back to Belfast.'

'Nothing's that important. Not when we were about to put that lot away.'

'You tell me.' The team leader drove the Range Rover hard, squealing it on its tyres towards the main road. 'You tell me what can be that important.'

Duncan looked at the men in the back, incongruous in their camouflage as the vehicle hurtled on down the country lane. He turned forward again.

'Fuck it.'

The Range Rover came into Belfast and was picked up by an army escort of two personnel-carriers on the outskirts. The small convoy made its way to the fortified barracks, where the Range Rover went through the gates on its own, the armoured escort returning to duty in the scarred city.

Colonel Carson, the SAS commander, was waiting for Duncan as the Range Rover pulled up. As Duncan got out, Carson signalled him to follow. Carson led the way into the small brick and concrete building, along the corridors to the small green-painted interview-room at the rear. He opened the door and waved Duncan in.

'Captain Duncan.' Carson announced Duncan to the man in the room and, once Duncan had entered the room, closed the door on the two men.

The man was sitting behind the single wooden desk that was, in addition to three chairs, the only furniture in the room. Duncan looked at him, immediately disliking the pin-striped civilian who was obviously responsible for his present situation. Duncan took off his pack and helmet, put them on the table, a gesture of defiance and annoyance.

'Kto vi?' The man spoke to him in Russian.

'You know who I am.'

'Izvineetye, ya plokho guvuryu po-roosky.' The man apologized for his bad Russian.

'All right, we both know I speak Russian. What is all this about?'

'Please sit down.' Duncan pulled up one of the chairs and sat opposite the man. 'You've been seconded to my department. My name is Laurence Woodward, and you will be under my control.'

'Under whose orders?'

Woodward paused, the dislike now mutual. 'Until further notice, you are transferred to MI5. You do know what MI5 is, I presume.'

'Of course.' Duncan was taken aback.

'Well, we agree on something. Things are looking up.' Woodward opened the folder that was on the desk and took out a paper. He glanced through it. 'I want to know if all this is correct. You are Mark Duncan, a captain in the 14th INT, based here in Belfast. You're third-generation Russian, your grandfather escaped during the revolution and came here via Switzerland and France. You are what used to be called a White Russian.'

'Wrong. I'm British.'

'A technicality. Please don't interrupt until I've finished. Some of your family had already emigrated during the last century and set up as moneylenders. Your family now control Duncan Pharsee Schiller, one of the city's major merchant banks. You were educated at Gordonstoun, but ducked out of university to take up flying. You have licences for both rotary and fixed-wing aircraft. Slightly different from your grandfather. When he came here from Russia, he was penniless, which is why he became a doorman at the Ritz. I wonder why he didn't go and work at the bank?'

'Probably earned more in tips.'

'Well, your father did. Join the bank, that is. And very successfully. Knighted in 1986, I see.'

'Just tell me where all this is getting to.'

Woodward put down the sheet. 'You're fluent in Russian, aren't you?'

Duncan nodded his affirmation.

'Learnt, I presume, from your family.'

'I also did a course at Leeds University.'

'As part of your SAS training.'

'You don't expect me to go off and spy in Russia, do you? Your latest secret weapon.' Duncan laughed at the absurdity of the situation. 'In this period of *glasnost*, I thought we'd stopped all that.'

'More serious than that, I'm afraid.'

'Then, you think I'm a spy. How absolutely absurd. Is that what all—?'

'You do have the privilege of mixing in royal circles. Prince—'

Duncan stood up, angrily pushing the chair back. 'Before we go any further, I want to know what all this is about.'

'In good time, in—'

'No. Now.' Woodward saw that Duncan would go no farther until he had a satisfactory explanation.

'Whatever is said in this room must stay between us. You accept that?'

'For the moment.'

'You know that the prince and the duchess are due to visit Russia next month. That's the official state visit. The prince's aide-de-camp, Victor Oldenburg, is in Russia now, arranging the details of the trip. During Oldenburg's visit, it was agreed that he and his family would stay at a secluded dacha outside St Petersburg. I believe it was once the private property of Tsar Nicholas. I believe you are a good friend of the Oldenburgs.'

'Yes.'

'Godfather to one of their children.'

'Yes.'

'You are also both of Russian descent.'

'So are a lot of other people. It doesn't make us agents.'

Woodward shook his head. 'Not everything we do comes out of a Len Deighton book, you know.'

'Then, get to the point.'

'Victor Oldenburg, or Count Victor Oldenburg and Hess, to give him his full title, has been kidnapped in Russia.'

'Kidnapped?'

'Family and all, just disappeared. Yesterday. And we want you to go in and find them.'

Both men stared at each other in silence. Woodward waited for Duncan to absorb the awful truth before he continued.

'Why?' Duncan broke the long silence.

'We don't know. No ransom notes, nothing.'

'What're the Russians doing about it?'

'All they can. Trouble is, both governments have agreed a total news-blackout on the situation. For obvious reasons, after all, we don't want to upset this particular cartload of royal apples, do we?' Duncan ignored the joke. 'Apart from a few people at the Kremlin and at Number Ten, you and I are the only people who know of the situation.'

Woodward slid the folder across to Duncan.

'You need to read this,' he continued. 'It's as much as we know, or as much as the Russians will tell us.'

Duncan opened the folder and took out the slim report. He sat down again, skimmed it, then looked up at Woodward.

'That's all?'

'I'm afraid so.'

Duncan put the sheet down. Victor had taken his family on a short private holiday to St Petersburg before attending to his duties as co-ordinator and organizer of the forthcoming state visit. Accompanying them were two police officers to look after the security arrangements. One of them was Inspector George Leeming, one of the royal bodyguards. There was also an American girl who was the interpreter for the two policemen. After two days, when the family were fishing in the river which

53

ran through their holiday home, a group of horsemen approached them. The men had been dressed in traditional Cossack outfits. They had waved and shouted greetings at the Oldenburg party, who in turn had waved back. When the group got closer, they broke into a gallop and charged the small party. Some carried guns and opened fire, the others brandished swords. Before reinforcements from the police at the dacha could reach the scene, the horsemen had lifted the children and Anna Oldenburg on to their horses to ride double. A spare mount had been brought and Victor was ordered, under the sharp blade of a Cossack sword, to mount. The group had then ridden away across the river. By the time the armed police had arrived, the kidnappers had disappeared with their victims, deep into the forests that surround St Petersburg. The horses were found three hours later, wandering in the forest. There were no other clues. Victor and his kidnappers had disappeared into thin air. Inspector Leeming was also abducted, and the interpreter. The other bodyguard was being kept out of sight while the Russians decided what to do.

'The prime minister has insisted that we are part of the investigation,' said Woodward, when he saw that Duncan had finished the report. 'I needn't tell you that that created a howl of protest from the Russians. They usually like to tidy up their own mess. He told them the only way we could agree to a news-blackout was if they co-operated with us and gave us a free hand in the investigation.' Woodward took the folder back from Duncan. He went on: 'We had a choice. Either send in a large team, which would eventually draw attention to itself; use a sleeper, which would only cause its own problems; or call in a loner. In the end we decided on the loner. Your advantage is that you know Oldenburg, that you speak Russian, that you're a trained professional and that you have an excellent cover.'

'Which is?'

'That as a member of a large merchant-banking family, with some ties to the Soviet Union, you will be over there looking at the country with a view to future investment opportunities. You will, of course, be working with a Russian. They've already nominated a Moscow policeman. Odd chap, half Russian and half Muslim. But he's one of their top men. Apparently kidnapping is quite common. Boosts the black economy, I suppose. Should you, at any stage, decide you want to work on your own, then you may give this Moscow policeman the slip. Our code of operation in this case is quite simple. We're not worried about any potential diplomatic fallout due to your conduct. Anything goes. Our only concern is to find the family.'

'Why're they getting the red-carpet treatment?'

'Because we want to know if it is in any way connected to the prince's state visit. Kidnapping some minor foreign royal isn't that important on its own. But it is when it might be used as a springboard against similar action against a member of our own royal family.'

Instinctively, Duncan knew the man lied. But now was not the time to rock the boat. The answers were in Russia, not here in a windowless room in Belfast.

'When do I leave?'

'When you're ready. As befits a member of the millionaire class, we've arranged for your family's private jet to take you to Moscow. I suggest you fly yourself. We've already cleared you into Russian airspace. Your contact will meet you and transfer with you to St Petersburg. It'll fit in with your cover.'

'I need to stop over in Geneva.'

'Why?'

'My business. I'll be there for a few hours.' Geneva was the centre of the terrorist trade; it was the one place where Duncan would find out if there had been any international involvement in the kidnap.

'Is it necessary?'

'Yes, I've got to refuel somewhere.'

Woodward paused before answering. Although he didn't trust people outside the department, this time he knew he had no alternative. If Duncan failed, then there would be no blame attached to the department. Woodward and MI5 were covered. He nodded assent.

'Time is short on this one,' he went on. 'You've got just over a week. I can't see it being kept quiet from the press for too long. In truth, it'll probably blow before then. Oldenburg needs to be back by July the eighteenth.'

'Has anybody got any ideas?' asked Duncan.

Woodward shook his head. 'Not unless the Russians are holding something back. Ever been to Russia?'

'No.'

Woodward pushed the folder back across the table. 'There're maps in there, your contact's name and various diplomatic contacts.' He took a separate piece of paper from his top pocket and handed it to Duncan.

'Memorize those names, addresses and numbers. They're sleepers. If you get into trouble, or need something fast, get in touch with them. But don't abuse it. It could cost them their lives. The Russians will expect us to use our agents.' Woodward didn't tell Duncan that he had fought against giving out the names. As far as he was concerned, the young SAS officer was going into this one alone.

Duncan read through the list, imprinting the information into his memory. Igor Yakovlev, a schoolteacher; Natasha Leonova, a secretary in Gum, the Moscow department store; Oleg Stolypin, a state lawyer; Karim Ishkent, a trade union official. In all there were eleven names, and Duncan had absorbed them all within five minutes. He handed the sheet back to Woodward. Woodward tore the paper into little strips, took out a Zippo lighter and burnt them in the ashtray.

'I don't have to tell you how important these people are, how much at risk you could put them.'

'No, you don't.' Duncan's answer was short; he objected to being treated like a child. He picked up the folder and stood up, the chair scraping noisily against the concrete floor as he pushed it back.

'Who's my contact if I want to get in touch with you?'

'Go through the embassy. You'll find all the names you need in there.' Woodward pointed to the folder. 'There'll be a plane waiting to take us back to Northolt.' Northolt was the West London RAF airport that was used for both military and VIP civil flights. 'I'd like you at the airport an hour from now, at six.'

'Is the plane there?'

'Yes. Also charts, anything you need for your trip.'

'I need to flight-plan to Geneva tonight. I can sort out everything I need there in the morning. I'll be ready to leave for Moscow by twelve.'

'Use a phone from here.'

'No.' Duncan was certainly not ringing Geneva from anywhere that the phone could be tapped.

Woodward held out an American Express card for Duncan.

'What's this?' said Duncan, taking it. 'For expenses? Very considerate.'

Woodward ignored the sarcasm. 'The Americans have offered us all the help we want. This is your safety-line. Keep it on you and you'll be tracked by satellite. Something they cultivated after the Iraqi Gulf War. We'll know where you are all the time. If you have a problem, if you need help, burn the card. It'll trigger off a signal which means you need assistance.'

'Who're you going to send in? The cavalry? And John Wayne?'

He picked up his pack and helmet, turned and left the room. Outside in the hall, his team leader waited for him.

'Everything all right?'

'Yes, Tim,' Duncan answered his superior.

'Important enough to fuck up the raid?'

'I'm afraid so.'

'They all got away. Two squaddies were hit, one's critical.'

The two men looked at each other, the senior officer accepting that Duncan was about to enter a more serious and dangerous assignment, whatever it was. His was not to ask.

'I've to get you to the airport once you've changed. Come on.'

Woodward came out as the two men turned and walked away in step. He was unhappy. As far as he was concerned, it was the Russians' mistake and up to them to sort it out. After years of plotting against the Russians, he found it difficult to trust any of them. He wouldn't be surprised if it was a KGB plot to uncover his sleepers, to trace Western intelligence in the Soviet Union.

He hoped that Duncan was up to it. He shook his head. There was too much riding on one man. Too much bloody risk.

The Kremlin
Moscow
8 July

Captain Ahmed Alekseevich Myeloski sat on a wooden bench outside the minister's office. He held a folder in his hands, similar to that which Duncan had. At forty-six, he headed the Kidnap and Terrorist Bureau arm of the Moscow Police. He had been a detective since he was twenty-five and, although unorthodox in his methods, had waged a successful war against the criminals he came up against.

Although respected by both his superiors and those who worked for him, Myeloski was never totally trusted.

The product of a mixed marriage, his father had been a Muscovite, his mother an Uzbek Muslim. He fitted into neither camp. The Muslims saw him as a Russian, the Russians saw him as a Muslim. The matter was exacerbated by the recent troubles in provincial republics as Muslim groups fought for their independence. His colleagues expected him to take sides; he was only interested in doing his job. To him, there were citizens and there were criminals. Race, religion, that's just how you were born. It wasn't how you were made.

The door opened, and his boss, Leonid Yashkin, came out. He sat next to Myeloski.

'Well, what do you make of it?' Yashkin asked him, referring to the contents of the folder.

'Unreal. These things don't happen.'

'It's happened.'

The two men sat in silence for some time, each in his own thoughts. A woman click-clacked past, her high heels dragging along as she carried a pile of heavy papers into a side-office.

'Shoes,' said Yashkin.

'Shoes?'

'The same. I remember when we used to queue for hours to buy shoes. To buy anything. But the shoes, they were always plain shoes. Now we have shoes like that. With style, cutaway sides, thin straps on the back. All sorts of shoes from the West.'

'You mean Taiwan and Hong Kong.'

'Whichever. The other day, one of the boys wanted Reeboks. You know Reeboks?'

'I have a pair.'

'You have a pair. You're lucky. They're difficult to find. Anyway, I looked round the shops for some. You know what I thought? That we have more shoes, more choice, but still the same queues. Did you black-market your Reeboks?'

'Yes, tovarich.'

Yashkin shook his head. 'Is that the way for a policeman to behave?'

'I can get your son the Reeboks. If you want? They're not too expensive through my contact.'

'If it saves standing in queues, why not?'

'You must give me the size,' said Myeloski.

'Nine. Size nine.' Yashkin turned to his junior officer. 'I wonder if they knew of the plan.'

'I think they did. You don't kidnap a whole family unless it's for a reason. If it was just for money, then we would have had a ransom demand by now.'

'Unless they didn't know who . . . No. They knew what they were doing. And when to strike.'

'There are many who would not like to see this thing progress.'

'I agree. Ahmed Alekseevich, when you meet this Englishman, he will not know the whole story. It must remain like that.'

The door opened, and a male secretary called them. The two men rose and went through the minister's anteroom into his main office.

As they entered the room, Myeloski saw the minister standing by his desk. In his chair he saw the familiar features of the president looking back at him, the face he knew so well from his television set and the newspapers. He stopped short, surprised to see the man. Yashkin was also taken aback; he had not expected him, either.

The president got up from the chair and came round the table, his hand outstretched in the Western style. Myeloski took his hand and shook it. The same welcome was then extended to Yashkin. He turned back to Myeloski.

'I wanted to meet you. To see the man I must put my faith in. Your superiors tell me that you are the best officer they have. That is what we need. Your best endeavours. Nothing is being hidden from you. I want to tell you that personally. All doors are open to you. I know you have to operate in secret, but we must keep it that way. An office has been prepared for you in the Kremlin. Is there anything you need?'

'Not yet, Comrade President,' Myeloski replied. 'Apart from some luck. But I will do my best. That I promise you.'

'Good.'

He put his arms on Myeloski's shoulders, leant forward and kissed him on both cheeks. Then he turned and walked out of a side-door, out of the office.

'Right, then,' said the minister. 'You heard. Everything is at your disposal. Keep me informed every day.'

And the two policemen were ushered out of the office and found themselves once again in the hallway.

'Did you know?'

'No,' replied Yashkin. 'I don't think he liked the crack about luck.'

'That's all we have at the moment.'

'We know that. But outsiders, they think we have a magic formula. Don't disillusion them. Any ideas?'

'Start where it started. St Petersburg.'

'The Englishman will be here tomorrow.'

'That's something I can do without. Wet-nursing a foreigner. Still, it gives me time to see if any of my contacts has heard anything.'

'One of the reasons you were chosen is because you speak English. From your time in London.'

Myeloski shook his head. His tour of duty as security officer in the Soviet embassy in London had been a miserable period of his life. He had found the English so dull, preoccupied with strikes, a falling balance of payments and high unemployment. They were always more interested in their past than in the future. He smiled to himself. It was a bit like modern-day Russia since *perestroika* had been introduced into the Russian culture.

'When you read his report, you will see that he is of

Russian descent. He knows the family well. That will help. He is also a serving officer in the Army. Holds a desk job somewhere. Comes from a rich family. Very rich.'

'Another chinless wonder.'

Yashkin looked at him quizzically. 'Chinless wonder?'

'English slang. Means no brains and no balls. I shall look forward to meeting him,' he sighed.

The two men walked down the hall.

'I bet he doesn't have problems getting Reeboks,' said Yashkin. 'How soon can you get them?'

Hôtel Le Richemond
Geneva
9 July

Duncan sat on the terrace of the hotel looking out over Lac Léman. It was a clear hot day, and he watched the fountain in the middle of the lake shoot its single needle-like spout over a hundred feet in the air.

He always stayed at Le Richemond, one of the few hotels still in private hands in Geneva. Owned by the Armleder family since 1875, the hotel was where his grandfather had first come when he escaped from Russia. It was here that he had become a doorman before going on to live in England. As a mark of respect, and in keeping with the tradition of the family, all the Denknetzeyans stayed at Le Richemond.

He remembered the arguments he had had with his father over the years. He'd once walked out, in a sixteen-year-old child's sulk, on a family dinner-party, and his father had always chided him about it – it had become one of those family memories that everyone always laughs at, always shares. He smiled, remembered his ambition to have a holiday with his friends instead of with his family. His father saw it as an act of treachery, his mother silently agreed with everyone as she saw their separate points of view. Given the choice now, he wished the old holidays could be taken again, that things were not as different as they had become. His parents were separated, one sister dead from a drug overdose, his younger brother on his way to becoming a merchant banker.

He shook his head. Now was not the time for reminiscing. He needed clear thoughts, a positive, not reflective attitude.

He had landed the night before at Geneva airport. He was used to flying the small Citation twin jet, and it was now parked, refuelled and ready for his journey to Moscow. Both the prince and Victor Oldenburg had flown in it with him, once to St Moritz for a skiing holiday and once to Gibraltar for an official visit. As he watched the fountain, he remembered the flight in, over the Jura mountains and along the lake. It had been a bumpy ride, through the tail end of a thunderstorm. When he had got to the hotel, he had looked for Carver, but to no avail. He had been concerned that the message hadn't got through.

Woodward, the MI5 man, had watched him closely at Northolt. But he'd managed to get to a phone near the toilets in the operations centre. He'd called Geneva and left a message on Carver's answering machine.

In the morning, when it was time to leave, he had paid at the desk with the American Express card Woodward had given him. He watched the cashier ring through for a clearance and had been surprised when it was accepted. Trust the Yanks, always covering the technical points. He grinned, wondered if they'd charge MI5 when the account arrived on their desk.

It was now eleven in the morning, and Duncan sipped a cappuccino in a café at the lakeside. He was restless, impatient in the knowledge that time was limited.

At the next table, the black African diplomat was

impressing the girl he was with. She looked Italian, was well dressed and was probably a secretary at the United Nations. Duncan, with nothing better to do, leant back and listened in on their conversation.

'I really am sorry I did not call you,' the smart-suited diplomat urged the girl on, his accent heavy Nigerian.

'You said you would ring me,' she chided him.

'I did. Many times,' he lied, 'but you were never in. You have other boyfriends, no. I know this.'

She smiled. 'Of course not,' she lied back.

'But I have been so busy. I was in Buenos Aires, then London, then I have to go back to New York, on to Montreal and then Frankfurt. I have only just got back. And the first thing I do is call you.'

'Why you call me?'

'Because I miss you. I want to take you out, to shop with you, buy you nice presents and have a nice time with you. Would you like to go shopping?'

She nodded, and he smiled back. He knew he was on the home straight.

'But I have to get back to work,' she said.

'No problem. I meet you after work. What time you finish?'

'Three o'clock.'

'OK. I have a suite here. Upstairs. Five hundred and ten. When you finish, you come to me. We have a little drink, OK.'

She looked unsure; the cart was going before the horse, the extension to her wardrobe now under threat.

The diplomat eased her fears. 'Then, when we have had a little early supper and a drink, we go shopping. I buy you something nice.' His dirty-intentioned words hit home.

'OK. I come here after work.' She smiled, the deal done. She rose from the table. 'I see you later. Ciao.'

The black man stood up, and the girl departed down

the steps. He sat down again, took a sip from his drink and leant back.

'You really are a dirty old man,' said Duncan.

'You know what they say. Once you've had black you never go back.' The accent was now East End London, the Nigerian one cast aside. The two men never looked at each other, their conversation a secret between them.

'What's the problem, Mark?' Carver asked Duncan.

'I need to know if there's been any action planned or executed in Russia.'

Maurice Carver was the centre of the terrorist trade. As 'Mr Fixit', he arranged arms, travel, false documents and any other of the paraphernalia that is the currency of modern-day terrorists. The authorities knew this, but left him alone. At least this way they could keep an eye on the supply source. Carver dealt with all the major terrorist and criminal organizations. If he didn't know about it, it wasn't going to happen. And he owed Duncan a favour, not once but many times over. The SAS officer had saved his life during a raid in Northern Ireland, let him escape during a terrorist ambush. This was the first time Duncan had called in a favour.

'What sort of action?' Carver asked.

'Anything that's out of the ordinary, Maurice. I don't want to say any more.'

'I need to know what type. Different groups do different things.'

'Kidnapping. I presume for extortion.'

'No. Not that I know of. Anything else?'

'Attacks on the royal family.'

'They're always open to that. There was some small group of Irish, bloody crackpots, who wanted to do it, but that never got off the ground. Ever since the Mountbatten thing, they've all been nervous of the publicity. It turned a lot of their own against them.'

'What do you know about Russia?'

'All internal stuff. No money for the big-time operators.

Kidnapping's the main stuff, but it's all small-time. There's a lot of brigands; yeah, that's what they call them, live up in the wilds, the forests and steppes. The authorities can't shift them. Place is so damn big that they can't find them. They're pretty well armed – blackmarket stuff stolen from the Army. I can't help you, son.'

'Are you lying to me, Carver?'

'Fuck off. Come on, I pay my debts, you know that.'

The two men sat in silence, a couple of strangers to any passer-by.

'How long're you here for?'

'I'm leaving after this.'

'I'll see what I can dig up. Where can I contact you?'

'British embassy, Moscow. Leave any messages with George Richardson on the trade desk. Use the contact-sign "Falkland".'

'Need any hardware?'

'No.'

'Be careful. The Russians don't like outsiders bringing in their own machinery.'

'I'll be OK.' Woodward had cleared Duncan to be armed. 'The Russians won't dare search you,' he had said. 'On this one, we're meant to be working together.' The young soldier felt reassured when he knew he could take his American Coonan 357 Magnum pistol. A copy of the Colt handgun, it was one of the most accurate and reliable handguns on the market.

Duncan stood up, left some Swiss francs on the table to pay for his coffee and walked back into the hotel.

Geneva had been a wasted visit and, more important, wasted time. Duncan picked up his bag and caught a taxi to the airport.

'Land of my fathers.'

As the Citation jet crossed into Soviet airspace, above the radio beacon at Myatyalyay where Poland borders with Russia, Duncan thought of his grandfather.

Looking down on the land over seven miles below from the lofty heights where jet streams vaporize behind you, it was hard to imagine the difficulties the old man must have faced.

Grandfather, the youngest son of Count Nikolai Denknetzeyan, was nineteen when the revolution broke out. He was a cadet at the Imperial Military Academy in Moscow when he heard that the emperor, Tsar Nicholas II, was under house arrest. It was March 1917, and the young officer-to-be immediately went north to Petrograd (now St Petersburg) to see if he could be of help to the royal family. A provisional government had been formed under Alexander Kerensky and the Soviet and was based at the Winter Palace.

By the time Grandfather Ilya Denknetzeyan got to Petrograd, the royal family were under house arrest in the Alexander Palace in Tsarskoye Selo. He tried to go to see the family, but the palace was surrounded by Bolshevik guards and Russian soldiers. After spending a futile week there, he returned to Petrograd where he found lodgings.

The revolution was based in Petrograd. Lenin, Kerensky and the other leaders of the new order all met there. The streets were busy all the time, great crowds milling around, all day and through the night, as the people of Russia tried to understand what was happening.

After a week in this confusion, and because the innkeeper, a fervent anti-royalist, suspected that Grandfather

Denknetzeyan was not the commoner he pretended to be, the young cadet decided to return to his family home in Talica, a small farming community between Ekaterinberg and Tobolsk in western Siberia.

He spent the next six months travelling. With little money in his pocket, and in fear for his life in those troubled times, he crossed the two thousand miles to the east well clear of the main highways and the great railways. He worked on farms to pay for food and hitched a ride wherever he could. He saw a Russia that was confused and hungry and hopeful and tired. Times were changing, and he began to realize that things would never go back as they had once been. He realized that because he saw the new world in the people's eyes; and if the populace wanted change, then there could be no return to what had been.

All he wanted was to return to his family, to their home in Talica, Villa Destayala. There, he decided, he would start again with a new life and a new Russia.

When he finally got there, when he walked through the town, he sensed a tension amongst those who saw him. When he waved or smiled at those he knew, they turned away, as if they didn't know him.

He continued to the outskirts of town and through the gates that led the half-mile to Destayala. The fields were deserted, no workers in evidence. Only when he came through the trees and round the small hill that sheltered the house, only then did he see the soldiers who had camped in the house and the grounds.

He pulled back, stayed hidden in the trees. As he waited for night to fall, he saw no movement in the house of anyone who resembled his father. Near nightfall he saw his younger sister Katya come out of the kitchens into the yard, saw her empty some slops for the few chickens who scuttled about. One of the men called her, was rude and irreverent in his gestures and words. Katya ignored him and returned to the kitchens.

At last, under the cover of a black moonless night, Grandfather Denknetzeyan stole over to the house and peered in through the kitchen window. He saw Katya and their cook Esmereldi. Once he had confirmed they were alone, he knocked on the window, startling the two of them. It was Katya who recognized him first, excitedly letting him into the kitchen, hugging him and kissing his cheeks and his eyes.

Then they were both fearful for him and they took him into the cold scullery, where they hid him from the intruders.

Eventually, when it was safe, Katya joined him. He demanded to know what she was doing as a kitchen maid, who were the soldiers using their house and where were their parents.

The story she told broke his heart.

The soldiers had come five months earlier. They had commandeered the farm and the villa in the name of the Ural Soviet. Their parents were ordered to live in one small room; the rest of the villa was shared by the officers of the new revolutionary army. Katya had been moved into a small room near the kitchens, which she shared with Esmereldi, and she was told to cook for the soldiers. The farm produce was now used exclusively to feed the troops.

One night their father had come down to see her. A group of revolutionary officers had been drinking and were in the room with her, some in a state of undress. Katya looked away at this point, the shame and embarrassment of that recollection burning in her eyes.

Her brother waited for her to collect herself.

'It was not my choice,' she said, 'but there was nothing I could do. Or else they would have killed us all, shot us in our beds. They came most nights. If I had refused . . . they threatened they would take our parents' lives.'

Grandfather Denknetzeyan had put his hand out, held

her hand. She drew some comfort from him and then continued.

The scene the count saw incensed the old man. He shouted at the men, came into the room and flailed at them. They laughed and pushed him around, from one to the other. Then the officer who had been on the bed with Katya drew his pistol and shot the old man dead.

They had dragged the body of the count from the room and continued where they had left off, their animal lust fuelled by the smell of death and the anguished screams of his sobbing daughter.

Their mother died a month later, heartbroken by the loss of her mate. She never knew the real reason for the count's death; it was something Katya told no one, not until that moment when her brother had finally returned.

'Where are they buried?' he had asked.

'With the family. By the chapel.' It was the family chapel on the north side of the estate. 'With Esmereldi's help, at night, we managed to bury them both. They are side by side.'

He put his arm round her, held her as she cried the tears she had wanted to cry since that evil night when their father had been murdered.

When she had calmed down, Grandfather Denknetzeyan took his sister Katya away from Villa Destayala. They visited the chapel on the north side and said their final farewell to their parents.

As they travelled west, along the same route that the young cadet had come, they met travellers who told them of the horrors of the revolution. They tried to ascertain news of the tsar and his family, but to no avail.

When they reached Perm, to the north of Ekaterinberg, they came across a White Russian force. They were about to attack Perm and then go on to rescue the tsar who, rumour had it, was imprisoned in Ekaterinberg.

Grandfather Denknetzeyan joined the Whites in their march on Perm. Katya, with some other members of the group, continued on to Moscow, where she was to stay with their Aunt Elisaveta. The brother and sister kissed goodbye, not knowing that they were never to see each other again.

The Whites took Perm and then moved on Ekaterinberg. But they arrived too late. The royal family, in the House of Ipatyev, had already been brutally murdered eight days earlier. There was no trace of the bodies, only a basement room with shuttered windows where Grandfather Denknetzeyan had seen the walls smashed by the bullets of Nagan revolvers. There were some dry stains of blood, although the room had been washed clean. Bayonet-marks grazed the floor and walls. No one could tell how many people had died there, just that people had been killed. The bullet-holes and bayonet-marks bore testimony to that.

Soon afterwards the Bolsheviks retook Ekaterinberg and the Whites were finally defeated.

The young Denknetzeyan fled to Moscow, once more following the backwoods routes. When he arrived there, he went to his Aunt Elisaveta's home. The pretty yellow building now housed over twelve families, a sign of the socialist times. Of his aunt and Katya there was no sign. Nobody recollected seeing them. Aunt Elisaveta had simply disappeared months earlier.

After living as a vagrant for several more months and getting nowhere in his search for Katya, Grandfather Denknetzeyan decided to leave his beloved Russia. As a soldier under the Whites there was a price on his head; someone would soon discover his true identity. He left one morning, striking out to the west.

Before he left, he went into the Cathedral of the Assumption, in Cathedral Square within the walls of the Kremlin. It was a place he visited often, at night, a place where he always felt at peace. He said his last prayers there, thought only of Katya and wished her well. He prayed for God to look after her, to protect her from any undue harm.

Eventually he crossed into Poland, and from there into Switzerland via Germany. The Great War was over, and Europe was learning to live with itself again.

He had never been close to his son, Mark's father, but had doted on his grandson and had often talked to him of the old Russia.

One night, Grandfather Denknetzeyan sat down and told the story of his escape from Russia to his grandson. He had never talked of it with anyone else.

He died three months later.

At the funeral Duncan had stood apart from the rest of the family. His grandfather had never liked his own son, always felt he lacked principle and sensitivity. Duncan understood why the old man felt like that, but he was Duncan's father and he would always be loyal to him. After the service, when everyone had gone to the reception at his father's house, Duncan had returned to the fresh brown earth mound and prayed for his grandfather's soul. He thought of his Katya and wondered if she was still alive, or whether Grandfather Denknetzeyan had now finally been reunited with her again.

He hadn't cried. It was not in his nature.

Well, if Grandfather Denknetzeyan never got back to Russia, then his grandson had. Maybe not on a white charger, as the old man had hoped, but in circumstances as strange as anything his grandfather had encountered. And on wings of steel.

'Welcome home, Grandfather. I hope I meet your spirit here.'

The small jet battled against a strong headwind and took nearly an hour and a half to cover the four hundred nautical miles from the Polish border to the Gagarin radio beacon.

Even though the winds were not as strong lower down, Duncan maintained his 41,000 feet altitude so as to save fuel. All jets burn less fuel the higher they go, and in order to fly non-stop from Geneva to Moscow he sacrificed air speed for fuel economy.

Now, with under a hundred miles to run to Moscow, he crossed the Gagarin beacon and called Air Traffic for descent.

'Golf Charlie India Tango India is cleared to Flight Level One Hundred, to be level by Ivanovskoy.'

'Roger,' replied Duncan as he started his high-speed descent to ten thousand feet. With sixty-seven miles to run he needed to lose height at nearly three thousand feet a minute. He set his autopilot for the descent and checked his charts for Moscow's Sheremetyevo Airport.

He was glad that he didn't have along the customary Russian navigator which was the standard requirement for all private flights over Russian airspace. They were usually minor KGB agents, and the two-thousand-dollar charge was nothing more than a way of increasing the Soviet Union's foreign exchange.

It had left him alone to think about the problems he had to face and how he would overcome them.

Less than a hundred miles away, in the small darkened room, the man at the screen watched the jet descend. The satellite pictures were clearer than normal, and he had no trouble in tracking the fast-moving aircraft. He reached for the phone and pressed the 'call' button. The phone was a direct link to the Kremlin.

'He should be landing in the next half-hour, comrade.'

'And the policeman?' a metallic voice came back at him.

'At the airport. We've picked up his transmitter. He won't get away from us.'

'Call me when they're on their way into Moscow.'

The line clicked off. The watcher put the receiver down and went back to his screen.

Twenty-five minutes later Duncan descended through the thick-formed low-hanging stratus cloud and landed uneventfully on Sheremetyevo's Runway 23 Left. He turned off on to the taxiway and followed the green 'go' lights to a corner away from the main Terminal One. As he powered the jet down, a yellow Lada came out of the shadows and towards him. By the time he had locked off the plane's controls and opened the door, Ahmed Myeloski was out of the Lada and waiting for him by the side of the executive jet.

Duncan climbed out of the jet as Myeloski came forward, hand outstretched. Duncan took the hand in greeting. For both men the handshake was warm, the eyes wary.

'Welcome to Moscow.' Myeloski spoke in English. 'Captain Ahmed Alekseevich Myeloski, Moscow Police. We'll be working together.'

'Mark Duncan,' replied Duncan. 'I'll need some fuel.'

'I can arrange that later. I think we should go to my office and then to your hotel.'

'All right. But I need to be here when they refuel.' Duncan, like all good pilots, liked to be present when others took over responsibility for his aircraft. He turned and took out his suitcase, then locked the door.

'I know you speak Russian,' Myeloski said as he waited for the Englishman, 'but it would be better if we spoke only English. This way, not everyone will understand us. Also, if I am not there, some people might have loose tongues if they think you do not understand.'

'That's fine with me,' replied Duncan.

'It's a fancy plane. Yours?'

'No. To a company I'm associated with.'

'Yes, your bank. It must belong to them.'

'Not my bank. My family.' Duncan immediately

regretted what he said. He never liked making excuses for his wealthy background. Typically English, he thought. Always bloody guilty.

The Russian smiled. He still knew how to get under their skin.

They walked towards the car. Myeloski, for all the seriousness of the situation, had a mischievous streak that was always present.

'It is only a small car. In London, I suppose, you only drive big cars. In Russia, only big cars for big important people.'

'How big are you?' Duncan knew that the policeman was trying to annoy him.

Ahmed held his thumb and forefinger together. 'This big.'

'That's small.'

Although he pretended to share a joke with the burly captain, Duncan was concerned. This was an important mission, yet they had sent him a minor police official who seemed to have little standing or influence.

Myeloski sensed the Englishman's nervousness.

'It would not be good to be noticed. We do not want them to know we are coming.'

Duncan nodded. But the Russian saw the look in his eyes. He knew he had not convinced him.

As Duncan opened the back door to put his suitcase in, Myeloski came round to the passenger side of the car.

'I can open any door in Russia.' He took Duncan's suitcase from him and put it on the back seat. He shut the door. 'And close them just as quickly. I have no Rolls-Royce, no Zil. But where I go I don't need them. You are here because your people wanted this. But this is my country. This is my crime. I tell you now, you keep up with me. I won't be waiting for you.'

This time it was Duncan who was pleased. Two could play the same game, and the Russian was now riled. When you don't have money, position matters.

The Lada pulled away from the parked jet and towards a gate at the side. As it approached, a guard stepped forward and hit a switch. The gate swung open, and the Lada pulled through.

The car joined the evening traffic as it swung southeast towards Moscow.

The two men travelled in silence for some time. It suited Duncan; it gave him a chance to absorb his new surroundings, to get used to Russia.

The motorway they followed was the M10. This highway, the main link between Moscow and St Petersburg, is one of the busiest in Russia, and the traffic was heavy even at that time of night. As well as trying to avoid the numerous pot-holes along the route, not always successfully, Myeloski was not the most accomplished of drivers, being one of those people who were never quite in tune with their machine. He spent much of the time swerving and cursing other drivers. Duncan wondered how long he would last in London or New York traffic.

'I spent many years driving in London, when I was stationed there.' It was almost as if the Russian had read Duncan's mind. 'Your traffic is heavier, but not as well mannered.' At that moment Myeloski lurched to the left to avoid a heavy truck that swung out in front of him. Duncan said nothing, but remembered the words of a friend who used to have a Lada and Skoda dealership in Putney. 'Every time I sell one of those things I'm committing a crime against humanity,' he had told him. Duncan decided at that moment that if things got really bad he would blitz the Russian with some of the Skoda and Lada jokes that were popular in the West.

They came into Moscow, past the vast Aeroflot Hotel which is still the main watering-hole for tourists. Duncan was staying at the Savoy Hotel, not far from the Kremlin. Unlike the big tourist hotels, the Savoy was for favoured and important visitors. Originally the old

Berlin Hotel, the refurbished and renamed eighty-six-room Savoy offered air-conditioning, videos, direct-dial telephones and much more. Although it was usually fully booked, Duncan had, with the help of the Foreign Office and probably the Soviet authorities, no problem in getting accommodation.

'They have given me a special office in the Kremlin. We will be there soon.' The traffic was heavier; Myeloski was trapped in the inside lane.

Duncan looked at the people passing by, wondering if he would have been one of them had Grandfather Ilya Denknetzcyan decided not leave Russia. He searched for any sign of recognition, of familiarity, but there was none.

The long queues outside certain shops surprised him.

'What're they queuing for?' he asked.

'For vodka. It's all people queue for now. That and McDonald's.'

He turned to look at Myeloski, peering urgently out of the window as the traffic stacked up and made movement impossible, and knew that he had nothing in common with these people, nothing that could be shared because of his blood. Then he thought of Victor, of what he and Anna and the kids would be feeling. And in his silence, in that tooting impatient traffic-jam, for the first time he wondered whether they had been killed. And suddenly he was impatient. He knew time was short. And here he was, stuck with a minor policeman who didn't even have the authority to use the exclusive fast-moving middle lane of the road that was available to important officials. He began to realize the possibility that he was being taken for a ride, that he was the stooge in a deadly game in which he was not being allowed to play a part.

The traffic moved slowly forward, down the Gorkova and into Red Square from the north.

'There – the Kremlin,' said Myeloski proudly.

Duncan looked at it, awed by its size and beauty. The Kremlin is Moscow's castle, the centre from which the city expanded. First built in the twelfth century, the Kremlin is ringed with high crenellated walls and crowned with the golden domes of the cathedrals. It had also been the seat of Soviet government since March 1918.

The Lada came past the Historical Museum in the centre of Red Square and turned right, just before the Lenin Mausoleum, into the Nikolskaya Vorota entrance. An armed soldier, a member of the Taman guard, flagged them down at the barrier. Behind him stood another soldier, a KGB trooper, and Duncan saw further guards hidden in the shadows. It was not a place that was easy to get into, or out of. Myeloski flashed his pass, and the steel arm was lifted, allowing the car into the parking area by the Arsenal.

In front of him, the young Englishman saw the splendour of the Great Kremlin Palace, the domes of the Church of the Deposition of the Robe and the Cathedral of the Assumption. The car pulled up opposite the Tsar Cannon, one of the largest cannons ever made. Weighing over 80,000 pounds, it has a barrel of more than 16 feet and a bore of 890 millimetres. But the gun had never been fired.

It was as his grandfather had said many times. 'The Kremlin cannot be described. It has to be seen, and felt, and only then can you understand the beauty of it and of Russia.' For a moment, for the first time in his life, he began to realize why his grandfather had never lost his love of Mother Russia, why it had always been in his blood.

But that was the past. What would he have thought of his beloved Russia now? The austere and dark side of the future lay in front of him. The Palace of Congresses, where the powermasters sat. Built in 1961, it made the rest look like what it was: a museum. And that is how it would remain, until such time as the people would be free to worship in their religion and be proud of their centuries-old heritage.

To the left of where they parked, there was the old Senate, itself a beautiful yellow triangular building. And there was the Praesidium of the Supreme Soviet. To their right was the massive Arsenal.

It was in here, on the north side of the Kremlin, that Myeloski had been given an office.

Duncan let himself out of the car as Myeloski walked round to him.

'They have given me . . . us an office here. It will be our headquarters.'

'We won't find anyone while we're sitting at desks.'

'But we must start somewhere. We have files to read. And my secretary will take messages for us.'

He turned and led the way into the Arsenal. They climbed the steps to the third floor and walked down a darkened corridor on the west side. The offices were small, and *apparatchiks* scuttled round between rooms. At the end, to the north side, the policeman led Duncan into a small suite of offices. The outer room was empty, but the lights had been left on. It was obviously the secretary's room. The office that led off it was larger, with two desks positioned so that they faced each other. The windows had blinds, which were drawn shut.

Yashkin stood up as they entered. He came towards Duncan, arm outstretched in welcome.

'Welcome to the Kremlin. I am Leonid Igorevich Yashkin, Ahmed Alekseevich's superior officer.'

Duncan looked round the room. 'Thank you. I presume this is where we are to work.'

'I hope it is all right.' Yashkin's English was poor, so Duncan answered in Russian.

'The office is fine. But we won't find the prince and his family here.'

Yashkin looked at Myeloski for support. He hadn't

expected to find the Englishman so hostile and direct.

'I will show him all the information we have.' Myeloski took over. 'And then we shall decide what we have to do.'

'That is how we must do it. Look for the clues and then chase them.' Yashkin held out his hand to Duncan. 'I must have your passport.'

'Why?' Duncan was alarmed.

'To stamp your visa, of course.'

Duncan took out his passport and handed it to the older man, who opened it to the relevant page and stamped it with a small stamper he had with him. He handed the passport back to Duncan.

'At least you won't be arrested as an illegal immigrant. Although some would say more people are trying to get out of Russia than in, these days,' Yashkin joked. It was lost on Duncan, who smiled courteously at the police inspector. Yashkin turned and went to the door, the small stamping machine now back in a small box and in his pocket. 'I shall return this to the Immigration Department. Everything you want is at your disposal. We are as determined as you to find your friends. But it is a secret matter, which gives us many difficulties. Which is why you are in a secret office here and not at police headquarters. But all our resources are there to be used. It only takes Ahmed or yourself to press the button. But remember, the more people who know, the more chance there is of it all getting out. I wish you all the luck.'

Yashkin left the two men in the room, closing the door behind him.

'Would you like a coffee? Or something stronger?' Myeloski asked Duncan.

'No. I just want to get on with it.'

Myeloski shrugged and sat at one of the desks. Duncan sat on the edge of the other desk as the policeman opened a drawer and took out a bottle of vodka. He also took out a tumbler, poured himself a short drink and put the bottle away. He drank some of the vodka before opening another drawer from which he took out a large folder. He opened the folder and spread its contents across the table. There were photographs on the top. He handed some of them to Duncan, who recognized Victor Oldenburg's features. The other glossies were of the family.

'I know what they look like.' His temper was getting the better of him.

Myeloski ignored the outburst. 'Apart from the family there are photographs of the rest of the party. There is a personal bodyguard, Inspector George Leeming.'

Duncan held up Leeming's photograph. 'I know him.'

'What do you know of him?'

'That's he's a good man. Very loyal and devoted to his duties. You do know he's one of the special police force responsible for the security of our royal family?'

'And are those his only duties?'

'Yes. His prime responsibility is the security of our prince. He was here, which I presume you know, to clear the visit from a security point of view.'

'You understand that I have to question everything.'

'I said he's a good man. You surely don't think he was involved?'

'Can you guarantee that he wasn't?'

Duncan stopped. The policeman was right. Everyone was a suspect. 'If we need it, I can get you any information on him, or anyone else, from London. I don't know his background, apart from the fact that the British police are very careful in how they screen royal and political bodyguards.'

'Do you know that, or do you presume it?'

'I presume it.'

'Then, we must disregard it. I have already asked for information on all members of the party. Your embassy has promised it for tomorrow.'

81

Maybe Myeloski was better than he had previously thought. Duncan looked through the rest of the pictures.

'I don't know all the others.'

'The second picture is of Sergeant Thomas Williams. He was seconded for this trip as a back-up to Inspector Leeming. Both men, I am assured by your embassy, are trained with weapons and in unarmed combat. They were also both armed.'

'Who's the other girl?' Duncan held up a photograph of a beautiful auburn-haired woman in her mid-thirties. The picture was unusual. Unlike the others, which were basically snapshots, this was one which would have fitted comfortably in any model's portfolio. It had been taken professionally, in a studio, with all the lights and equipment that top photographers use.

'That is a picture we found in the holiday dacha. It was in her bedroom, so we included it. The others are passport snaps, apart from those of the family. She was their interpreter. We have asked your embassy to see if she has any connections that may be of interest to us. Has she an Irish boyfriend? This could always be a terrorist attack.'

'Or a Russian boyfriend?'

'We have asked for a full investigation. All this is, of course, a slow process. Your police cannot be told why we need this information. And your Foreign Office . . .' He shrugged. 'Like treading on broken glass.'

Myeloski knew that Duncan had not been told the whole truth. Typical of the British. Send a man into the field only half-armed with the facts and expect him to do a professional job. 'The girl is American,' he continued. 'Louise Taylor. From Phoenix, Arizona. Would . . . uh?'

'What?'

'Would Oldenburg have brought her with him? As his—'

'We leave that to the French. No, she's not his girlfriend. And that I can guarantee you.'

'As a policeman I must—'

'Question everything. I know.'

'As well as the family, Inspector Leeming and the girl Taylor were also kidnapped. I don't know why the inspector didn't use his gun.'

'Probably because, in a crossfire, some of the family could've been killed.'

'Maybe.'

The two men sat in silence. Duncan threw the pictures back on to the table. Myeloski collected them together, then passed the Englishman a set of larger pictures.

'These are our pictures of the dacha and the gardens.' He rose from the desk and came round to Duncan's shoulder. 'That is the dacha itself. On the eastern out-skirts of the Nikolskaya Vorota Forest, near St Peters-burg. An attractive house, used by the State to entertain foreign visitors. It has security gates and a high wall that runs along the front and side. There were no high walls to the south, only a fence to separate the grounds from the woods and the river. No one expected an attack from there. No one expected an attack. The wall is there only for privacy from the road. There, in that picture' – Myeloski took a photograph from the pile and put it on the top – 'they came along that river-bank. The family were all there, the prince fishing, the others playing on the bank. Your Inspector Leeming was last seen here, by this tree. The girl was with the children.'

'Has nobody any ideas?'

'No. Unless it is the brigands.' Myeloski went back to his desk and sat down. He drank from the glass, then held it up to Duncan, a gesture indicating an offer of a drink. Duncan shook his head.

Myeloski continued: 'It is a common crime. Kidnap-ping. State officials are always under threat, always being kidnapped. After all, only the Government has the money with which to pay a ransom. In the West, it's the industrialists who are targets. Here, state officials. This year, in St Petersburg alone, there have been an army colonel, two Communist Party officials, a university teacher and a tax collector kidnapped. They were all ransomed and returned unharmed. Even the tax collector.'

Duncan smiled. 'Who are the brigands?'

'Wild people. Criminals .who live in the forests and mountains. The worst are in the east, in Siberia. They hide in the birch forests and in the Ural Mountains. Most of them are ex-soldiers, many from the Afghan campaign, who have not settled back into civilian life. They live as outlaws, raiding the villages and towns for food and clothing, for petrol. They are all armed, some with the most modern weapons. I have even heard of some who have helicopters, some say even tanks.'

'Why doesn't the Army go in after them?'

'Because they cannot find them. Have you any idea how big our forests are? Some are bigger than England and France together. And the brigands move around, never stay in one place for too long. But it can't be them. They're two thousand miles to the east of St Petersburg. It may well have been local brigands, but we've found no clues.'

'And there's nothing else? Nothing?'

Myeloski shook his head. 'Not even a ransom note. If we made it public, then they might kill the family. To protect themselves. The only strange thing was their outfits.'

'Cossack clothing.'

'Only some wore that. When the police from the house rushed down and saw them riding away, they say some of them wore military uniform.'

'The Army?'

'Old uniforms. From the First Great War. And also the Cossack-horseman outfits were traditional, from that period. Dressed as they would have during the revolution.'

The two men looked at each other quizzically, then Duncan handed the pictures back to the policeman and stood up. 'When can I go to St Petersburg?' he asked.

'Tomorrow morning.'

'Good. Why did they come to Moscow first?'

'Only one day. They stayed in the hotel you will be in. I have locked off their suite. I thought you might want to see it.'

'There must have been a reason to come here for a day.'

'They met with the president. Privately.'

'Nothing else?'

'No. Apart from one visit at night to the Cathedral of the Assumption.'

'Where's that?'

'You were just looking at it, when we drove in.' Myeloski was annoyed by his own cheap joke. He continued quickly: 'Here. In the Kremlin. We can go there.'

'I'd like that.' Duncan had his own reason for wanting to visit the cathedral.

Myeloski stood up. 'I know that you must wonder if the Soviet authorities have a hand in this kidnapping. I would, if I were in your shoes. I have even considered it myself. I must tell you that I see no advantage to them in this situation. You would also expect me to say that. But it is the truth. We are all in the dark.'

Duncan searched his face, saw the honesty in the eyes. But, as a soldier, he was trained to be wary. 'I hear what you say. But, just as you're a policeman and suspect everyone, so I'm a soldier and don't trust anyone. I'm here to defend the royal family. I will do that at whatever cost.'

'At least we understand each other.' Myeloski walked to the door, Duncan behind him. As the policeman reached to turn off the switch, he said: 'You are good friends? You and Count Oldenburg.'

Duncan realized it was the first time Myeloski had mentioned Oldenburg's Russian origins. 'We were in the Falklands together. We shared a common danger.'

'I've never been in a war, but in the police we also have a need for comradeship. It's not all parking tickets and queue-jumping. We can eat afterwards. I'm afraid I can't offer you fish and chips. But we can get a pizza or a McDonald's.'

'No, thank you. I'm trying to get away from all that.'

Myeloski laughed, switched off the light, and the two men walked out of the room.

A small apartment
Chistoprudney Boulevard
Moscow
9 July
9.45 p.m.

General Dmitry Vashinov sat in the curtain-darkened room, the only source of light a red lamp by the bed.

He was naked, apart from his polished calf-length military boots. He sat astride a ladder-backed wooden chair, his legs splayed out in front of him. As he watched the young couple make love on the small bed, he lit another cigarette with the lighter that lay on the table beside him.

The two lovers who excited him with their performance were both young KGB officers. The girl, twenty-two-year-old Vera Kasyanova, was one of the general's favourites. She had been discovered as a fourteen-year-old Moscow prostitute when she decided to take on the whole of a KGB barrackroom who were in need of relief. Her sexual appetite and expertise at that early age had endeared her to a senior officer who then enlisted her as an agent. Since then she had become one of their most successful 'pillow talk' operatives. Her conquests included black African diplomats, Japanese business-men, American studs and senior party officials. On her odd nights off she still managed to keep some of the barracks satisfied.

The young man writhing underneath her was another of Vashinov's unnamed young officers. They were both totally naked and exuberant in their lovemaking. The general loved watching her; she was totally insatiable, yet capable of multi-orgasms that lasted as long as she was making love. He could tell that the young man was near to coming, but would not dare until Vashinov allowed him to.

Vera looked over to Vashinov and grinned. She knew she had her partner on the verge of an orgasm, but that he would have to work harder at controlling himself. She leant down and started to lick out his ear, bit his lobes, started to tell him of all the things she had done with other men.

At that point the young man lost control and came, his white juices exploding inside her. She came at the same time; then, as he lay there, quivering in his spent heat, she rolled off him and on to her knees. She lifted her buttocks up into the air, taunting Vashinov as he saw the white sperm slide out from inside her.

Vashinov stood up and came to the bed, his penis erect before him. Like its owner, it was short and stubby, not long like the young man's, but thick, so thick that it was impossible for most women to put their hand round it.

'Turn over. Do it,' he commanded the man.

The young man leant in the same position as Vera; they both now offered their buttocks upwards to Vashinov. With the cigarette between his lips, he ran his hands over both their bodies, inserting his fingers deep into them. Vera squealed. Who, she wondered, would be his choice tonight? She started to come again as he tried to slide his whole hand deep into her soaked vagina. Then he lifted his hand from the young man's buttock and felt under his legs, squeezed his balls gently, then firmer, then hard. The young man gasped, the pain between his legs searing through him.

Vashinov laughed, and as he brought Vera to a climax with one hand he took his cigarette from his lips with the other and burnt the young officer's left cheek with its glowing end. Then he threw the cigarette away as the young man started to sob and mounted him, pushing his thick erection deep into his anus. Vera had started to climax again as she saw Vashinov pump away at the young man, his breathing rapid as he reached towards his orgasm.

The phone rang. Its shrill jangle shattered the intense silence. Vashinov tried to continue, but the phone was stubborn, refusing to give up. He pulled out of the young officer, kicked the sobbing man off the bed, then finally answered the phone.

'Vashinov.' It was the old man, Marshka.

The general tried to regulate his breath, tried to speak normally. 'Yes, Comrade Marshka.'

'Bring it forward twenty-four hours.' The old man's voice cut through his sexual heat, brought him straight back to earth. How the hell did the old man know he was here? Only his secretary knew of this place. How did he—? Marshka's voice cut through him again. 'Did you hear what I said, Vashinov?'

'Yes, comrade. Bring it forward twenty-four hours.'

The line disconnected. He put the receiver down, looked round the room. Vera grinned back at him; the young man was still writhing on the floor. Dammit, thought Vashinov. How did he know I was here? And did he know about all this?

'All right, out!' he boomed at the others. 'I have work to do.'

'Aah,' said Vera, her night's entertainment suddenly cut short. She smiled at him as the general hurriedly got dressed. Whoever had called him must have been someone very powerful to make the head of the KGB jump like that.

Vashinov suddenly turned towards her, a grin forming on his lips.

'Ready for some more action, Vera?'

'Always ready, Comrade General.' Even in bed she knew her place.

'Good. Get dressed. Look sexy. I've a little job for you. And get that wimp out of here before you go, will you? Send him back to the Army. I want my officers made of sterner stuff.'

The Cathedral of the Assumption
The Kremlin
Moscow
9 July
9.50 p.m.

The massive Cathedral of the Assumption stands on the north side of Cathedral Square, within the walls of the Kremlin. Crowned with five gilded domes, the cathedral is probably the most important church in Russia's long and turbulent history.

Duncan and Myeloski entered the cathedral through the copper-plated doors of the south portal. The spaciousness and grandeur of the interior of the high domed building stopped Duncan inside the door, its beauty awe-inspiring to the young Englishman.

This was, to him, the Russia of his grandfather, the motherland he had so often been told about. This was where his grandfather had come as a young man, to worship and to be at peace with himself. It was here that Grandfather Denknetzeyan had spent many hours in deep contemplation while the seeds of revolution were scattered all around him, here that he spent his last moments in Moscow before setting out on that final and fateful journey to Petrograd. He saw the old man's face, the half-smile he still remembered so well.

Myeloski stood by his side, unaware of the emotions that raced within his companion.

'It is magnificent, is it not?' he said. 'It was built in 1475 and took only four years to complete. Only four years. Now it would take four hundred.'

It was not Duncan's instinct to share his innermost emotions with Myeloski. He cleared his mind and went farther into the vast cathedral. The policeman followed him, and their shoes clattered eerily in the stillness of the now empty cathedral.

'Was this the only place Oldenburg visited in Moscow?'

'Yes, apart from the hotel and the president's office.'

'Was he on his own or with the family?'

'With his wife. Also the policeman, Leeming.'

'I presume this is on the itinerary for the royal tour.'

'Possibly.' Myeloski shrugged, but the answer surprised Duncan. Why else would the Oldenburgs have visited this great cathedral if not to check it for security?

The Englishman walked to the white stone, the patriarch's seat, and sat on a guide's wooden chair next to it. Even with the few night-lights burning, the cathedral gave an appearance of lightness and spaciousness. As he looked towards the Iconostasis, the wall that is filled with important and unique icons, he tried to re-create his grandfather's torment, his inner pain and despair. The cathedral, for all its size, was a place where you could be alone with your own thoughts, with your soul.

He realized he was wasting time; the past could wait, the future was running on a short time-fuse. He forced his thoughts to Victor. Why should he come here? Why make this his only visiting-place in Moscow? Victor was not an architectural buff. What did this magnificent cathedral hold for him?

He stood up and turned to Myeloski.

'Time to go,' he said. 'To the hotel.'

The policeman walked to the south portal with him, and the two men left the cathedral to its history.

What Myeloski had not told Duncan was that the Cathedral of the Assumption was where the coronation of Russia's rulers had traditionally taken place, that the last of these great ceremonies was in 1896, when Nicholas was crowned as tsar and became Russia's last Romanov emperor.

The Savoy Hotel
Moscow
9 July
11.20 p.m.

Duncan slung his small case on to the bed and zipped it open. He had left Myeloski downstairs at the Hermitage Bar, seated on a stool with a Budweiser light beer and vodka chaser. He was surprised by the Russian's ability to absorb and hold his drink without losing any of his faculties. They had eaten a snack together before coming to the hotel. Myeloski had insisted on buying Duncan a pizza at the latest Pizza Hut. Duncan, not the greatest fan of junk food, had picked at his while the policeman enthusiastically devoured his. He had then polished off Duncan's leftovers before driving him on to the hotel. They had agreed to have a final drink after Duncan had unpacked.

He hung a spare suit and some shirts in the wardrobe and put his washing kit in the bathroom. He plugged in his razor to recharge it and washed his face in the gold-tapped sink. He then returned to the bedroom and carefully folded his socks, underwear, jeans and other casual wear before putting them in a drawer by the bed.

His actions were deliberate, his trained eye looking for

any bugs that might be hidden in the room. He didn't expect to find any as the hotel had recently been refurbished and the KGB would have used the latest available technology, burying it in the plasterwork, the heating and the plumbing. He grinned when he picked up the phone to check the dialling tone. The small sign beside it proudly stated 'Direct Dial Telephone'. Yes, direct to the KGB listening service.

As expected, he found no tell-tale clues that revealed any devices. He left the room, switching off the light behind him. He left the television on. The show was 'Happy Days', and the Fonz grinned into the empty room, his hip American coming out in dubbed Russian.

After he had freshened up, Duncan went into the casino and watched some of the players. One of the croupiers, a blonde girl, beckoned him to join the blackjack table. He grinned back and shook his head. Although he enjoyed gambling, this was not a time for such activities; he needed a clear head at all times.

The simple gambling-chamber was quiet. It had been the first casino in modern Russia, had operated out of a converted bedroom on the second floor. With bored businessmen and other visitors, it hadn't taken the authorities long to realize that gambling was an important source of foreign currency. The casino now extended into what had been five bedrooms. And you could still, as ever, pay with an American Express card. He remembered the card in his pocket. His sense of mischief almost prevailed; he wondered how the Americans would have dealt with his losses at the gaming-tables.

Pushing temptation aside, he left the casino and walked into the crowded bar next door. Myeloski had been joined by a young woman in her early twenties. She was dressed fashionably, mini-skirted with black high heels and a fawn-coloured high-necked blouse. At the back, the blouse cut away in a big yawn down to the wide plastic-belted top of her mini-skirt. Although there were many attractive women mingling with the tourists and officials in the bar, she stood out as the most desirable of them all. She listened intently to Myeloski, who was in full flow, as Duncan approached them.

Myeloski turned as he got there.

'Good, you're back,' he welcomed. 'I have your whisky here. This is Vera. Russian and very, very beautiful.'

The young KGB girl, who only a short time earlier had been the eager recipient of General Vashinov's favours, smiled at Duncan. It was an open smile, attractive and willing. Duncan returned the welcome, with his eyes and his grin.

'Her English is good,' Myeloski continued, warning Duncan to ensure he didn't converse in Russian. 'We were discussing politics. Don't mock, my friend,' he warned. 'All Russians talk of politics.'

'And what were you discussing?'

'The good, or bad, of Western influence.' Myeloski smiled at Vera. 'She does not believe in Western culture. She believes in communism, the way it was. Don't you, Vera?'

'Sometimes. There's nothing wrong with it. Too many people criticize, yet it has given them what they have today. They should not forget it.' Her answer was directed at Duncan.

'Too much change for the sake of change. Not always good,' he replied.

'You see.' She turned back to Myeloski. 'He agrees with me.'

'You can't argue politics with foreigners,' sighed the policeman. 'They always take the easy way out.'

He turned back to his drink, shaking his head in mock despair.

'What are you doing in Moscow?' she asked Duncan.

'Business.'

'You mean, making money.'

'Nothing better. What do you do?'

'I am a secretary and interpreter. For Intourist. I meet many foreigners.'

Behind them, a row was developing at a table between a drunken American and two girls. The man had asked the girls to go to his room, and they had refused. He had obviously spent a lot of money on them and he felt cheated. He was determined to share his viewpoint with everyone else in the room. The girls got up to leave, and he grabbed one of them by the arm, rough in his treatment. From nowhere, a Russian bouncer appeared, dinner-jacketed and big. Before the American could go any farther, the bouncer had grabbed his wrist and forced him to let go of the girl. The girls hurriedly departed, and the bouncer withdrew as quickly as he had appeared. The American sat there, mouthed a few more obscenities before sinking into a deep sulk as he nursed his hurt pride.

The room returned to normal, the incident forgotten.

'Gone are the days when you could buy what you wanted with a pair of Levi jeans and a Jerry Lee Lewis album,' commented Myeloski. 'People are too smart now.'

Duncan looked round the room. Drink was flowing and voices getting louder. It was time to bow out.

'I'm off to bed,' he announced. 'Nice to meet you, Vera. I hope you don't think we're all like that.' He indicated the slouched American. He turned to Myeloski. 'When can I see their suite?'

'First thing in the morning, before we go to St Petersburg. I will pick you up at seven o'clock.'

'See you then.' Duncan gave them both a farewell smile and left. The policeman turned back towards the girl; she followed Duncan with her eyes.

The car, a 1986 Chaika that owed its style as much to the 1958 Cadillac Eldorado as it did to the people's revolution, sped along a country road.

Inside the car, there were five people, the driver and passenger in the front, a girl sandwiched between two burly men in the back. The girl had a black balaclava over her head, and her hands were handcuffed in front of her. She wore a simple summer dress of Western origin.

'How long?' one of the men in the back asked the driver.

'We'll be there in half an hour,' came the reply.

'Then pull over. Let's do it now.'

'You're too eager. It's not meant to be fun,' the front-seat passenger joked, the others joining in the dirty insinuating laughter.

The Chaika pulled into a rutted cart-track and stopped. The doors were flung open as the occupants climbed out, one of them dragging the girl behind him.

The men formed a circle round her; she didn't know where she was in her hooded world. Then one of them, the driver, came forward and grabbed her dress at the front, just under the neck. He pulled sharply on the material, tearing it as he did so. The girl yelped, startled and frightened. The other men moved in, and between them they tore all her clothes off, an intense frenzy, until she stood in front of them, whimpering naked in nothing more than her flat walking-shoes. She tried to tear off the balaclava, but it was tied around the neck, so in her shame and fear she attempted to shield her body with her handcuffed arms.

One of the men laughed, a nervous betrayal of his obvious lust. Three of the men moved closer, the driver stood back and watched. Then they pushed her, from one man to another, making her stumble as each man greedily explored her body before shoving her on to the next man. She was passed around the small circle, turned and fondled, from man to man. Then one of them held her, threw her on to the dry dirt road and started to undo his belt.

'No,' commanded the driver.

'Why not?' came back the reply. 'No one will know.'

'Do you really want to risk that?'

'It'll be her word against ours, even if she dares to say anything,' one of the other men argued.

'No,' said the driver. 'We follow orders. As we were told. Harm her and we're all dead. Now, get her back in the car.'

The others looked at him, but knew that he was right. The man who had sat in the front passenger-seat leant down and grabbed the girl's arm, dragged her through the dirt towards the car and pushed her in.

He climbed in beside her, eagerly rubbing his hands over her body, jostling her in the back seat. The others laughed and got in. Then, with a slam of ill-fitting doors, the Chaika drove off towards Pushkin.

The Savoy Hotel
Moscow
9 July
12 a.m.

Vera Kasyanova came out of the lift on the fourth floor. What she liked about the Savoy was the lack of babushkas, the old women who sat on every floor in all the other hotels and recorded all the movements.

When she had first plied her trade as a child prostitute,

she had always been embarrassed by their silent knowing stares. But as time progressed, and as she became 'official' as a member of the KGB, it was always the babushka who averted her gaze and looked away.

Still, she knew she was being watched. With modern technology, the KGB didn't need the old ladies any more. In fact they now covered every angle in every room in the hotel. And that turned her on. Knowing that she turned the peeping Toms on with her performances – and that they could do nothing about it as they sat there, transfixed by her sex and her flagrant use of it.

As she walked down the corridor, she gave it that bit extra. She really wanted them to burn tonight, to feel the heat between their legs as they watched the glowing monitors. She felt good. She had liked the Englishman, and it was always better when she was attracted to her prey.

She looked for the room and, finding it, knocked on the door.

Almost immediately the door was opened. She smiled, warm and inviting. Duncan stood there, naked apart from a towel wrapped round his mid-section. She had been right. Under his suit she had sensed a hard fit body. It was a body shaped not by exercise machines and aerobics gyms, but by hard endeavour and an active life. In the background she heard the nasal tones of the latest hit television show, 'Sergeant Bilko'.

'Can I come in?' she asked, her smile and body transmitting her availability.

Duncan grinned back at her, then shook his head. She was perplexed; she had sensed his interest in the bar downstairs.

'Why not?'

'Where's Myeloski?' Duncan asked, ignoring her question.

'Your friend? Gone home.' She didn't say that he had

drunk three more large vodkas before leaving, without even a backward glance at her. 'I am an interpreter. If you let me in, I can tell you what Sergeant Bilko is saying.'

'I'm tired. I've travelled a long way today.' He shrugged as he spoke. Then he shut the door in her face.

Vera didn't like that. She was about to knock again when she remembered the peeping Toms. No bonus points for losing face in front of them. She knew the Englishman's type – no meant no. Unless they were queer. She turned and walked back down the hall to the lift.

When she was in the lobby, she went to a phone and called General Vashinov. But he wasn't in to hear of her failure. She returned to the bar and was soon the centre of attention. But, for all her new-found success, she regretted not being with the Englishman. He had got under her skin, and after half an hour she went home alone, not content with second-best.

By the time she left the hotel Duncan was in bed, the light and television both switched off.

He was annoyed with Myeloski. The policeman should have known better than to expect Duncan to fall for a cheap trick like that. But, if that was what he had to expect from the Russian, then that is what he would beware of. He grinned; at least Myeloski had sent him a beautiful woman and not a dog. In any other circumstances he would have warmed to her; he had found her especially disturbing.

He switched off from the incident, lay back and analysed the day's events. He hadn't learnt much. It was a confusing situation, no real clues, nothing concrete. Maybe the Russians were screening something from him; he could only presume that they were. The business with the whore had proved that they were up to no good.

Tomorrow was St Petersburg, and maybe that's where he should have started. The morning visit to Victor's hotel suite would be a waste of time. The Russians would have removed any possible clues from the suite by now.

Duncan shut his eyes and was asleep within two minutes.

The nightmare had begun when the phone rang. It was the same nightmare, Duncan wrapped within the swirling crashing helicopter, flames reaching out to burn him. Only this time there was no Victor, only the emptiness of his own fear and his own death.

He was instantly awake, the sweat on his face the only reminder of his terrible dream. He reached for his watch, checked the time. It was four in the morning. He sat up, switched on the light and answered the phone.

'I am sorry to wake you.' It was Myeloski. 'But we must leave for St Petersburg immediately. Something has happened. I will pick you up in twenty minutes. Be ready in the lobby.'

Myeloski hung up. As he swung his legs out of bed, Duncan wondered if this was the next move in the Russian's game. If it was, he would be ready for him.

Twenty minutes later Duncan was waiting in the lobby. He had shaved, had a shower and was fresh for another day. When you were part of the 14th INT, sleep was something you never took for granted.

Myeloski arrived ten minutes later. He looked terrible as he came up the stairs. Sleep was something he obviously didn't have under control.

He beckoned Duncan to follow, and the two men left the hotel and got into the Lada parked outside, Duncan putting his bag on the back seat. Myeloski started the engine, and the car pulled away.

99

'The girl, Louise Taylor, has turned up in Pushkin. It is a town near St Petersburg.' Myeloski battled with the Lada as he spoke. 'We must go there. The local police have her. Luckily, one of my men intercepted the message and we have kept the news quiet.'

'Has she said anything?'

'No one will speak to her until we arrive. We must use your plane. We can be there in two hours.'

'I wanted to see the hotel suite they stayed in.'

'A waste of time. There's nothing there. I'm sorry I spoilt your sleep.'

Duncan was silent. Maybe the girl hadn't reported back to Myeloski, told him that she had failed to seduce him. And why didn't the policeman want him to see the suite?

The two men sat in silence all the way to Sheremetyevo Airport. One to concentrate on his thoughts, the other to concentrate on the flight ahead that was alien to his being.

The journey, at that hour of the morning, took thirty-five minutes. This time Myeloski broke the speed limit without hesitation.

KGB Headquarters
2 Dzerzhinsky Square
Moscow
10 July
4.50 a.m.

General Vashinov, now fully uniformed, sat at his desk. Even at this late hour, he wanted personally to ensure that the plan was carried through successfully. Now that the old man knew of his weakness, Vashinov did not want the project to fail and thereby have the finger of incompetence pointed at him.

He knew Marshka would destroy him as effortlessly

and unthinkingly as shelling peas. It was not a risk he was likely to take, even if it meant him staying at his desk for the next twenty-four hours.

The phone rang, its soft warble loud in the quiet of the room. He picked it up.

'Well?' he barked into the phone.

'Like clockwork, Comrade General,' came the reply. 'The local police rang our people in St Petersburg. They wanted to know what to do with her, as a foreigner. I told them to say we weren't interested. Our head of bureaux suggested they ring the Foreign Office. He gave them a number. The number was, of course, our own. We told them to contact Captain Ahmed Alekseevich Myeloski. He is now, with the Englishman, on his way to the airport. Officially it is a police matter, and they are dealing with it.'

'Good.' Vashinov scented success.

'The girl is under lock and key. As she will remain until the good captain arrives.'

'Keep me informed,' Vashinov instructed his caller. Then he clicked the line dead with his finger and dialled the president's bedside number. He heard the sleepy voice answer the phone.

'There's been a breakthrough, sir,' he said. 'We've found one of the party.'

He waited, knowing the president was waking up. He then told him what had happened. The president thanked him and told him to keep him in touch with any further developments. The call was then terminated.

Vashinov never rang Grigory Marshka. The old man had gone to bed with instructions not to be disturbed, not unless the plan failed. It was not a call that he would now have to make.

General Vashinov relaxed in his chair. Things were going smoother than expected.

It was a strong cross-wind gusting to over thirty knots across the runway when the Citation touched down.

Duncan landed it on the port main wheel with the wing dipped into the strong cross-current. As the speed bled off, he turned the aircraft on to the runway heading by kicking hard on the right rudder-pedal. The executive jet settled on its main wheels and braked sharply as the thrust-reverse and spoilers were deployed.

As Duncan taxied off the runway, Myeloski silently breathed a sigh of relief. Not the greatest of air travellers, the policeman had accepted Duncan's offer to sit up front in the cockpit. He had been impressed by his companion's expertise, with the way he handled what seemed the most complex manoeuvres with a cool and detached ability.

Duncan had tried to explain what he was doing, but most of it went straight over Myeloski's head. All he remembered was that they had flown on an invisible road in the sky called Red One from Moscow to St Petersburg at 33,000 feet. The Englishman, not concerned with fuel-burn on such a short leg, had kept the plane at an altitude where he sacrificed fuel economy for speed.

Myeloski had enjoyed the flight, once they had taken off and the jet had settled into its smooth high-altitude cruise. That soon changed once the jet had started to descend into its approach and landing into Pulkovo Airport.

The severe turbulence, with the jet bucking up and down as it encountered windshear, had Myeloski wishing he was sitting in the back. At least out of the small side-windows he would not have seen the effects on the

102

aircraft of those gusting winds. But what really unnerved him was the landing. The plane had dipped wildly down on its left wing and skidded on the runway with only one wheel in contact with the ground. Eventually Duncan had managed to slew the aircraft round before it settled on all wheels on the runway. What Myeloski didn't appreciate was that that was how the plane was meant to be landed in such terrible conditions, that he had witnessed a superb piece of flying by a highly trained pilot.

As they taxied in, Myeloski decided he would not comment on what had obviously been a most difficult landing with a lucky outcome.

In Moscow, the screen-watcher was unaware of all this drama and emotion as he tracked the Citation across north-west Russia and into St Petersburg.

He leant back and pushed himself away from the table, sliding backwards on the castors of his typist-style chair. It was a shift-change, and he watched his colleague take over. Then he swivelled round to a side-table and started to write his report. It had been an uneventful night, the bugged policeman doing no more than was expected of him. But soon that could change, when he got closer to his prey and his detective instincts took over. That was when the watchers would have to be at their best.

As he wrote, the new shift operator tracked the Citation towards the parking-ramp, his face lit up by the screen in front of him.

What he didn't know was that the secret military satellite launched on the Columbia space shuttle in the summer of 1989 also had the capability of following the Citation. In Houston, over eight thousand miles away, a similar operative watched a similar screen. The Americans were beaming in on Duncan's credit-card transmitter, his whereabouts constantly monitored by American and British intelligence.

On the ground, when they had left the parked plane, Myeloski excused himself and went to the men's room. After he had been sick in the handbasin, which he diligently cleaned up with paper towels afterwards, he joined Duncan for their drive into St Petersburg.

4

TAKING THE BAIT

Police interview-rooms
Chaykovskovo Avenue
St Petersburg
8.30 a.m.

Louise Taylor sat in the corner of the room, her legs
tucked under her; she rested her chin on her knees.

She was on the small cot bed. The rest of the room was
sparsely decorated and had only two wooden-backed
chairs and a small steel-legged table.

The interview-rooms were away from the main police
station. It was where informers and witnesses could be
taken in private, away from prying eyes. It was also
where criminals could be questioned, with varying
degree, away from the more public places.

Louise Taylor, the girl in the picture that Duncan had
been shown the night before, was now dressed in an ill-
fitting cheap Russian dress. It was all that the police
could find, from a caretaker's wife, after Louise was
discovered, naked and handcuffed, in the Alexander
Palace on the north side of Pushkin. Her body was
bruised, from the beatings she had received, and a

balaclava had been placed over her head.

She was found by the caretaker, whimpering and exhausted on the ground floor of the east wing. The caretaker, an old man and frightened by what he saw, went to his wife who then called the police. The Pushkin police officers had intended to take her to St Petersburg police station when they discovered she was a foreigner. On the fifteen-mile drive, they had been instructed over the radio to stop on the outskirts of St Petersburg, where the woman was transferred to an unmarked car.

She was then taken to the police interview-rooms in Chaykovskovo Avenue, the handcuffs were finally removed and then she was left alone.

At seven-thirty an officer brought in a tray with a bowl of semolina mixed with stewed dry fruit. She devoured it, not having eaten for twenty-four hours, and then stayed on her cot until Duncan and Myeloski arrived.

She looked up as they entered, her eyes tired but wary. The two men could see that she had been crying, that she was still extremely distressed.

Duncan stood back, against the wall, as Myeloski picked up one of the wooden chairs and pulled it up to the cot. He sat on the chair, perched forward on the edge.

'I'm Captain Ahmed Alekseevich Myeloski, Moscow City Police,' he started, speaking in English. 'I am here to—'

'I'm an American citizen,' she interrupted. 'I want to see the ambassador.'

'Do you have proof that you are American? Your passport?'

'You know how they found me. I didn't have any clothes, let alone a passport.' She was contemptuous in her reply.

'When the caretaker found you, you spoke to him in Russian. Also to the local police. How do I know you're an American?'

'Look, I'm not prepared to discuss this with anyone until I know you're who you say you are. And not until I have someone from the American embassy present.'

Myeloski reached into his pocket and took out his warrant-card. He showed it to her, but she turned away.

'I'm English,' Duncan spoke quietly. 'I'm here to find the Oldenburgs. We can either waste time or find the family.'

She swung round, her swollen eyes searching Duncan for the truth. He realized that she wanted to believe him. He came forward and took his passport from his top pocket and handed it to her. She flicked through it, suspicious.

'Before you say it's a forgery,' he went on, 'let me assure you that we are all after the same thing. The safe return of the Oldenburgs. And George Leeming. We already know who you are. Louise Taylor. Interpreter. You're over here to help organize the royal visit.'

The girl looked hard at him, then handed the passport back. As he put it away, she turned to Myeloski.

'What do you want to know?'

'What happened. Anything that can help.' He pulled a small tape-recorder out of his pocket and put it on his lap, switching it on as he did so. 'You were all fishing. By the river. Then what happened?'

She stared at Myeloski, still tense from her ordeals. Then she shut her eyes and took a deep breath, collecting herself. After a moment, she opened them again.

'I was with two of the children, the baby and Jemma. Victor and Anna were fishing; they'd just caught something and were shouting to us. Then, from across the river, these horsemen appeared, riding along the bank and waving. They had old clothes on – you know, period stuff. We thought it was a display for the family; everyone started waving back and cheering. Then they rode across the river, across the shallow bit. That's when

George saw the guns they were carrying. They were modern – automatics, I think.'

'George?' asked Myeloski.

'Inspector Leeming,' said Duncan, reminding Myeloski of the policeman.

Myeloski nodded, then turned back to the girl. 'I'm sorry. Please go on.'

'He started to shout, warning us. But it was too late. The horsemen just charged forward, guns aimed at us. By the time George got his gun out, they were right there, on us. I don't know exactly what happened, but they seemed to lean down and grab us, just pull us up on to their horses. One of the men came straight up to me and grabbed the kids. I tried to stop him, but he just knocked me down. Then another man picked me up, swung me in front of him and we rode off. Victor and George ended up riding a spare horse – I don't know where it came from – and then we went to where they'd come from. I saw people running down from the house, I heard some shots, but that was all. Next thing we were in the woods and away. All I really remember is the kids crying and no one doing anything about it.'

She stopped, her breath now coming fast. Myeloski leant forward and put his hand on her arm to comfort her. She started to sob, slowly at first, then harsher. It was a sob of relief – she knew she was finally safe; then the cries turned to ones of anguish.

The two men left her to her grief. Neither spoke; they knew that it was a trauma she had to face. After nearly five minutes, Louise started to calm down, her breathing slowly becoming shallower and more regular.

'I need to know more,' said Myeloski, his voice gentle. 'To help find them.'

She nodded. 'I don't know how long we rode for. I just know we went deeper into the woods. Then, after quite a while, we came to a small clearing. There was a truck there, on the road.'

'What sort of truck?'

'Military. Camouflaged. Sort of truck you carry troops in.'

Duncan and Myeloski looked at each other; things were starting to take a new direction.

'Did it have any signs on it?'

'Like what?'

'Like a red star, or anything that could identify it?'

'No.'

'Was it green or blue?'

'Grey. Camouflage grey. Blue grey.'

'Are you sure?' Myeloski snapped at her, a dog straining at its lead.

'Yes. Grey.' She was startled by his intensity, withdrawing into herself.

He smiled at her, trying to win her confidence back again. 'I just wanted to make sure. Different colours for different services in Russia. Grey – it isn't used by any of the armed forces, you see. You said it was on a road. What sort of road?'

'Just a track. In the forest.'

'A dirt track?'

'Yes.'

'But wide enough for a truck?'

'Yes.'

'So you got to the truck. Then what happened?'

'They put us in the back. All of us. I held the children with their mother. Some of the men climbed in after us and put the cover down on the back, so no one could see us. They made us all kneel, made us put our heads between our legs and clasp our hands behind. Then they handcuffed us. George, at one stage, tried to get up, but one of them hit him over the head with his rifle. He was knocked out for a time. We were facing the front of the truck, so we couldn't see the men. We travelled for a long time. Because the children were crying, they picked them up and put something in their mouths. The kids slept after that, on some sacks in the corner.'

'But they were all right after that?' asked Duncan. Little point in saying he was godfather to one of them.

'Yes. We were scared for them, but one of the men said it was a small drug. They were OK afterwards.'

'Did the men speak English or Russian?' Myeloski asked her.

'They always spoke to us in English.'

'What sort of English?'

'Foreign. It wasn't their natural language.'

'Did they speak to each other, say anything?'

'No. Throughout the whole thing, even when they took us to the palace, nobody said a word. Not when they were near us anyway.'

'The palace?' said Duncan.

Myeloski held up his hand to Duncan to silence him. 'Tell us what happened after the truck ride.'

'We drove for a long time. It must have been an hour or more. When we stopped, they came and put hoods, woollen knitted ones, over our heads. I noticed it was dark outside when they opened the back. I noticed, just when one of them put the hood over me, that they had changed.'

'How?'

'Into army clothes. They had different boots on, modern army ones. One of them – I didn't see his face – looked like a soldier.'

'Officer or enlisted?' asked Duncan.

'I couldn't tell. I don't know the difference. And it was only a glimpse.'

'They took you out of the truck?' Myeloski took her back into her sequence.

'Not straight away. After maybe another half-hour. Then they led us into a building and kept us there, all together.'

'They took the hoods off?'

'Yes, but they always left the lights on.'

110

'You must've seen the men, then.'

'No. They made us stay at one end of the room. Then they cut small square holes, four of them, in the door opposite, which they kept closed. They watched us through the holes, and always had two guns pointing directly at us. We were about – I don't know – fifty feet from the door. There was nothing we could do.'

'Did you talk to each other?'

'Not a lot. We had to sit with our backs to the wall, facing the door. Our hands were handcuffed in the front. We had to keep at least ten feet from each other. If they came in, with food or to check us over, we always had to put on our hoods first.'

'You must've discussed what was happening, even in whispers,' said Duncan.

'We couldn't. They always had one child with them, outside the room. They told us they would kill them if we didn't follow orders.' She was suddenly angry. 'What would you have done? Taken that risk? Easy when they're not your kids.'

Myeloski interrupted, his tone gentle. 'You said a palace. What palace?'

'The room we were in. It was big, very ornate. Like you'd expect in a palace. But it was run-down, plaster missing, streaks on the walls. There was no furniture, just sacking for us to sit and sleep on. Even when we slept, we had to spread out, heads towards feet, always facing the door.'

'Did you go anywhere else?'

'No. Then – I don't know how long we were there – they came and got me, dragged me away from the rest. I got taken outside, thrown in a car and squashed between two men and driven for quite a while. Then they stopped, got me out of the car, still with my bloody hood on, and ripped my clothes off.' She looked defiantly at them both. 'I don't know why they did it and no, don't even think it, I wasn't raped. Then they took me to

111

where the police found me. Just dragged me into the building, threw me down on the floor, made a lot of noise and left.'

'Did they say anything, while you were in the car?'

She caught her breath, looked down in her shame. 'Only that the reason they didn't rape me was because if they were found out they would be killed. I know that because I heard them.' There was a silence and then she swore, remembering the fear that had convulsed her. 'Bastards!'

'There was no message to give, nothing about a ransom or anything?' Myeloski brought her back to the present.

'Nothing,' she replied, suddenly washed out.

Myeloski stood up. 'We will need to go with you to where you were found.'

'Now?'

'Yes. I know you're tired and hungry. Time isn't on our side.'

'Can I get a sandwich and a drink at least?'

'Of course,' answered Myeloski. You could sense the urgency in his tone. There wasn't a lot to go on but, whatever little there was, he didn't want the scent to go cold.

And then he led them out of the small room.

The Kremlin
Moscow
10.30 a.m.

Marshka was late. When he finally wheeled himself into the Politburo meeting, all the others had arrived. They knew he was deliberately late. It was all part of the game that he enjoyed playing.

The president sat at the head of the long mahogany table. It had been a gift to Tsar Nicholas from Queen

Victoria. The meeting had not yet opened, and he was in deep conversation with Boris Telskyn, former mayor of Moscow and one of the leading democrats in the Soviet Union. It had always been the president's strength, the way he managed to keep all the different political factions under control, to keep them talking as the Soviet Union underwent her tremendous social change.

He stopped talking as Marshka entered and wheeled himself into the empty space at the table, at that end farthest, on the right-hand side, from the president.

'Apologies, comrades,' he said, 'but in today's enlightened consumer age the traffic problem seems to get worse day by day.'

'Welcome, Grigory Mikhailovich,' said the president. He looked round the room, taking his time, being deliberate before he spoke. 'This meeting has been called because of the urgency of the situation. There is only one matter on the agenda.'

As the president spoke, Marshka looked round the room. At eighty-two, he was the oldest there, well over the compulsory age of retirement. But he knew his position was safe, that no one dared challenge his seat on the Politburo. General Vashinov sat opposite him, to his left and halfway up the table. They had carefully avoided eye-contact since the old man had entered. But they had already spoken that morning, their plans drawn up ready to be activated.

The other twelve members were a mixture of the old and the new. Since the loss of their monopoly as the ruling party, the communists now accounted for half the Politburo; the rest represented the different parties who now shared power. Under the president's leadership, there were now more radicals than conservatives. But, with his perception and wisdom, he had managed to move matters forward in a way where compromise was not a weakness but a strength. The only odd man out was Marshka. Yet, because of his knowledge, he had powers

113

second only to the president. He was the arch-socialist, the keeper of the past, the living conscience of Lenin and those revolutionary ideals.

'You have all seen the report from Captain Myeloski.' Marshka had received it by fax at his dacha, as they all had. The president waited before going on, to confirm that no one had missed the report.

'As you can see, there is still no obvious reason as to why they were kidnapped. No ransom demands, nothing. The release of the girl is also confusing. The family were here, with other security representatives, to prepare for the forthcoming royal visit.'

'It's a warning,' said Alexander Alexandrovich Vasily, the youngest of the Politburo members, a writer by profession and the first non-politician on the ruling body. He had also been a trade union official, once leading a strike of railway workers in 1989. The president had silenced the vociferous strike-leader by bringing him on to the ruling body. 'To stop us going ahead with the tour.'

'Why?'

'Because it reminds us of our past. For all this talk of democracy, some still remember the days of the Romanovs. And they were supported by the British. I have to say I am amazed to find you have called a special meeting of the Politburo over a simple kidnapping.'

'Unless there is more, something you couldn't put in the written message.' Marshka's words hit home, all eyes turned towards the president.

'Nothing escapes you, my friend,' replied the president. He waited before answering, making sure his audience was totally prepared for what was to come.

'The family, the Oldenburgs, are also descendants of the Romanovs.'

The disbelief round the table was sudden; it was the last thing they expected to hear. The gasps of shock built into a cacophony of questions. The president raised his hand to silence them before going on.

'You can see now why this matter is so important.'

'Did we know they were Romanovs? Before they were kidnapped?' asked Vasily, leading the pack once more.

'No,' lied the president.

'Then, the British got us into the mess.'

'That isn't the point. What is important is determining why they were here, and who kidnapped them.'

'Call in the KGB?' asked Vasily.

'Too big a risk. The less people who know, the better. The last thing we want to do is broadcast this information.'

'What does the KGB think?' Marshka asked. 'Do they think it's too big a risk?'

They all looked at the president, and then at General Vashinov. The old man was again openly questioning the leadership. But the president was quiet. The KGB would have to sort itself out.

Vashinov's answer was simple and direct. 'There's no point in us getting involved at present, although we are closely monitoring the situation. The policeman is doing the best he can, under impossible conditions. Anyway, where would we start? There're no real clues. Too many investigators would all fall over themselves in the confusion. Let the policeman go on, as he is, until he finds something which we can follow up. Until then, we must wait and watch for something to turn up.'

Vashinov sat back, his viewpoint terminated. He looked straight at Marshka; it was a look that could only be recognized by the others as defiant. Marshka shrugged and looked down at the report in front of him. He was pleased. It was going as they had planned.

'Does that answer your question, Grigory Mikhailovich?' asked the president. Marshka nodded, his gaze held in front of him.

'I agree with the KGB,' the president went on. 'We

must sit and wait. And ensure that the news-blackout remains.'

His words were leaden, heavy on the room, as truth often is.

'Do you agree with that, Grigory Mikhailovich?' asked Vasily of the old man.

Marshka looked round the table. 'I agree that we do nothing. For the moment anyway.'

The old man turned his wheelchair and left the room. The door was opened for him by a secretary who sat alone in a corner. As his driver took charge of the wheelchair in the hall, Marshka looked behind him and noted with satisfaction that the meeting was already breaking up.

The road to Pushkin
11 a.m.

Myeloski struggled with the Lada, making slow time even though the traffic was light and the road clear.

It was an unmarked car and it now carried the three of them towards Pushkin. Louise Taylor was asleep in the back, a half-eaten sandwich, made of chorny bread and salad, still in her hand. She had changed into some clothes brought for her by a clerk who had been sent out with a handful of roubles to a nearby shop.

The car smelt of fish. Myeloski, not having had his customary oatmeal porridge for breakfast, had stopped at a shop to buy some vobla, a dried Caspian roach. He had returned to the car, after having pushed his way to the front of the queue shamelessly brandishing his police warrant-card, with the fish in a rolled-up newspaper.

They had then rolled off towards Pushkin with Myeloski eating the vobla out of an old copy of *Izvestia* which was unrolled on his lap. Duncan wasn't too concerned because he soon realized that there was little difference in the policeman's driving whether he used one hand or two. The girl in the back was too exhausted to worry anyway.

As he sat there, he though about the interview, about the girl's story.

'You seemed surprised,' he said to Myeloski, 'about the army truck being grey.'

'It was nothing. Only that it wasn't the Army. We have no grey colours in the armed forces. It was a private vehicle, painted to look like the Army. That was all.'

Duncan didn't believe him.

But there was nothing to be gained by challenging him now. He remembered the girl Vera, and how Myeloski had tried to set him up. He probably wasn't a policeman anyway, more likely a member of the KGB.

Duncan closed his eyes, settled back. His instincts, honed over the years as he lived continuously on the threshold of danger, warned him that things were about to change. Soon something would open up and give him a path to follow.

Until then, he, too, would wait.

They arrived half an hour later.

Pushkin, named after the Russian poet who studied there, was once the prettiest town in Russia.

In pre-revolution times it was known as Tsarskoye Selo, which is 'Royal Village' in Russian. It had been the summer home of the Russian monarchy since 1716 and housed some of the greatest imperial palaces and parks in Russian history. It was where the court gathered in summer, and those who followed royalty built many great houses in Tsarskoye Selo.

After the revolution, the town was shortly renamed Detskoye Selo ('Children's Village') and many of the great houses were turned into sanatoria for children.

During the Second World War, the Germans destroyed the town. Although the art treasures had long since been taken to Moscow, many of the palaces were in ruins after the fearful fighting between the Russians and the Germans. With the Germans finally driven out, some restoration work was undertaken. But money was short and other priorities more important.

In this climate, it was only within these last few years that serious restoration work was initiated. The result is that most of the great palaces are only partly restored, the parks only just beginning to take shape again. Most of the restoration has been on the exterior of the buildings; most of the interiors are still as they were the day the Germans were defeated.

As they drove along the wide boulevards, Myeloski was expansive in his description of the history of the town. It was the first time he had been there, but he had learnt about the town from the captain in charge of the St Petersburg interview-rooms.

Duncan half-listened. In his mind he saw his grandfather; he must have visited here as a young man. He couldn't recall the name, but the old man had often talked about a magical place where the family stayed in the summer months, a home that was part of the Romanov court. He sensed it was here; this must have been the place. He suddenly wished his grandfather was alive; how he would have enjoyed showing him all this, listening to the old man and reliving it as it must have been.

Louise was still asleep in the back, her exhaustion now complete.

They came off the St Petersburg road and into Boulevard Vasenko. The Alexander Palace, yellow and white in its beauty, was on the left, and Myeloski turned the car into the great driveway at the front of the palace. He parked by the entrance as a steward came up to them, signalling them to park elsewhere. Myeloski got out and waved the man away, holding up his warrant-card as he did so. After having woken the girl, Duncan led her into the palace as they followed the policeman, past the small queue of tourists and other visitors who were waiting to sightsee.

The Alexander Palace was one of the imperial family's smaller homes. Crescent-shaped, it has an austerity that is unusual compared to other palaces. From 1904 it had been the last Romanov's main home. It was here, on the ground floor of the east wing, that Louise Taylor had been found, in the same room that had been the royal family's drawing-room. As with much of Pushkin, the Alexander Palace had survived the revolution but not the Germans. Although there were some rooms open to the public, most of the interior was desperately in need of restoration.

Myeloski led them to the room where the girl had been found. She sat at the window, looking out on the gardens, not wanting to be reminded of her ordeal as her two companions searched for any clues that might have been left.

When they had fruitlessly exhausted their task, Myeloski called the caretaker to guide them round the rest of the palace. He led the girl, was gentle with her, wanted to see if any of the other rooms held any memory for her. But, after nearly an hour, it was obvious that she had simply been brought to this near-empty building and left for the police to find her.

The three of them returned to the car. It was now nearly one o'clock, and Myeloski was ready for his lunch. He trundled the Lada into Pushkin, down the Boulevard Vasenko, looking for a restaurant, preferably a McDonald's. At the end of the Boulevard there sits the enormous Catherine Palace, baroque and three times the size of the Alexander Palace. Still being restored, over half the Catherine Palace is closed to the public.

Just opposite, next to the Church of the Sign, there was a new Wendy's Hamburgers drive-in. Myeloski went for a big order while the other two ordered coffees.

The policeman then pulled the car across the road, crossed the Lycée and with a wave of his warrant-card was soon parked in the officials-only area in the palace grounds.

He said little, concentrating on his meal, but obviously deep in thought. The other two sat in silence; there was nowhere they could go.

He broke his silence once, talking through a full mouth as the hamburger sauce ran down the side of his mouth. 'How long were you driving for after they took you away from the family?'

'Not long, about half an hour.'

'In a straight line? Or were there many corners?'

She reflected before answering. 'The car seemed to turn a lot. And stopped many times.'

'Were they driving fast?'

'No. It didn't seem fast. I can't remember that well; they all kept talking a lot.'

Eventually, when he had slurped his way through the two cheeseburgers and large French fries, polished off an apple pie and a strawberry milkshake, he got out of the car and walked over to a litter-disposal unit. He trashed his rubbish, then signalled the other two out of the car. He then led them into the Catherine Palace, once more brandishing his authority whenever an official came forward to stop them.

They found the room in the deserted area, up on the third floor. It was where the bedrooms had been; they were later to discover that it was where the Romanovs had lived for a century and a half and had been the favourite apartments of Nicholas I.

The girl recognized the room immediately. It was at the top of a small staircase, well away from the heart of the building. As they entered the room, Duncan saw the four square holes in the door, big enough for men to look through and also rest the muzzle of their guns on.

Louise was at first excited; then, when the recollection

had overwhelmed her, collapsed in a corner, her body racked with sobs. Myeloski, hands and lips greased with hamburger oil, sat beside her on the sacking that covered the floor and tried to comfort her.

Duncan searched the rooms, but found only some soiled children's clothing and their excreta. In the room where the guards must have remained, there were no clues, no cigarette butts, no sign of anyone having ever been there.

When Louise had collected herself, Myeloski took her through her story again, this time asking her to point out where incidents had occurred, where the hostages had been held.

Her story was as before, but Myeloski wanted to make sure that he missed nothing. After he had checked her account, he then spent nearly an hour searching, with Duncan, for clues.

But there were none; the kidnappers had taken their charges and disappeared. As a matter of course they checked the rest of the disused area before leaving the palace. Myeloski took some Polaroid pictures before they left, having sent Duncan to the car for his camera.

On the drive back to St Petersburg the girl once again dropped off to sleep. Only then did Myeloski open up to Duncan.

'They knew what they were doing,' he said, 'cleaning up after themselves like that. I don't think they're common criminals. These boys are professionals.'

'What made you go there?' Duncan had been surprised by the policeman's astuteness in deciding to investigate the Catherine Palace.

'Just a hunch. Luck, I suppose,' he replied.

'Are you going to call in your people to check for fingerprints or anything?'

'We could, but I don't think they'd find anything. If you remember, the girl said they always wore leather gloves. And this is meant to be hush-hush. Put the lab boys in and . . .' He shrugged. Duncan realized he was right.

They drove back to St Petersburg in silence.

What Myeloski didn't tell Duncan was that things were slowly beginning to take shape in his mind. There was a pattern forming, loose and ragged, but a pattern. And the policeman wanted to check his facts before deciding to take a chance on a long shot. It was a crazy idea, but it was all he had at the moment.

What he didn't know was that the captives had already been moved over two thousand miles to the east. As the Lada sped towards St Petersburg, the hostages were being moved into a spacious townhouse that was now empty and had once been a district governor's home.

The prey was distancing itself fast from the hunters; the scent, as Myeloski knew, was still cold and getting colder.

Astoria Hotel
Herzen Street
St Petersburg
6 p.m.

Duncan's room was on the seventh floor.

The Astoria, one of St Petersburg's finest, had been refurbished in 1989. Not as plush as the Savoy, it was another hotel designed specifically for visiting business-men and other important visitors.

Part of the top floor had been sectioned off by the police and now housed those involved in the kidnapping. The cordoned-off area, quite common in Russian hotels when special guests were being entertained and there-fore not something that would cause suspicion, was served by its own lift from the lobby. Two plain-clothes policemen, acting as hotel security men, kept watch at

122

the lift. Any unwanted guest soon found himself bundled down to one of the lower floors.

Duncan sat in his room with Sergeant Thomas Williams, the second royal policeman, who had accompanied Leeming on the visit. Williams had received the George Medal for saving three young children who were taken hostage during a bank robbery. He, like most of their bodyguards, was devoted to the royal family and would give his life for them.

Half an hour later Duncan was no farther in his quest. Williams had not been there during the vital moments when the kidnapping had taken place. He had heard shots, including the rapid fire of automatics, but when he rushed down to the river-bank the kidnappers had already vanished with their victims.

He knew nothing of the girl Louise Taylor, other than that she had arrived at Buckingham Palace three months earlier and had spent time coaching the prince and the duchess in Russian. She kept to herself and didn't seem to act in any suspicious manner.

'When do you think they'll let us go home?' asked Williams at the end of the questioning.

'When we've found them,' answered Duncan. 'Not until then.'

When Williams finally left the room, the phone rang.

It was Myeloski.

'Where've you been?' asked Duncan. Myeloski had left him and Louise Taylor at the hotel entrance after the drive from Pushkin. He had been preoccupied and seemed impatient to get on his way.

'Just checking on some things. I am at police headquarters now. I have the replies from London. How did your meeting with Sergeant Williams go?'

'I didn't learn anything.'

'I told you that!' Myeloski's arrogance irritated Duncan.

'Where're you off to now?' he said, not allowing his annoyance to show.

'To get some food. And to do some reading.' The phone went dead.

Duncan put down the phone. He went to the side-table and poured himself a glass of water. Then he waited for Louise Taylor to wake from her exhausted sleep.

Marshka had arrived late and now sat with Vashinov in his office waiting for the latest report.

'Have you dug up any further information on the SAS captain?'

'Very little. He's one of their best men, with their intelligence arm. Russian descent, but no emotion for the motherland.'

'What was his family name?' The old man was suddenly interested.

'Denknetzeyan. White Russians, from the Tiumen area in western Siberia.'

'Count Nikolai Denknetzeyan. From that family?'

Marshka never ceased to amaze Vashinov. 'That was his great-grandfather.'

'Then, his blood will still be hot for Mother Russia.' Marshka smiled at the general as he spoke. 'Don't look so sceptical. I just hope that he believes what he sees, that you don't become too obvious and make him realize that he's being set up.'

'That will not happen. Of that I'm confident.' But inside himself Vashinov knew that something would soon go wrong. That was Boris's Law. Something would soon get buggered up.

'Is that policeman out of that library yet?' asked Marshka.

124

The general picked up the phone and dialled. As he asked for the latest report, Marshka thought about the policeman and the Englishman. He knew, from their records, that they could be a formidable pair, if they worked together. He wanted them to continue to distrust each other, continue to irritate. In that way, it would be easier to plant the clues and let them stumble on them. He had been surprised that they had discovered the Catherine Palace hideaway. That must have been down to the policeman.

'He's on his way back to the hotel,' Vashinov reported as he put down the phone.

'Good. I feel happier when they're all under the same roof. I hope they go to bed early. Otherwise they're going to have another sleepless night, and we need them fresh for the next stage.'

Dvortsovaya Embankment
St Petersburg
10 p.m.

The Dvortsovaya runs along the Neva river and in front of the State Hermitage. It looks out where the river widens and splits at Vasilyevskiy Island. Across the waters, the magnificent Peter and Paul Fortress looks back at the shoreline. It was here, on 'Bloody Sunday', that the shooting and killing of thirty people started the First Revolution of 1905. Twelve years later, the square at Dvortsovaya became the centre of the Bolshevik uprising.

Duncan and Myeloski walked side by side. The view was breathtaking, and even in this period of crisis both men found time to absorb St Petersburg's beauty.

Duncan had learnt little from Louise Taylor; she had woken earlier than he expected, had wanted to eat.

He took her down to the brasserie, sat with her at a

corner table away from the main body of the room. While she ate he sipped a Miller Lite, watched her devour the meal as her appetite returned. Things were getting back to normal.

'Feels good,' she said when she had finished.

'Returning to the land of the living always does,' he replied.

She looked at him quizzically. 'What're you doing here?'

'Keeping you company.'

'I meant in Russia.'

'You know exactly what I'm here for.'

'You're not a policeman.'

'How can you tell?'

'Easy. Your feet are too small.'

He laughed, shook his head.

'So what are you doing here?'

'Helping find the family.'

'And George.'

'Of course.'

'Are you Intelligence?'

'I passed a few exams.'

'Very funny.' She smiled at his deliberate avoidance of her questions. 'If you're a policeman . . .' She paused.

'If I'm a policeman . . .'

'Policemen always ask questions. Interrogate me.'

'Were you sleeping with George?'

'Bastard.' She caught her breath, surprised by the suddenness of the question. 'Policemen don't ask that sort of question. Not straight away.'

'Were you?'

'No.'

He saw she lied. Leeming's reputation with women was well known.

'What if I was?' she continued.

'Makes no difference. I was just interested.'

She shook her head, saw the humour in his eyes. 'If

you're not a policeman, then who are you?'

'Just a soldier. A friend of Victor's. And the family. Just like I said.'

'So why did they send you? Why not a policeman?'

'I don't make decisions. I'm just here to help find them.'

'What sort of soldier?'

'A captain type.'

'An officer and gentleman.' She looked him over, cool and casual in her appraisal. 'Not so much the gentleman.'

Duncan shrugged.

'SAS?' she asked quietly. 'You've been sent in case there's trouble.'

'Just an everyday captain,' he replied, equally quiet.

They stared at each other, she questioning in her gaze, he stonewalling her with a half-smile on his lips.

It was the girl who broke the silence. 'I hope you find them. Alive.'

'I'm sure we will.'

'Have you any clues? Apart from those today in the palace.'

'We'll get there.'

'With your fat friend?'

Duncan grinned, remembered Myeloski's eating habits. 'A clever fat friend. He worked out where you'd been kept prisoner.'

She nodded, suddenly remembered her ordeal. He saw the pain cross her face.

'Sorry. I didn't mean to remind you.'

She looked at him, warmth returning to her eyes. She moved her hand across the table, touched his arm, squeezed it for comfort.

'All things pass,' she said. 'In time. I wish you luck, soldier boy. You're going to need all you can get.'

When Myeloski had returned to the hotel, after the girl had gone to her room, Duncan had suggested they

127

go for a walk. The policeman had been genuinely pleased by the invitation, and the two had set off for the river.

Myeloski nudged Duncan and signalled him to watch a scene farther on, just by a small playground.

A young girl, no more than eighteen months old, dressed in a pretty pink outfit, was playing with some fallen leaves. She picked one up, stood there swaying in her newly learnt balance, and crumpled the leaf. It sprang open again, and this made the girl laugh – a crackle of pleasure from her tiny mouth. She did it again; once more the leaf sprang open. She turned to her mother, a young woman who was watching her, and did it all again for her benefit. Mother and child laughed, sharing their love and their joy of discovery.

'Whatever the difference, children are the same the world over.' Myeloski turned away and walked to the river-wall, leant against it. Duncan came alongside him. The two men stared out, their eyes searching in the dark for the brightly lit fortress on the other side.

'The car, the one the girl was in, if it was a Zil as she says, then it was seen by a policeman,' Myeloski told Duncan.

'Did they get a number?'

'This is Russia. Policemen don't take numbers of official government cars.'

'Official! Government!' Duncan was alarmed.

'Zils are used for visiting VIPs and government officials only. Nobody else could afford one. But it was night-time, and anybody could have borrowed it – a chauffeur, anybody.'

'Anything else?'

'Nothing.'

'I can't go on just standing by, you know.'

'What else can you do? We have to wait. Something will happen. Have you been involved with hostages before?'

'Yes.'

'Tell me about them.' Myeloski, although dealing with kidnappers in other cases, had never known how the hostages survived their isolation and their fear. As soon as he had apprehended any kidnappers, the state prosecutor moved in on the hostages and he never saw them again.

'It's a strange relationship between hostages and captors.' Duncan remembered an Irish businessman his unit had rescued from the IRA two years earlier. The man had been held for nearly four months in a blacked-out room. He had been like an animal when they found him. They hadn't let him go home for nearly a week; there was no way he could have coped with his freedom or his family.

'They become dependent on their kidnappers,' he went on. 'Like a dog you keep chained up in a dark room. It hates you for putting it there, but is loyal to you because you bring it food. In all the cases I've seen, when the hostages have been freed they have always understood the kidnappers' motives, always sympath-ized with them. And still went on hating them.

'I remember one incident.' He recalled the business-man again, saw his face, framed in the night-light outside the small house they had kept him captive in. 'He'd been held for four months. Never left his room in that time. When he saw the terrorists, the people who were responsible for his plight, he lunged forward, grabbed a rifle off one of the soldiers. He had it up there' – Duncan touched his own forehead – 'the gun cocked, ready to blow the kidnapper's head off. Then he just started to cry, just dropped the gun and put his arms round the man. He just sobbed until someone came and took him away.'

'How did the kidnappers react?'

'Thought he was a nutter. They don't give a damn, do they? Just want their money.'

129

'Your friend. Can he handle it?'

'I think so. It's more difficult with the family there. He can't try anything, couldn't risk trying to get away.'

'I don't think it will last long, this kidnapping.'

'Why?'

'Because when it gets into the papers, which it will, things will happen fast. That is, if they want their money.'

'I don't agree. There are terrorists who want nothing more than publicity. You've got all these regions after independence; it could be any one of them, using the situation to highlight their struggle. You've also got various religious freedom fighters. They could even end up in Beirut, if some of those Muslim fundamentalists get their hands on them. I don't think it's as cut and dried as you think.'

'You can't blame us Muslims for everything.'

Duncan squirmed; he had forgotten the policeman was a Muslim.

Myeloski laughed. 'But you are right. We mustn't discount anything.'

The men turned together and started to walk back to the hotel. Duncan knew that Myeloski had more to tell him, that he was holding back. But he also realized that the policeman was not a man who trusted easily. He would have to wait, and until then he would keep as close as he could to the Russian. He regretted leaving Myeloski alone in the afternoon. He should have insisted that he go with him. He decided then that he wouldn't let that situation occur again.

What he didn't know was that Myeloski wanted to share his knowledge with the Englishman. If what he believed was really happening, then he would need Duncan's support.

Myeloski was beginning to realize that he could be taking on forces that encompassed the very people who ran the Soviet Union, the powermasters who employed him to keep the peace as a police officer.

It wasn't just a kidnapping. It was about the future of the Soviet Union.

Astoria Hotel
Herzen Street
St Petersburg
11.30 p.m.

Duncan had left Myeloski propping up the bar, drinking his customary vodka and Budweiser chaser. He himself had drunk one quick light beer before excusing himself for an early night.

The room was hot when he entered, and he turned down the thermostat on the wall. Then he went to bed, having checked the room for electronic bugs and found one in the base of the lamp. He knew it was a decoy, but could find no other.

The knock on the door came just after he had put out the light. He got up, slipped a towel round his waist and opened the door.

Louise Taylor wore a white bathrobe that ended halfway up her thighs. 'I can't sleep,' she said. To highlight her legs, she also had on a pair of black high heels. Duncan knew she was naked underneath. He also knew the room was bugged.

He stood back, inviting her in. He also held his forefinger to his lips, indicating that they might be overheard. She nodded, understanding his signal, as she came into the room.

By the time he had closed the door and turned into the room she had slipped the towelling robe off her shoulders. She stood there, beautiful and tall, in nothing but her high heels.

They looked at each other, neither saying a word, silent in their understanding of each other. Then she

131

stepped forward and pulled at his towel. It fell away and she saw that he was already excited.

She knelt in front of him, took his manhood into her mouth. He watched, excited yet dispassionate. It was something they both needed, a release from the events of the day.

He leant down, put his arms on her shoulders and lifted her up. Then he kissed her, felt her breath release as she felt the force of his passion as he put his arms around her waist, as he pulled her towards him.

Then he swung her round, lifted her with his strength and pushed her against the wall. Then he entered her, harsh in his passion but warm in his need.

Before she could cry out, he put his left hand over her mouth to silence her.

They made love like that, standing up, silent in their lust.

She came three times before he did, her legs wrapped round him, her screams muffled against the force of his hand.

When they had finished, he still held her to him, gentle in his embrace. She started to cry, silent sobs as the tears ran down her cheeks. He wiped her face, licked the tears from her.

Then he led her to his bed and let her sleep, childlike in her position as she sucked her thumb. Duncan lay next to her, his arm behind her head as he stared at the ceiling. She woke once, nuzzled in to him.

'I just needed someone,' she whispered.

Then she fell asleep again. In time, at half-past midnight, Duncan finally dropped off. The two of them slept deeply, unaware of the camera that had watched their silent lovemaking, the camera that was so small it could be hidden in the face of the heating control on the wall by the window.

132

Railway marshalling-yard
Tobolsk
Western Siberia
3.30 a.m. (St Petersburg time)

They found Inspector Leeming in a boxcar on the outskirts of Tobolsk.

Two thousand miles to the east of St Petersburg, the boxcar was part of a long train that had started out in St Petersburg a week earlier and had gone along the Trans-Siberian Railway.

In the boxcar there were also sheep. They had been loaded on at Perm and were being shipped for slaughter and wool to Irkutsk, the great Cossack camp in eastern Siberia.

The boxcar, one of ten, had been parked in the marshalling-yards at Tobolsk for nearly twenty-four hours when the railway workers had come along to feed the sheep and hitch the cars on to a new engine.

They had heard loud banging from the boxcars, as if someone was trying to attract their attention. Then they saw some men, running away from them, but shouting and laughing loudly.

The workers decided to investigate the carriages, to see what was amiss.

Leeming was standing in the middle of the third car, surrounded by sheep who milled round his feet.

He was warmly wrapped up in a fur coat and had gloves on. His gloved hands were handcuffed behind his back. When the railway workers slid the door open and saw him, they shouted at him, demanding to know who he was. He gave no reply, just stood there, his back to them, his head tilted backwards and upwards. The men climbed in and pushed their way through the animals towards Leeming.

When they finally stood in front of him, they realized why he had not answered.

A thin steel cord was bolted to the beam that supported the boxcar roof. The cord hung down, straight above Leeming, and then went down his throat. There were some fish-hooks attached to the cord higher up, tiny little fish-hooks.

One of the men swore, then came towards Leeming to help him. The Englishman stepped back, shook his head, uttered a guttural sound. Then he started to cough, forced himself to control the tickle he felt at the back of his throat.

The men saw the blood at the corner of his mouth.

'They've shoved a bloody fish-hook down him!' exclaimed one of the men. They stepped back, examined Leeming.

'I'm going for the police.' The man who had tried to help Leeming spoke. 'You stay here. And keep him upright. If he slips, that fish-hook will rip his guts out.'

George Leeming, who didn't understand Russian, relaxed as the other men stepped forward to support him; he knew they were going to help him.

No trace was found of the men who had left him in the yard.

The road to Pulkovo Airport
St Petersburg
6.30 a.m.

The Lada raced along the road towards the airport. Myeloski was still half-asleep and seemed more in control of the machine in that state.

Duncan had been asleep when the policeman burst into the room to give him the news that Leeming had been found.

As Myeloski switched on the light, he had caught a glimpse of Louise Taylor before she disappeared under the cover. He said nothing, just that he wanted to see

134

Duncan in the hall. He then left the room, closing the door behind him.

Duncan had pulled on his trousers and gone into the hallway.

'They've found your Inspector Leeming. In Tobolsk. We have to go there.'

'You could've told me that inside the room, not drag me out here,' Duncan replied, irritated by the policeman's need for secrecy.

'The girl is an American,' came the quick answer.

'So?'

'Old habits die hard.' Myeloski shrugged.

'She's an interpreter, not a CIA agent. She's part of it, you know.'

'No. Only you and me. The two of us. We're the only two who're part of it. And that's how it has to be, if we are to succeed.' Myeloski was angry in his reply, mostly because he knew he was in the wrong. 'Even so, there's little point in staying here. The clues are in Tobolsk. I'll ring my superior and get air clearance for you.'

'I won't be long.' Duncan turned to go back into the room.

'Will you tell her?'

Duncan didn't answer, just went back into his bedroom, packed and left. When the girl asked him where he was going, he told her that they had to return to Moscow. As he spoke, as the words came out, he cursed himself. He was behaving as irrationally as Myeloski. She asked if she could join him; his answer was short and negative. She decided not to push the point any further, could see he had switched off. As they spoke, neither of them reminded each other of their passion a few hours earlier; it was as if it had never happened. It had been a welcome respite in a cruel and anguished time.

They politely said goodbye, and Duncan left to catch up with Myeloski.

'The Tobolsk police, when they realized they had got

135

an Englishman, rang Moscow. The night-duty man had rung Yashkin at home. He rang me,' Myeloski explained.

'Why a fish-hook?' Duncan had asked, when Myeloski told him of the strange situation in which they had found Leeming.

'It's like a warning. Just as the girl was naked when we found her. It's their way of telling us they're in control, that we're hooked on their line.'

When they got to the airport, Duncan went to the Air Information Service (AIS). He only had charts for western Russia, primarily Moscow and St Petersburg. The AIS officer in charge was helpful, once Myeloski had shown him his warrant-card, and helped the Englishman plan his route. It was over the Citation's flying range, and Duncan flight-planned the first leg to Kirov where he would refuel.

It was cold as they walked out to the executive jet. Duncan unlocked the door and supervised the fuelling from a small bowser as Myeloski made himself comfortable in the rear seat. He had decided he would not be sitting in the front any longer.

When the refuelling was complete, Duncan climbed in and started the engines. Once the left engine was turning over at 45 per cent, he switched on the right engine, using the live engine's generator to save the battery.

While the engine was spooling up, igniting to go to full power, he saw the right-hand thrust-reverser warning-light flash on and off very quickly. He watched it for a moment, but it stayed off. He had never seen that happen before, and decided to get it checked when he finally returned to England.

With both engines turning, he called for his clearance and taxi instructions.

The tower, knowing the Citation was on a priority flight, gave him immediate taxiing clearance to the runway. An approaching Ilyushin passenger-jet was told to overshoot as the tower lined Duncan up on the runway. He had already done his instrument checks as he was taxiing and the only warning-light that had not flickered was the right thrust-reverser one. He pulled the cover off the switch and realized that the bulb had gone.

As he swung on to the runway, he saw the Ilyushin start to overshoot, a mile from the end of the runway. He knew the airliner would be turning right at the end of the runway and that he would be turning left.

As St Petersburg aiport called him with take-off clearance he applied power and started to roll. He hit V1 (the speed at which a takeoff cannot be aborted) at 97 knots and pulled the stick back for rotation at 106 knots. Duncan enjoyed the moment of take-off, that split second when the bird starts to fly as it comes free of the land. In the back, Myeloski shut his eyes; it was the moment he hated the most.

As Duncan left the ground, as his undercarriage started to retract, as the Ilyushin started to turn right four hundred feet above him, his right-hand thrust-reverser popped out.

Now, a thrust-reverser is there for only one reason. It is a bucket-shaped attachment that deploys when a plane lands; it is designed solely to stop the plane flying. When a pilot activates his reversers, he also pours on the power to create reverse thrust, to have the blast from the jet engine going forward over the wings instead of backwards. It's like putting a car into reverse.

It is not something any pilot would wish to happen on take-off, when power is at full thrust and the plane has only begun to fly as it approaches the end of the runway. To make matters worse, the deployment of only one thrust-reverser meant that there was a tremendous drag on the right engine.

The Citation, at the most vulnerable time of any flight, now had full forward power hurling it upwards on its left

137

side and full reverse power dragging it downwards on its right side.

The small jet yawed sharply to the right, upwards and towards the Ilyushin airline. Four hundred feet may seem high, but to these small executive jets it is an altitude that can be covered in just ten seconds.

Duncan hit the emergency stow switch, next to the indicator with the failed bulb. All jets have an immediate fail-safe switch that retracts a failed thrust-reverser. Only this time nothing happened; the reverser stayed deployed, continuing to drag the aircraft to the right.

Duncan knew he couldn't level off. Once he pulled the nose down, with all the power on one side and the drag on the other, the plane would simply flip on to its back and crash.

He chopped back on the right engine, closed it down. At least he didn't have any reverse thrust left, just a bucketful of drag. He applied hard left rudder and left aileron, attempting to pull the aircraft back to the left. It responded slowly, now only a hundred feet below the Ilyushin. The Citation rolled slowly on to its left side as Duncan fought to keep it flying and to keep it away from the airliner.

In the back, Myeloski suddenly opened his eyes and found himself staring straight above, straight into the great silver underbelly of the Ilyushin. He believed then that he was going to die.

The pilots in the airliner above were unaware of the drama being enacted only a hundred feet below them. They continued their gentle turn to the right as they cursed the tower controller for making them overshoot.

When he was only forty feet from the Ilyushin, with his right wing now pointing straight up, its tip just a few feet from the airliner's belly, Duncan pulled back on the left engine and then let the drag pull the plane level. The Ilyushin pulled away to the right, the Citation started a gentle power-off glide.

Disaster was averted. The whole incident, from the moment that the jet had popped its reverser, took no more than thirty seconds.

As the big jetliner continued its turn back to the airport, Duncan applied some power back to the left engine. He waited until the Ilyushin was clear and then started a slow turn to his right, using the power on the left engine in conjunction with the rudder. The small jet wallowed in the sky, on the edge of the envelope of control.

Duncan knew that one small move would knock the plane out of the sky. At four hundred feet he hadn't enough altitude from which he could recover if he went into a spin. He kept the turn going to the right, using the drag of the extended reverser to make the turn easier.

He called the tower, told them he had an emergency and that he was returning for a landing. The tower acknowledged him, once more ordering the Ilyushin to overshoot. Duncan could imagine their anger at being forced into another emergency manoeuvre. He thought of all those white-faced passengers, panic-stricken as they peered out of their windows when they heard the engines spooling up again, wheels rumbling as they were noisily retracted, finally followed by the sharp upward tilt as the plane climbed out from the airport at full power.

He turned to look at Myeloski. The policeman glared back. Duncan shrugged and returned to his task.

He coaxed the Citation through the downwind leg and turned on to final runway heading, some five miles out from the airport. The critical stage would be when he lowered his undercarriage. The resultant drag could topple the plane from the sky. His control of the power through the throttles had to be accurate. The difference between a propeller plane and a jet is the time it takes to apply power. A piston engine reacts immediately to power, just like a car. A jet engine can take up to six

139

seconds to spool up. That meant that Duncan had to be six seconds ahead of the plane, applying power before he needed it.

With a mile to run, he reduced power and rolled the plane to the left, counteracting the drag on the right side. As he pushed the nose down for the final approach, he extended down the undercarriage.

The plane slewed sharply, dipping towards the runway. He banged on the power and felt it start to right itself. As they crossed the end of the runway, he slapped the big flaps on, chopped the power and extended the airbrakes.

The Citation rolled on to the runway for a near-perfect landing. He kept it rolling and swerved off at the first exit on the right. Clear of the runway he stopped the plane and switched the engine off. He saw the emergency vehicles rushing towards him, their lights beaconing in the morning light. Overhead the Ilyushin passed by as it set itself up for its final landing.

He turned to Myeloski. 'What was that about Boris's Law?' he joked.

The policeman smiled back weakly. There is a life after death, he thought.

5

HOOKED

**Marshka's dacha
Outside Moscow
8 a.m.**

As he drank his morning tea, the old man lived in his memories. It was something that he did regularly, a habit brought on by the onset of old age.

He thought of Andrei Gromyko, the great survivor of the different regimes that had followed the revolution. They had been good friends, had helped each other over the years. And yet, a few years after Gromyko's death, Marshka had proved himself to be an even greater survivor.

He recalled that the president hadn't gone to Gromyko's funeral. Politically necessary, but a pity. Then he thought of his own death, of his own funeral. He hoped it would be a state occasion. Then he smiled, laughed at himself for his arrogance and vanity. When he died, when they found out what he had done, he would be lucky to be buried at all.

The phone rang beside him, and he answered it. He

listened intently, trying to collect his thoughts away from the past of his dreams to the present of reality.

It was Vashinov. The old man listened as the general told him about the incident at Pulkovo Airport.

'I said we were to incapacitate the aircraft, not destroy it,' Marshka said when Vashinov had finished his report. 'And, if it had hit the airliner, Russian lives would have been unnecessarily lost.'

Vashinov sensed the old man's fury. 'I agree that our operatives in St Petersburg were over-zealous in their work, comrade. They will be reprimanded accordingly.' He shifted the blame down the line, remembering to ensure that their punishment was harsh enough so that it would be noted by Marshka.

'The other problem was the over-eagerness of the air-traffic controllers at Pulkovo,' he went on. 'If they had allowed the airliner to land first, there would have been no problem. The Englishman is a first-class pilot and handled the emergency well.'

'Where are they now?'

'About to catch an internal flight to Tobolsk.'

'At least they will not have the availability of their own aircraft. Now it will be easier to monitor them. Call me when they have arrived at their destination.'

Marshka put down the phone. He sat back, closed his eyes. Then he remembered the time that he had walked in on the Politburo meeting and arrested Beria. That had been a great and memorable moment; that was when they knew he was a man of substance. He remembered the look on Beria's face. The hunter had finally been hunted.

Aeroflot Flight 366 lifted off from Pulkovo's runway on schedule. The plane, a Tupolev 154, was a three-engined jet based on the Boeing 727.

Duncan and Myeloski sat in the front half of the plane. All the seats had been taken, but once Myeloski had waved his warrant-card at the ticket-desk they had been given seats. Myeloski had then insisted that they commandeer the seats on either side, thus ensuring them of privacy on the journey. The result was that four travellers were now sitting in the airport terminal waiting for the next flight, which was probably full anyway.

Internal flights on Aeroflot are basic by nature and design, unlike the comfortable, if not luxurious, services offered by its Western rivals. It was untrue that passengers travelled packed together like cattle. The great Russian joke was that cattle, as part of the expanding Soviet economy, travelled in better style than people.

Within ten minutes of take-off, Myeloski had insisted on being fed. When the sullen male attendant had ignored his request, the policeman had pulled out his warrant-card and shouted at the man, threatening him with everything including deportation. The attendant, now adding a sulk to his sullenness, had shuffled off to the kitchen area. Myeloski had settled back, watching hawk-like for the man's next move.

Fifteen minutes later the attendant returned with two bowls of soggy rice and boiled chicken. When Duncan had refused his, Myeloski took charge of both bowls and set about lustily devouring their contents. The attendant returned to the kitchen area where Duncan spotted him taking a deep swig from a bottle of vodka that was then passed round the other members of the flight crew.

Duncan hoped that the drink wasn't going to end up in the cockpit. He knew now why Aeroflot was known as the worst airline in the world.

As he watched Myeloski eat, he thought back to the incident of the failed thrust-reverser. After he had taxied in to the terminal and parked the plane, he had checked the right engine and its hydraulic system with one of the Aeroflot engineers. It hadn't taken long to determine that the plane had been sabotaged. The springs that hold the reversers shut had been loosened, the bolts securing it removed. As soon as the plane had hit any turbulence, the springs would have popped off the arm that held them and the two buckets would have automatically deployed. The take-off run and its resultant vibration were enough to shake the spring loose. The bulb had obviously been hit hard so as to break its filament, to ensure no warning light came on. It was a simple attempt to bring the plane down, but one that required sound engineering knowledge.

Duncan had wanted to wait the few hours it would take to fix the Citation and run checks on it, but Myeloski was anxious to get to Tobolsk. As Duncan had already decided not to leave the policeman to his own devices, he had no alternative but to join him on the next available flight to Tobolsk.

After he had eaten, Myeloski settled down to sleep. Duncan stayed awake, looking out of the window at the cloud-covered land thirty thousand feet below. Although he mistrusted the policeman, he realized that they could have both died if the Citation had crashed.

That meant that there were other players in the game, that Myeloski was just as much under threat as he was. Maybe it was time to start trusting the policeman.

Duncan turned and looked at his sleeping companion, now slumped in his seat, his mouth open as his snores rumbled across the cabin. Duncan shook his head. He wished there was someone else he could trust, someone else to form an alliance with instead of this comic figure of a Russian policeman.

Myeloski awoke like a grizzly bear with a sore head. Two hours into the flight, and he was hungry again. He growled at the attendant, by now quite tipsy, and demanded another meal.

The attendant giggled and came back a few minutes later with another bowl of rice and chicken, which Myeloski despatched with his customary enthusiasm.

'You must eat your wife out of house and home,' commented Duncan.

'No wife. Divorced five years ago.'

'I'm sorry.' Duncan realized that this was the first time they had discussed their private lives since they had met.

'Why? She was a pig. Good riddance to her.'

'Any children?'

Myeloski shook his head. 'Maybe, if we had had children, she would have been better. I am a man who should have children. The only trouble is that they grow up. Then they end up like her. Oink, oink.' He laughed at his own joke. 'You married?'

'No.' Duncan didn't tell him that he would never marry while he was a serving officer in the SAS. He had seen the pressure army wives were under, had seen their faces crumple when their men went out on a mission. He remembered when he had told a young woman that her husband was dead, killed by a sniper in the Falls Road area of Belfast. It was not something he would want to put anyone he loved through.

'Everyone should be married, if only once. If only to stop you making the same mistake twice, eh?'

At that moment, on his instinct, Duncan decided to trust Myeloski.

'The girl in the Savoy. Why did you send her up to me?' he asked.

'What girl?'

'The one you introduced me to. In the bar.'

'That good-looker? So she followed you. No taste, some people. That's why she wanted to get away quickly.' Myeloski laughed. 'And you think I sent her up. Listen, someone as good as that, you keep.'

Duncan was annoyed at Myeloski, at his dirty laugh.

'Was she good?' the policeman went on. 'She looked good.'

'She didn't stay.'

'Because you thought I had . . . To spy on you.' Myeloski's laughter grew; other passengers now looked in their direction. 'You missed a great night. Because you thought I'd sent . . .' He couldn't go on, his laughter turning to tears that ran down his cheeks. Duncan leant back, not enjoying being the object of the Russian's amusement.

'Why should I send her to you?' Myeloski eventually asked, when he had brought himself under control. His eyes sparkled with good-natured humour. 'We're on the same side. After the same fucking crooks. Why should I spy on you?'

'Why should someone sabotage the jet?' Duncan's point hit home.

'Why indeed?'

'If I am to help on this, then I should know what's going on. You said we're on the same side. Is there something I don't know?'

Myeloski looked away, his mind split between his distrust of strangers and his need to share his thoughts with another. This game was big, big enough for him to need support in the future.

'Whoever tried to kill us in the plane, whoever that was, has put us on the same side.' Duncan's blunt statement answered his own question.

Myeloski was about to return Duncan's trust. But he wanted the Englishman to earn it.

'Tell me about yourself. You say you work at a

desk. Why should they send me a pen-pusher?'

'I'm an army officer. A captain serving in the SAS. That's a—'

'Yes, yes. I know the SAS.' Myeloski was impressed. 'With field experience?'

'Northern Ireland, and before that the Falklands.'

'We could have done with you in Afghanistan.'

'Victor Oldenburg, as I said, is my friend. We served together in the Falklands. I'm also godfather to one of his children.'

'That's all?'

'Our people think this kidnapping could jeopardize the whole state visit. I was seconded to MI5 to report back to them on this one. You'll know that anyway.'

'Old habits die hard. These *spion*' – Myeloski used the Russian word – 'have a lot to answer for.'

'I'm not *spion*. There's nothing else.'

'Can you kill a man?' Myeloski knew the answer before he had finished asking the question.

'Yes.'

'You may have to, before this is over.'

'Can you?'

'I have never killed anyone in my life, never even come close to it.' Myeloski paused and considered. 'I don't know.'

'Are you KGB?'

'No. Nor GRU.' Myeloski referred to the smaller intelligence service that dealt with embassies and foreign missions. 'I am, as I said, a simple policeman from Moscow. But on this case I go directly to my superior, Colonel Yashkin. You met him at the Kremlin. He reports only to the President of the USSR.'

'When the girl, Louise Taylor, and then Inspector Leeming were found, I don't believe it didn't get back to the KGB. So why aren't they crawling all over the place?'

'Ah, just my thoughts,' Myeloski confirmed. 'It's

almost as if they've been told to keep their distance.'

'By the president?'

'By somebody. You remember the truck the girl said the family were transported in?'

'After they were kidnapped? The grey military one?'

'Used by the KGB when they are observers during special forces' exercises. Or for their troop movements. Blue grey is their colour.'

Duncan whistled through his teeth. It looked as if he was taking on the whole KGB. 'What's going on, Ahmed?' He used Myeloski's first name.

'I don't know. But it's a big game. Big players. And you and I might be the only ones between your friend and the bullet. Tell me.' He paused before he went on. 'What do you know about the assassination of the tsar and his family?'

Soviet airspace above the Urals
33,000 feet
1.50 p.m.

The T154 had entered high cloud and severe turbulence as it crossed the Ural mountain range on its journey eastward.

The 'No Smoking' and seatbelt signs were on, although this made little difference to Myeloski who had clamped himself into his seat as soon as he had boarded the aircraft. He somehow felt safe, locked into his seat, as if no harm would come to him if he stayed like that.

He had also, as soon as the 'No Smoking' sign was illuminated, lit up one of the strong cigarettes he used. At a time of stress they were his comfort, and any warning light, even the 'No Smoking' sign, brought on an attack of stress. The attendant, now well into his second bottle of vodka, decided to ignore Myeloski's indiscretion. The last thing he wanted, as the airplane was tossed round the sky, was another of the policeman's abusive onslaughts. He repaired to his kitchen area, flagrantly disregarding the woman who was being sick three rows behind the two men.

Duncan was unconcerned about the conditions. He knew that planes were designed to withstand violent airwaves, that the real danger came when they were close to the ground. Apart from the discomfort, he knew there was no danger. Unfortunately, the onset of severe flight conditions had stopped Myeloski from continuing his discussion with Duncan about the kidnapping.

Duncan sat back, shut his eyes and went over what the policeman had said. It was a startling and unconventional theory. But they were in a startling and unconventional situation. At the end of it, just before Myeloski had given in to the rough flight conditions, Duncan had come to realize how sharp the policeman was, how through his individual approach he had put together clues that most others would have missed.

'I couldn't understand why the kidnappers should wear old uniforms, old clothes and costumes from the past,' Myeloski had said. 'It was as if they were trying to give us a clue, deliberately toying with us.'

'Could the guards have been mistaken?' asked Duncan.

'No. I checked that carefully myself. Yesterday afternoon, when we came back from Pushkin, I interviewed the guards who were on duty when the family were kidnapped. One of them was a student of military uniforms. I took him to the St Petersburg library, let him show me pictures of the uniforms. He had not made a mistake. They were the uniforms of soldiers during the revolution, in St Petersburg where it all started.'

So that's where he had disappeared to, Duncan thought. Then he remembered how the policeman had hurried off after leaving him and Louise at the Astoria.

'When the guard – he was a KGB man' – Myeloski had raised his eyebrows at that point – 'had gone, I wandered

149

around the library. There are many revolutionary artefacts there. I tried, for the first time in my life, to understand what it must have been like then, under tsarist rule, where people, peasants, were no more than livestock, to be dealt with by the aristocracy as they saw fit.

'Then I thought about the girl. Why should she be found in the Alexander Palace? Did it have a significance? Now, although St Petersburg is full of some of the greatest treasures of the world, full of riches that have been handed down from the imperial days, there is very little about the tsar and his family at the time of the revolution.

'I then went to various museums and institutes. I found nothing; it was as if they had vanished at the end of the revolution. Yet everyone knows they were shot and killed. Finally, at one of the smaller institutes, one on the Restoration of Palaces, I found what I was looking for.

'The Alexander Palace was where Tsar Nicholas and Empress Alexandra had been placed under house arrest by the revolutionaries. The royal family had lived on the ground floor of the east wing.'

Myeloski paused, but Duncan had already realized the coincidence. 'That's where we found Louise Taylor.'

'That's where they left Louise Taylor. For us to find her.'

'Another clue,' said Duncan.

'Maybe.'

'So what made you go into the Catherine Palace?'

'A lucky guess. A policeman's hunch. But afterwards, in the Institute, I also read up on the Catherine Palace. Guess what?'

'The tsar's family were also taken there?'

Myeloski nodded. 'The Bolsheviks were worried that a rescue attempt would be made on the Alexander Palace. So they moved them to the Catherine Palace.

Easier to defend, you see. A few weeks later they were taken away from Pushkin, away from St Petersburg and the European side of Russia where they had many supporters. They were taken east, to an area that was a stronghold of the revolutionaries.'

Duncan felt the hairs rise on the back of his neck. 'Tobolsk,' he said quietly.

'You should've been a policeman. Tobolsk. East of the Urals, the mountains that were the stronghold of the revolution.'

The two men sat in silence. The plane had started to shudder as it entered some turbulence, and Myeloski was startled by it.

'Don't worry about it. These planes eat up turbulence. They're designed for it.' Duncan had tried to calm his companion.

'If Allah had intended us to fly, he would have given us wings, not arms,' the policeman had replied.

'Where were they taken in Tobolsk?' Duncan pushed the conversation, not wanting Myeloski to stop.

'To a district governor's house. But they were only there a short time. The trouble is I don't know where they went afterwards. That is, if the kidnappers are following the same route.'

'Can't we get that information from your people?'

'Can't trust them! Look, if it is the KGB, then we don't know how high this goes. Alert them to the fact that we're on to something, if they know we've out-guessed them in their stupid game, then we don't know what they might do. If you want your people back, then we've got to do it ourselves.'

'What we need is information about what happened to the tsar's family. I can try to get it from the British embassy in Moscow.'

'The phones will be tapped. By the KGB.'

'I'll find a way.' He remembered his list of contacts, stored away in his memory.

151

'Let's see Leeming first.'

Duncan understood Myeloski's caution. If the police-man was right, if it was a deadly game played by professionals with the resources of the KGB behind them, it was important that they didn't suspect their plot had been uncovered. There was also the possibility that Myeloski was wrong, that it was nothing more than a string of coincidences.

The plane bucked sharply. Duncan saw the panic in the policeman's eyes. He went on, trying to keep him talking.

'Why the game, Ahmed? What do they hope to prove?'

'Your people have not been honest with you.'

'So tell me. What is it I don't know?' Duncan was beginning to wonder which players were playing on which side.

'Not now.'

The plane hit an air pocket, and the crash of the wings slapping against the high pressure outside reverberated through the cabin. Duncan saw the panic in Myeloski's face, saw he was out of control. The policeman franti-cally lit another cigarette, then leant back, his eyes closed as he took a deep lungful of tobacco smoke.

'Will you tell me? For God's sake,' pleaded Duncan.

'Afterwards. After we have seen Leeming.' And with that the policeman shut off, into his world of foreseeable death and crashing, screaming engines.

Duncan knew it was hopeless to push him any farther. He sat back himself, looked out of the small window at the heavy, storm-laden, bulbous clouds they were flying through. It would be an interesting landing, if his experience of weather patterns was anything to go by.

He looked at his watch. Twenty minutes to run. He knew they'd be starting their descent in another five minutes. He settled down, trying to curb his impatience.

At last, events were beginning to move.

Hospital No. 9
Tobolsk
Western Siberia
4.15 p.m.

Tobolsk is a small town that somewhere missed its way in history.

Situated on the banks of the River Ob, it developed into a great regional centre in 1584, when the Cossack adventurer Yermak, with his band of mercenaries, crossed the Urals into Isker. Yermak concluded a deal with the then tsar which wiped out his past crimes for a surrender of his conquests. Within six years, Tobolsk was the main fortified trading-post in western Siberia.

Then, over the centuries, as trade moved eastwards and the Trans-Siberian Railway was built, eventually linking St Petersburg and Moscow over 5,700 miles to Beijing in China, Tobolsk diminished in importance. During the revolution, the Bolsheviks saw Tobolsk as one of their strongholds and used the town as a springboard into the rest of the Urals. Since then, the town had once again withdrawn into a sleepy backwater. The airport was shared between the military and civil air services. The two sections were split by a 4,000-metre runway, with the military on the north side and the civilian area to the south.

When Duncan and Myeloski had come through the small terminal, they soon found that no car had been sent to greet them. Myeloski, still unsteady on his feet from the effects of the flight, had weakly harangued a local taxi-driver into driving them to the police station.

The taxi, an old Moskvich with torn upholstery, had laboured its way through the gears into Tobolsk, to the square brick police station that lay in the centre. Myeloski, now feeling stronger as he had returned to terra firma, told the driver to send his bill to the Moscow Police transport department. The taxi-driver had given a rude sign to Myeloski's disappearing back before turning to a bemused Duncan for support. Duncan had simply shrugged and followed the policeman into the building, knowing that he would now be getting a repeat performance from the taxi-driver.

Once inside the building, it took Myeloski nearly twenty minutes to find the officer in charge and determine that no word had been received by the Tobolsk police regarding their impending arrival.

The senior officer, an inspector, realizing that Myeloski was an important personage because Myeloski told him so, immediately set about arranging transport for the two visitors as well as booking accommodation in one of the local hotels. While he did that, Myeloski commandeered his office and rang Yashkin in Moscow for any further news. There being none, the two men decided to book into the hotel and then go on to see Leeming.

The transport arranged was the same taxi-driver who had brought them from the airport. After a short heated argument, the inspector agreed to pay the costs in cash from his local station funds. A sulking Myeloski climbed back into the Moskvich with the sulking driver getting in the front. Duncan, quietly amused by the whole situation, sat in the front with the driver and they drove to the hotel.

After they had deposited their bags at the hotel, itself ramshackle and run-down, they had gone on to the hospital. It was a modern building, bright and spacious. Leeming was on the second floor, a police officer on guard outside his room.

He was asleep when they entered. Duncan saw that he was in a bad way, his face grey and wan. He lay there, a saline drip in his arm, his head tilted back and held in a vice-like contraption. Duncan felt sorry for the policeman. He had always liked him, always respected the quiet authoritative way he carried out his duties and was fiercely loyal to his royal charges.

A doctor entered almost immediately behind them.

'Who're you?' he demanded.

Myeloski produced his warrant-card and showed it to the doctor.

'We've got to talk to him,' said Myeloski, once the doctor was satisfied with his credentials.

'Not for some time. He's under sedation now.'

'What's wrong with him?'

'You heard how he was found?' asked the doctor.

'Yes. With a fish-hook inside him.'

'That's right. We've X-rayed him. It's a very small hook, with a small weight tied to it. We can't pull it out. Could tear his throat and his insides. All we can do is wait for it to pass through. It's further complicated by the wire it's attached to. When we brought him here, we put him under an anaesthetic and then cut the wire down here.' The doctor held his finger at the base of his throat. 'Now we just monitor him, check the progress of the hook as it passes through. If it gets stuck, or tears anything, then we'll operate.'

'Did he say anything?'

'What do you expect him to say with a fish-hook down his throat?'

'Then, how did you find out he was English?'

'His police identity-card and passport were tied with string around his neck. I have them, with all his clothes, next door.'

'We'd like to see them now.'

The doctor led the two men out of the small private room and into an office next door.

Leeming's clothes, consisting of his woollen suit, shirt, underwear, white socks and black shoes, were laid out on a chair. His gun-holster, without his weapon, and other belongings lay on the table.

Myeloski examined his belongings, went through his pockets. There was nothing unusual there – a few receipts, a letter from a friend.

155

'Where is his watch and his tie?' Myeloski asked the doctor.

'No watch or tie. Everything is there.'

The policeman looked across at Duncan. 'Can you remember if he wore a watch?'

'A Cartier watch. I remember because he was very proud of it. Gold, with a gold bracelet.'

'Russian policemen can't afford gold watches,' Myeloski replied ruefully. 'It was probably stolen before he got here.'

'By the police?' Duncan asked, surprised by Myeloski's statement.

'By anybody who thought he could get away with it. But we're not here to solve the robbery of a watch.' He turned to the doctor. 'We have to talk to him. As soon as possible.'

'Not for at least an hour.'

'Can't wait, Doctor.'

'I don't—'

'Now.' Myeloski was firm, his authority complete.

The doctor considered before speaking. 'I will need to be there. In case there is a problem.'

'No. This is state security. If he gets worse, I'll call.'

The doctor was concerned; he didn't trust Myeloski to honour his word. He was about to stand up to the policeman when Duncan spoke.

'I am an Englishman, Comrade Doctor,' he said, pulling his passport from his inner jacket pocket. He showed it to the medic. 'Your patient is a colleague of mine, also a good friend. I will not allow him to suffer. But we do need to speak to him alone.'

The doctor looked into the Englishman's eyes, saw that he was telling the truth. He nodded assent.

'I suggest we give you some paper and a pencil. That way he can write things down,' he added. 'Give me fifteen minutes. It'll take that long to bring him round.'

The three of them went into the hallway, the doctor

156

leaving them while he went into Leeming's room to carry out his duties.

Myeloski turned to the policeman on duty.

'Is there somewhere here I can get some food?' he asked.

Duncan grinned. His companion had returned to full strength.

Twenty minutes later, George Leeming lay as they had first seen him, except that his eyes were now open and his back arched as the doctor had placed a pillow under him to make him more comfortable.

Duncan and Myeloski sat on his right side, near the bedhead so that he could see them without having to turn his head. His discomfort was extreme and obvious, but he did his best to ignore the pain in his usual stoic manner.

The smile of recognition and welcome for Duncan had been followed by a fit of coughing. His two visitors had sat still, waiting patiently until the coughing subsided. Leeming tried to speak, but Duncan silenced him by putting his finger to his lips to soothe him, to help relax him. The doctor, realizing that Duncan was as good as his word, quietly left the room to wait outside.

'Don't speak unless you have to, George,' Duncan started. 'The man with me is Captain Ahmed Alekseevich Myeloski of the Moscow Police. He's on the case and, from his actions so far, I have to say I've come to trust him. He speaks good English, so he'll understand everything we say.' Myeloski smiled at Leeming, a lame attempt to gain his confidence. The man in the bed was defensive in his look.

'I know it's difficult to talk, but I don't have to tell you that time is short. If it'll help, I've got some paper you can write on. Otherwise just nod or shake your head, unless you want to take a point further. OK?'

Leeming nodded, his eyes fixed on Duncan.

'We've been to St Petersburg already, where you were kidnapped from. We found nothing. Was there anything that you remember at that stage that was unusual, that made you suspect something was going to happen?'

Leeming signalled no.

'The interpreter, the girl, Louise Taylor, turned up two nights ago. She was alive, but in a state of shock, in an old tsarist palace near St Petersburg. She was hand-cuffed and had a hood over her head.' Duncan didn't feel the need to say she had also been naked. 'She told us that you had all been kept in what looked like some palace rooms, about how you were all positioned, never allowed to touch or speak, and that you were watched through little holes in the door. How'm I doing?'

Leeming nodded.

'Good. She said the family were fine when she last saw them. Are they still all right?'

Leeming nodded again, tried to speak and started to cough.

'Easy, George. Come on, don't rush it.' Duncan squeezed his arm to calm him. When the coughing stopped again, he signalled Myeloski to give him the pad and pencil. He handed it to Leeming, who wrote on it.

'FAMILY OK. NO ROUGH TREATMENT. YOUNGEST HAS COLD.'

'Good.' Duncan felt a wash of relief overcome him. He knew they were in danger, but at least they were still alive.

'Bad cold?'

Leeming shook his head.

'Fine. Louise Taylor said the men wore uniforms. First of all, old-fashioned uniforms; then modern combat gear.'

Leeming nodded again.

'We found the palace where you were kept. Near St Petersburg. The girl recognized it, the room, the holes cut in the door, everything. There were no clues left at all; it was a professional clean-up.'

'Ask him if he knows where he is now,' said Myeloski.

Leeming shook his head, answering the question before Duncan needed to repeat it.

'We're in Tobolsk.' Duncan saw the look of mystification on Leeming's face. 'Siberia. Two thousand miles east of St Petersburg.'

The alarm in Leeming's face was obvious; the confusion that followed brought on another bout of coughing.

'How did they bring you here?' Myeloski said when Leeming had settled once again.

Leeming signalled for the pad and took it from Duncan. 'TRUCK. TROOP-CARRIER. THEN PLANE FOR LONG JOURNEY. THEN TRUCK. SMALL HOUSE. THEN TAKEN TO TRAIN.' When he finished, he pointed to his throat, signifying that that was when they had pushed the fish-hook down him.

Duncan read the scrawl, then passed it to Myeloski.

'Jet plane?' Duncan asked.

Leeming shook his head. 'Propeller,' he said, his voice distorted by wire still in his throat.

'Don't speak unless you have to,' Duncan said, his voice soothing to the man on the bed. Then he remembered their arrival at Tobolsk airport. 'Was it a transport plane? Like a Herc?' 'Herc' was a service name for the Lockheed Hercules, a vast four-engined turbo-prop that was the backbone of Western military transport fleets. The Russians had an equivalent, a two-engined high-winged transporter known as the 'Curl'.

Leeming nodded.

Duncan turned to Myeloski. 'There was a Russian military transporter at Tobolsk airport when we landed. It's called a Curl.'

The Russian had seen nothing; he had been too preoccupied with his own problems on the flight.

'I remember it because it had grey military markings,' added Duncan.

* * *

The drive to the airport was too slow for Duncan.

The taxi-driver, refusing to be hurried by Myeloski's threats and curses, kept the Moskvich firmly planted behind a big lorry for most of the journey. The road, narrow as any country road, was a single-lane journey for any vehicle.

They had spent another fifteen minutes with Leeming before the doctor had come in to check on his patient. They had got no farther. Leeming had written that no member of the party had any idea why they were kidnapped or who the kidnappers were. Apart from the seclusion and pressure of being watched under a gun, they all seemed in good spirits.

They used the doctor's appearance and concern as a reason for stopping the interview and made plans to return the next morning. Duncan had taken Leeming's hand, promised him that he would do his utmost to find the family and deliver them safe from harm. Leeming had seemed comforted; he knew Duncan's awesome reputation.

It had taken them a while to find the taxi-driver. He eventually surfaced in the hospital kitchens, where, through his flirtatious manner with a fat lard-like female cook, he had managed to scrounge a free meal.

An hour later they arrived at the airport.

Myeloski, not trusting the taxi-driver, told him to wait until they returned. He then followed Duncan through the small terminal to where they could look out of the window at the tarmac ramp, on to the military side, where Duncan had seen the transporter.

The aircraft had gone, the space it had occupied now filled with a small single-engined plane.

'Fuck it!' said Duncan.

'Fuck it!' repeated his companion.

'We have to find out where it went.'

Myeloski turned and walked towards the gate. Duncan

followed him right through the gate as Myeloski flashed his warrant-card. They climbed up to the small tower that was perched on top of the terminal building.

There was one air-traffic controller on duty. He sat with a small radar screen in front of him, writing up the small strips that are used by controllers all over the world, strips that have all the different aircraft information on them. He turned as they came up the spiral wrought-iron staircase.

'Nobody is allowed up here,' he barked, irritated at their intrusion.

'Police.' Myeloski held up his credentials. 'Where has that military transporter gone?'

'Which one?'

'The Curl. The one with grey markings. It was parked over there.' He pointed at where Duncan had looked.

'I don't know.'

'Don't argue with me,' Myeloski shouted, 'or I'll make sure your stay in Siberia is permanent. In a funny farm. Where did it go?'

'I don't know.' The air-traffic controller was obviously frightened.

He half stood up as Myeloski came towards him, when an aircraft called him over the radio. He started to answer, but the policeman pushed him down again, pulled the headset off his head.

'Where did it go?'

'I really don't know. Look, I have no flight-plan.' He shoved a batch of papers towards Myeloski. 'Military planes do not have to report where they go. We just clear them on to the runway and tell them what other traffic we expect. Sometimes we guide them towards a beacon. After that, military radar does the rest.'

The Tannoy crackled again as a pilot asked for landing instructions.

'Which direction did they go in? You had them on radar for a while,' asked Duncan.

161

'South, then they turned east. About twenty miles out.'

'Did you see who got on board? It's important. Otherwise, I'll let my partner deal with you.' The threat of a maddened Myeloski was too much for the controller. He turned and pointed to where the aircraft had been.

'They came in a military truck. Right up to the plane. I couldn't see too well, but it was about ten or twelve people. The engines were already turning over. They took off immediately the passengers were on board.'

'Any children?'

'Some small persons. Possibly children.'

'And the truck? Where did it go?'

'They left it. Over there, by the fuelling station.'

The voice on the Tannoy came again, the pilot's tone anxious.

Duncan looked at Myeloski; they had gone as far as they could with the air-traffic controller.

Myeloski turned and left the tower, Duncan following.

On the Tannoy the anxious voice continued to crackle.

The truck had nothing of consequence in it. Painted in military grey, it was parked, as the controller said, behind the aircraft-fuelling pumps.

After a cursory check, Myeloski went off to talk to the guard at the gate and find a torch. Duncan got in the cab and searched for anything that might have been left. There were only three crumpled cigarette-packs, a sign that whoever had been in the truck had possibly been waiting a long time. The key had been left in the ignition.

In the back he found nothing. The truck was bare down to its wooden boards. In the darkness, he felt above his head, under the canvas canopy. Again, nothing. He heard Myeloski returning and went to the back of the truck. The policeman had found a torch, which he shone at Duncan.

162

'The truck was left here last week,' said Myeloski. 'Official military business, according to the policeman on the gate.'

He lumbered into the back of the truck, pulling himself up and over the tailboard. Duncan could tell all the exertions of the last fifteen minutes had exhausted him. The policeman sat on the tailboard and shone the torch into the covered area, at the same time wheezing and catching his breath.

'The police were told that the truck was to be left alone until someone came and got it,' Myeloski went on, having regained his breath. 'He says all he saw was two men in the front when it arrived. He said the canopy was down; he couldn't see inside.'

He got up and, with the torch shining into the corners, checked to see if there was anything unusual. He came to the same conclusion as Duncan. They were empty-handed once again.

They both climbed down out of the truck and went round to the cab. Even with the torch, Myeloski found nothing. He disregarded the cigarette-packs, after having checked inside each one carefully to see if a note had been left.

'I want to check where the plane was,' said the policeman.

'Let's use the headlights.' Duncan climbed into the cab and started the engine. Myeloski stood on the running-board as Duncan drove to where the transporter had been parked. Myeloski then stepped off and walked in front of the truck, while Duncan followed, lighting up the area for the policeman.

Duncan leant out of the window and shouted at Myeloski. 'The wash. It could've blown something.'

'What?' shouted back Myeloski.

'From the propellers. The plane was facing that way. When the engines were going, the propellers could have blown something in that direction.'

163

He turned the truck in the direction he had pointed, Myeloski once again walking in front of the two headlights that lit his path for him.

They found the baby's bootee tucked under a rubbish-bin next to the terminal. Inside the bootee was wrapped a small gold ring. Duncan recognized it as Anna Oldenburg's wedding ring. It must have been blown there by the propwash.

So it was them, and they were alive, and they had disappeared once again.

Tsentralny Hotel
Tobolsk
Western Siberia
8.15 p.m.

The hotels in Tobolsk, as in all Russian towns off the tourist map, are basic in their design, functional in their service.

Duncan's small room, with a metal-framed cot, small table and two chairs, was one of the best in the hotel, having been repainted a sickly pale green only six months earlier. 'Refurbished,' the desk clerk had said, when Myeloski introduced Duncan as a foreigner. Tobolsk was not a town where foreigners were common currency.

Duncan, seeing that there was no phone-extension in the room, asked if he could use the manager's. Although this caused some small problem because the manager had gone home and taken his office key with him, a duplicate was soon found and Duncan let into the sparse office.

The phone was not direct-dial. Duncan picked up the receiver and waited for what seemed an eternity before the operator answered. He gave the number of the British embassy in Moscow.

After nearly five minutes the call connected through. The operator, surly in her attitude, didn't inform Duncan that they had answered, and it was a moment before he realized that there was someone on the line.

'Hello,' Duncan tentatively called.

'Trade desk.' It was the usual nasal high-pitched voice that the Foreign Office always sent as their emissaries abroad, a caricature of the British past, a service packed with Hooray Henrys.

Duncan realized the number he had been given was a direct line to the trade section. 'Jack Richardson, please.'

'Who is calling him?' It was a lazy insolent answer.

'Kittyhawk.'

There was silence at the other end. When the man spoke again, the voice had changed, now urgent, now conspiratorial. 'This is not a clean line, Kittyhawk.'

That was obvious to Duncan. He knew the call, even from Tobolsk, was probably going through a series of monitoring stations.

'Call Woodward,' he went on. 'The interpreter and policeman in fine health. Family definitely well. On trail. Repeat exactly as stated.'

He put the phone down. He hoped Woodward had the intelligence to work that one out. He would have liked to give more information, ask someone to research the final days of the tsar; but he knew that would only have got back to the KGB, and in this game secrecy was the only key he held. He left the office and returned to his room.

Myeloski, who was in the next room, heard him return. He, already having made his report to Moscow, banged on the thin wall.

'Did you get through?' he shouted.

'Yes.'

'Good. I'm coming round.'

The policeman left his room and came to Duncan's.

165

The Englishman had already opened the door. Myeloski sat on a chair and heaved a big sigh, a theatrical moment signifying that the day had been hard.

'So what is it that my people didn't tell me?' Duncan asked, now sprawled on the bed, his legs crossed and his head resting against a thin cushion that passed for a pillow.

Myeloski looked round the room, worried.

'It's clean. No bugs.' Duncan had already checked for surveillance equipment. The Tsentralny Hotel in Tobolsk was not usually what one considered a top security risk.

'Whatever I tell you has to remain between us.' Myeloski raised an eyebrow, quizzical of Duncan. 'I need your word on that.'

'I can't guarantee that.'

'Then, I can't tell you. Otherwise my people will have my balls for breakfast. We're meant to be trusting each other.'

'OK. But don't compromise me.'

'I won't. It's a fantastic story,' Myeloski reflected. 'One that even I didn't believe at first. But it's true, no fairy-tale.' He could see the apprehension on Duncan's face. It was best that he knew.

'Russia, as you know, is fucked up. *Perestroika* is struggling; there are groups everywhere clamouring for independence. We have strikes, food is short, queues grow longer, the Russian spirit is strained. This is not what the revolution was for.

'But, deep down, every Russian knows that our strength is in our unity. Together we are a great nation. But we need our independence and freedom within that unity. *Perestroika*, even if it is creaking, is our only hope for the future. Trouble is, under communism, people have learnt not to look after themselves. The State does it all for you. It's a simple contract. You behave yourself, and we'll feed and clothe you. That's what they led us to believe anyway, even if they were the ones who had most of the food and clothes. That was Russian democracy. Now we are having to stand on our own. That's difficult, when you were brought up to believe you would be looked after from the cradle to the grave.

'Anyway, what the Government want is a symbol of unity. Something to unify the people. Like Germany. Like so much of Europe. Even Europe is becoming a united country, not a continent any longer. Communism, and the Party – nobody trusts it any more. Not when we're moving to a democracy, not with a multiparty system.

'The president, who is a great man, and some of the Government, some of whom are not so great, want a figurehead, a new symbol for our people. With our long history, with our traditions, what they have decided they want is a constitutional monarchy.

'They want to bring back the tsar.'

6

SLIPPING THE BAIT

Tsentralny Hotel
Tobolsk
Western Siberia
8.45 p.m.

Duncan sat in stilled silence, Myeloski's words sinking in.

The policeman watched him, letting him settle his thoughts.

'So that's the real reason for the state visit?' Duncan eventually spoke.

'Your royal family have experience of a constitutional monarchy. It would also help tie the links between East and West. Britain has always been close to America – their "special relationship".'

'A radical idea.'

'For radical times. It worked in Spain; Juan Carlos has been a symbol of their progress into the modern world. And look at the rush of monarchs all desperate to get back to the eastern European countries. In Spain, Parliament still rules, as does your Parliament in England. And don't forget we had royal rulers for centuries. The revolution is not yet a hundred years old. Just as religion is now playing a major part in our future, so could a monarchy.'

'That's mind-blowing.'

'You remember the Cathedral of the Assumption, where we went in the Kremlin?'

Duncan nodded.

'That was where all the coronations of our kings have been. It was where Nicholas II, the last tsar, was crowned. It is where the coronation would take place. The state visit was designed to see how the Russian people would take to royalty. If they welcomed them warmly, then the president would have continued with his plans. If not, then that would have been it. It's to be an extended state visit, not just visiting Moscow and St Petersburg. The tour was to include all the fifteen Soviet republics. They were to meet and mix with ordinary people. Then, if it was successful, the president would have announced his intentions and put it to a referendum of the people. The final decision would be theirs.'

'My people should have bloody told me.' Duncan was angry.

'Leave it. That's for later on. But the clues – the traditional uniforms, the path of the tsar's last days. Someone is telling the president to stop, not to continue with his plan.'

'So they kidnapped the Oldenburgs as a warning?'

Myeloski stopped suddenly. He realized that Duncan had misunderstood him. 'You don't understand. It's not your prince who's the candidate. It's Oldenburg.'

'What?' Duncan was stunned.

'You know his heritage. I thought he was your close friend.'

'I knew he was very distantly related to the Romanovs. His parents, all his relatives, died when he was young. He was brought up by an aunt.'

'His family always kept their links to the tsar secret.

Always a fear of assassination. No, your man Victor is the Grand Duke Victor, the great grandson of Tsar Nicholas's younger brother, Mikhail.'

'I didn't know.'

'Neither did he, until recently. The secret was well kept by his aunt. She never wanted him to be one of those exiled Romanovs who were always claiming the throne was theirs. The Grand Duke Mikhail, the tsar's younger brother, was killed in a town called Perm at about the same time as his elder brother. But Mikhail was married, and there was a son. I don't know what happened then, except that the rest of the family escaped from Russia.'

'And now they want him back.'

Myeloski shrugged. 'That's not our problem. We're just here to find him.'

'You're the policeman. This is your patch. Where next?'

'What we need is information about the tsar, about what happened over seventy years ago. There's also another problem.'

'It can't get any worse.'

Myeloski smiled ruefully. 'We're running out of time. The Romanovs were executed on July the sixteenth.'

The two men looked at each other. It was now 14 July.

They only had two days left.

Tsentralny Hotel
Tobolsk
Western Siberia
10.20 p.m.

Myeloski and Duncan split up for the evening.

After they had both eaten in the hotel restaurant, Myeloski had decided to use his authority and get the local librarian to open up the library. He wanted to see if there was any information on the tsar's assassination.

Duncan decided to go to the one place he always felt at peace in, a place in his own mind that was far away from the pressures he now found himself under.

After Myeloski had gone off in the taxi, the driver still grumbling that it was well past his bedtime, a complaint that fell on deaf ears, Duncan had taken a walk towards the outskirts of town.

When he was clear of the people and the buildings, when he could see the countryside in front of him, he stopped walking and started to run.

It was what he enjoyed most, away from people, with the weather blowing in his face. As he ran, up into the woods and the low hills, he started to wait for the pain that would come. He had never been a good cross-country runner; it was not his natural inclination. He had been a top sprinter at school, having run as a schoolboy international. But since he had joined the Army, and then the SAS, he had come to enjoy the peace that came with the pain of long-distance running.

It had started when 'yomping' became part of military street-talk. Soldiers, with heavy packs on their backs, would run for at least ten cross-country miles. It was 'yomping' that gave the SAS and paratroopers a war-winning advantage over the Argentinians during the Falklands campaign.

Although still in his street-clothes and wearing his walking-shoes, Duncan was determined to keep in training. Stamina would be important in the next few days, and he didn't want to fail because he had allowed his fitness to slip.

The pain started sooner than usual; he had only covered three miles when he felt the sharp stab across his chest. He had learnt, over the years, to withdraw into his thoughts when the pain began.

As he ran, he thought of Myeloski's theory. The coincidences were solid, but one factor stood out that disproved the policeman's supposition. If the kidnappers wanted to kill Victor and the family, they would have done so already. Why were they playing a cat-and-mouse game? Did they want to be discovered and, if so, why? He didn't discount Myeloski's theory. He couldn't, because it was the only game in town. But it didn't make sense.

He realized he needed the time up here to clear his mind. He had already broken his golden rule: 'Never trust anyone.' He had started to trust Myeloski.

The hurt in his chest had spread to his thighs, to the muscles in his back. He rode the pain-barrier, pushing along, pumping his legs forward along the path and through the undergrowth.

'Think, think your way out of pain.'

As Duncan ran he started to form his strategy. He would go with the policeman, but watch him closely. Myeloski was, at the end of the day, a servant of the Kremlin. The Englishman realized that the time would come when he would have to strike out on his own, take on not only the policeman but also the KGB and any other agency the Russians decided to throw at him.

He would need his strength, his fitness. And he had his list of contacts that Woodward had given him. He went through the names, refreshing his memory with the telephone numbers and addresses.

He hoped his transmitter was working. Up there, outside the blackness of night, he knew a satellite was passing on his position to the watchers at home. He also remembered that by burning the small credit card a 'help' signal would be alerted on the watcher's screen.

Not that they could do a lot, he thought, but at least he knew he wouldn't die alone.

Whilst Duncan ran, Myeloski went through the history books at the library. In a room to the side, the spinsterish librarian waited for him, angry at being dragged reluctantly out of her warm bed, but too frightened to refuse this pompous ruffian of a policeman his request.

But in this small provincial library he came up empty-handed. It was as he expected: he knew that he would have to contact Moscow over the phone. Once he did that, from that moment on, he knew he risked any advantage of surprise he might have. His biggest concern was as to how far up the ladder of power this thing went. Once he had reported back to Moscow, asked for their help in tracing the tsar's final days, forces over which he had no control could move against him and crush him.

Unlike Duncan, he had already worked out why the family hadn't been killed yet. The only way the kidnappers could gain maximum publicity and still get their message over was by linking Oldenburg's death with that of the tsar. The only way he could stop the massacre – and that's what it would be – was by getting to the end of the trail before the kidnappers did. Ringing Moscow had to be his last resort. Secrecy and his policeman's instincts his only defence.

He swung round in his chair, drawn up to the reading-table, and looked through the glass divider into the small room where the librarian sat, hawkishly watching his back.

He signalled to her, inviting her to sit with him. She rose from her desk and came into the main room, approached him.

'I'm sorry I have kept you up so late,' he said to placate her. 'Unfortunately I will need some more of your time. Please sit down.'

She sat opposite him, watching him warily as a mouse watches a cat.

'I can't find what I am looking for,' he said. He had already told her he needed anything to do with the revolutionary period in 1917, his reason vague except that he was looking for information that would help trace

173

a witness in an old crime they wished to close their books on. It had been a weak reason, but he knew the older provincials still remembered the Stalinist period and those dreadful purges. They always reacted immediately to authority and the policeman's uniform. 'Do you have any old newspapers of the period?'

'No,' she answered, defensive in her manner. 'All newspaper cuttings are kept for only five years, then they are sent to the State Archives in Moscow.'

'Then, I shall have to ring Moscow,' he concluded. 'You must be very proud to run this library. I am impressed with the neatness of it. It is an efficient system. I found my way through the list of books very easily. Is it your system?'

'Yes, Comrade Captain,' she preened. When Myeloski wanted people to talk, he always started by getting them to talk about their work. It was the one thing that people were proudest of, the one thing they would happily pass hours discussing. It also opened up a bridge of trust between them and the policeman.

'My father worked in a library,' he lied blatantly. 'In Moscow. Just a small one. He never achieved the post of librarian, as you have done. But he taught me how important a role librarians play in the community, that they are the pathway to the past and the signpost to the future.' He smiled, pleased with his little metaphor.

She smiled back. Maybe this policeman wasn't as bad as he had at first seemed.

'This is true,' she replied. 'A library is not just a place where books are kept. It is a meeting-point for the townspeople. They come here to research for local events, to plan for gatherings. In my small way, I always help where I can.'

'That's important in a town like Tobolsk, one with such a great tradition.'

'It is,' she answered proudly. 'It was founded in 1581, and became a great trading-fort. Since then, although

174

much of the trade to Asia passed to the south, this town has remained the gateway to northern Siberia.'

'A great part of our history. I once read that the tsar and his family were brought here during the revolution. They were kept here, under arrest.'

'That's true,' she replied, surprised by his apparent knowledge. 'Not many people know that.'

'I've always been fascinated by the history of our revolution.'

'They were brought here from Tiumen, up the river by steamer. They were kept at the governor's house for nearly eight months.' She was warming up, starting to gossip as if the events had only taken place a few days earlier.

'When they arrived, all the local people took up petitions against them, marched for days past the governor's house carrying placards and singing revolutionary songs. But after a while everyone settled down again. The tsar and his family used to come out in the streets. The people spoke to them, but there were always guards. They would sit on the front steps in the sun. And they had a big conservatory at the back. The tsar built some wooden chairs, and they would sit there, on the roof of the conservatory. I have seen photos of them.'

'Where? Where did you see them?'

'At the house.'

'The governor's house?' Myeloski froze; he thought the house had been pulled down.

'Yes. It is in Liberty Street. No one lives there. It is a museum, which is only opened for special visitors, usually from Moscow.'

'Tell me more. About those days.' He could hardly contain his excitement, but he knew he must go on, seeing what else came up.

'They lived on the first floor. I have been inside. It is comfortable, nothing more, not like you would expect for them. There are still people who remember when

175

they were here. Very old, but they still have their memories.'

'Where did they go? When they left Tobolsk?'

'To Ekaterinberg.'

'Of course.' He didn't really remember, but he would look up a map afterwards, find the town.

'The daughter of Commissar Yurovsky lives in Tobolsk now.'

'Really.' The name meant nothing to Myeloski.

'He came here from Ekaterinberg. Married here and lived for many years. He was a watchmaker. Then they divorced and he went to Moscow, I think. His daughter is an old woman now, nearly seventy. If you are interested in history, you should talk to her. After all, he was commissar of Ekaterinberg and in charge of the tsar's family.'

'Where does she live?' he asked, his interest suddenly sharpened.

'In Sverdlov Place. In the old people's Home of the Fighters of the Great October Revolution. But not now, I hope. It is very late.'

Myeloski laughed. 'Not now. And thank you. I have kept you very late.'

She smiled at him as he rose from the table.

'I shall give you a lift home in the taxi,' he said. She rose to join him. He wasn't so bad after all, she thought.

Myeloski escorted her from the library, ignored her soft-lidded invitation to go into her apartment for tea and an evening meal, and returned to the Tsentralny Hotel. On the way there, he saw the taxi-driver's smirk in the rearview mirror. Dammit, he thought, the Englishman gets the interpreter and he turned down a spinster librarian who probably hadn't had it for the last ten years.

Life sometimes really was a bitch.

Duncan saw the moving flashlight on the first floor before Myeloski. The policeman was more concerned with opening the side-door to the old district governor's residence.

He had found that the keys were kept in the local police station. He had gone there after dropping the librarian home and then proceeded to the Tsentralny Hotel, where he interrupted Duncan in the shower. After Duncan had got dressed, they had gone back to find the taxi-driver, who had been told to wait, had decided that enough was enough and had gone home. After a flurry of phone-calls, Myeloski had arranged for an unmarked police car, another Lada, to be brought to the hotel. The bemused driver, on delivering the car, was told to find his own way home as Myeloski and Duncan had driven off with the necessary instructions as to how to get to Liberty Street.

Myeloski had taken Duncan through the evening's events. They would have to find a map in the morning to determine where Ekaterinberg was. There would, no doubt, be one at the police station.

'I didn't want to ask anyone where it was,' explained Myeloski. 'You never know who's watching us.'

'You must've heard of it.'

'I remember the name, I think, from my schooldays. Probably some small village somewhere.'

They had parked away from the governor's residence and walked down Liberty Street towards it. It was a large rectangular house, ringed by a six-foot wooden fence. There were two floors, and the main entrance was on the side of the building, behind the fence.

When they had confirmed that no one had seen them,

177

Duncan helped Myeloski over the fence. He was as out of condition as he looked, and it was a struggle to get him over the wooden slats. In the end, to Duncan's dismay, as he didn't want to be discovered, Myeloski rolled over the top. He couldn't help but grin as he heard Myeloski land with a soft thump on the other side, cursing and groaning. Myeloski was still trying to get up when Duncan slid over and joined him on the other side.

'You all right?' he asked.

No, Myeloski was not all right, as he made obvious with his glare at the Englishman. Duncan left him to dust himself down and went up the steps to the front door. The policeman joined him and started to try the various keys he had been given. Duncan went back down the nine steps to see if anyone had noticed them.

It was then, as he turned back to join Myeloski, that he saw the light on the top floor.

He watched from the corner of the balustrade at the bottom of the steps. There was someone up there, someone who didn't want to be seen. Someone looking for something.

'Are you sure there's no caretaker here?' he climbed the steps and asked Myeloski, who had just managed to find the right key and unlock the door.

'No one. This place is off-limits.'

'There's someone up there. Top floor. With a torch.'

'You sure?' Myeloski was alarmed.

'Absolutely.'

'No, they said no one was here.'

'It could be them. And the family.'

Myeloski took his hand away from the door-handle; he had been about to open it. 'Or it could be an intruder. We can't take any chances. We need reinforcements.'

'No. Let's handle this ourselves. We've more of a chance that way.' If they were all up there, the last thing he wanted was a vanload of flat-footed Russian police-men bursting in on the place.

Duncan pushed past Myeloski, put his hand on the door-handle. In his other hand the policeman glimpsed Duncan's black-barrelled Coonan 357 Magnum.

'Where did you get that?' asked a nonplussed Myeloski.

But Duncan was gone, silently slipping through the door. Myeloski looked round, then followed the Englishman into the residence.

They came into a big hallway with a minstrel gallery running round. A wide staircase on the left led to the first floor. Duncan quietly closed the door behind Myeloski.

'Are you armed?' he asked the policeman.

Myeloski nodded and pulled out a small police-issue revolver. 'Never used it,' he whispered.

'Even at a firing range?' Duncan was surprised.

'Once. I fired ten shots.' Myeloski was apologetic. 'I don't like them. Too bloody noisy.'

'Give it here.' Duncan took the small firearm from Myeloski and quickly checked it. He snapped the safety-catch off and handed it back to the Russian. 'Safety-catch is off. Don't squeeze the trigger unless you have to. And keep it pointed away from me. OK?'

Their conversation had been in whispers, and Duncan moved to the bottom of the stairs. He listened for a moment, heard nothing. He returned to Myeloski.

'I'm going up. Stay here. If anyone comes down, challenge them and, if they don't reply immediately, open fire. Got that?'

Myeloski nodded lamely and stepped back into the shadow away from the window. Duncan turned and climbed the stairs.

He moved silently, his instincts and training taking over. Like all members of the SAS 14th INT, his speed of thought was based on reaction. The trick was to clear your mind of everything except the task in hand. Duncan's sole thought as he climbed the stairs was to

179

identify the intruder and then react accordingly.

At the top of the stairs he paused, working out which door opened on to the room where he would have seen the light. There were two doors to his right. Either door could open into a single room or share access into one large room.

He moved to the first door, his handgun now cocked as he kept close to the wall. He knew never to approach a closed door in such a way that surprise fire through the thin door could catch him unawares.

He stopped at the side of the door and listened. He heard no movement. He dropped silently, crouching on one knee; and, when he felt safe, lowered his head to look into the room through the keyhole. He saw no light, no movement in the large high-ceilinged room. He then knelt down and looked under the gap between the floor and the door. He still couldn't identify any movement. He stood up, and quickly crossed to the next door, where he followed the same procedure. Once again there was no sign of any movement.

He heard Myeloski clear his throat down in the hallway. He lifted his gun with both hands, ready for any sudden movement. If he had heard Myeloski, so could the intruder.

Still silence. He decided to remain where he was, his back covered by the wall. If either door on each side opened, he could react immediately. Any movement further down the minstrel gallery was also covered. His eyes, now used to the darkness, took in the surroundings. It was as if time had stood still in this house. On the wall, to the left, there was a family photograph of the last Romanovs. Farther along there was another picture, a pencil sketch of a young girl. Duncan presumed it was one of the tsar's daughters.

If Duncan was used to silence and keeping still, Myeloski wasn't. It had been many years since the policeman had been involved in a stake-out. Although a brilliant detective, he wasn't at his best when it was time for action.

The tickle in his throat was developing into a cough. He knew it was nerves, and he fought to keep the cough from getting out of hand. But the harder he fought, the more he lost the battle.

By holding back, Myeloski made matters worse. The tickle became a tank rolling down his throat. As he started to cough, he kept his mouth closed, to block out any sounds. This had the result of choking him on his cough; his eyes started to water, and he broke into a coughing fit.

Upstairs, Duncan waited for something to happen. There was nothing he could do about Myeloski's cough, except turn it to his advantage. He hoped the intruder hadn't heard him come up the stairs, that he would presume the coughing was from someone who had only just entered. He hoped Myeloski could cope; he was on his own now.

A door slammed at the back of the house on the ground floor.

Duncan stayed where he was. He knew the intruder couldn't have gone out of the front room in the time it had taken Duncan to enter the house quickly and climb the stairs. That meant that there was more than one, or the rooms upstairs all had connecting doors. The intruder could have gone to the back of the house without coming on to the minstrel gallery.

As he stepped forward, knowing he would have to investigate the sound from the back of the house, two things happened simultaneously.

The lights in the hallway snapped on, a brilliant chandelier filling the hallway with light.

A door at the other end of the minstrel gallery burst open, and two men ran out. Both were armed, one with a machine-gun.

Duncan turned, twisted the door-handle and spun into

the room. As he hit the floor, the machine-gun exploded in his direction, the bullets biting great chunks out of the walls in the hall and in the room he had entered.

But he was low, on his stomach and bringing the Coonan Magnum into play.

The two men were halfway down the stairs, the machine-gunner about to take aim at Myeloski. Duncan, with only the top half of the intruder's body in sight, aimed at his torso, the biggest part of a moving target.

Myeloski saw the black-holed smoking muzzle being aimed at him. He brought his handgun up, frantic and hurried in his action. But, before he could fire, he saw the intruder with the machine-gun falter in his step, as though stopped by a giant invisible wall. He saw the hole that had appeared in his chest, just above the heart; then he saw the man crumple and deadfall down the stairs. Only then did he hear, in his shocked state, the boom from the Coonan Magnum, muffled from above.

The other intruder, seeing his stricken companion, fired wildly with his handgun in Myeloski's direction. His shots missed, and the man, fearing for his life, ran out of the back to where his other companions were obviously waiting.

Myeloski stood shock-still as Duncan came down the stairs fast. By the time he had reached the bottom, the back door had been slammed again, no doubt by the escaping intruder. Duncan rushed past Myeloski and out of the front door. By the time he got to the fence, he was just in time to see the tail lights of a car disappearing around a corner.

He holstered his gun and went back into the house.

Myeloski had brought himself under control; guns and sharp swords were not his idea of policing. He knelt over the intruder's lifeless body as Duncan entered.

'He's dead,' was his blunt statement, as he stood up to face Duncan.

'Let's check the house,' answered Duncan, the dead

man no longer of any concern to him. 'I'll take upstairs, you search down here.'

'I'm getting the local police.'

'With all that noise, somebody will have called them.'

Without waiting for an answer, Duncan went up the stairs to search the rooms. Before he entered the first room, he drew his Coonan Magnum. It was a precautionary measure, but he knew he couldn't take any chances.

The rooms were all empty, from the bedrooms at the front to the servants' quarters at the rear. All the front rooms were linked by an interconnecting door. That was how the intruders had got through to the back.

The rooms were unchanged from the days when the tsar had been held captive. Except that there was evidence that someone had been there recently. In the back rooms, where the maids and tutors must have lived, there was bedding rolled up on the floor. Some of the bedding was still unrolled, and Duncan realized that they had interrupted the kidnappers whilst they were clearing the house of any sign of occupancy. That meant they were getting close, that the kidnappers would start to make mistakes if they were pushed.

The trouble was that, if they were going to kill the family, then they could bring the moment of execution forward. It was a risk that the two hunters were now committed to.

Apart from the bedding, there were two plastic bags of half-eaten sandwiches, chocolate-bar wrappers and the general debris of people living rough. He gave the contents a cursory inspection, then picked them up and returned to the ground floor.

As he got to the bottom of the stairs, Myeloski returned from the rear of the house.

'Nothing,' said Myeloski. 'What're those?' he asked, referring to the plastic bags that Duncan was carrying.

'They lived upstairs, at the back. The family were

here. This is the rubbish I found. The bedding is still there, some of it rolled up, ready to be moved. I think we caught them as they were packing up to go.'

'But the family's already gone. Earlier, by plane. That means they're rushing, that we've caught up with them quicker than they expected.'

'Which puts our people in more danger.'

Myeloski nodded his agreement. Then, over Duncan's shoulder, he saw another family photograph from the past, hanging just inside the door. In the corner of the frame there was a smaller picture, a coloured Polaroid snap. He walked over and took the picture from the frame. He looked at it, cursed under his breath and passed it to Duncan.

It was Victor and the family. Duncan recognized the room upstairs where the picture had been taken. The family, for all their ordeal, looked well. Victor had a small growth of beard, Anna looked natural and beautiful without any make-up. The children were all smiling. He was sure the parents were making them feel it was all a great escapade. At that age, anything out of the ordinary was always a great adventure, great fun.

He put the picture into his pocket. Myeloski said nothing, his mind working feverishly.

'I'm going to rip this place apart. There must be a clue somewhere,' he said.

At that moment there was a loud commotion outside and the front door opened as the local police walked in.

Myeloski and Duncan never found the clue that was meant to be planted. In their hurry to get away, one of the escaping men dropped the book that told the story of the tragic events at the House of Ipatyev that would have led them directly to Ekaterinberg.

The book, an old weathered edition, was picked up by a policeman who, after an uninterested flip through its pages, put it back in the nearest bookcase.

General Vashinov had his usual private dining-room upstairs. The head of the KGB was entertaining three black African diplomats who, through their dealings with the general, had substantial numbered accounts in various Swiss banks. To lighten the conversation and give the diplomats a night to look forward to, he had also arranged for three young women to join them at their supper-party.

One, the girl Vera, sat on his right. He had spent the last half-hour stroking her thigh, working his hand up and into her silk underwear. She, concentrating on her black charge who sat on her right, gave no sign of the game that was going on under the table.

The Lefortovo Restaurant is next to the Lefortovo Prison, a security interrogation-centre. It is a favourite haunt of KGB and army officers. Many tourists, on giving the name 'Lefortovo' to taxi-drivers, find themselves delivered to the forbidding-looking prison, rather than to the eating-place. This joke is shared by the guards at the gate, who often escort would-be diners through the steel gates and into the first level of the prison before explaining their mistake.

As Vashinov explored his companion's nether regions, he thought about Vera. Of all his women, she was his favourite. She enjoyed sex for the sake of it; she had never known any different since she was a child. There was no emotion in her lovemaking; she simply did it because it was there to do, and it was fun.

But he had noted a change in the last few days. She seemed distant, somehow going through the same exciting and innovative motions without actually joining in. It had been like fucking a robot.

He watched her with the African. The diplomat was enjoying himself hugely, his eyes shamelessly exploring Vera's body. He regretted bringing her along for the African; should have kept her for himself, as he had done for the last few weeks.

He smiled to himself, surprised by his twinge of jealousy. Middle-age crisis, he thought. Always wanting what you can't have. She was untouchable; somewhere in her mind, in a part that no one got through to, there was the real Vera. All the other girls, the women over the years that he had used, they were affected by the life of sex and shared debauchery. They became emotional, let the life get to them. Twenty-five-year-old girls looked forty. But this one, this young girl, it was as if she was still a virgin, had been touched by no one.

He withdrew his hand suddenly. Damn the black African, he thought.

It had been the same with his mother. He suddenly remembered her and realized he hadn't thought about her for months. She was dead now, the victim of a lifetime of heavy smoking which finally caught up with her eight years earlier. She had lived her life for his future, fought to give him the chance to succeed in a hostile world after his father had left her pregnant in a Kiev suburb. She had come to Moscow, the young child only two years old, and set about building a base of respectability for the young Vashinov to grow in.

She had been beautiful and soon gained employment as a clerk with a branch of the city's local Soviet. Her boss, a boozy old reprobate with a sexual desire far greater in his thoughts than in his deeds, soon bedded her with the threat that she either put out or lose her job. It hadn't been a difficult decision for her as sex was the currency she had already used to buy tickets and food for her journey to Moscow. She rose rapidly through the ranks, spending her days working hard and studying, her nights fucking hard and ingratiating. As her new bosses and subsequent lovers grew in importance and stature, so her own position in the party hierarchy grew more secure. During this period, the boy Vashinov grew into his teens and then into manhood. He was educated in the best schools and often headed the school lists as a brilliant student.

He was seventeen and about to take his final exams for a place at the Patrice Lumumba College for Foreign Affairs when he unexpectedly walked in on his mother in a compromising position with the deputy head of the KGB on the floor of their apartment in Moscow. It was a tense moment, she shamed because her son had seen her at her worst, he because he had not expected her to be there with a mouthful of KGB general in their home. He had stormed out, ignoring her pleas as he slammed the door behind him. In all those years he had never considered why the apartments they had lived in were always being visited by her male superiors, had always considered it was in the line of duty. As he walked the streets, he realized that they were all there for one reason only: that their only line of duty had been to fuck his mother.

He returned late that night and was surprised to find the KGB man still there. His mother, afraid of losing both her son and her job, had been drinking heavily and was unaware of what was to follow. Her lover, a cruel man with a bent for the unusual, was not backward in making his intent known to the young Vashinov. It was a simple deal, and the seventeen-year-old agreed. After all, he was his mother's son.

The next morning, the unfortunate woman woke up from her drunkenness to find not only her lover in bed with her, but also her son. It didn't take long for her to understand that her son had finally lost his virginity. Not only to the KGB officer, but also to her.

And so life went on in the apartment. The young Vashinov never enrolled at Patrice Lumumba, but joined the KGB where he was protected by the general. In time, and after his protector's execution in one of the many coups of the period, Vashinov used his ability and gained rapid promotion within the security organization. He had jumped at the chance of going to Afghanistan to head the anti-terrorist wing and returned with full military honours for his successful campaigns.

While he was on that tour of duty, his mother died of lung cancer. When they had passed him the telegram informing him of her death, he had felt nothing. They had gone on living together, even continued their acts of incest for the KGB general over the years until he was finally destroyed by the firing squad's bullets. They had lived in the same apartment, but had become strangers. They had had to live together, for they both knew any hint of scandal would ruin his career and her lifestyle.

That's why he liked Vera. Because she reminded him of his own failings, of his own sordid introduction to the cruel reality of life. They were kindred spirits in a tough world.

He thought of the morning, when the tapes would be delivered to him. The video of the African and Vera together, she pleasing his every whim, he wanting the pleasure and degradation of a white woman. He always watched the tapes alone, locked in his office, his trousers round his ankles as he masturbated slowly in front of the moving images that filled his television screen.

He wondered what the African would do. In his mind he could see Vera with the African, his blackness rammed into her receptive mouth, the grin of pleasure on his face. She always told him she never enjoyed it with the others. It wasn't what the videos showed; either that or she was a brilliant actress.

A waiter came into the room. It was a call for him.

He excused himself, saw the look of surprise from Vera, no doubt a comment on the sudden withdrawal of his hand, and went to answer the phone.

That's when they told him one of his operatives had been shot dead in Tobolsk.

That's the moment he suddenly realized that things were starting to go wrong.

'They want to know why a foreigner is carrying a gun.'

'For health reasons. Tell them to mind their own—'

'Tsk, tsk. There's no need to be rude.'

The two men were tired and irritable. After the police had turned up they had treated Duncan and Myeloski as criminals. They had both been kept under armed guard at the house until the district police commissioner had turned up. Myeloski's warrant-card had finally proved useless; they were being handled like murderers.

Myeloski, for obvious reasons, could not give the true reason for them being there. His claim of 'official security' was wasted on the Tobolsk police. There was no identification on the dead man, and that made matters worse.

Eventually, when the commissioner had spoken to Yashkin in Moscow, he sullenly let them go.

Duncan had asked for his gun back, and he was told it would be returned, with Myeloski's, in the morning.

While the police cleaned up the mess, took photographs and checked for clues, Duncan and Myeloski went over the house.

Apart from the bedding and the rubbish, they found nothing else.

The house was a museum. Duncan had been fascinated by the photographs that filled the walls and the tables. They were of the tsar's family, reminders of a bygone time. They showed Nicholas II as a dedicated

189

family man, always surrounded by his family. In addition to his wife there were five children.

Alexis, the tsarevich, his son, was in his fourteenth year. If he had lived he would have just turned ninety. Then there were his elder sisters, Olga, Tatyana, Maria and Anastasia. He remembered the name Anastasia. She was the one who was supposed to have escaped. It reminded him of a film he had seen on television, some years ago, with Ingrid Bergman. They looked happy as a family, but no doubt lived in fear, knew they would probably be killed.

There were photographs everywhere, reflecting their life at Tobolsk and before.

The saddest picture of all was of the tsarevich, Alexis, on his thirteenth birthday, waiting by a train to take him into exile. It had been taken by his father, and showed the sickly boy in army uniform, eyes frightened yet bright with hope, waiting to go wherever they were told. What a way for a young man to spend his first teenage birthday.

The pictures brought back memories of his own grandfather. About that time he would have been making his way east, back to the estate. He probably passed through here, with the Whites, probably saw this place in his quest for the tsar. He quickly cleared his mind of his personal thoughts. The job at hand still had to be completed.

They had returned to the hotel at four in the morning, Myeloski clutching the two rubbish-bags. After only two hours' sleep, about which Myeloski complained bitterly, they had driven to the police station. It was here that Duncan had asked for his weapon back.

The Coonan Magnum was returned grudgingly. It was a powerful weapon and obviously impressed the local officers.

Duncan then sat back and watched Myeloski go through the rubbish-bags. He found nothing that was of help. Duncan had smiled when the Russian had put his hand into a soiled nappy by mistake. The policeman had almost vomited on the spot, then rushed out to wash his hand.

'Royal excretion's no different from anyone else's, is it?' Duncan had joked on his return. Myeloski's dismissive expression showed he didn't share the Englishman's sense of humour.

The commissioner came in at eight and said that the local KGB had been on, that they wanted to interview the two men. Myeloski had called Yashkin – it was three hours earlier in Moscow – and got him to use his authority to divert the KGB.

While they were waiting for that clearance, Myeloski had asked if they had an area map. One was produced, and the two men pored over it.

They couldn't find Ekaterinberg.

'Probably changed its name from pre-revolution days,' said Myeloski. 'Anything that was associated with an imperial name was changed. That's why St Petersburg became Petrograd, then Leningrad.'

To the west there were the main western Siberian towns of Perm, Sverdlovsk and Chelyabinsk, to the east the city of Omsk. It was a comprehensive map yet there was no sign of the town they wanted. They had already decided not to ask any of the local police. If they were to move on, it had to be in secrecy. It was still their main weapon, as they had shown the night before by catching the kidnappers unawares.

By nine, Yashkin had ordered the commissioner, with a written command from the president's chief of staff, to allow the men total freedom. They were not to be interviewed by the KGB, or by anyone else for that matter.

Myeloski had then demanded that the commissioner send out for some breakfast. When it arrived, he had eaten two bowls of buckwheat before leaving the police station with Duncan. His companion watched as he sipped a cup of Russian tea. He had already decided to balance his diet with one main meal a day. After the previous night's activity, fitness was now a top priority.

They had already decided on their plan of action. It was to find the daughter of the old commissar of Ekaterinberg. She would know where the town was.

The Kremlin
Moscow
9 a.m. (Moscow time)

All the members of the Politburo, with the exception of the president and General Vashinov, were assembled. Even Marshka had arrived on time.

They waited for nearly twenty minutes for the president. Although they grew restless, they knew it was important, otherwise they would not have been called to a second extraordinary meeting within twenty-four hours.

Vasily had grumbled to the member on his left, but it was more to pass the time of day. Marshka sat stony still in his wheelchair, reading a document that he had brought with him. The document was his standard cover; he hated sitting in his wheelchair with others thinking he had nothing to do. He also took great delight in knowing that others believed he was reading secret papers of great importance. Russians, with their great sense of intrigue and drama, couldn't stand being kept in the dark.

He hoped that Vashinov was playing his part.

'I'm sorry to keep you,' the president said, sitting down at the top of the table. He waited for Vashinov to take his seat.

'Things are moving faster than we expected.' He looked round the table. 'Captain Myeloski gave a full report to his superior earlier this morning. Things are progressing satisfactorily.'

'How satisfactorily?' Marshka prodded again.

'Their report was brief.' The president remembered Yashkin's warning that there may be forces who were acting against him, probably someone in this room. 'The good captain was concerned that something might be overheard on the telephone line from Tobolsk.'

'What are they doing in Tobolsk?' Vasily's turn this time.

'That is where they believe the family was taken.' Vasily started to go on when the president interrupted him. 'There was also a shooting in Tobolsk last night. A man was killed. By the Englishman who is with Captain Myeloski. It appears the dead man was one of the kidnappers. Unfortunately, there was no identification on him. We have absolutely no idea who he was, even if he was Russian.'

'Where in Tobolsk?' Marshka planted the time-bomb.

'At a museum.'

'Which museum?'

'Just a local museum,' the president lied.

'The police must have some idea as to why he was there, as to why he was killed there.'

'I told you before, it was a brief conversation. For good security reasons,' he lied again.

Before Marshka could continue, Vasily jumped in. 'What was the Englishman doing with a gun?'

'Again, that point was not covered.' The president decided to steer the conversation away from the house in Tobolsk. If Myeloski wanted a security blackout, then he would support him. 'General Vashinov has spent this morning ensuring that no information about the killing has been made public. Not easy, as you appreciate, in a time of press freedom.' He smiled; it was ironic that it was he who had created such an environment. He imagined how the story would be blown up by the Soviet tabloids, not something imaginable only a few years earlier.

'My main concern', he went on, 'is to help identify the perpetrators of this crime. It is something we should spend more time considering. It could be more than just a terrorist plot. Let's not forget the revolution started because of the Romanovs. We don't want another revolution because of them again.'

'They don't matter any more,' interrupted Vasily. 'Save them if we can. If not, then hard luck. Where the Soviet Union goes, our future, is more important than the lives of a few privileged people.'

'We invited them here. They are our responsibility.'

'They came because of the past. Because they want things to be as they were, because of their greed. We must look to our future. If this gets out, then the riots and strikes we have seen will be nothing to what will happen. We will have betrayed our people. Are you prepared to send the troops in to quash them? Like Stalin did. Thirty million people died in those purges. My own father was one of them. Do you want to send us down that road again? Is that to be the new *perestroika*? At this rate, when you finally have free elections, the Communist Party will be lucky to poll even one vote, let alone stay in power.'

'What you say, Alexander Alexandrovich, is true.' The president spoke directly to Vasily. 'It is a great risk. But it is one we all believed in at the time. Russia still needs a symbol to unify her republics. That need has not changed. For the same reason that we set out on this course, for that same reason we must continue. I see no other way.'

'At this stage, I see no harm in the KGB being involved. They have trained agents who could help the police. There is no reason why they shouldn't assist.' Marshka's quiet flat words cut across the emotion of the moment.

The president considered. 'I agree with you, Grigory Mikhailovich.' He turned to Vashinov. 'Draw me up some plans as to how you can help. Then come and see me.' He smiled that famous smile, now so well known across the television screens and newspapers of the world. Then he stood up. 'Let's hope that Captain Myeloski finds the family before any harm comes to them. Thank you. I shall keep you informed of any developments.'

He turned and left the room.

As Marshka looked round, as he saw that the president's words had little effect on the other members, at that moment he knew that he would have to progress matters to a satisfactory conclusion.

At least it meant, after all these years, that he was safe and that he would never have to unleash the terrible truth of the Beria Archives.

Sverdlov Place
Tobolsk
Western Siberia
11.30 a.m. (local time)

They found the old people's Home of the Fighters of the Great October Revolution at the top of Sverdlov Place.

As with many buildings in provincial Russia, little had changed since the revolution. Having once been the home of a rich merchant, the house had been commandeered in 1935 as a hostel for the elderly. Apart from the odd lick of paint and a brand-new central heating system, the house had remained unchanged since that time.

They were shown into a small waiting-room and told that Anna Yurovskaya would be brought to them. After five minutes the door opened and she was led in, clinging to the arm of a young male nurse. They both stood up as she entered, remained standing until she was lowered into a chair, then sat down again.

'Anna Yurovskaya?' asked Myeloski, gentle in his approach.

She nodded, wary of the policeman. Why did they want to see her, an old lady of seventy? Myeloski saw the mistrust in her eyes. He turned to the nurse.

'You can leave us now,' he told him. 'We'll call you when we've finished.'

The nurse left them; as he walked out of the door Myeloski saw the panic in her eyes. She didn't want to be left alone with them. Good, he had her rattled. He beamed a big smile, the smile of a friend for life.

'You mustn't be worried,' he started. 'There's nothing you've done wrong. As well as being policemen, we are also students of history, of the revolution. We were here, in Tobolsk, on another matter, and were told you lived here, that you were the daughter of Yurovsky, the famous commissar of Ekaterinberg. It was not an opportunity to be missed. To talk to someone who was a part of our great history. That's not something you get from textbooks.'

His charm worked. Her features relaxed; her eyes softened. But there was still something in her eyes that worried Myeloski, something dark and hidden.

'What did you want to know? About my father.' It was a strong voice for a woman of her age.

'What really happened. The truth of Ekaterinberg.'

'It was as has been said. It is true that it was he who pulled the trigger. It was he who killed Nicholas and the boy.'

Myeloski drew back. He felt Duncan shudder behind him. Neither of them, until that moment, had realized that Yurovsky had been the High Executioner, the arch-assassin of modern times. She stopped, startled by his sudden move.

'He was a watchmaker, wasn't he?' Myeloski pulled

196

the first fact he could remember from his memory, remembered the librarian's words.

'Yes. From Tomsk. He came to Tobolsk after the revolution was over. He met my mother here, and this is where I was born.'

'Did he talk to you of Ekaterinberg?'

'Only sometimes. My mother and he divorced many years ago. I was fifteen. He went to live in Moscow. I never saw him after that. I had some letters, but that was many years ago. Then they wrote to me, a long time ago, nearly thirty years now, and said my father was dead. He died in bed, after a long and painful illness. They said he was rewarded for being a hero of the Ural revolution with an official funeral at the Novodyevichy Cemetery.' She stopped, losing herself in the thoughts of her father. Myeloski was later to find out that Yurovsky had died in 1962. The 'long and painful illness' had been cancer of the lung, brought on by the Jew's fondness for his pipe.

'He didn't steal the jewellery, you know.' She spoke sharply, suddenly cautious about Myeloski again.

'What jewellery?'

'Are you not here about the jewellery?'

'No. We are here to learn about a hero of the revolution. To inspire us.'

'But you are police?'

'We are Russians. Who says he stole jewellery?'

'Everyone. After the executions, nobody found their jewellery. They thought the jewels were sewn into their nightgowns and corsets. My father told me this was not so. Ever since what happened in Tobolsk, the tsarina made her daughters wear underclothes, special ones, like chastity belts.'

'What happened in Tobolsk?'

'Everyone knows what happened.' She spoke as if it had only been the other day. 'The soldiers tied the young ones to the chairs. Then they . . . beat them. And . . .' Her voice tailed off. After a while she spoke again.

'That's why they had the special clothes. Not for the jewels. My father said they had no jewels, only small trinkets, the sort young people have. It was because he was a Jew. That's why they said it. He told me once that he believed in the revolution because it freed him from being a Jew. It was the reason he was a Bolshevik. But after the revolution, he said, nothing changed. Always a Jew, always to be different. He even told me that they let him kill the family because he was not a Russian but a Jew. They said a Russian could never have done it. That's what he said. Afterwards, even when he wrote to me from Moscow, he was bitter that nothing had changed. It is why he left Ekaterinberg when he was commissar.'

'Did they go to Ekaterinberg – the family, that is – when they left Tobolsk?'

'I think so. By boat. By river-steamer. The same one that brought them here.'

'Is Ekaterinberg on the river?'

'Yes. But they didn't go there. The ferry only goes to Tiumen.'

'I know Tiumen.' It was south of Tobolsk. 'But where were they taken after that?'

'To Ekaterinberg, of course. I thought you said you studied history.'

'As a Russian, to learn of my past. Not as an academic. When did they change its name?'

There was a pause. She shut her eyes; they watched her closely. Finally she opened them, looked directly back at Myeloski. They could both tell her mind was beginning to wander, that she was growing tired.

'I never went to Ekaterinberg, even as a little girl, with my father. He never went back, either. Not once he had left. The townspeople were frightened of him. They knew what he had done. Even though he had liberated them, they were terrified that he could do such a thing. They all stayed at the Hotel Amerika. It's where they used to have their meetings. When he and Voikov – that was his friend – came into reception, people always made way for them, got out of their way. He said some people called him a devil.' She laughed. 'He liked being called a devil. Said it made them respect him. Look, there in that picture on the fireplace.'

Myeloski rose and went to the mantelpiece. He lifted the faded black and white photograph of a group of men lined up outside a brick-building entrance. He brought it over, passed it to Duncan.

She leant forward, so she could share in the picture. She pointed at two of the men in the front row, one a tall bearded man in a fur hat, the other shorter yet more distinguished. Both smoked cigarettes and looked satisfied.

'That is my father,' she said, pointing to the taller of the two. 'The other is Voikov. Like I said, it is outside the Hotel Amerika. This was just before the execution.'

Duncan passed the framed photograph back to Myeloski.

'I am tired now. I want to go to my bed.' Her voice was suddenly old, the effort of her conversation and her memories tiring her.

As she struggled to get up, Duncan came forward and helped her. When at last she was standing, leaning on Duncan's arm, she turned to Myeloski.

'They were all killed, you know.' The policeman was surprised by the look on her face, one of fear, yet of persuasion as if she wanted him to believe her. Like a child about to be spanked and desperately trying to convince the parent that it has not lied. 'Some said the Grand Duchess Anastasia escaped, fell in love with a guard and was hidden after the killing. Others said the bodies were from the local morgue, that none of the family was killed, only taken away and kept prisoner. They even said that Papa had deliberately missed the tsarevich, the boy. When he put his report in, they said he left the name of Alexis off the list of dead. So what? Anyone can make a silly mistake. Those stories upset him, as if they were ashamed of what had been done. But he told me it was necessary, it was to liberate Russia. They were coming to rescue them, you know. They knew they were at the House of Ipatyev. The Whites. With those terrible foreign soldiers. Not Russians, but foreigners.'

Duncan remembered his grandfather's quest and difficult journey, of his hope to save the tsar. He had mentioned a group of Czech soldiers who had marched with them. The old lady stumbled as she leant on his arm, the fatigue affecting her. He steadied her.

'I hope I have been of help to you.'

'You have.' Myeloski got up from his chair as he spoke. 'Very much so. Thank you. Just one last thing. When they changed the name of Ekaterinberg, did they not ask your father back, as its most famous commissar?'

'No. But they named it after a Jew. He laughed at that. Sverdlov was a Jew, you know.'

She cackled. Myeloski smiled. He remembered Sverdlov from his history lessons. He had been Lenin's deputy, the most notorious of all the Bolsheviks.

Then he looked at Duncan, and the Englishman knew that Myeloski had the answer.

A clearing in the Koptiaki Forest
The Urals
2.30 p.m.

Although one of them had been there before, it took some time for the three men to find what they were looking for.

The Koptiaki Forest is thick with silver birches, the ground swollen with forest moss that has lain in the shadows of the sun for thousands of years.

They had parked their transport, a grey army troop-carrier, a half-mile from the entrance to the mine-shaft. The only path leading up here had long been overgrown, although its track could still be seen under the moss and the fern.

Their leader, pushing forward in the falling drizzle, had not realized he was at the mine-shaft until he stumbled and fell into the shallow pit that marked its opening. He had got up, cursing as he did so, and wiped the mud from his knees and elbows.

He turned and shouted, calling the others.

When they eventually got to him, they stopped and looked about the area. The two newcomers had not been there before; they only carried maps given to them by their colleagues.

It was nothing like they had imagined. An innocuous place that could be found in any forest. But this place, they knew, was not just any place in any forest. For all their military training and their discipline, each man wondered what it must have been like on that terrible night so many years before.

'No birds,' one of them commented. It was true; there were no sounds of birds singing as there had been at the bottom of the forest.

'Come on,' said the leader, 'we have work to do.'

The two others joined him in the shallow pit and started to clear the boarded-up entrance to the mine-shaft that had lain undisturbed for over seventy years. The entrance had been closed after the Russian authorities, under the direction of Investigator Nikolai Sokolov, searched for the acid-burnt bodies of the tsar and his family. The men moved the rotted wooden covers away from the entrance, opening it up as it must have been in 1917.

As they worked, at the site still known as the Four Brothers, a young bearded Cossack with an Israeli Uzi machine-gun slung over his shoulder settled down to watch their progress. Hidden behind a tree, his head no higher than the forest ferns which surrounded him, he had been left there by the small group of men who had, by chance, stumbled on the scene.

They had gone to get their leader, to show him what they had found.

Twenty minutes later, whilst the men still cleared the mine-entrance, the leader, Ivan Bakor, had arrived. He, also with an Uzi strapped over his shoulder, sat down with his scout and watched the men's progress. Five minutes later, one of his men reported back that a truck, grey in colour, was parked away from the clearing. The leader acknowledged this fact; he didn't need telling that it was a KGB transporter. It was something they all knew.

Within the next fifteen minutes he had spread his men through various parts of the forest. There were now scouts in all directions, all the way down to the truck.

Nothing would move in the Koptiaki Forest, around the area of the Four Brothers, without Bakor's knowledge.

Unaware of all this, the three KGB operatives worked on, clearing the pit, just as they had been instructed to.

Like all things in life, nothing is smaller or greater, save by position.

As the watchers hid low in the forest and watched their prey clear the area, so the satellite spies in the sky relayed the information on Myeloski and Duncan to their masters.

What they couldn't transmit was the sense of urgency, or the sense of discovery, that both men felt.

Neither could they foretell that events, like all well-planned and well-executed events, were about to be overtaken by the most simple of scientific knowledge. To the Americans it was Murphy's Law; to the Russians, Boris's Law.

And no amount of technology, no amount of expertise, and certainly no amount of planning could compete with Lady Luck. From now on, chance was to play its hand. And just as night follows day, so bad luck inevitably follows good.

The Lady was about to join the game.

7

IN THE NET

Duncan watched the Mig 29 twin-jet fighter, known as the Fulcrum, taxi off the runway and park next to the terminal.

It was a two-seater trainer, and as the plane braked to a stop, hunching down on its front gear-springs, the canopy lifted up, revealing the two helmeted pilots.

Duncan, sitting on a tubular-steel bench seat by the window, watched as the support-vans drove out to the fighter. A fuel-bowser appeared from the other side and crossed the runway towards the jet.

Around him, the few passengers who were waiting in the terminal crowded to the windows to catch a glimpse of the plane. Duncan smiled to himself, wondered how they would react if they knew there was a British army officer sitting amongst them. The two pilots, now with their helmets off, waved at the people in the terminal, their proud young faces beaming. Duncan joined in the mood of the moment and waved back.

After a few moments the small crowd broke up. Duncan sat on his own, watching the air force crew refuel the plane. He had been on his own for more than ten minutes, Myeloski having gone off to find some form of transport to take them on to their next stop. There was no civil flight until lunch-time the following day, and they both knew that they needed to move before then, or lose to the kidnappers.

Everything had slowed down after they left the old lady, Yurovsky's daughter, over four hours ago. When they had returned to the police station in order to determine the flights out of Tobolsk, the commissioner had been waiting for them. Myeloski was instructed to ring Yashkin, his superior in Moscow. That had taken over an hour, most of which was wasted in trying to connect to Moscow and find Yashkin.

When Myeloski returned to Duncan, his face was furrowed in concern.

'Let's go and get something to eat,' he said, and was out of the police station before Duncan had a chance to object.

The Englishman followed him out of the building and round the corner, where Myeloski had stopped.

'What's up?'

'They want to bring the KGB in.' Myeloski was angry.

'They?'

'Some of the Politburo. Yashkin says we must continue. The president is to approve a KGB plan later today, one he asked for.'

'What does "continue" mean?'

Myeloski grinned. 'It means we keep going and try to avoid working with the KGB. I think I must now go on alone.'

'No.' The look on Duncan's face was final.

'Look, if the KGB is involved – and, remember, we don't know how deep – then we can't risk a foreigner in there. If Yashkin tells me to continue, then that order has come from the president. All I do is obey it.'

Duncan flicked back his jacket so that Myeloski could see the Coonan in his shoulder holster. 'This may be the support you need. Especially after your heroic efforts last night.' Myeloski ignored Duncan's scathing criticism. 'It may be your crime, but it's my responsibility. I'm staying right next to you. And if you try to slip me, then, I promise you, not only will the publicity I generate back in England destroy the president's credibility, but I'll also come looking for you. Then it'll be my crime and my solution.'

The Russian's face broke into a huge grin. He grabbed Duncan by the shoulders and shook him. 'Good. It will be dangerous, but I wanted to hear you say it. You understand, if you use that' – he nodded towards the Magnum – 'then I may not be able to help you next time.'

Duncan nodded as Myeloski stepped back.

'My friend. We will find your family. And, whatever game the KGB is playing, we will make sure we stay one step ahead.' Myeloski was elated.

They went to the hotel, packed and checked out. Then they went to the library. Myeloski introduced Duncan to the librarian and then, leaving the Englishman to his own devices in the reading area, disappeared into one of the small reference sections at the back with her. Duncan passed the time reading the newspapers on display, all the time checking that Myeloski did not catch him unawares by slipping out of the library.

A good half-hour passed before the two of them returned. The policeman thanked the librarian for her help and the two men departed.

'I know where we're going now.' Myeloski was obviously pleased with his efforts. 'It's all falling into place.'

They climbed into the Lada, Duncan deciding not to

question Myeloski. He knew the policeman would tell him in good time, when he had put his own thoughts in order.

They returned to the police station, where Myeloski went through a charade of ordering food and complaining about having to wait for further orders from Moscow.

When they were alone, Myeloski moved his chair closer to Duncan and spoke to him in a low voice. 'We have to get to Sverdlovsk.'

'Ekaterinberg.'

'You're right. One and the same.'

'Where is Sverdlovsk?'

'About five hundred kilometres from here. To the south-west. It is a big city. A steel and coal city. We call it the Pittsburgh of the USSR. You know Pittsburgh?'

Duncan nodded; everyone knew the large steel city of North America.

'We will go to the airport soon. When they are not suspicious. I hope we do not get any orders from Moscow in that time.' Myeloski slid his chair away and lit a cigarette. After a few puffs, he said: 'You are privileged, you know.'

'Why?'

'Because Sverdlovsk is off-limits to foreigners.'

Duncan was surprised. 'I didn't know that still went on.'

'Oh yes. It is a closed city. No non-communist has ever visited there. You will be the first. You can put that in your memoirs, if you live that long.'

'Why is it closed to foreigners?'

'I don't know. I suppose, if that's where the family were killed, that it would be a tourist attraction for the wrong reasons. It's not something the Government would want to be reminded of. Now, or in the past.'

Eventually, after two nervous hours, and one large, gruesome and soggy meal, Myeloski told the commissioner that they would be going for a drive to look at

207

the local countryside and would then return to the hotel. He explained that he had already booked out, but would be returning there for the night by 7 p.m. The commissioner, a local policeman, had accepted Myeloski's statement as a matter of course. He understood that waiting for fresh orders from Moscow was boring. Might as well be out driving than sitting in a cold room waiting.

Once they had left the police station and driven round the corner, Myeloski slammed his foot down on the accelerator and sped off towards the airport.

That's when they found there were no flights until the next day.

While Duncan waited in the passenger area, Myeloski went off to quiz the air-traffic controller as to the availability of any military or other flights to Sverdlovsk.

And that's when Duncan saw the Antonov AN-2 land and taxi in to park on the far side of the two Migs.

The AN-2 first appeared in 1947 and became the workhorse of Russian airspace. It fulfilled the same role as the DC3, the Dakota. But, unlike the DC3, the AN-2 has only one engine and is a biplane. The earlier models were powered by a Shvetsov radial engine, although the modern versions have a turboprop unit up front. The plane Duncan saw was of an early variety.

Although primarily a cargo-plane, the AN-2 could seat up to sixteen passengers. With a top cruising speed of 115 miles per hour and a ceiling of 14,000 feet, the plane became a legend in the Russian outback. It could take off on a grass strip of only 600 feet and was as solid as a London double-decker bus, and about as comfortable. With a stall speed under 50 miles per hour, the aircraft seemed to hover over the end of runways like a helicopter before landing.

The plane parked at Tobolsk airport was a freighter, and the two pilots climbed out through the side-door. They were followed by a man in a white coat and a nurse.

The pilots opened the freight-doors and climbed back into the plane as an ambulance drove out to them. Through the wheels of the Mig undercarriage Duncan saw a stretcher being unloaded and put in the back of the ambulance. The man in white, obviously a doctor, and a nurse climbed into the back of the ambulance, the pilot in front with the ambulance crew. The vehicle left the ramp as the other pilot closed the freight-doors.

Behind him, Myeloski pushed through the crowd and sat down next to Duncan.

'No flights at all. And no trains, not until tomorrow. I think we'll have to take the car.'

'That'll take forever. Can't Moscow help?'

'Not unless we want to get stuck with the KGB. I know Yashkin. We have worked together for many years. He will not want me to call him.'

'It's over five hundred kilometres. We wouldn't get there till lunch-time tomorrow. That's if we left now.'

Myeloski puffed up his cheeks and let the breath noisily escape from his clenched lips. He stared ahead, at the Mig which was now being refuelled.

'It's a pity we haven't got one of those,' he said, indicating the fighter. Behind the jet, a bowser had arrived to refuel the AN-2.

'No harm in asking, is there?' Duncan stood up. 'After all, we've nothing to lose.'

'The Mig – I suppose you can fly it also. But it only has two seats.'

'Come on. And bring your police warrant-card with you.'

Duncan set off towards a side-door, carrying his small case. Myeloski jumped up and followed him.

A guard barred their way to the apron, Duncan stopped and indicated Myeloski, who pulled out his warrant-card and showed it to the guard.

'Police business.' Myeloski fell into his role, his voice dismissive and gruff. The guard checked his credentials and then stepped back, opening the door for them. He was about to end his shift and wanted to get home. If he detained them, he would only have to wait for a senior officer to turn up. And that could take a long time.

As they moved on to the apron, Myeloski fell in beside Duncan. 'We cannot steal a Mig. However important it is.'

'But you can commandeer that one.' Duncan pointed at the AN-2. Myeloski stopped dead and stared at the old biplane. His fear of the skies took hold again. 'It's been used as an ambulance flight. When they've finished refuelling, just order him to fly us to Sverdlovsk. You said you could open doors, remember?'

Myeloski slowly and painfully came to terms with the situation. He knew the Englishman was right. This was their one chance to keep up with the kidnappers. He walked forward, towards the plane that was being refuelled and up to the pilot. The pilot was of the old school, a grizzled war veteran in his sixties who had never flown the airlines but knew the Siberian terrain like the back of his hand. While Myeloski spoke to him, Duncan kept back, in the shadows. He surveyed the Mig, appreciating its powerful and clean lines. They had finished refuelling, and the bowser and ground crew moved away. The twin jet engines whined as they started to turn and then surged into a thunderous roar as the igniters sparked the fuel that exploded through the turbines.

Duncan put his hands over his ears and turned away, back towards Myeloski and the pilot. The policeman was shouting above the roar, holding his warrant-card up for the pilot to see. The Mig bounced on its brakes as the pilots released the plane, turning it away from the ramp. It taxied towards the runway, its canopy still open. Myeloski walked towards Duncan.

'OK. He will take us. But he wants to wait for his co-pilot. They are part of the air ambulance service. I told him that you were a pilot and that it was important we go now.'

'What did you threaten him with?'

'Prison. What else?'

So much for *perestroika*. Duncan walked with him back to the AN-2. The bowser-man had refuelled the plane and was disconnecting the fuel-lines.

'I need to get a flight-plan. From the tower.' The pilot spoke to Myeloski, who looked at Duncan for help.

'Do it over the radio. Say we have received an emergency and need to go now.' The pilot watched Duncan as he spoke, realizing he was a foreigner.

'They will not accept it.'

'Yes, they will.' Duncan moved between the pilot and the fuel-truck. He pulled his jacket back, and the pilot saw the Coonan Magnum. Its shape was brutal in the dusk of the day. Duncan smiled at him. 'On the radio.'

Myeloski, now knowing that they were committed to a new course, came closer to the pilot. As he spoke, he looked away from the refueller, so as not to be heard. 'Comrade, we are not enemies of the State, or spies. We are here on government business that is of a secret nature. We need your plane. If you are not going to help us, then my friend will shoot you. Have no doubt of that.' He saw that the pilot believed him, not by his words, but because of the look on Duncan's face. 'He is also a pilot and will fly this plane if you do not.'

The refueller came towards them, waving a sheet of paper. 'I need your signature for the fuel,' he shouted.

Duncan stepped back, his jacket closed. The pilot took the sheet from the lineman and read through it, checking the contents, taking his time. The Mig on the runway turned on full power as it started its take-off run.

'We must hurry, comrade. We must get to the patient quickly.' Myeloski spoke up, taking the pilot by the arm. The pilot took the pen offered to him by the refueller and signed the sheet. He was then given the top copy, and the refueller returned to his bowser. He stopped to look at the Mig, its lights blazing, reach the halfway point on the runway.

'Wouldn't you rather be flying one of those?' he shouted across the engine roar.

The Mig swung its nose up, lifted off the ground and seemed suspended in time and stillness for a moment. Then the wheels tucked up, the nose lifted sharply skyward and the jet roared into the air, its ear-shattering blast shaking the ramp and the small terminal building. The fighter pilots were giving the spectators a show, and the refueller saw some of the waiting passengers by the windows applauding the take-off. He grinned and turned to the others, but they were gone. He saw the small side-door of the aircraft close. He shrugged. Bloody pilots, always in a hurry. Then he got into his bowser and drove away.

Inside the plane, Duncan slid into the right seat, next to the pilot. Myeloski was busy strapping himself into a small tubular-steel seat in the fuselage. Both men in the front put on their headsets.

'Call up the tower; say we're going south, to Tiumen. That it is an emergency. Tell them you are refuelled and that you are taxiing out whilst waiting for them to get your clearance. Start the engines first.'

'It is most irregular. I always get clearance from the tower first.'

'Not this time. Just do as I've told you.'

Duncan picked up the map that lay next to the pilot and attempted to identify the landmarks. It was a topographical map, and he found Tobolsk marked on it. At the same time, he watched the pilot go through the start-up procedures. He saw the battery-switch, the magnetos and the fuel-cock. In essence, that was all he needed to know in case he had to start the plane at some future date. The pilot primed the engine, still warm from its previous flight, then applied the starter. As the big radial spluttered and came alive, he fed in the fuel and then applied the throttle. The engine rattled for a few more seconds as fuel was fed into each cylinder and finally exploded into life. The pilot pulled the throttle back to idle and turned on the radios.

In the tower, the controller was surprised to see the AN-2 start its engine. He was even more surprised to hear the pilot ask for taxi instructions and for a clearance. It was most irregular, but he had only been stationed here for a short time and accepted that it was an emergency. He cleared the AN-2 to taxi for the runway.

Myeloski sat quietly in the dark of the fuselage. He had tightened when the giant Shvetsov radial had burst into life, sending a metallic shudder through the cabin. As they started to taxi, the fuselage had groaned, its age very apparent. The policeman shut his eyes, bowed his head and prayed to his God.

The biplane turned on its tailwheel and taxied to the runway.

'Line up,' ordered Duncan when they reached the end.

'I haven't got—'

'Get on the runway.' The pilot gave up, followed Duncan's command.

In the tower, the controller stood up and reached for his binoculars. The AN-2 was taxiing on to the runway, and he hadn't got his clearance yet. He reached for the microphone to stop him, but the teleprinter chattered from the area control. He looked at the printout. It was the pilot's clearance to Tiumen.

'Line up,' he called and then read out the clearance. When he had finished he gave permission to the AN-2 to take off.

After using only a fraction of the runway, the biplane laboriously strained to lift into the air.

The controller watched it depart to the south.

The KGB men searched the terminal for Duncan and Myeloski. When they didn't find them, they questioned the air-traffic controller. He had nothing unusual to report. The only flights to depart in the last two hours had been a Mig fighter and an air ambulance for Tiumen.

The guards on the gate couldn't help the KGB men, either. They had only just started their shift.

And across the other side of the runway, near the fuel-tanks, the bowser-driver slept peacefully in the line shack and dreamt of Fat Katerina and her ample delights that waited for him when he finally went home.

The watcher sat at his screen in Moscow, the green light reflected in his eyes. He watched the slow-moving white dot that was the AN-2 leave Tobolsk and go south towards Tiumen. He sent his report by phone, then continued to track it. It took over an hour to get a distinguishable picture from the satellite. He recognized the shape of the slow-flying Antonov and passed the information on to his superior.

North of Tiumen the plane changed course, heading directly towards the small town of Talica. Over Talica it turned west towards Sverdlovsk and followed the track that the watcher knew was the Trans-Siberian Railway.

His report was passed to two sources, one official and one secret.

The official report went to the president who, after reading it, sent for the police chief, Yashkin. When he arrived, the two men discussed the situation and pondered why Myeloski was travelling west. Yashkin believed his officer had uncovered a clue and was now keeping clear of the KGB. He would, of course, report back immediately to the president once Myeloski had contacted him. The meeting broke up, and the president

214

asked to be informed as soon as Myeloski had landed.

The other report, by black-leathered despatch-rider, went to General Vashinov at KGB headquarters. After he read the document, he called Marshka and told him of the latest developments. The old man said little, asked to be kept in touch when Myeloski's destination was clear. Both men agreed that it was probably Sverdlovsk. When he had hung up, Vashinov sat back and examined the situation. The policeman was good, had picked up the clues faster than expected. He and the Englishman were a formidable team. The killing of the KGB agent in the governor's house had proved that. They had also managed to get away from Tobolsk, from both the police and the KGB. With the plan so close to fruition, he didn't want them changing the ending the old man had planned. He picked up the phone and ordered his deputy to call off the men in Tobolsk, and organize a surveillance team in Sverdlovsk. He also arranged for his private jet to be prepared in case he needed it. Sverdlovsk wasn't the most inspirational town in Russia, but a few days there with Vera to help pass the time would make life most enjoyable.

The men at the mine-shaft in the Koptiaki Forest finished their task and departed down the hill towards their vehicle.

Eventually, when the forest had returned to its natural sounds, only then did Ivan Bakor come out of the undergrowth and to the mine-shaft. He found little, except that the shaft had been opened and prepared for habitation. There were sleeping-bags and canned food ready in boxes. The shelter had been prepared for a short stay.

Bakor and his men left everything as they found it. He knew the men would be back. He knew that now was not the time to act.

His men melted back into the forest, into the

undergrowth to wait for the intruders' next move.

Vashinov's surveillance team were waiting outside the terminal for Myeloski and Duncan.

They had watched the AN-2 land on the shorter of the parallel runways and taxi towards the civilian ramp. The plane had been surrounded immediately by local uniformed police. Its unplanned flight to Sverdlovsk had prompted the air-traffic controllers to call in the local gendarmerie.

Myeloski was first off the plane, his warrant-card out in his hand before he had touched the ground. As he spoke to the superior officer in the group, Duncan stepped out after him, followed by the pilot. The senior officer went with Myeloski to one of the parked cars, and Myeloski spoke over the radio. After ten minutes, when the Sverdlovsk police had finally contacted Moscow by phone, Myeloski and Duncan were allowed to go free.

The pilot, who had wanted to tell the police about Duncan's death threat, decided that discretion was the better part of valour and headed for the terminal. Myeloski, now back firmly in command, insisted on an unmarked police car for the two of them.

Half an hour later, a grey Lada was delivered to the airport for their use. During that time, Myeloski had gone to the cafeteria and replenished his strength. Duncan had walked round the terminal, which was modern and much bigger than the one they had left in Tobolsk. It was when he went up to the observation-platform that he picked up the surveillance team. There were two of them, at opposite ends of the observation-tower, watching him. He left the platform and returned,

216

by the escalator, to the ground floor. As he walked to the main entrance, as if to leave, he saw the third member of the team, a woman in a red coat. So much for unobtrusive wear. He turned sharply, catching all three of them flat-footed, and went into the cafeteria. He joined Myeloski at a window-table and drank tea while the policeman finished his meal.

They left the terminal soon after, with the policeman who had brought the Lada. He had been nonplussed by Myeloski, who had ordered him to catch a bus home. Only when they drove away, towards the Hotel Amerika, did Duncan tell Myeloski about their tail. In his surprise and eagerness to see their pursuers, Myeloski almost lost control of the Lada. After he had settled down again, with the curses and honks of angry drivers still ringing in their ears, they finally sped towards the city. Duncan relaxed, now anaesthetized to his companion's driving, and looked at his surroundings, at the city he was being driven into.

Sverdlovsk, the Ekaterinberg of old, is one of the biggest cities in eastern Russia. An industrial monument to modern Russia, its prosperity was based on coal and steel. With over one and a half million inhabitants, Sverdlovsk was a sprawling ever-growing metropolis of low-rise buildings and vast cooling-towers. But in the centre the charm and style of old Ekaterinberg remained. A commercial area of banks and government departments, little had changed since the revolution.

The Hotel Amerika, when they eventually found it, looked just as it did in the picture they had been shown by Yurovsky's daughter. They parked the Lada outside the front entrance, on the Vosnesensky Prospekt, not far from where the photographer must have stood.

They took two rooms on the second floor. The hotel, as old and faded inside as it was outside, was the haunt of local party and trade union officials. While they had checked in, the small group of prostitutes who sat in the

217

lobby stopped their gossip and watched the two men. When they saw no interest for their wares, they returned to their chatter, yet still keeping one eye on the men, in case they should change their mind. As Duncan and Myeloski were led by the porter, an old man in a purple threadbare uniform, to the stairs, the Englishman nudged his companion and indicated a framed photograph on the wall. It was a larger photograph of the tsarist conspirators outside the hotel, the same picture they had first seen in Tobolsk.

The porter noticed the look of recognition that passed between the men.

'You know who these men are?' the porter stopped and asked Myeloski.

'Some of them.' Myeloski was cautious, surprised by the old man's question. 'It is an old picture. A famous picture.'

'Yes. An old picture. Maybe not so famous.'

The porter turned away and led them towards the stairs. Myeloski looked at Duncan and shrugged. The two men followed the porter, carrying their own cases as they went.

From his window, which looked out on the front of the building, Duncan saw the green KGB Lada parked at the opposite kerb. The woman in the red coat had left, and the two men sat in the front, keeping a watch on the hotel entrance. Neither of them saw Duncan at the window.

Twenty minutes later, the Englishman went down to meet Myeloski. As he came down the small main staircase, he heard the Russian's voice, loud in its discussion. Myeloski was near the front entrance, talking to the old porter. So as not to break the policeman's progress, Duncan sat on a small wooden chair on the landing. He simply became one of those ever-present people who always seem to hang round hotels doing nothing.

'The Pittsburgh of the Soviet Union. It is a terrible name for such a pretty town.'

'Here, in the centre, yes. But you should see the rest of Sverdlovsk. It has grown too quickly. An ugly place.'

'I envy you. To live here, in such a place of history.' Myeloski fought to get the old man's confidence.

'Moscow has even greater history.' Duncan heard the suspicion in the old man's voice. 'I thought you said you were from Moscow?'

'But it's not the same. It's all too grand, like living in a museum. And you lose the sense of the past; it's all lost in the rush-hour traffic and the queues in the streets. Here, in the centre of Sverdlovsk, time has stood still.'

'We have our rush-hours. And our queues.' The old man cackled. 'It's been like that as long as I can remember. Ever since I was a boy.'

'How old are you?'

'Sixty-eight. I can retire, you know. But I would have nothing else to do. People die when they retire, you know. And I intend to live for ever.'

'I bet you know some stories. I bet you've seen some things.'

'More than you can imagine.'

'Tell me.'

The old man shook his head. 'I would need for ever. So why are you and your friend here?'

Myeloski leant forward, was suddenly conspiratorial. He spoke in a low voice; Duncan didn't hear what he said. 'My colleague is from Hungary, a famous writer and journalist. He is here to research the early days of the revolution. In these days of *perestroika*, all it seems we do is change history. I don't see what good it all does. So I'm a nursemaid, here to make sure he gets all the help he can. In Sverdlovsk, he is to see the House of Ipatyev.'

The old man gasped as Myeloski leant back, watching to see the effect the name had on him.

219

'Is it far from here? The infamous house.' Myeloski asked the question softly.

'Which house is that?'

'You know. The one in which the tsar and his family were killed.'

'There are many old houses in Sverdlovsk. And plenty of rumours. But it was a long time ago. It is not something that is advertised. I must work now.'

Duncan heard the old man move away from Myeloski. He got up and went down the stairs. Myeloski saw him and took his arm and led him towards the small restaurant at the rear.

'Time to eat,' he told Duncan. 'I asked the porter if he knew of the House of Ipatyev. He said no, but I know he's lying.'

The old porter watched them from the front desk as they went into the dining-room. Then he picked up the phone and made a call. Myeloski watched him through the glass door, watched him speaking frantically to someone. When the porter finished his conversation he put down the receiver and looked towards the restaurant.

There was no sign of Myeloski.

Marshka didn't attend the Praesidium assembly. He sat in his sitting-room in the dacha and waited for General Vashinov's call. It had gone well, each piece in the jigsaw had fallen into place as well as could be expected. He thought of the president's face, at the surprise he knew that would register when he told him the reason for the plot.

He smiled warmly, thought of his 'little reindeer' and hoped that he would understand. The president's father had stood beside him in Leningrad when the Germans had attacked. The two of them were part of a small guerrilla sniper force that moved from area to area, from house to house. Younger than Marshka, the president's father was a schoolteacher from the Ukraine who now fought the Germans with a ferocity that was rare in any human being. He hated the Germans for what they were doing to his country, to the land that they were trying to usurp. It was a cold hatred, steel in its resolve and cruel in its execution. Marshka had never known him take a prisoner; to him the only good German was a dead one.

The two became friends when the younger man realized that Marshka was as committed as him to the destruction of the Germans. They always hunted together, in the darkness of the burnt-out buildings where they waited for the Nazi soldiers to pass by.

Marshka remembered once, when they had both come face to face with a young Wehrmacht officer in the shadows of the Peter and Paul Cathedral. The surprised officer, his hands bandaged against the cold of the Russian night, had turned to run, trying awkwardly to pull out his pistol at the same time. The young Ukrainian had overpowered him quickly, knocking him to the floor. As the German lay there, with his attacker standing over him, he had reached into his tunic pocket and pulled out a battered leather wallet. He took out a picture of his family, a blonde wife and two children aged between six and seven. He held the picture up, sobbing hysterically as he did so, pleading for his life. Marshka's companion watched him, his face impassive. Then he drew out the long hunting-knife he always carried, forced the German's head back, and calmly cut the officer's throat. The photograph fluttered to the floor, sprayed by the pulsing blood of the dying man, before being picked up by the Ukrainian. He wiped the blood off the photograph with his sleeve, pocketed it and left the dead officer as a reminder to others who would find him the next morning.

After the war he had returned to his village and the school in which he taught. Occasionally, when Marshka needed to get away from the pressures of Moscow, he

221

would go to the village and visit his friend. The photograph of the dead German's family was always on the mantelpiece, near the religious icon that had been in their family for generations. There was always a candle lit in front of the photograph and the icon.

It was in this atmosphere that the president, an only son, had been brought up. Marshka got to know him as a child and then a young man. He had opened doors for him into government service and helped him when help was needed. He called him 'little reindeer' because of his nimbleness as a young man when he had been one of the best mountaineers of his time.

Now, years after the president's father and mother had died, he still saw the gleam and energy of commitment in the son's eyes. In his friend's son, the Soviet Union had a leader of worth, a leader of destiny. *Perestroika* would work, but it needed time. And Russians, as Marshka knew, were not a people who were always prepared to give up such a precious commodity.

The phone rang, and Marshka answered it at the same time as his secretary picked it up in the anteroom. It was Vashinov. Marshka waited for his secretary to put down the receiver before he spoke.

'Give me the latest report,' he said. He listened to Vashinov, frowned as he heard the news from Sverdlovsk. When Vashinov had finished, Marshka spoke. 'No, there is no need for you to go there yet. But keep yourself on standby. The policeman is clever, but he still has a way to go. Make sure your people report immediately if they move from the hotel. And, if you want to, bring everything forward to a conclusion.'

Marshka paused before he continued. Then he said: 'The point is made. It is near the end.'

And he hung up on Vashinov. He leant back and took a Kosmos cigarette from the pack on the table. It was too late for anything to go wrong. The plan would soon be complete.

* * *

The restaurant of the Hotel Amerika was full, and an anxious waiter hovered around Duncan's table. He wanted them to finish their final cups of tea so that he could clear the table and bring in more diners. There was a queue at the door which reached out into the hall.

Myeloski drained his cup and signalled the waiter over.

'Another tea. For me and my friend. And a vodka with a beer.'

'Could you have your drink in the bar? There are people waiting for tables.'

'No. Bring them here.' Myeloski turned his back on the waiter and spoke to Duncan. 'Bloody pigswill. They must be mad to queue to eat here.'

Duncan smiled, remembering the gusto with which the policeman had devoured two helpings of the main course. Appreciation of the culinary arts was not one of his prime strengths.

'So what is this Victor of yours really like? The one who will be a tsar.'

'He's a good man.'

'Good men don't always make good leaders. Can he handle it?'

'He can handle it.' Duncan was firm in the defence of his friend. 'I've seen him face danger many times. His sense of responsibility is inborn. He'll be a good king. Will you be a good subject?'

The question made Myeloski laugh. 'Who knows? Will Russia accept a tsar again? Do the people want one? Why should we have one? Does your queen make any difference to you?'

'Yes.'

'Why? The Americans, the French, none of them needs a royal family. Why is it so important?'

Duncan had never queried the monarchy's role. It was his instinct to be loyal to them, to accept their position as

223

constitutional rulers of the country. 'Because they are constant. Our governments change. All the time. And they both stand for completely opposite philosophies. Not like the Yanks, where there's no real difference between the Democrats and the Republicans. The queen is our symbol. She's the unity in the United Kingdom. As a soldier, my allegiance is to queen and country. But they are really the same. By voting we can change our government, can make them bend to our will. That means we have the ultimate responsibility for the land we live in. And she symbolizes that land. That's why it's so important.'

'And will a tsar make such a difference to the Soviet Union?'

'I don't know. But, from what I read, this country is tearing itself apart anyway. Is that really what the people want, or is it just breaking from the oppression of the past?' Duncan stopped, but Myeloski didn't answer, just shrugged. 'If communism is no longer the bond and symbol of the people, then why not a tsar? Why not a symbol under which each republic can live to its own local laws, yet have a national purpose? It happens in America. The states have their own individual laws, but the constitution and democracy are their flag.'

'You forget, it was the tsars who fucked us in the first place. It was they who conquered the republics and made them part of Russia. The revolution was to break free from that oppression. Only we got new masters, a new oppression. America is a new land; they've no tradition. Not like the British and the Soviet people. Our tradition is in our blood. The people of the Soviet Union want their own traditions back in their hands.'

'So you don't want the tsar back?'

'No. But that does not stop me doing my job. I am a policeman first; that is my duty to the Soviet Union.'

The waiter scurried back with two cups of tea, a beer and a vodka, and put them on the table. Myeloski ordered him to put the bill on his room account. The waiter hovered behind Myeloski, waiting for a tip, but the policeman turned his back on him, faced Duncan again. The waiter turned away in disgust and went to another table. The vodka was gulped down instantly, causing Myeloski to choke and then break into a fit of coughing.

'You all right?' asked Duncan.

The policeman nodded, wiping away the tears that the coughing had brought on. 'Damn it. I forgot. This Siberian vodka's 200 per cent proof.' He looked up, caught the derision in Duncan's eyes. 'Don't doubt my commitment to finding the family.'

'I don't.' Duncan's answer wasn't completely honest. 'But we're not going to get very far just sitting here, are we?'

'You never know. Somebody wants a word.'

Duncan half-turned and looked at where the policeman indicated. It was the old porter Myeloski had spoken to. He signalled to Myeloski from the restaurant entrance and then went back into the reception-area.

'You wait here.' Myeloski rose from the table and followed the porter. Duncan sat there, sipping his tea, feeling the eyes of the waiting queue burning into his back. He ignored them and slowly sipped his drink.

Myeloski returned five minutes later.

'Let's go! The mountain has finally come to Muhammad.' He looked pleased, his expression eager as he once again sensed his quarry. Duncan rose and followed him into the reception-area. The porter was at his position, his head down as he read a paper. He ignored the two men who passed next to the reception-desk and slipped out of the back of the hotel.

The woman in red saw them come out. She stood in a shop doorway, huddled against the cold evening wind that had started to blow. Duncan saw her as Myeloski led him across to the small taxi-stand that was tucked away behind the bus-shelter. They were fortunate, as there was no queue waiting and they climbed into the first Lada taxi in the line.

'Club Panther.' Myeloski leant forward and instructed the driver where to take them. As the taxi pulled away, he leant back and turned to Duncan. 'At least the KGB won't be following us,' he said smugly.

Duncan decided not to disillusion him. He had already seen the woman in red scurry across the road and into the hotel. She would have run through the lobby and out of the entrance to where her two colleagues were waiting.

'Is this a mystery tour, or are you going to tell me where we're off to?'

Myeloski laughed. 'To a nightclub. For a good night out.'

Duncan knew he didn't want to discuss matters within earshot of the taxi-driver. He sat back and took in his surroundings. The drab greyness of the city was accentuated by the few neon street-lamps that half-lit the streets. After a few minutes they had left the old centre and entered the newer part of Sverdlovsk. The greyness continued; the only difference was the square-blocked small-windowed housing estates which spread outwards.

Duncan saw the green KGB Lada pick them up before they left the centre and keep a discreet distance behind them.

The Club Panther was down a side-street sandwiched between the residential area and the steel-mills. It was a dark street, some two hundred metres long, which was only lit at each end. The houses, prefabricated in their design and only one storey high, were individually illuminated by different-coloured lights above the closed windowless front doors. This was where Sverdlovsk drank after a hard day's work in the heat of the steel-mills.

The taxi drew up outside one of the buildings on the

left-hand side which had a single blue light above the door, rather in the fashion of a British police station in the 1950s. As Duncan climbed out and heard Myeloski go through the now familiar routine of ordering the taxi-driver to invoice the local police, he saw the green Lada pull up at the top of the street.

Eventually, when the complaining taxi-driver had departed, Duncan asked Myeloski what they were doing there.

'Welcome to the black market,' answered Myeloski, a huge grin on his face.

'Will you stop playing games?' Duncan showed his irritation.

'In the Soviet Union everything is still on the black market. Even information. The porter told me that someone here can show us the House of Ipatycv.'

'A black-market guided tour, eh?'

Myeloski's laugh bellowed across the deserted street. 'That's very funny. Very good. A guided tour, on the black market.' Still laughing and shaking his head with amusement, he turned to knock on the door.

'While you're in a good mood, you should know the KGB have followed us here.' Duncan's statement brought Myeloski's laugh to an abrupt stop. 'Down there, the green Lada on the entrance.'

As Myeloski swung round he saw the Lada lights blink off. 'You should've told me,' he said.

'Why? They'd've traced the taxi anyway.'

Myeloski, now angry at being followed, turned back and rapped sharply on the door. As it swung open, Duncan heard the loud blast of music from inside the building.

The two of them walked in as the doorman, a young sharp-featured man in jeans, purple Cossack shirt and Cuban heels, closed the door behind them. They were in a small anteroom with whitewashed walls on which were pictures of strippers in various pouting poses. It would

227

have fitted neatly into the gaudy and cheap fleshpots of Hamburg or Soho. Behind the small cubicle set against a wall, a bored gum-chewing, red-headed girl watched them.

'You're not members,' the purple-shirted doorman stated firmly.

Myeloski shook his head. 'We're staying at the Hotel Amerika. The porter said we should come here.'

'OK. But you have to be members. That's twenty roubles. Membership fee. You pay the girl.'

'He never said anything about paying.'

Duncan stepped forward before Myeloski took the matter further and, Duncan was sure, insisted it be billed to the local police. He pulled some notes from his wallet and slid them under the glass partition to the girl. She put the money in a drawer under the counter.

'Another five roubles to go in,' she said.

'But we just paid,' snapped back Myeloski.

'That was to become members. Now you pay the entrance fee,' said the doorman, moving towards them.

'You never told us that.'

'You never asked.' The doorman shrugged. 'You don't want to go in, that's fine with me. Come back another day.'

'And you keep the twenty roubles?'

'That's for your membership. I told you. As members you can go in any time you want.'

Duncan had pulled out the extra notes and passed another ten roubles to the girl, who deftly slid the money into the drawer.

'You see. Your friend doesn't argue. He knows a bargain when he sees one.' The doorman opened the inner door, and they followed him through. 'As new members you are allowed one free beer. Then you pay.'

It was a large rectangular room. There was a small raised stage at the far end which was illuminated by a series of flashing lights. A stripper was halfway through her act; the music was Jimi Hendrix's 'Purple Haze'. The room, with painted nudes on the walls which had long since lost their glow under the layers of forgotten nicotine, was packed. It stank of sweat and stale tobacco. As they were led to a table at the side, Duncan noticed one of the prostitutes who had been at the Hotel Amerika. She was entwined round a large pot-bellied steelworker who was much the worse for drink.

The doorman signalled a waiter over as he sat them down.

'A free beer for these new members,' he said to the waiter. 'Enjoy. Girls, dancing – whatever you want.' With that, he turned and pushed his way through the crowd.

On the stage, the stripper, a thin blonde girl with nipples for breasts and bruises on her left thigh, took off her final garment to the raucous jeering and catcalls of the audience. 'Purple Haze' finished before she did, and the last minute of her act was completed in mime against the general cacophony of the patrons of the club. When she finished, she grabbed her clothes from the stage where they had fallen and rushed off behind the curtains. Two minutes later, as the waiter approached the table with the two free beers, another stripper came on and started her act.

'What do we do now?' Duncan asked Myeloski. 'Watch the cabaret all night?'

'We wait. When you're dealing with the black market, you always play by their rules.' He held up his glass to Duncan. 'Enjoy. To friendship . . . and to success.'

The policeman emptied his beer without taking the glass from his lips. The music competed with the shouts of the crowd; it was Elvis Presley's 'One Night with You'. On the stage the new stripper, this time a dark-haired plump girl with a bushy growth of hair under her arms, mouthed the words to the music and pretended to do an Elvis impersonation as she removed her clothes.

Myeloski stood up and beckoned the waiter over.

As he sat down, the purple-shirted doorman came through the crowd and knelt down between them.

'Why do you want to see the house?'

The man's bluntness surprised Myeloski. 'My friend wants to see it. He is a foreign journalist. Another beer.' He shouted at the waiter who had come to the table.

The doorman waited for the waiter to go before continuing. 'Why do you think I know where the house is.'

'I don't. We were told to come here by the porter at the hotel.'

'You were followed.'

Myeloski looked round. Duncan, who had seen them enter the club, leant across and pointed his finger across the room. Myeloski saw the two men and the woman in red at another side-table.

'KGB,' the doorman stated flatly. 'Why are they following you?'

'The KGB still follow everyone. Old habits, you know.' Myeloski's answer didn't convince the doorman. 'Look, I am from the Secretariat for the Interior. I am here to show this journalist where—'

'If it is an official visit, why do you need me?' The doorman stood up to go.

'He's a policeman from Moscow.' Duncan's cold hard tone stopped the doorman. 'I'm from England. One of my countrymen, a diplomat, has been kidnapped. We think we'll find the answer in the House of Ipatyev.'

'And the KGB?'

'I don't know. Either they're involved in the kidnapping or they want to get there before us and claim the credit. I really don't know.'

'We're not trying to trap you, to find out about your little game.' Myeloski took out his warrant-card and showed it to the doorman. 'See for yourself.'

The doorman glanced at it and acknowledged it. He

spoke as Myeloski put away his card. 'How do I know you're not trying to trap us?'

'Because I'm too bloody important to come all the way to Siberia to catch a small-time crook. That's why. And, if you don't help us, I'll make sure this place closes down for good. That I guarantee you.'

'Can he do this?' The doorman asked the question of Duncan, who nodded his answer. He turned back to Myeloski. 'The police always threaten to close me. All that happens is that I disappear and open again in a few weeks. You can stuff that in your Moscow pipe and smoke it, arsehole.'

Myeloski puffed up, his face red with anger. Duncan leant over and put his hand on his arm to calm him.

'Look, this is an important matter,' Duncan pleaded with the doorman. 'There's a hard way and an easy way. Nobody wants you to close down. So why force it? All we want is information and directions.'

The doorman considered before replying. 'How much?'

'You tell us.'

'A thousand rubles.'

'OK.'

'No, two thousand.'

'Don't get too greedy.' Duncan leant back, and the doorman saw the flash of the Coonan Magnum under the Englishman's jacket. He looked into Duncan's eyes and saw that he had reached his limit.

He looked away from Duncan as he spoke. 'Cash.'

'Traveller's cheques.'

'Dollars?'

'Dollars.'

'OK. Five hundred dollars. Now, finish your beers. I will be back in a few minutes. We must give the KGB the slip. Leave it to me.' The waiter came back and put Myeloski's beer on the table. The doorman grinned as he spoke. 'Three roubles. For the beer.'

Duncan reached in his pocket and gave the waiter the money. The doorman turned and went back to the foyer.

'Greedy bastard.' Myeloski picked up his beer and drank it as quickly as he had the first. He put the empty glass down. 'There was no need for the money. He bluffed you. He would have taken us anyway. There was no way he wanted this place closed.'

'I know that. But at least this way he won't run and tell the KGB.'

'You want to bet?'

Myeloski nodded his head towards the other table. The doorman, his purple shirt a bold banner across the room, moved toward the KGB group.

As he reached the table and knelt down to speak to them, the stripper, in her last moment of jaded sexuality, fell across the stage as one of the audience grabbed her ankle and tripped her over.

The crowd jeered and shrieked at the unfortunate girl as Duncan and Myeloski saw the doorman point across the room at them as he continued his earnest conversation with the KGB operatives.

'To make my dreams come true,' sang Elvis as chaos reigned in the Club Panther.

At that moment a grey army truck pulled up outside the large deserted house which was screened from passing traffic and chance intruders by a high concrete security-wall. The solid metal gates, over three metres tall, at the entrance to the road were closed as the driver got out and went to the front door.

A man dressed in traditional army uniform of the First World War came out on to the veranda. The driver saluted him.

'Is everything ready at the Four Brothers?' the officer in the old uniform asked.

'Yes, Comrade Captain.'

'Good. Wait for us. We will not be long.'

The officer returned to the darkened house. From inside there came the sound of a child crying as it was awakened in the early hours of the morning.

The Club Panther exploded into action fifteen minutes later.

A big steelworker, his shirt-front peeled open to his pot-bellied navel, went up to the KGB group and asked the woman in red to dance. The girl declined; but her would-be suitor was heavily under the influence of drink, and this refusal excited him more. He pulled up a chair from the next table and sat down, leaning over the table as he leered at the woman. One of her companions warned the intruder, but his words were ignored. The woman shook her head again, told the steelworker that she wouldn't dance with him. Not to be outdone, he took some money from his pocket and offered it to her. She, appalled at being mistaken for a prostitute, turned her back on him in disgust. The KGB man on her left shouted at the steelworker to leave them alone. All this did was further incense the steelworker, who stood up, leant over the table and grabbed the woman by her arm, turning her roughly towards him. As she pulled back from his bruising action she tore her red dress at the shoulder. He pulled her towards him, knocking the table over as he did so. One of the KGB men fell over backwards in his chair as the other one got up to help the woman, but the steelworker hit him across the face with the back of his free arm. The KGB man shot backwards, tripped over his companion who was trying to get up from the fallen chair, and crashed into the next table. The occupants, a peroxided elderly whore and two steelworkers, all fell to the floor as the force of the KGB man landing on their table sent them all sprawling.

The steelworker who had started it all dragged the woman in red on to the dance-floor and clutched her to him with both arms, her face buried in his naked heavy

233

chest. Behind them, the two steelworkers who had been knocked to the floor got up and attacked the KGB man they saw as responsible for their situation. The fight spread, and within seconds the second KGB man was punched in the face by another steelworker.

While this was going on, a young man in working clothes and a heavy woollen jacket sat down at Duncan and Myeloski's table. They recognized the grinning features of the doorman, now changed out of his purple shirt.

'We'll get out the back way. When I go, follow me, and keep low. Give me the traveller's cheques now.'

Duncan reached in his pocket and took out his wallet, from which he pulled out some traveller's cheques. He tore five one-hundred-dollar cheques from the stubs and then signed each one. He handed them over to the doorman, who confirmed they were authentic.

'What about the KGB?' Myeloski asked.

'No problem. They'll be occupied here for a long time.'

'Did you tell them why we were here?'

'No. Just that you wanted information about the tsar's death. By the way, my name's Morrison.'

'Morrison?' Myeloski was surprised.

'You know, the Doors.'

Myeloski shook his head, but Duncan remembered the 1960s pop group.

'Jim Morrison,' Duncan replied on Myeloski's behalf.

'Good. A civilized man.' Morrison looked pleased with himself. 'I will take you to the house, show you how to get in. We must be no more than half an hour in there.' He turned and looked at the developing fight. 'Good. Let's go now.'

He rose from the table and led them, in a half-crouch, towards the stage and out through a small side-door.

They went through the strippers' changing-room. Three girls looked up; one of them smiled at Morrison, recognizing him. The room had a stale smell about it; there were over ten sweaty girls crammed in there. They left the changing-room by another door and walked down a long corridor. There were bedrooms on each side, and Duncan realized this was where the prostitutes conducted their business. As they reached the end of the corridor, a door was open and Duncan saw a girl, no more than fifteen, naked on a bed with a heavy, raw, red-bodied man about to climb on top of her. Another man sat naked on the end of the bed, obviously having already been satisfied, with his head in his hands as the drink played havoc with his brain after his exertions. The girl, seeing Duncan, smiled weakly at him from under the red-bodied man. The smile was welcoming, the eyes were old and tired and said the smile lied.

At the other end of the corridor the door from the club swung open and the steelworker came through, dragging the woman in red behind him. She was screaming, but it did no good. Join the KGB and see the world, Duncan thought.

'She'll be OK,' Morrison spoke, as though reading his thoughts. 'They're just going to keep them busy for a while.'

As Duncan followed Morrison and Myeloski out of the back door, he doubted the doorman's words. The screams from behind told a different story.

There was an old Datsun 240Z sports-car, red in colour, parked outside the door. It was obviously Morrison's pride and joy. He opened the driver's door and signalled them to climb in from the other side. The small rear seats of the 2+2 dismayed Myeloski, who stepped back to let Duncan in first. The Englishman shrugged and climbed into the back, allowing Myeloski to ride in the front.

With a spin of his rear wheels, Morrison pulled away from the kerb and took off down the road, the engine obviously well tuned as its resonant roar indicated.

'Is it far from here?' asked Duncan.

'Twenty minutes, no more.'

Morrison swung the car on to the main road, away from the old centre, and swept through the steelworks and coke plants that lit up the night, a giant firework that sweated and belched across the skyline. Both Duncan and Myeloski were impressed by the sheer size of the industry, by the industrial endeavour that had made Sverdlovsk the powerhouse that it was. But it was also the city that hid the shame of the revolution, the nemesis of death that had been shielded from the world for over seventy years.

'Nothing like this in Moscow, eh?' Morrison joked to Myeloski. 'Leave us to live in the shit while you lot pamper your arses on the Metro.'

'We have our problems, too.' Duncan sensed Myeloski's defensive attitude as he spoke.

'Yeah. Well, I'll trade your problems any day for the smoke and heat and sulphur we have to breathe in. Those workers back there in the club. Don't look down on them. It's the only break they get in a pretty shitty life.'

'Nobody's looking down on them.'

They continued in silence for a while, past the steelworks and up the hill that led away from the industrial area.

'You like the Doors' music?' Morrison asked Duncan.

'I've heard some of it. Good stuff.'

'Who's Jim Morrison?' asked Myeloski.

'He was the lead singer,' said Duncan.

'The greatest. I have all his records, all his tapes,' broke in Morrison. He reached into his top pocket and took out a battered photograph. He handed it across to Duncan.

'He signed it,' said Morrison as Duncan looked at an old publicity photograph of the original Jim Morrison with his disdainful look at the camera. It was the type of pop picture Duncan had seen many times, the sensual portrait of a young god with a wide ruffled shirt splayed open to the navel and disappearing into sprayed-on leather pants. 'See, see. At the bottom. He signed it. Jim Morrison signed it.'

'That's great,' replied Duncan, not wanting to tell the club-owner that most publicity shots were usually signed by girls in the mailing office. He handed the picture back to Morrison, who tucked it back into his pocket. 'Where did you get it?'

'In Liverpool. In England. I was there, many years ago, working on a ship. I bought it in a club. For only twenty pounds. Cheap, eh?'

'Yes. A good bargain.'

'One day, one day, I will buy a guitar he used. That is what I really want. They sell these things in the West, yes?'

'Sometimes. At auctions.'

'He's a big star?' Myeloski asked of the Englishman.

'Was. He died of drugs,' replied Duncan.

'Another great Western import.'

'Rubbish,' shouted Morrison. 'He died because he was a genius. And geniuses are different from us. They need excess; they're bigger than life itself. And here, in this fucking death-hole, if you can't escape into music or something, you'll kill yourself before the day's out. Fucking hole.'

'What do you know about this place? About Ipatyev.' Duncan leant forward as he changed the subject, his head between the two in the front. His question was directed at Morrison.

'It was a fucking hole for them, wasn't it? It's where they were killed. The Romanovs. The house is sealed off, the whole area for hundreds of metres is deserted. One road goes past; it is hardly used.'

'How do you know so much about it?'

'Because it's business. Just because the authorities . . .'

Morrison stopped, looked quizzically at Myeloski.

'I'm not interested in your scam, I told you,' Myeloski answered the unasked question.

'What about the authorities?' Duncan reminded Morrison of his last remark.

'They may not be interested, but plenty are. We have a lot of people come here, want to see it. Ghouls. I can think of better ways of passing the time. They should've pulled it down years ago. But, then, I wouldn't have had the tours, would I?'

'How many tours?' Myeloski asked.

'Plenty. Used to be a necessary stop in the days of the Party.'

'Anyone recently?'

'Like who?'

'You tell me.'

'No. It's been quiet for a few weeks. That's 'cos the officials came down.'

'What officials?'

'I don't know. Maybe they run their own tours. Out-of-towners. Moscow clothes. They stay there a few days, then move on.'

'When did they come last?'

'Two weeks ago. They stay there. They could be there now. We'll see.'

The Datsun had entered a clear area. The houses which had once stood nearby were demolished, but the rubble had never been cleared away. Morrison switched off the lights and pulled off the road, behind a pile of brick and concrete rubble.

'We walk from here,' he said, switching off the engine. 'Stay close to me, and if we see anyone there, then we come back here.' He took two torches from the glove-compartment and got out, the others following. He handed one of the torches to Duncan, who slipped it into his coat pocket.

As they picked their way through the rubble, Duncan

238

felt an excitement within him, such as he had not felt since the Falklands. Not only was he near to finding the royal family, but he was also on the verge of touching the spirit of his grandfather. He would have come here, all those years ago when the Whites tried to save the tsar.

They rounded the corner and saw the high concrete wall and the metal gates. Morrison stopped for a moment, checked the area and then whispered: 'It's behind there, behind those walls. Just keep close to me.'

Over the top of the walls, in the hazed cloud-thin moonlight, Duncan made out the roof of the white building. It was bigger than he had imagined, a stone balustrade encircling the roof. He reached for his Coonan Magnum, clicked the safety-catch off and loosened it in its holster.

Morrison led them towards the left side of the building, away from the high metal gates. Down there, near the corner at the rear, he stopped at a smaller metal gate. From his pocket he produced a key and unlocked it slowly and silently. He pushed it open gently and signalled the two men through. Then he followed them into the courtyard behind the house, closing the gate behind him.

The courtyard was overgrown and had not been tended for many years. But there was a small path through the long grass and weeds, cut no doubt by Morrison as he had used the entrance over the years.

The white house was two-floored, rectangular and impressive. There were no lights from within the house, no sign that anyone was inside.

'Stay here!' Duncan's voice was authoritative, and the others obeyed him. The gun that had appeared in his hand also impressed them.

He circled the house slowly, keeping close to the white peeling walls. The windows were all covered with corrugated iron, the doors sealed and locked. At the front, near the main entrance, he saw that the gardens had been trampled down to the gravel below the undergrowth. There was a large archway into a smaller courtyard on the opposite side, and the wooden double gates hung open. Duncan noticed the deep tyre-tracks that meant a truck had been there. He felt the tracks, felt the fresh earth and realized that the truck had not been long gone. He continued his search of the exterior and came on his two companions where he had left them. He reported that there was no sign of activity within the building.

'Good. Take us in,' Myeloski told Morrison.

Morrison nodded and led them to a side-door, one which opened on to a half-basement. He pulled back one of the corrugated-iron seals which revealed the door behind it. He took another key and unlocked it, pushed it open and went into the house. The others followed, first Myeloski, then Duncan. Duncan closed the door behind him, closing out the night light. They all stood silently in the black, listening for any sounds of occupants in the house. The silence was complete, the atmosphere heavy and clinging. Then a light came on, surprising them in the darkness.

It was Morrison's torch. It shone on the double door at the opposite end of the room.

Keeping his gun in his left hand, Duncan reached in his pocket and took out his own torch. He switched it on and swung the wide beam around the small room.

Next to the double wooden door, to its left, splattered across the faded striped wallpaper, he saw the gaping pink red mess of the bullet-holes. The damage to the wall spread halfway round the room and covered the floor as well as the wall. Duncan knew this was the room in which the tsar's family had been brutally murdered. The air was lifeless, and he gulped as he swallowed, then started to cough. He put his hand over his mouth to stifle it.

He heard Myeloski gasp next to him, realized that he was shocked by what he saw.

'Everyone reacts in the same way.' Morrison walked into the beam of Duncan's torch, his eyes squinting against the light.

'We need to search the rest of the house.' Duncan's voice was calm in its authority, the professional taking charge.

He walked past Morrison and ran his hand over the bullet-holes. Satisfied that the blood was not fresh, that the damp was that of age and decay, he moved to the door and turned the handle. The door opened, and Duncan slipped through it and up the stairs. Myeloski and Morrison looked after him, surprised by the speed with which he had moved, and then followed. But Duncan was gone, deep into the house, his gun in his hand, the torch illuminating his path.

He searched the floors, from room to room, but found the house empty. When Myeloski and Morrison eventually caught up with him, he was in a room on the second floor, at the front of the house, which had a balcony that overlooked the courtyard below. He had opened the doors, torn back the corrugated-iron covers, and the room was flooded with moonlight.

On the floor there was bedding and full rubbish-bags. It was as it had been at the governor's residence in Tobolsk. And once more they were too late.

Myeloski looked round the room. Like all the others, it had fallen into disrepair and was bereft of any furniture or decorations. The whole house was a shell, nothing more than a memory of pain and shame.

Myeloski walked past Duncan and out on to the balcony. In the distance, over the high concrete walls, he saw the lights of Sverdlovsk. Now where? What next in this deadly game?

Morrison came and stood by him, looking out towards the city. In the room Duncan poured the contents of the rubbish-bags on the floor and started to search through them.

'What happened to the bodies? After they were killed here?' Myeloski asked the question of Morrison.

'I'm not sure. There's only rumour and gossip.'

'Tell me the rumour.'

'There're lots. Even one that says they weren't killed, but taken away and hidden.'

'Forget that. Tell me about what happened if they were killed. Weren't they taken somewhere and burnt? Where were they buried?'

'In the forest. Buried in a mine-shaft.'

'Where?'

'I don't know.'

'Then, find someone who does. We have to go there. Now.'

'At this time of the morning? You've got—'

Duncan called to them from behind. 'Maybe this is what we're meant to find?'

He knelt amongst the rubbish as the others joined him. He held a large print of an old photograph in his hand, illuminated it with his torch. It was a picture of a bearded man with a flat peak cap who knelt on the forest floor and looked down at a hole in front of him. On the bottom, written in a thick Pentel, was a handwritten inscription: 'Sokolov finds the bodies near the Four Brothers in the Koptiaki Forest.'

'Who the hell's Sokolov?' asked Morrison. They were later to find that Nikolai Sokolov had led the investigation into the death of the tsar's family.

'It's an old picture. He's probably dead by now.' Myeloski took the photograph from Duncan and held it closer so that he could examine it more thoroughly. 'More important, where's the Koptiaki Forest?'

'To the west. About twenty kilometres,' said Morrison.

'And the Four Brothers?'

'No idea.'

'We're staying here. To search the place. You get back to town and find where, or what, the Four Brothers are.' Myeloski stood up and looked round for further clues. Duncan went on searching in the rubbish. Morrison, not knowing what to do, followed Myeloski.

'Where am I going to find out something like that? At this time of the morning?' he asked Myeloski.

'Look' – the policeman turned on him, the anger in his voice genuine – 'I'm here to find the hostages before any danger comes to them. Just accept that. Now, time is against us; it might already be too late. There must be people, old people, who know where this place is. Find out. Don't fuck me around. If you let me down, if you con me, there won't be a place anywhere that I won't find you. Just get it done and get back here. As fast as you can.'

Morrison realized that Duncan had risen and stood behind him. He knew he was trapped. The policeman had the authority, the Englishman the determination.

'I'll see what I can do.'

'And get that car back here within the hour. We'll need it by then. Leave me the torch.'

Morrison handed Myeloski the torch and then left them. They heard him go down the hall and to the stairs, they heard him crashing around in the darkness.

'Anything else in there?' Myeloski referred to the rubbish in the bags.

'No. The picture was on top, obviously planted for us to find.'

'You look downstairs. I'll check up here. And let's open this place up. Use the moonlight.'

The two men looked at each other, weary in the knowledge that they had arrived too late and that they were still the pawns in someone else's game. They had come a long way together, their brotherhood was formed.

And they were both impatient for the end.

'Shit, shit, shit, shit!'

Duncan sat on the balcony, out in the early-morning cold, and watched Myeloski pacing up and down in the room, the photograph in his hand, swearing at no one in particular.

Their search had been fruitless. The house, an empty damp mausoleum, gave up no secrets. It had been stripped of its furniture and belongings decades before, sealed off from the world in a forgotten corner of history.

Dawn was beginning to streak the night sky, and Morrison had been gone over an hour. They had decided to split up if Morrison had not returned within two hours. Myeloski was to return to Sverdlovsk, to the Hotel Amerika, and pick up the car. Duncan was to wait for Morrison to return, or for Myeloski to come and collect him. They both felt a sense of hopelessness. So close, and yet no nearer a satisfactory conclusion than when they had first started.

Duncan heard the 240Z first, its engine roaring in the distance, coming up the hill from the direction of Sverdlovsk. It was the first sign of life they had heard since arriving at the House of Ipatyev.

He came off the balustrade and into the room. 'Come on. I think our friend's back.'

Myeloski followed Duncan down the stairs, through the room of death and into the courtyard. They met Morrison as he pulled up at the side-gate. He got out of the 240Z, a big grin on his face.

'I got it!' Morrison shouted, excitement in his voice.

'You know where it is?' Myeloski asked, over Duncan's shoulder.

'No problem,' came the cocky answer.

'Come on, let's go!' Duncan, urgent in his command, climbed into the car. Myeloski and Morrison followed him. 'Just get going. Tell us what happened on the way.'

Morrison spun the wheel, and the car U-turned back in the direction he had come from. He drove fast, falling in line with their sense of urgency.

'They're trees. Fucking trees,' Morrison told them as he drove.

'What trees?' asked Myeloski.

'The Four Brothers. Trees. In the forest.'

'Do you know how to get there?'

'I know just where they are. Only they're not there any more. It's just an area. Where these trees used to be.'

'What else?'

'There was this old feller. Always said his father was a Bolshevik, said he was one of the assassins. Nobody believed him; just an old man wanting to impress. Anyway, I always had a soft spot for him. No point kicking an old man, no point in taking away his dreams.'

'Every Russian's a Dostoevsky. Come on, what the hell did he say?'

'About the trees, about the mine-shaft. There was a mine-shaft, you know. Grisly ending.'

'We know.'

'Burnt 'em with acid, tried to dissolve the bodies. Bloody sick. Then threw them down the shaft.'

'I said, we know.'

'Just put your foot down. You can find it, can't you?' asked Duncan.

'I think so. Unless his memory was playing tricks.'

They arrived at the Koptiaki Forest fifteen minutes later. It had started to drizzle; a mist had settled on the trees. Morrison, after traversing the road twice to make sure he was in the right spot, parked the car in a small opening. In the distance, from the direction they would be going in, they heard a helicopter skimming low-level away from them. Eventually the sound of the turbine-powered rotors disappeared into the distance.

They had decided to walk the last half-mile, not wanting to warn the kidnappers if they should still be in the forest. As they started to move into the forest, Morrison produced a small automatic pistol from his waistband. That's all I need, Duncan thought. A Saturday-night special.

They followed the path that ran alongside the small river, where the old man had told Morrison to go. It was slow going, the earth muddy wet underneath them. Duncan stayed some twenty yards ahead; they knew he was the professional, and they bowed to his leadership. Every so often, when he was sure that they had not been spotted, he signalled them to follow. Myeloski was impressed with Duncan's natural ability to merge into his surroundings. Even though he knew he was ahead of them, he had difficulty in seeing him through the mist and the undergrowth. The gun that Myeloski carried suddenly felt heavy against his chest; it was because he knew that he might soon have to use it. He slipped and clawed his way after Duncan, his breathing laboured.

Morrison, younger and fitter than the policeman, also found the going difficult. The farther they went into the forest, the farther into the wall of white birch trees, the steeper became the terrain.

Duncan noticed the grey truck in the clearing after they had covered about a quarter-mile. He signalled the others to approach him quietly, and then, when they had reached him, made them lie low, hidden from the truck.

Morrison looked pleased. 'Looks like the old man was right,' he whispered.

Duncan silenced him with a sharp gesture, then left them there and circled the clearing. He saw no obvious sign of life, no movement. His two companions saw him suddenly appear in the clearing, right next to the truck. They saw the big gun in his hand. When he had determined that there was nobody there, he signalled them out into the open.

When they got to him, he pointed up the hill, along a narrow path. 'Tracks lead up there,' he whispered. 'About nine people. Including some children.'

So they were there. Maybe it wasn't too late.

'Same procedure. Wait for my signal before you move on. And, if you see any movement, just freeze. Stay still, whatever happens.'

With that, Duncan moved on and upwards into the trees again, the other two following.

Duncan was frustrated by his two companions; they slowed him down. He was also concerned about their safety, knew that they were not experienced in terrain warfare as he was. But he knew he had no alternative. Move too fast and they would stumble, possibly give away the element of surprise that he needed.

The birch trees thinned out as they climbed higher. Eventually he reached the top of the first hill. He dropped on to his stomach and crawled over the brow. He could see, through the thickness of the trees, another opening some hundred yards ahead and below him. He signalled the others to catch him up, and to keep low. A few minutes later the three of them lay side by side, looking down over the hill.

'You two break down there to the left. Keep some distance between you, at least twenty feet.' Duncan explained the plan to them – soldiering by numbers. 'If somebody starts shooting, don't just start firing back. You might hit one of the family. And don't yell out. Keep low and behind the trees. I'll be the other side. When you get down there beside the clearing, don't show yourselves until you see what I'm doing. And take your time getting down there. Don't rush it; it isn't a race.'

He slid over the hill and went down into the trees to the right of the clearing. The other two looked at each other, both suddenly feeling vulnerable without Duncan in front of them. Myeloski nodded to Morrison and rolled over the top and down into the trees. Morrison watched him go, and when he felt that there was enough space between them he followed the policeman into the trees.

When the two of them got within full view of the clearing, they realized that it was deserted. They could see the entrance to the mine-shaft; it was a hole in the forest floor. They stayed where they were, in sight of each other and hidden from the clearing. Considerable time passed before Duncan appeared silently behind them, surprising them both.

'There's no one here,' he reported. 'Anywhere around here. Only more tracks to the east. Riders. On horses.'

'Where now?' Myeloski's concern showed in his question. This was the end of the line as far as clues were concerned.

'Cover me.' Duncan drew his gun and waited for the others to follow his example. When he knew they were ready, he left the cover of the trees and moved into the open space of the large clearing.

He moved slowly, his eyes scanning the surrounding trees and undergrowth. But there was no one there; they were on their own.

He signalled the other two to come out into the opening.

Morrison stayed to Duncan's left, while Myeloski skirted round and walked towards the mine-shaft opening. He knew that this was where they had thrown the tsar's body, and those of his wife and young children. Was this where the trail was to end? Was this where the English family had come to a bloody termination? He felt the anxiety in his throat, the fear of what he knew he would find.

It was Myeloski who first saw the rivulets of blood that had formed in the mud.

It was Myeloski who also saw the bodies heaped up, lifeless and dumped in the mine-shaft.

The sheer magnitude and surprise of the carnage sickened him. The face of the body on top of the others had been sliced in half with a machete-type instrument.

He turned and vomited, right there in the middle of the clearing, next to the mine-shaft.

Duncan put his arm out and held Morrison back. He came forward and looked down on the piled, mutilated corpses.

That was when one of the bodies, under the pressure of those above, slipped in the mud and its hand fell loose from the heaped pile.

Strapped to the wrist, shining in the greyness of its surroundings, Duncan saw the gold Cartier watch. He didn't need to inspect it closely to know that it was the same watch that the prince's bodyguard, George Leeming, was now missing.

8

SLIPPED THE HOOK

**A clearing in the Koptiaki Forest
The Urals
10 a.m.**

The first members of the Sverdlovsk police arrived in the clearing two hours after the bodies were found. There were six of them, their high shiny boots covered in mud as they slithered down the path.

They were led through the undergrowth by Morrison, who had been despatched by Duncan to the nearby village of Koptiaki to phone for assistance.

When he had gone, Duncan and a chastened Myeloski had searched the area for clues, but found none. The only tracks leading away from the area had been those of the riders. There were also the imprints of heavy tyre-tracks in the mud. But they went nowhere, and Duncan remembered the helicopter that they had heard when they first arrived at the forest. Whoever had been responsible for the killings had left by air.

Myeloski didn't have the stomach to help Duncan pull the corpses from the mine-shaft. But he knew his duty, and helped the Englishman, regularly breaking away from the opening so as to retch in the undergrowth. It was a most unpleasant duty, but Duncan was made of sterner stuff and he simply got on with the business.

There were seven corpses in all, most of them riddled with bullet-holes and then mutilated. Five of the seven were dressed in period army uniforms.

There was no sign of the Oldenburg family.

When they had laid the corpses out in a row, they checked deeper in the mine-shaft. There was bedding there, and cans of food, as though it had been prepared for a short stay. There was also a primus stove, no doubt for the family's use. The entrance to the shaft looked very much like a Second World War air-raid shelter. Apart from the preparations for a stay, there were no other clues.

They then searched the corpses, went through their clothing. They found no identification-marks, no clothing tags to help them. The Cartier watch, which they presumed was stolen from Leeming, was the only obvious link. Myeloski said nothing when he saw Duncan remove the watch and slip it into his coat pocket. He knew it would be returned to its rightful owner. There were also no arms; whoever had killed them had taken away their weapons. Duncan commented on the state of the bodies; he said that each man had been superbly fit and obviously well trained.

'Probably KGB,' Myeloski had commented, trying not to look too closely at the bullet-ridden corpses. Duncan had not pushed him any farther on his comment.

The two men then sat at the edge of the clearing. Duncan brought a can of corned beef with him and opened it, offering some to Myeloski. The policeman refused, shook his head in disgust. Duncan ate sparingly of the contents, just enough to keep his energy-levels high.

'You see their faces?' he asked Myeloski.

'What about them?'

'Surprised. Total fucking panic. I think they were ambushed, caught in a crossfire. If you look round the edges, you can see where people were hidden in the undergrowth.'

'What the hell's going on? Where're the family now?'

'You tell me. This is your country, your crime. Isn't that what you keep telling me?'

'Are you saying I'm not doing my job?'

'If the cap fits. I just think it's time we changed direction. Got a little tougher in our approach. And if you don't want to, then I'll move on my own.'

Myeloski was angry; he objected to the Englishman's criticisms. 'We've moved as quickly as possible. In a matter of days we've come this far.'

'Not far enough. We still haven't got the family. And, while we've been pussyfooting around, the KGB and God knows who else have all been getting involved. It's time we knew why the KGB's involved. Moscow must know. And who's been planting all these clues?' Duncan stood up as he heard the sound of men shouting in the distance, coming towards them along the path from the road. 'Look, if you're really genuine, then it must have crossed your policeman's mind that somebody's setting us up. Just playing along with them isn't working. It's time to change tactics. Time to shake the bastards up. I don't know where to go next, but the next time I see the family I don't want to see them like this.' He pointed at the row of corpses.

Myeloski knew the Englishman was right, knew that they had been set up. But he also knew that the answer wasn't necessarily in Moscow. He decided not to share his speculation with the Englishman at this stage. What puzzled him most was that if the bodies were KGB, then what rogue act had brought about their deaths?

'As the Americans say, it's time we kicked some ass,' Duncan went on.

An hour after the police had arrived, and Myeloski had stamped his authority on them, the two KGB operatives and the woman in the red dress had arrived. She had changed into uniform, and Duncan noted that she was a lieutenant. Her eyes gave little away; she kept them averted, and both men wondered how the situation with the big steelworker in the Club Panther had been resolved. The KGB officers showed Myeloski their identity-cards and then remained in the background. They knew it was a police matter and, unless ordered to, knew better than to get involved. After all, their directive had been to follow Myeloski and report on his movements, not to solve a murder, however sensational it appeared to be.

More police arrived and a doctor. Whilst the doctor examined the corpses, Myeloski organized a search of the area around the mine-shaft. Nothing was found. The trail of horses led deeper into the forest and eventually joined a small tarmac road some three miles from the clearing. It was impossible to gauge which way they had then gone.

By one o'clock Myeloski knew that he was wasting his time. There were no clues to follow; the trail had dried up.

He decided to return to Sverdlovsk with Duncan and Morrison. It was time to make his full report to the president.

Sheremetyevo Airport
Moscow
9 a.m. (Moscow time)

General Vashinov missed the Politburo meeting that had been called for 10 a.m. As soon as he had heard the news of the Koptiaki Forest massacre, he had rung Grigory Marshka. After a brief conversation with him – the old

253

man had been surprised and horrified by the news – he then contacted the president.

The president was already aware of the situation and was in the process of arranging an emergency Politburo session. He instructed his KGB chief to fly to Sverdlovsk and investigate the situation. He was to make a full report to the Politburo of events over there. He was not to interfere with the investigation, was to leave it in the charge of the police. Captain Myeloski was to remain in control of the investigation. He was also told that the president's private jet was being prepared for Vashinov and would be ready at Sheremetyevo Airport.

When he had finished with the president, he rang Marshka back and reported the conversation to him. Neither man went into too much detail. There was always the possibility that someone might be listening. If they had been, they would have heard only a conversation of concern between two Politburo colleagues and friends.

'Any idea who the dead men are?' Marshka asked Vashinov.

'No. Maybe we will never find out.' They both knew that the dead men were KGB agents. It was up to Vashinov to ensure that their real identity was never discovered.

The question neither of them could honestly answer was asked by Marshka. 'So where is the family now?'

Shortly afterwards, when he had finished speaking to the old man, Vashinov rang his assistant and told him to prepare for their trip to Sverdlovsk. He also asked him to contact Vera Kasyanova. They would need a secretary on the trip, he said. He grinned as he put down the phone. At times of crisis, sex was Vashinov's release; the thought of moments spent with Vera excited him. She would be of great comfort while he tried to determine what had happened to his men in the Koptiaki Forest.

The president's plane, a Yakovlev Yak-40, was a small

three-engined civilian jet that had been converted two years earlier for his personal use. It had been refurbished in Hungary, a country that somehow managed to retain its grandeur and entrepreneurial spirit despite years of communist rule. It was now the most successful trading nation in Eastern Europe.

Vashinov sat in the president's seat as the tri-jet lifted off the runway and flew east. Not a fast plane, it had a cruising speed of only 340 knots; the journey was to take four hours. Vera sat across the aisle from him in her service uniform, his assistant in the front compartment where the *apparatchiks* always sat.

When they had climbed to their cruising height of 35,000 feet and the seatbelt sign was extinguished, Vashinov called his assistant through.

'Close the connecting door!' he ordered. 'I want some privacy to dictate a report for the Politburo. I don't want to be disturbed for any reason.'

When the assistant had gone, closing the door behind him, Vashinov signalled Vera to follow him through the door that led into the president's sleeping-quarters, an essential requirement on the regular long tours that the president made both in the Soviet Union and abroad.

He closed the door behind her, put his arm round her and grinned wolfishly.

'Bet you've never been fucked in a president's bed before,' he joked.

She stepped back and looked at the wide double bed. Through the portholes she saw the bright blue of that sharp sunlit sky that can only be seen at high altitude, away from the earth's impurities.

'Never done it in a plane before,' she answered matter-of-factly.

'Then, it's time to become a member of the Five-Mile-High Club.' He moved towards her, expected her to be excited by the new thrill, by this most original of sexual adventures.

In his eagerness and his lust he never noticed how, although her physical movements were as exciting as ever, her commitment was distant.

As Vashinov pawed the girl and made love to her on his president's bed, as he reached into the bestiality of his inner self where he found his only sexual relief through the degradation and shame of others, as he turned over the pictures in the dirty book of his mind, she looked out of the window and wondered what she was doing there.

Vera Kasyanova, as innocent as any virgin, her soul untouched by the multitude of men who had enjoyed and despoiled her body, had finally tired of her games and started to grow up.

The Kremlin
Moscow
10 a.m. (Moscow time)

Marshka watched him. 'If this gets out, we'll be the laughing-stock of the whole world,' said Vasily angrily. He looked the seedy little trade union official he was. The old man had never forgiven him for selling his principles down the river for a seat on the Politburo. The country needed men of principle and vision, not party officials who dived for cover at the first hint of trouble.

'What would Comrade Vasily have us do? Join in the laughter? Our concern should not be what others think of us, but that we do what is right.' As Marshka said the words, he wanted to reach out and claw them back. It was not his style to rise to the weaknesses of others.

'What do you think is right, Grigory Mikhailovich?' The president's question drew Marshka further into the discussion, something he had not wanted at this stage. The death of the KGB men had come as a bolt out of the blue. By now, the plan should have been completed, the result as he had planned. Now he was just as helpless as the rest of the Politburo, as helpless and as useless as any other old man in a wheelchair.

'Wait. For Vashinov's report from Sverdlovsk,' said Marshka.

'We did that before. Waited. Just got us deeper into trouble, didn't it?' Vasily was running with the hounds, felt he was on safe ground.

Marshka controlled himself, fought hard not to let Vasily get under his skin. His voice was tough and unemotional as he spoke, as they would expect him to be. 'Our concern is not what others think of us, but to identify the truth.'

There was silence. Marshka looked round the room; he saw that he had hit the mark.

'What if it is a monarchist group?' The president's question was addressed directly to Marshka. 'They will say they have rescued the family. They will openly blame us, criticize us for not safeguarding them.'

'No matter. Not if we make a statement first. After all, we didn't kidnap the family. Our hands are clean.' Only Marshka knew he was lying.

'If there are no dissenters to that viewpoint – and I agree with Grigory Mikhailovich – then that will be the course we shall take.'

With the silence that continued, the president knew that they had all agreed to follow the old man's advice. 'Good. Then, that is what we shall do.'

The president rose and left the room. As the others started to talk amongst themselves, Marshka wheeled his chair and left by the other door.

At least, he thought, the effect of the plan was now being executed. But who had interfered in Sverdlovsk? Why had they kidnapped the family and killed their guards?

As he left the room and turned the corner, he took one last look at the other members of the Politburo.

Could one of them have taken the reins from Marshka's hands? If so, what terrible twist was about to be unleashed on Marshka and the game that he had started?

After a life of living on a knife-edge, Marshka had never lost the instincts that had protected him when others around him had fallen. He had always had an uncanny sense for impending danger, had always managed to change course before being overtaken by any disaster. As he sat there, alone in the wheelchair, his eyes still on the blanked-out screen, his instincts told him that this time it would be the greatest threat he had ever faced.

Marshka thought of Vashinov, on his way to Sverdlovsk. If he was being double-crossed, then he didn't believe the KGB general was the man. He couldn't be trusted, but he would only strike when he knew that the old man couldn't hurt him.

Whoever had kidnapped the family and killed the KGB guard would have to show his hand soon. He hoped no harm would come to the Oldenburgs; it had always been his intention to protect them. But, even if they were killed, the result would be as he had planned.

So who was the new player in the game? Were they to force his hand so that he had to reveal the awful truth of the Beria Archives?

Hotel Amerika
Sverdlovsk
2 p.m.

Morrison was waiting for them when Duncan and Myeloski returned from the forest.

Myeloski had given instructions to the local police to search the area. He had also cordoned off the mine-shaft after the local photographer had taken pictures for him.

The corpses had been removed to the mortuary in Sverdlovsk, and a post-mortem was ordered on each body.

On the drive back, the two men had said little to each other, not wanting to share their thoughts with the police driver who had been assigned to them.

At the hotel, Myeloski called Moscow and gave his report to Yashkin. His superior, after listening at length to Myeloski, told him that the head of the KGB, General Dmitry Vashinov, was flying to Sverdlovsk to prepare a full account for the Politburo. Myeloski was instructed to stay in the region and to give the general any assistance he required. But – and Yashkin was firm in his words – the investigation was to remain under Myeloski's authority. He added that he understood the strain this would put on Myeloski, but those orders came from 'the highest authority'. He was also in the process of setting up a direct telephone satellite link between Moscow and the local police station for faster communication.

After his call, Myeloski went looking for Duncan, who had also been on to Moscow, to his contact, Jack Richardson, at the trade desk of the British embassy. Richardson had nothing to report, apart from informing him that he was to continue to work with the Russian authorities. Duncan informed him that the Russian company he was avoiding were now in a terminal state. He hoped that Richardson could work that one out.

The two men, after swapping notes from their respective conversations, went downstairs into the lobby.

The prostitutes, who were normally at home at this time, had arrived early when they heard of the activity at the Hotel Amerika. They hoped business was going to be good.

Fortunately no one recognized Duncan and Myeloski. They, after speaking to the manager, requisitioned the library at the side of the lobby for their own use. After

259

he had cleared the room of other guests, the two men moved in. Morrison, who had been hanging round the lobby, followed them in. The police driver who had brought them back from the forest was positioned at the door and ordered not to allow anyone in.

They sat at an Empire-style gilt table. The top was pitted with tea-cup ring-marks and cigarette-burns. What they didn't know was that it was at this same table that the council of the Ural Soviet had passed sentence of death on the Romanovs. The table, then as now, had remained in the library of the Hotel Amerika. On the walls hung faded photographs of the Bolsheviks who had played such an important role in the bloodiest days of the revolution. This was a historic room that had faded beyond memory and lost its meaning.

Unaware of all this, pleased only to find the sanctity and privacy of such a room, Myeloski needed time to reflect on the situation. Like all investigators he needed information. The trail was cold; it was up to them to open it up again. Morrison was as good a starting-point as any.

'You said that there had been activity around the House of Ipatyev for some time.' Myeloski asked the question of Morrison. 'How much activity?'

'Enough to keep me away. I tried to get in three times last month. Just to show people round. I saw lights on the top floor, so I didn't go in.'

'What sort of lights?'

'Torches.'

'Only on the top floor?'

'That's all I saw. You've got to remember I never took anyone over the rest of the house. People only wanted to see that room.'

'Any vehicles parked there?'

'A car, once. And a truck was in the courtyard.'

'A grey military one?'

'Yeah.'

'And you never saw any people?' Duncan joined in the questioning.

'No.'

'When you left us at the house, who did you go and see?' Myeloski took over.

'I told you.'

'You said an old feller. Who?'

'He was an old steelworker. Before the club, in the days before social enterprise, I worked in a drinking bar. It was a workers' club; that's what we used to call them then. He used to come in, every day, regular as clockwork. Sat quietly in a corner and drank nothing more than beer. Over the years I got to know him. He told me about the old days, things his father had told him. He's nearly a hundred now. And the older he gets, the more he seems to remember.'

'An old man's memory playing tricks.'

'No. Not with him. He's never said one thing one day, then something else the next. It's just new things, new memories. He told me about the Ipatyev place, about the murders there. I learnt more about the history of the revolution through him than I ever did in any school. He's a good old—'

'Shit and dammit!' Myeloski's outburst cut across Morrison. The other two looked at him, surprised. 'Maybe the mine-shaft wasn't the end of the line. What was that you said earlier about those rumours?'

'Which rumours?'

'About the Romanovs. About the rumours that they weren't all killed.'

The question stunned Duncan. Maybe Myeloski had finally found another door to open. They both stared at Morrison, waited for his answer.

Duncan had gone to meet the old man with Morrison, leaving Myeloski to wait for Vashinov.

The general had arrived three hours earlier with Vera in tow and had insisted that Myeloski take him to the House of Ipatyev and then to the mine-shaft in the Koptiaki Forest. The policeman recognized Vera as the girl from the Savoy Hotel in Moscow. She had looked for a sign of recognition from him, but he gave none. He remembered Duncan's annoyance at her visiting his room, realized now that she had been a KGB plant. At least that was one mystery resolved.

They travelled in a stretched Zil limousine which the local KGB office had procured for the great man's visit. The car was used by a local party boss who was also the region's head. During the journey, Vera had looked anxiously across at Myeloski in the front seat, but he took no notice. It confused her; not many men didn't remember seeing her after a few days, even if it had only been a meeting in a hotel bar. She wanted to know if the Englishman was still there.

They had found nothing new at either site. This had infuriated Vashinov, who did not want to report back empty-handed to Moscow. He was in an impossible position. It was his men who were dead, and yet he had no choice but to disown them.

He had been fascinated by the room of murder in the House of Ipatyev. It had surprised him; its stark simplicity and untouched history, as though the murders had only taken place a few months earlier, had taken his breath away. He tried to get rid of Myeloski, to stay in that room with Vera. The excitement of fornicating with her in those surroundings had stimulated him so strongly that he had had to turn away from the policeman so as not to show his protruding sexual arousal. Vera had noticed, but she ignored him, had not even smiled at his predicament. But Myeloski stayed with him, refusing to leave the general.

He asked about the history of the assassination, but the policeman gave nothing away, simply stating that he knew only that the tsar's family had been killed there. They drove back to the Hotel Amerika in silence. Vashinov knew the policeman was holding back, yet he had no authority to insist on the truth. Even if he did, he believed Myeloski would stonewall him.

Duncan's journey was far more fruitful. The old man, pleased to have someone to talk to, was willing to answer the Englishman's queries.

Igor Mischnev was a young ninety-three. He had led a life full of sex, tobacco and drink and never had a serious illness. Like most Siberians, Mischnev was tall, over six feet three in his youth. Now, stooped with age, his ambition was to live to a hundred. Although sex had long since stopped being part of his life, he smoked and drank with the same enthusiasm he had always done. He was convinced this was his secret to achieving his personal centenary.

He lived on the top floor of a retired steelworkers' home for the old. On the eighth floor of an old concrete 1950s tower-block, he had a small balcony which was his pride and joy. Mischnev would sit there, on a small wooden-backed chair, looking out over the city and towards the hills. It was an easy place to recall your memories, to escape the drabness and uselessness of old age in a bustling industrial centre. From this height one could see, on a very clear day when there was no smog, the House of Ipatyev nestled in the shallow hill and the forests beyond.

Morrison introduced Duncan as a foreign journalist. The old man had been suddenly frightened, not wanting to see his name in print. He still vividly remembered the days of the Stalin purges. Morrison calmed him down, told him that Duncan was only after background information, would not reveal Mischnev's identity.

Duncan could see the old man trusted Morrison, who was a frequent visitor and enjoyed the peace he shared with the old man and his memories. Morrison produced some vodka he had brought, gave Mischnev the bottle. The old man shuffled away and produced three small tumblers. Morrison opened the bottle for him and poured out three measures, the largest going to Mischnev. They all drank a toast.

Mischnev had been in his late teens when the revolution started, when the tsar had been murdered. His father had been a farmworker on one of the local estates. When the revolution came, the land had been confiscated from the landowner and set up as one of the first collectives. His father, well into his forties, had been put in charge of production by the local Ural Soviet.

Duncan let him ramble through his past, through the stories of intrigue and change of those early revolution days. As the old man spoke, the Englishman listened intently, trying to understand the times that his grandfather had lived in. He wondered if the family estate at Talica had been similarly commandeered. It probably had.

'What happened to the landowner?' Duncan's question surprised Morrison; he didn't see the point of it.

'A bastard. Treated his workers like shit. I think he went to Moscow or somewhere.' Mischnev then launched into an attack on the unfortunate landlord, who had probably died in a pauper's grave many years earlier. Duncan regretted asking the question. After a few moments, he steered the old man back to the assassination and other doings of the time.

The assassination story was as he had heard before. There were no new discoveries. The people of Ekaterinberg knew nothing of the deaths until after the event.

264

They had known the tsar was there, under guard in the house, but very few townspeople saw them; in fact they were actively discouraged from visiting the area. They all knew the guards and the captors. After all, they lived in the Hotel Amerika; that was where they had their meetings. He himself had see the Jew, Yurovsky. Afterwards, they said it was the Jew who had actually killed the tsar with his Nagan revolver.

'What happened after that?' Duncan led Mischnev on. 'They buried them all in the forest, didn't they?'

The old man didn't answer, suddenly looked mischievously at Morrison. Duncan saw Morrison nod imperceptibly, and the old man turned back to the Englishman.

He was suddenly secretive in his tone, his voice lowered to a whisper. 'So they said.'

'If not in the forest, where?'

'Maybe they weren't all killed.'

'The tsar not killed?'

'Oh, he was killed. They couldn't leave him alive. It was definitely him they carried out and took to the forest.'

'Who else?'

'The German. Rasputin's tart.' Mischnev meant the tsarina.

'The children?'

'They say that Olga, Tatyana and Maria were also killed.'

'There have been rumours about Anastasia for generations. That she escaped, that she went to live in France and then in America. They even made a film about it.'

'Then, you must believe it is a rumour. Nothing more.'

Duncan realized he had said the wrong thing, that the old man was clamming up. 'There was also a story that the entire family had been taken to America. They were impostors, although nobody ever proved it. It's good to talk to someone who knows the truth. You must tell me. I want to believe you.'

Mischnev considered for a moment, appeased by the young man's apologetic approach.

'It's all rumour. Just tall stories.'

'Most of history is rumour. What you tell us could change our understanding of history.'

The old man preened, was flattered by the compliment. 'My father, visiting the Hotel Amerika on the day that they were to be executed, overheard an argument between Yurovsky and Voikov, who was the commissar of the Ural Soviet. He was waiting to see Voikov about the farm quota, and they didn't know he was there in the waiting-room.'

'What was the argument?'

'From Moscow, Kerensky had ordered Voikov not to kill the family.'

'Kerensky?'

'I thought you knew about history.'

'I'm here to learn.'

'Bullshit. Trouble with people these days. They don't do their homework.' He saw that Duncan looked suitably admonished. 'Kerensky was the prime minister. Not for long. He wasn't a Bolshevik. That's why they saw him off. He hated them. Helped start the revolution, but was a democrat and a republican.'

'Why didn't he want the family killed?'

'He wanted them to stand trial for their crimes against the State. But Yurovsky said they must die. He said Sverdlov—'

'Who?'

'The Commissar of the Interior. What did they teach you at school? He wanted them executed. Sverdlov had informed Yurovsky that Lenin also wanted this before the Whites got into Ekaterinberg.'

'And Yurovksy won.'

'The Jews always win. There was much shouting, and then they came to a compromise. They would all be killed, except for the boy Tsarevich Alexis and the

266

Grand Duchess Anastasia. They would be taken away and hidden until such time as a trial could be arranged. Yurovsky was to visit the local morgue and arrange for the bodies of two children to be taken to the House of Ipatyev, where they would be swapped with those of Alexis and Anastasia. My father, fearing for his life, then left and waited elsewhere for Voikov.'

There was a long silence before Duncan spoke. 'Were there any rumours as to where the two survivors were taken?'

'No. But people knew they were alive. They say that Yurovsky shot the boy in such a way that he would live. When Voikov and the Jew were left alone in the room, after the execution, they switched the bodies and dragged them out of the room. Afterwards, when the house was clear, the young ones were taken secretly to another safe place.'

'And you don't know where?'

'I said it was only a rumour. Some even say they were killed elsewhere, after they decided not to hold the trials. Who knows? I even heard that they were taken to an asylum near Tiumen. That they were locked away with the mad ones, and after the decision was made not to have a trial they were just left there, shut away to rot with the rest of the madhouse. It would be justice. After all, it was at Tiumen that Rasputin lived.'

The old man had little else to add. After some further questions, Duncan indicated to Morrison that they should leave. They shook hands with Mischnev, and Morrison promised to see him again soon. He promised that he would bring more vodka.

The two men returned to the Hotel Amerika. On the way, Duncan thought about Yurovsky's daughter's words. She had also mentioned the rumours about the family not being killed. But she had denied them, said they were only rumours.

Morrison, pleased to be alone with the Englishman,

regaled Duncan with stories of the sixties pop scene, of the Doors and Jimi Hendrix and the Beatles and anything else he had picked up from his imported pop magazines over the years. He told him of his life in the merchant navy and of the ports he had visited, of the world beyond the Soviet Union he had discovered.

'So why did you come back here?'

Morrison shrugged. 'It's home.'

'That's the only reason?'

'Well, I'm also special here.'

'Special?'

'There're hundreds, thousands of Jim Morrisons in the West. Even Moscow has them now. And Elton Johns. And George Michaels. Everyone's a pop star, or looks like one. But here I'm the only one, eh? Here I'm special.'

The two men laughed at the shared joke as they made their way back to the Hotel Amerika.

Myeloski had not returned when they got back. Morrison said he was going to the club and would be there if he was needed. Duncan went to his room to wait for Myeloski. He lay on the bed and fell asleep; he needed to catch up on his rest after the last few days.

The nightmare came very quickly, even before he had fallen into a deep sleep. He was walking in the snow, up in the forest with the outline of the steelworks behind him, when a helicopter came over the trees towards him. He started to run, knowing that the aircraft meant him danger. At the control column, wearing a flying helmet with goggles across the eyes, he saw the MI5 man, Woodward. He was laughing, his left thumb over the button on the yoke that fired the machine-guns. Duncan sprinted in short bursts, swerving from left to right and back again, but he was no match for the helicopter. As Woodward got closer, he opened fire, the bullets streaking towards Duncan, cutting up the ground around him as he ran. He fell forward, the big blades of the helicopter now thrashing the air over his head, forcing him down into the ground. He lay there, still, as the chopper hovered only inches over him; the huge wheel-supports had only to drop a few inches and they would crush his head. Men climbed out of the helicopter, men dressed in army uniforms from the First World War. They dragged him into the forest, through the snow, towards the mine-shaft that he knew was there. The helicopter stayed over him, making sure that he wouldn't break for cover. When the mine-shaft appeared, when they had dragged him there to its great ugly hole of an opening, they threw him in. As he struggled to get out, one of the men – he recognized Yurovsky from the photograph – held up a large metal container and poured the contents over Duncan. Before the liquid hit him, he knew it was acid. He felt no pain, but saw it burn into his skin, strip his flesh from his body. The rest of the men drew revolvers, old-fashioned in design, and opened fire on him. Again he felt no pain, but in the heat of that moment he knew he was dying. Then they suddenly stepped back. Over them the helicopter came in, settled itself right over the opening. Before he could move to defend himself, he felt the searing heat and flash of the first napalm bomb. The hole exploded into a bright fireball, and the helicopter lifted away. Woodward looked down on him, mocking him. This was the price of failure. As he fell into the mine-shaft he saw the bodies under him move. They looked up at him; they were the dead, and he was joining them. They reached towards him, flesh hanging raggedly on their arms and skeletons. They grabbed him, pawed him, pulled him down. It was then he saw their faces, recognized Victor and the family. Their screams of anguish and pain and despair racked him, because then he knew that they were all dead, and that he had failed when it mattered most.

But the nightmare wasn't over; the despair went on.

Grandfather Denknetzeyan stood by the grave, his

expression gently mocking Duncan, reminding him that he had failed. Duncan wanted to speak, but there were no words, just an awful silence. The more he wanted to tell him how hard he had tried to save the family, the more difficult it became to speak, the words locked in his throat.

Then the grave had faded away and he found himself standing with Grandfather Denknetzeyan near a big house, an old house, a ruined house. As they stood there, a young woman came towards them from the debris of the house. He knew it was Katya, the great-aunt he had never known, the sister lost by his grandfather. He watched them embrace, watched them turn to him and beckon him over. But he couldn't move; he was the outsider who had failed in his duty. Then Grandfather, still with that mocking little smile, faded away into oblivion, left only Katya and him. Her smile was kinder, but he recognized his grandfather in it. Then the hands reached out, hands and arms, hundreds of them, out of the earth and dirt and towards her. She screamed and tried to run, but it was to no avail. The hands clawed at her, tore her clothes, pulled her down to the earth and devoured her body. She screamed, called to him for help. But it was no good; he was trapped in his own nightmare, unable to respond and save her.

Then, and for no reason at all, the screams stopped as she started to enjoy the hands that ruthlessly explored her body. Unseeing fingers, worm-like, caressed and violated her, probed and enjoyed her. When she looked at him, he saw it wasn't Katya, but Vera Kasyanova.

And like Grandfather Denknetzeyan she mocked him. Then she started to cry, but her tears became his tears and burnt his face, washed away the skin in deep rivulets that seared through to his cheekbones.

He woke up then and sat up sharply in the bed. He put his hand to his cheeks and was surprised that they weren't damp. There were no tears in the real world.

He knew sleep would be difficult, so sat there and thought of what he could remember of his nightmare. Katya. What had become of her, so long ago? What would she have done in Moscow? Had she married? Had children? A lonely young girl in a changing city. Anything could have happened.

With a start he realized that could have been Vera's story. A young girl, deserted in a big city to look after herself. He suddenly realized how wrong he had been to dismiss her. He had no right to treat her in such a curt and rude manner. No one had the right to do that.

When the nightmare and its aftermath had finally subsided, he slept for over an hour before Myeloski woke him by knocking on the door. He swung his body off the bed and let the policeman in.

'How did it go?' asked Myeloski.

Duncan told him about the visit to Mischnev and the old man's story. Myeloski listened without interruption until he had finished.

'And he had no idea of where they were taken?'

'He says not.'

'Shit. Mind you, he's an old chap. Maybe we could refresh his memory. He could've just forgotten.'

'It's a pretty wild rumour.'

'But it's all we've got. You better come down. The KGB brass wants to meet you.'

'Why?'

Myeloski shrugged. 'You know that whore, the one at the Savoy Hotel who you thought I sent up to you?'

'Yeah.'

'She's here.'

'One of your camp-followers.'

'Very funny. No, she's with the KGB. One of their officers.'

'So *they* sent her along to my room.'

271

'That's right. They knew what we were up to all the time. You should've given her one. Found out what she wanted.'

'What's she doing here?'

'She's with the big man from Moscow. Vashinov. Boss of the KGB.'

'So now they think it's important. Anything else?'

'I think she's his bit of stuff.'

'Jealous?'

'They don't make police officers like her. All ours are six feet tall and six feet wide. They frighten the life out of me. And they're on my side. Listen, don't mention those rumours. You say the old man's father actually heard them arguing?'

'So he says.'

'Well, it's all we've got.'

When they got downstairs, they found that Vashinov had taken over the top floor for his own use and the disgruntled guests were at the front desk, waiting to be taken to another hotel. There was a guard on the library door, who, on recognizing Myeloski, let him in.

Vashinov was on his own. He was looking out of the window as the two men entered. He turned and, seeing them, came forward with his hands outstretched to welcome Duncan. They shook hands, and Vashinov signalled them to sit at the gilt table.

'I am sure that Comrade Captain Myeloski has told you who I am and why I am here. I want you to know that it is our intention to do everything to resolve this terrible situation to your government's satisfaction. I know that you, and our good comrade here, have achieved remarkable results in a very short space of time. But, now that the whole thing is out in the open, we can pour more resources and more people into the investigation. There will be nowhere they can hide in the Soviet Union. Nowhere.'

'Have you any idea where they are now?'

Vashinov paused. The Englishman was clearly not frightened or impressed by him. 'Not yet. But, then, we have only just joined the investigation. I expect things to change rapidly.'

The door opened at that point, and Vera walked in, dressed in her KGB uniform. Vashinov's expression showed he was annoyed with the interruption, but he said nothing. Vera saw the look of cold dislike on Duncan's face.

'I'm sorry, Comrade General, I did not . . .' She turned to leave the library.

'Come in, Vera.' The general ordered her into the room. 'Let me introduce my assistant, Lieutenant Vera Kasyanova.'

Duncan stood up as she approached the table.

'We've already met.'

He turned away from her and looked directly at Vashinov, who didn't know that Vera had gone to Duncan's room when he sent her to the Savoy Hotel. She had told him that neither of the men was present. She had obviously lied.

'Was there anything else, General?'

'No.'

'Then, if you'll excuse me . . .'

Suddenly there was a great commotion at the door, and Myeloski heard his name being called. He went to the door, the others following. It was the local police chief and he had a note in his hand.

'I must see you immediately, Comrade Captain,' he shouted.

Myeloski, who would rather have seen the man privately, knew that he must share whatever information he had. He signalled him to enter the room, and closed the door behind him.

'I'm sorry to interrupt, Comrade Captain.'

'What is it? You can speak freely here.'

The police chief held up a note. 'This was delivered to

the police station. It was pushed through the door. We didn't see who delivered it.'

'What is it?' asked Vashinov as Myeloski took the note and read it. When he had finished he looked at Duncan, spoke to his partner.

'A ransom note. At last we know who's got them.'

9

MOVING UPSTREAM

Moscow
6 p.m.

Colonel Yashkin asked to see the president at the Kremlin as a matter of urgency.

When the Moscow police chief arrived, he had with him a copy of the ransom note which had been faxed to him by Myeloski. It was from a bandit group, brigands who lived in the forests and steppes of Siberia.

Their demands were simple. For the safe return of the family, they wanted a ransom payment of five million dollars to be paid at the time of transfer, a free and unconditional pardon for the thirty members of the brigand group, arranged transport to take them abroad to a country of their choice, and an amnesty for any other bandit group who might wish to take advantage of any such agreement. There would be a forty-eight-hour deadline on these terms and then the family would be killed. Agreement to the terms was to be broadcast simultaneously on an aircraft radio frequency of 133.77 from Sverdlovsk, Omsk and Perm air-traffic control centres. The brigands would reply by a method to be specified, but their code-sign would be 'Koptiaki'.

The ransom note was signed 'Bakor'.

The president put the sheet of paper down carefully, as if it were an explosive device in his hand that might blow up at any moment.

'At least we know who we're against now.' Yashkin was positive in his statement.

'But who were the dead men in the mine-shaft?'

'No idea. Maybe just thieves who fell out with each other.'

'And Bakor?'

'The only Bakor we have in our files is an ex-captain with the Red Army. He was a veteran of Afghanistan, highly decorated and one of the few leaders who had any success against the *mujahedin*. Unfortunately he was slightly over-zealous in his efforts, which resulted in his being court-martialled.'

'How over-zealous?'

'He and his commandos went into a village which they believed supported the *mujahedin*. There were some atrocities.'

'Go on.'

'The full details were not released to me by the Army. Neither were they revealed at the court martial. But I understand there were tortures . . . involving women and children. There were also some deaths. Once again, women and children.'

The president shook his head; he suddenly didn't want to know any more about the horrors that the army captain had inflicted on innocent villagers, whatever his motives. 'And this is the same Bakor?'

'Possibly. After he and some of his men were found guilty at the court martial, they were brought back here to serve their sentences. They were on their way to Yakutsk.' Yashkin spoke of the maximum-security army prison-camp that lay at the end of the railway line in eastern Siberia. No one had ever escaped alive from the army prison. 'Their two army helicopters, combat assault-craft, landed at Omsk to refuel. While they were there, Bakor and his men escaped. They killed the guards and the pilots. Some of his men, army veterans, knew how to fly the helicopters. They flew north, into the forests, into the taiga. That was over six years ago. Since then, we believe, they have organized themselves as one would expect of any crack professional army unit. They raid the villages in the region and have even attacked military establishments for arms. That may be why they want us to transmit on an air-radio frequency. They will pick up the message on one of their helicopters.'

'Then, let's trace them from the satellites. Surely we can pick them up.'

'Only if they're in the air, Comrade President. And to pick up the radio signals they can stay on the ground. There is no proof that this group is led by Bakor, or even that he's still alive. The signature on the ransom note is all we have at the moment.'

When Yashkin left, the president put in a call to the British prime minister. After he had informed him of the contents of the ransom note, the prime minister had been quiet for a moment.

'Our policy has always been never to give in to terrorist demands.' His voice was matter of fact, it was a situation he had faced many times before.

'That is also ours, Prime Minister.'

'Then, we must do all we can to find them.'

'All our resources are directed so as to come to a satisfactory conclusion.'

'They will be innocent martyrs to your cause, if it is not concluded in such a satisfactory manner.'

'I know that. And no effort is greater than mine in trying to save them, to ensure their safe return.'

277

Vashinov was in his element. He knew that the president had little choice but to release the full force of the KGB on to the investigation.

He had spoken to Marshka after they had received the ransom note. The old man had reacted badly, fearing that the Oldenburgs would be killed. He realized, as did Vashinov, that there was no way the president could agree to the ransom demands. But he wanted the family saved. This was not how it was supposed to finish. At the end of the call, Vashinov had heard the weakness and fear in the old man's voice. It was the first time he had realized that Marshka was vulnerable, that he was running out of time and influence.

It was then he decided to go it alone, to make the move that would make him the hero of the moment. He decided to play along with Marshka and wait for the president to react. But he had already decided on his course of action. To him, Marshka was out of it now. The old man could never reveal his part in the plan; it would simply destroy him.

He called his assistant and made arrangements with him. The KGB had secret funds that they could use at any time for their clandestine operations. The amount needed to pay for the release of the hostages was small; he was surprised that that was all the brigands wanted. They probably believed it was a vast sum. He also put the rest of the plan into motion.

While Vashinov was scheming, Duncan and Myeloski decided there was little they could do until morning. The policeman had already contacted Morrison, who said he knew nothing about Bakor and his group.

'It's killed off our theory about the tsar's family still being alive,' Myeloski had commented to Duncan. He

278

had laughed. 'Amazing what you consider when you're desperate. That would've been a turn-up for the books. Finding the tsar and his lot.'

While Myeloski went for a late, late supper, Duncan retired to his room.

He had not been there long when there was a knock on the door. He opened it and was surprised to see the KGB girl, Vera Kasyanova, there. She was still in her uniform.

'Can I come in?'

'Haven't we been through all this before?'

'Please.' He was surprised by the urgency in her voice. He stepped back, beckoned her in, closing the door behind her.

'I just wanted to explain . . .' she shrugged.

'What? That you weren't really trying to set me up? Just wanted some good clean fun?'

'No. I was doing as I was ordered.' Her candour surprised him.

'Are you still under orders?'

'I just wanted you to know.' She shrugged, a noncommittal reply.

'How long have you been in the KGB?'

'Why?'

'You're very young to be with them.'

'I am twenty-two.' Like all youth, she leapt to defend her age, or lack of it. He realized how young she was, how vulnerable.

'What do you do?' His question was harsh; for all her youth, she was still a KGB agent.

'I . . . General Vashinov's secretary.'

'And your duties include going out and fucking under orders.'

His remark stunned her, and she instinctively swung at him, tried to slap him across the face. But he was too quick. He caught her arm before she could complete the blow, held it rigid. She tried to move, but his hold was complete. Then he let her go. She stepped back from him.

'Go on. Get out of here.' He almost laughed at her.

'It's your loss, soldier,' she said defensively, a posture not lost on Duncan.

She regretted it as soon as she said it. Under her apparent cool, she knew she wanted him. It was a new sensation for her. She was always detached about others, but this one intrigued her. As she stood there, she realized she didn't want to go.

'Comrade Lieutenant Kasyanova. Hello.' She heard her name being called in the corridor. It was one of Vashinov's assistants looking for her.

'Your master's voice.' He walked past her and opened the door. The corridor was empty.

'Go on. Before they find you've screwed up again.'

She realized how cheap she had become, and she turned and hurried from the room. Embarrassment was a new emotion for her; it was not something that was to her liking.

He closed the door and went and lay on his bed. He knew she was a whore, but the girl disturbed him. Her vulnerability appealed to him, softened him. But this was not the time or place for any such distraction. He tried to forget her, undressed and then climbed under the covers, switched off the light.

But her face was still there. When he finally dropped off, it was Vera Kasyanova's face that said the final good-night.

He had only been asleep for a few minutes when Myeloski burst in to wake him up.

The House of Ipatyev
Sverdlovsk
12.30 a.m.

When the KGB driver dropped them outside the house, Vashinov led Vera to the entrance. They carried two stand-up battery torches with them. Vera had changed out of her uniform and now wore a long flowing cape of the sort that was fashionable in Moscow that year.

The two guards at the gate, on recognizing their chief, sprang to attention, their automatics displayed smartly at their side.

'Good night for guard duty, eh, lads?' Vashinov joked with them. 'Warm, dry. Better than being with the wife.'

The men joined in the joke nervously. They were local KGB men and not used to the big brass coming down to their level.

'My secretary and I will be in the house for a while. I'm going to look round, see if my men missed anything. I don't want to be interrupted. By anyone. Is that order clear?'

'Yes, Comrade General.' This was the language they understood.

He nodded and went through the gate with Vera following. One of the guards closed the gate after him.

They entered the house through the room of death.

As Vashinov shut the door, a shiver of excitement ran through him. He shone the torch around the room, the beam slowly highlighting the faded walls, the decay of the years.

'Do you know what this room is?' he asked her quietly.

'No.'

'A room of history. A room of death. The room that is now the shame of our country.' He laughed as he walked over to the corner where the bullet-holes riddled the wall. With the torch in one hand, he ran his fingers gently over the punctured openings where the bullets had struck.

'What a moment that must have been.' He turned and faced her. 'You have no idea what I'm talking about, do you?'

She shook her head.

'This room, my dear little Vera,' he went on, 'is where the tsar and his family were killed. Shot. Brains scattered all over the wall.'

He heard her gasp. It pleased him to know she was affected by this gruesome place. It would add to the enjoyment. He shone the torch back at the wall he had just been next to.

'The very bullet-holes. Still here after all these years. What a place to fuck, eh?'

He laughed, then put his torch in a corner, tooks hers from her and placed it in the opposite one, under the bullet-holes and faded blood. He turned to her, a huge leering grin across his face. He nodded to her, held his finger to his lips as a sign for her to keep quiet.

In the torchlit room, macabre in its grisly past and shadowy in the dim light, she removed her cape. Underneath it, she was naked except for a high-sided leather G-string, fishnet stockings held up by red suspenders and very high-heeled shoes.

The cape dropped to the floor; she felt the cold, and came out in goose bumps immediately. He made her stand there, enjoyed her body as one would enjoy a lovely painting, not touching, just admiring and imagining.

Then he took off his tunic, dropped it to the floor on top of her cape. He unbuttoned his trousers, let them fall to his ankles, then stepped out of them. He was naked, except for his shoes and socks.

He beckoned her over, stood her in front of the bullet-holed wall. Then he thrust himself forward, signalled her to take him in her mouth. She faltered; he sensed her resistance. He was unused to that from her. He grinned, grabbed her by her hair and forced her down, cruel and vicious in his action. She felt the hair being wrenched from her head as he pushed her down to his erection.

But she fought back, refused to be part of his sordid game. He pulled her erect again, pulled her straight up by the hair.

'What the hell's the matter with you?' he demanded, his voice low but angry.

She shook her head, was frightened to answer him. Still holding her head in a cruel vice-like grip, he forced her down again. This time he shook her head violently, pulled more hair out by the roots. The shock of it made her open her mouth in pain, and he forced his erection into her. Then he realized she was sobbing as he moved his body against her mouth. That pleased him; he enjoyed other people's pain. He started to ejaculate in his heat and excitement, but pulled out, didn't want to spoil the moment so soon after they had only just started.

He stood her up again, turned her round and tried to bend her over, to enter her from behind. But she continued to resist, to fight back. He became desperate to enter her, his thick shaft forced through her thick hair and into the dryness of her unwelcome entrance. He felt himself going in; she was held vice-like in his grip.

He managed eight strokes before she twisted away and forced him out of her.

It was time to tame her.

So he kicked her hard between the legs, his shoe burning into her flesh. She screamed as she fell, the pain searing into her. He was over her immediately, his hand over her mouth, forcing her to be silent. He didn't want anyone to hear.

Then, with one hand over her mouth, he beat her with his other hand, punched her face and body until she nearly passed out. Then he kicked her again, repeatedly in the stomach and in the back. He felt cold fury, knew that he would probably kill her, but was beyond the logic of fear. He'd get it covered up; she would become another person never heard of again. It was not the first time Vashinov had killed cold-bloodedly when the ice fury took him.

He didn't know whether he felt the cold muzzle of the gun against his temple first or heard the calm flat voice.

'One more kick and I'll kill you.'

He froze, recognizing the Englishman's foreign accent. He stood up slowly, knew the man wouldn't hesitate to pull the trigger. On the floor, the girl moaned in her pain, unaware that the situation had changed.

'Don't interfere in that which doesn't concern you.' Vashinov turned and faced Duncan. He wished he had his trousers on.

'Let's say I believe in fair play.'

'Another English weakness.' Vashinov was derisory in his tone. 'Just leave. I won't touch her any more.'

Duncan walked away from Vashinov and picked up one of the torches. He came back and held it closer to the girl. Her bruised and cut body shocked him, sickened him. 'Big man, aren't you?' He put the torch on the floor and slipped the Coonan Magnum into his shoulder holster. The warning look he gave Vashinov was enough. The general stepped away from the girl, his hands held up, palms outward, signifying that he would do nothing. He had seen enough fighting men in his life to know the dangerous ones. It was always in their eyes, in their stance. He knew this was one of the best. That had already been proved in the governor's house in Tobolsk.

Duncan leant down and helped the girl to her feet. She leant against him, her body frail and grey in the nakedness of the torch-light. The welts and bruises made her vulnerable, and Duncan instinctively put his arm round her naked shoulders as if to protect her. Vashinov knelt down, reaching across the floor for his trousers. He hated his ridiculous nakedness in front of the Englishman.

'Leave them where they are.'

Vashinov drew his hand back and stood up again. Duncan's voice brought Vera out of her semi-conscious state, and she opened her eyes, looked up and saw Duncan holding her. She shuddered, moaned in her anxiety.

'It's all right. You're OK.' Duncan tried to calm her, thought she was frightened of another beating. But Vera was ashamed and embarrassed. The last thing she wanted was for the Englishman to see her in such a sordid situation. She turned her head away from him, reached towards the cape that lay on the floor.

Seeing her discomfort, he took his arm from around her shoulders and picked up the cape, slipped it over her. She hugged it to her, wrapped her shame and nakedness under it.

'Can you walk?'

She nodded, her eyes averted from him.

'Do you want me to take you back?'

She shook her head, her eyes still downcast.

He turned to the naked Vashinov. 'No more, or you'll answer to me. And leave your people out of it. Your government have got enough problems without having to explain away any more dead KGB men. Or a dead KGB general.' He looked at Vera again, but she kept her eyes averted.

Duncan left the room, went up the stairs into the blackness and into the main house.

Vashinov hurriedly grabbed his clothes and got dressed. When he was fully attired, he picked up a torch and gave it to her. Then he picked up the other one and led her towards the back entrance, out into the courtyard.

'Hold yourself upright,' he ordered her, not wanting the guards to notice her condition. She straightened herself, the pain racking her body. He looked at her, wondered what he ever saw in her. She was a whimpering little slut.

As he led her out of the death room, he thought of what the Englishman had said, the words about dead KGB men. Was it possible they knew about the men in the mine-shaft? Had the Englishman and his fat police friend known all along?

It was time to speed up the game.

Further down the road, Duncan slipped into the Lada which was parked there. Myeloski was in the driving-seat. It was he who had seen Vashinov leave the hotel earlier and had warned Duncan. The policeman had decided to follow the general and his companion; there was no way he was to be left behind in any game the KGB were playing. They were surprised when Vashinov was taken to the House of Ipatyev, even more surprised when the guards in the house were sent out on to the road. That was when Duncan had decided to break into the house. Getting past the guards had caused no difficulties to the SAS man. He slipped over the high wall and into the house through the first floor.

'Well, what were they up to?' Myeloski's eager question tumbled out.

'Not a lot. Just fucking.'

'What? In that house?'

'In that room.'

Myeloski whistled through his teeth in amazement, shook his head, started the engine and drove back to the Hotel Amerika.

<h3 style="text-align:center">Hotel Amerika
Sverdlovsk
9 a.m.</h3>

Vashinov was still angry when Marshka's call came through.

He had been up since 6 a.m., in touch with Moscow as he laid his plans. He dealt only with his most senior officers, only those whom he trusted. He bypassed those he knew would report back to Marshka. Confident that the old man was losing control, Vashinov gave his subordinates the orders that triggered off his plan to oust Marshka. The money he had asked for the previous evening was already on its way from Moscow to Sverdlovsk by KGB courier.

He had seen the Englishman leave the hotel earlier, seen him go off on an early-morning run. He was bitter about the experiences of the night before, but would settle that debt before the soldier returned to Britain. He was only, after all, a hooligan who was trained to kill. Vashinov had dealt with his type many times before.

The girl, Vera, was in her room, the door locked. Like the Englishman, she was a debt to be repaid. There was nowhere she could go.

The policeman, Myeloski, was another matter. Vashinov knew he answered directly to the president. And he had proved that he wasn't the type who gave in easily. He needed to keep the Moscow policeman busy, needed to ensure he was out of the way when the big play was made.

He picked up the phone and spoke to Marshka. Bugger the old man's persistent interference.

'Grigory Mikhailovich,' he beamed into the receiver. 'I have been waiting for your call.'

'You must take control of the investigation.'

'How? The president insists that the police remain in charge.'

'I shall speak to Vasily.'

'As you think best.'

'The policeman is dangerous.' Marshka spoke of Myeloski. 'If he stays there, he will uncover the truth.'

'I spoke to him last night. He said he thought the

kidnappers had fallen out amongst themselves, that some of them had been killed.'

'Do you believe him?'

'No.'

'Has he passed that on to the president?'

'I don't know. The police have their own secured telephone line.'

There was a pause while Marshka considered. Vashinov smiled; the old man was hanging himself.

'No one will agree to paying the ransom.' Vashinov shook his head; Marshka was still stating the obvious. 'We must trace the brigands. We must pay the ransom.'

'As you said last night, Grigory Mikhailovich.' Vashinov stopped, tried not to reveal the sarcasm in his voice to the old man in his wheelchair. 'I have men out there, trying to find all they can on these brigands. If we can get to them first, then we shall arrange the matter as you ordered.' He knew he hadn't placated Marshka; the old man's continued silence suddenly made him uncomfortable.

'Report back as soon as you have news.' The line had clicked off; Marshka was gone. Vashinov slammed the phone down, furious at his own stupidity, his vanity. The old man wasn't a fool; he would have realized that Vashinov was hiding something from him.

The old instincts were in full flight. Grigory Marshka knew he was becoming a target, not for the first time in his life. The best reaction, as always, was to keep moving, change the rules minute by minute.

He called his assistant and immediately asked to be put through to the president.

When he was connected, he spoke quietly. When he had finished, the president suggested that he go to the Kremlin. But he could not meet him for two hours.

'In two hours, then,' Marshka replied. 'I shall be there in two hours.'

Soviet airspace over Tiumen
Siberia
10 a.m.

In Moscow, the watcher in the sky checked the blip on his screen that showed Myeloski's presence in Sverdlovsk. The satellite picture was powered off. There was no need for them to follow the policeman's moves; they knew of his exact whereabouts. He was not expected to leave the city.

In America, a continent and an ocean away, an American watcher saw the signal beamed up from Duncan's credit-card transmitter and filed a report that the target was stationary in the central Urals in Siberia.

Neither watcher saw the small single-engined plane that flew east from Perm, a city to the north of Sverdlovsk. After flying east for one hour, at a height of no more than three hundred feet above ground-level, the plane suddenly climbed to three thousand feet. When the plane levelled out, it flew at that altitude for two minutes before the pilot pressed the transmit button on his radio and broadcast on the 133.77 frequency.

'Koptiaki. Koptiaki. Terms agreed. Arrange further. Koptiaki. Koptiaki.'

Before startled air-traffic controllers could identify the aircraft, no more than a simple blip on the radar, it had dived down to below two hundred feet, below radar coverage, and turned north. Fifteen minutes later it landed safely in a small clearing, where two men rushed out from the trees and helped the pilot pull the plane out of sight.

The search helicopter from the Omsk air-force base found no sign of the hidden aircraft. By the time the watcher in Moscow had been ordered to tune his satellite to help with the search, over half an hour had passed since the aircraft first popped up on the air-traffic

289

controller's screen. He, too, saw nothing except the forests and hills of the Siberian region.

The president was in the Kremlin at a meeting of the heads of the Economic Research and Development Unit when he received a full report. He excused himself and went into the corridor, where his assistant gave him a complete account of the incident.

'Who authorized the message to the kidnappers?' he asked.

'No one, Comrade President.'

'Well, someone has!' he retorted angrily. The assistant was nonplussed; he had simply been the bearer of bad tidings.

'Call Vashinov,' the president continued. 'Find out if he knows anything. And don't interrupt me until Grigory Marshka arrives. With all this going on, it's easy to forget we still have a country to run.'

He returned to the economic forum, but his mind was elsewhere, far to the east in the early-autumn landscape of western Siberia.

Hotel Amerika
Sverdlovsk
11 a.m.

Vera Kasyanova stayed in her room for the morning. She could hide the marks on her body, but not on her face. Her left cheek was swollen, and both her eyes were puffed. She knew if she showed her face people would ask questions, would wonder what had happened to her.

She had returned the night before with Vashinov. She had kept her face hidden when they entered the hotel lobby and gone straight to her room. The general had said nothing, but she knew that it was only a matter of time before he would exact his revenge. There were no corners to hide in, nowhere that his evil influence didn't penetrate. She had lain awake all night, expecting him to come into her bedroom. Eventually, when the dawn light broke through the ill-fitting curtains, only then did she drop off to sleep. Her last thought had been of Duncan, her memory of his face her only comfort.

She was woken an hour later by the bedroom door opening loudly. She heard the sound in her sleep, had struggled to wake up, only to find the door had been slammed loudly before she saw who it was. She knew it was Vashinov. The fear had returned, and she sat up in the small cot, her knees pulled up under her chin, as she waited for him to make his move.

Later, Duncan was her first visitor. He carried a bowl of heavy porridge and a jug of tea. He had knocked on the door, and she had answered apprehensively. He was the last person she expected to see, the first she had wanted to.

'Thought you could do with something to eat.' He put the bowl on the table next to the bed and brandished the jug in the air. 'And something to drink. I presumed nobody else had considered your creature comforts.'

She smiled nervously as he poured a cup of tea for her. He put it on the table and picked up the bowl of porridge, passed it to her.

'You should eat.'

She took the bowl and started to eat with the spoon he had also handed her. She had little appetite and pecked at the food.

He sensed her embarrassment. 'You look terrible.'

She looked up sharply, then saw the humour in his eyes, the warm smile on his lips. She shook her head, laughed.

'How's the pain?' She recognized the genuine concern in his voice.

'Not bad. My stomach's the worst.' As she spoke, he remembered Vashinov kicking her as she lay semi-conscious on the floor.

'What about a doctor?'

She shook her head. 'No, I'm OK.' She knew no bones were broken and she hadn't coughed up any blood. She was bruised and hurting, but it was nothing that time wouldn't cure. She didn't tell him that this had happened before, not just with Vashinov, but also with some of the others with whom she had spent time. The bruises and pain had always been a part of her life.

'What're you thinking?' she asked sharply. 'That I'm not so pretty. How different from when I came to your room.'

'No.'

'Or that I only got what I deserved?'

'Nobody deserves that.'

'Even a whore. A KGB whore.'

'Don't push it.'

'You said it.'

'Only because you came on strong. I don't know who you are, where you're from. All I know is your name, and that you came on strong.'

'You thought I came to you because I was ordered to.'

'Didn't you?'

'No. Yes, the first time in Moscow. Not yesterday; I came because I wanted to.'

He said nothing. It wasn't a situation he was used to.

'Don't you believe that?' she asked eventually.

'I'm suspicious by nature. It goes with the job. Tell you what. Let's forget what's happened. New start. Get to know each other. What do you say?'

She smiled, nodded. It was a warm smile, and he was gladdened by it.

He had stayed with her for a while, but they said little, just sat in comfort and shared companionship. Duncan was surprised by his sense of ease; he had always felt restless in the company of women. He didn't dislike them, or look down on them, but because of the nature of his work and lifestyle he had never allowed himself to get close to them. He had seen the widows and fatherless children who were the victims of nothing more than love, had seen the hopelessness and despair in their eyes when they knew they had lost their men.

As he sat with her, he also realized how similar they were. They were both loners, isolated from normality because of the lives they had chosen for themselves.

When she finished the porridge he took the bowl from her and got up.

'Don't let things get to you.' It wasn't much, but he sensed the comfort she received from his words. He nodded and left her. As she sipped her tea she thought only of him.

Myeloski was waiting for him in the library. The look on his face told Duncan there was trouble.

'What's up?'

'Somebody's used the radio to contact the brigands. Vashinov insists that he's in charge, that it's now a KGB matter.'

'Who sent the message?'

Myeloski shrugged. 'Who knows? All we do now is wait. It's up to them to come back with instructions.'

While Duncan and Myeloski waited at the Hotel Amerika, Vashinov furthered his plan to take charge of the kidnap operation. More uniformed KGB troops were flown in from Moscow. When they landed at Sverdlovsk, they were airlifted by the giant Mil Mi-6 helicopters to a deserted KGB training-base at Irbit, some eighty miles to the north-west of Sverdlovsk. The helicopter, code-named the Hook, was designed to carry seventy combat troops. Four further helicopters, Mil Mi-28s, had also been flown in by the KGB. Known as Havok aircraft, they were to be part of the further assault group, which also included some two hundred troops. Each unit of fifty trained anti-terrorist soldiers was fully combat-equipped. Vashinov had chosen the site because it bordered the forests and plains from where his intelligence sources told him Bakor operated.

The base at Irbit had been abandoned in the mid-eighties by the KGB. A secret training-camp for anti-terrorist troops, there had been speculation that it was a training-ground for government forces specially designed to take on the growing nationalist groups who came to the fore during those early days of *perestroika*. The base had been closed as a symbol of *glasnost* and open government. But the KGB had maintained it on a skeleton staff; they, more than anyone, understood that all things were liable to change. It was not their style to be caught unprepared.

While the troops were being transported in readiness to the camp, Vashinov formally visited the Sverdlovsk police headquarters. The local police commissar was hugely impressed by the powerful KGB general who was also a member of the Politburo. Within ten minutes of Vashinov's arrival, he had agreed to three KGB men being left at the headquarters to monitor any signal that might be received from the kidnappers. He was a large genial man who was only used to dealing with drunks and domestic crimes, not with international kidnappings and the head of the KGB. The situation frightened him, and he was happy to hide under Vashinov's protection. He agreed not to tell Myeloski of their arrangement. He realized the Moscow policeman had no real power compared to Vashinov.

Vashinov then returned to the Hotel Amerika. He called a meeting with Myeloski and Duncan. When they came into the library to meet him, he ignored Duncan, made no mention of the night before. His conversation was with Myeloski alone; the Englishman was there so that he could not be accused of causing a breach in diplomatic relations.

'You've heard that someone has contacted the brigands by aircraft radio?'

'Yes, Comrade General.' Myeloski maintained the official greeting.

'Any ideas who?'

'No.' Myeloski was not about to reveal that he and Duncan thought it was the KGB themselves.

'I have spoken to the local commissar of police.' He saw the alarm in Myeloski's eyes. 'I have ordered him to contact us if he receives any message from the kidnappers. We will all stay here together, so that when something does break we can react immediately.'

There was little Myeloski could do. He knew they were being trapped at the hotel; Vashinov did not want them out of his control. 'As you wish, Comrade General.'

'I have also asked for any information on Bakor, the leader of the brigands. When I have that, I shall pass it on to you.' He didn't disclose that he had already received all the information that the KGB had on the bandit leader. 'Good. I will call you if something comes up.'

Myeloski and Duncan left Vashinov in the library. In the lobby they noticed the armed guards who had been placed at the hotel entrance, the gaggle of journalists now firmly established outside.

'Under house arrest, eh?' said Duncan.

Myeloski shrugged, and they went into the restaurant for tea. Duncan grinned; the determination in Myeloski's eyes told him that the policeman was not prepared to bend to Vashinov's will.

The president's office
The Kremlin
Moscow
11 a.m. (Moscow time)

The two men sat in silence, a samovar of tea in front of

them. The president had never doubted Marshka, not since he had been a small boy of ten. As he watched the old man in the wheelchair, he remembered how fit and strong Marshka had once been, this man who was as close to him as his own father. He never forgot the debt he owed the old man.

Marshka had been with the family on his annual holiday, away from the pressures of Moscow and its politics. He had taken the boy fishing in a small rowing-boat, out on the lake near a small village. The lake ran into a small but sharply inclined weir, constructed of jagged rocks, at the far end. Unaware of the weak current, they had let the boat drift slowly towards the white rushing water. The two of them had been engrossed in their endeavours, relaxed as they waited for the fish to bite.

Marshka had been the first to realize that the sounds of the fast-running waters had grown louder; he turned and saw that they were drifting towards the weir. Still some thirty yards from the incline, he could see that they were safe, that a few pulls on the oars would take them clear of the current and back towards the centre of the lake.

He lifted the oars and started to row gently, so as not to disturb the water too much and frighten any fish that might be lurking nearby.

He turned the boat just as the boy jumped up and shouted with excitement that he had got a catch. In his excitement as he stood up, just as the boat swung round when Marshka pulled hard on one oar, so he lost his balance and crashed over the side and into the water.

It wasn't very deep, only two or three metres, but the current was much stronger under the surface. The boy was a good swimmer, but not powerful enough to combat the current that sucked him under and towards the cascading weir.

Marshka didn't have time to turn the boat and go to

the boy's assistance. As he saw the boy swept along, he realized he had no alternative but to go in after him. He threw his jacket off, kicked his boots to the bottom of the boat and dived after his charge.

The strength of the undersurface current surprised him, but he was a fit man and the current not strong enough to force him under. He set out, with powerful crawl strokes, after the boy.

He reached him just before the weir. The boy, spluttering and short of breath as he fought to keep his head above water, saw Marshka approaching him. The older man shouted, but he couldn't hear his words in the swirling white-topped water. Just before he went over the edge of the weir, he felt Marshka's hands grab at him, felt his arms encircle his body.

They tumbled over the weir, into the rocks and the fifteen-metre drop where the water cascaded into the lower lake. The boy never felt the rocks; Marshka had wrapped himself round the youngster and took all the punishment himself. When they eventually reached the bottom, when Marshka finally let go of the unharmed boy, he had broken three ribs and fractured his left shoulder. As the boy swam to safety, he saw the blood that flowed through the torn shirt from Marshka's back. Only after they had climbed out on to the bank did he realize that the older man was in pain, that the blood came from cuts all over his body.

Some fishermen had rushed over and helped them rescue the boat, which had followed them over the weir. They lost one oar, but the boat showed little sign of damage. After apologizing to the owner, and paying him a substantially greater fee than he had expected, they returned by bus to the boy's house. Marshka had found his coat, but his boots were gone for ever. He sat in the bus, his wet, stockinged feet leaving small puddles on the bus floor.

Tired and exhausted, the boy had been sent to bed.

He couldn't sleep, and got up later to ask his mother for some water and a snack. In the small living-area he found his parents with Marshka and the local doctor. Marshka was naked from the waist up, and the doctor was cleansing the wounds in his body before bandaging him up.

The adults had looked up, startled by the boy's cry of anguish. His mother had rushed towards him, but he avoided her, ran to Marshka.

'I'm sorry, Uncle,' he cried, using the title his parents had conferred on Marshka. 'It was my fault. I'm sorry.'

Marshka had laughed, stretched out his arms and lovingly held the crying boy. He looked at the father, over the boy's shoulder, and they both knew that he would grow into a fine and compassionate young man. It was only when he returned to Moscow three days later and visited his own doctor that the full extent of his wounds was discovered.

The president had never doubted Marshka from that day. The older man had guided him, been his secret mentor. No one knew of their closeness; that had been at Marshka's insistence. He knew that jealousy and association of comrades could often lead to the downfall of the most able of men. Even now, in these days of open government, the two men never felt they could reveal the depth of their true friendship.

But now, after all this time, as they sat in silence, Marshka knew that his young friend now doubted him.

'They had another forum this morning.' The president referred to the many political forums that were publicly held on television. The programmes consisted of five or six officials from various departments and agencies who answered questions from interviewers and a selected phone-in audience. It had started in 1989 when the KGB's top officers had sat at a table and answered viewers' questions. Since then, it had become a staple diet of Russian television and always used when there was a crisis.

'I didn't see it. Who was on?' Marshka's question was indifferent; he wanted to repair the broken link of trust between them.

'Police and Army. No KGB. The topic was kidnapping and the outbreak of outlaws and bandit groups. The new economic black market, they called it. Money for lives.'

Marshka laughed. 'At least they aren't aware of the kidnapping.'

'Yet. Why are we, Uncle, in such a mess?'

'It's not as bad as some make out. As long as we find the family.'

'Alive.'

'Of course.'

'And if they're not alive?'

'These things happen.'

'Uncle?' The president paused, afraid of crossing the line that could break their trust.

'Go on.'

'It doesn't matter.'

'If it's in your mind, and in your heart, then it matters.'

He decided to break his silence. It was what his father and Marshka had always taught him. To go to the heart of the matter. 'There are rumours that the bodies in the mine-shaft were KGB.'

'I didn't know you were governed by rumours.'

'I'm not, Uncle. But I have a good understanding of their importance. So who were they . . . the men in the mine-shaft?'

'KGB.'

The president sighed; his worst fears were being confirmed. 'Is Vashinov involved?'

'Yes. But, if you were to ask him, he would tell you that his men were directly under his orders, working secretly on the case, close to rescuing the family, when they were ambushed and killed by the brigands.'

'But he would be lying?'

'He would.'

'Am I to be the last to know what's happening?'

The old man considered. He reached in his pocket, opened a packet of cigarettes and took one out, lit it.

'That's bad for you. I thought you'd stopped.' The president remembered the death of his own father from lung cancer.

'You're getting too westernized. From what I read, they're giving up everything, trying to live for ever. In life, little reindeer, only death is guaranteed.'

'And taxes.'

'In my case, for all my faults and bad habits, it'll be old age that kills me. Taxes are for capitalists.' He chuckled, hugely enjoying his own joke.

The president waited courteously for Marshka to finish before continuing. 'Am I to be told?'

'Once you know, you may have to act on it. That may not be a good thing.'

'Do you not trust my judgement?'

The old man puffed on his cigarette. He knew that the president would act in the best manner for Russia. But he also knew that it could be the end for him. How would he react when his loyalty to his 'uncle' was put to the test? He remembered the look in the president's father's eyes, all those years ago in Leningrad, when he had cut the German soldier's throat. He recalled the photograph enshrined on the family mantelpiece. He was about to find out if the president was his father's son.

'The plan, for the return of the monarchy, was always doomed to failure.'

The president shook his head. 'It was the right thing to do. We need a symbol, something to unify us. Communism, the gun, the threat . . . the gulags. They weren't symbols of unity.'

'Agreed. But your plan was a disaster.'

'It's what you always wanted. Father told me that. Many times.'

'Is that why you came up with the idea? Because that's what your father wanted? I never knew.'

'It was the only way. To restore the monarchy, but one that was constitutional and headed a democratic socialist Soviet Union.'

Marshka pondered for a moment. 'I never knew. You should have told me.'

'Did you tell *me* everything?'

'Not always.'

'Why was it doomed to failure?'

'Because there is too much change in this country. Too much turmoil. You could not have gone on television and simply announced that it was the Government's intention to reinstate the tsar. Even with a referendum.'

'The state visit. People would have met them, seen them. In real life and on the television. They would have realized they were ordinary people, not the monsters the Romanovs became, not gods. By seeing them it would have made our task easier. In that way, slowly, step by step, we could have reintroduced the monarchy. We would have gauged their reaction, seen the effect before deciding on a referendum.'

'No. Too simple. Our people like drama; they are an emotional people. That's what the revolution was about – about emotion. The French had it, two hundred years ago; and look what a disparate nation they have become because they remained a republic. To win the Soviet people over, to get them on your side, you must appeal to their emotion, to their sense of history and drama. This is the country of Dostoevsky, of Tolstoy, of Solzhenitsyn. Television announcements telling them that they are to have their tsar back is not the way, little reindeer.'

The president saw the awful truth. He saw what the

old man had done before he even spoke the words that confirmed it. 'So you decided to give it a little push.'

The old man smiled, pleased that the younger man had picked it up so quickly, the pride of a teacher with a star pupil.

'There was no choice. The kidnap was arranged—'

'With Vashinov's assistance?'

Marshka ignored the question. 'Clues were laid so that the family could be found. The policeman from Moscow and the Englishman moved faster than we expected.'

'Whose idea was it to copy Tsar Nicholas's abdication route?'

'I don't remember.' It had been Marshka's, one of which he was proud. But he had never been one to take credit or boast of his ideas. 'It gave your plan a chance. Once it was public knowledge that the family had been kidnapped, once that was out, the Russian people, all of the Soviet people, would have wanted their safety, would have been involved with them. Don't you see how much easier that would have made it for you?'

'A dangerous game, Uncle.'

'I have never played any other. How do you think I survived for so long?'

'And if our people hadn't picked up the clues?'

'We would have laid more. Until a child could have followed the trail. It was planned so that it would appear that bandits had kidnapped the family.'

'And now they have done. Or is there more to the plan?'

Marshka lifted his head sharply, jolted by the president's words into the reality of the situation.

'Has Vashinov taken the plan farther? Without telling you?' The president had never trusted the KGB chief, had learnt to live with his possible treachery.

'We must find them.'

'And if we don't?'

'We will. Anyway, then we can tell the people.'

'You always taught me that the people knew best in the end. You should have left it to them, Uncle.'

The words stung Marshka. He ignored the comment and continued. 'We must find who transmitted the ransom acceptance to the brigands. I think it was Vashinov.' His honesty startled the president. The cards were now face-up on the table.

'Why?'

'Just an old man's instinct.' Marshka's instinct had served him well over the long years. 'I know he lied to me. And, if you can, you must be prepared to pay the ransom. The last thing we want is for them to be killed.'

'We have never given in to terrorist demands.'

'Of course we have. Every country has. The secret is in not being found out. We must use what has already been set in motion. When the brigands come back with their arrangements, we have to be the ones who meet them.'

'You should have left well alone. The people would have made the right decision.'

'No, little reindeer. There is more. You don't live as long as I do, remain at the top for the time I have, without sometimes learning the awful truth of history.'

Then Marshka told a stunned president the truth of the Beria Archives. When he had finished, he left the office and returned to his dacha. He was sad. The last person he had wanted to pass the awful secrets on to had been his little reindeer.

10

FRESH BAIT

The Frozen Forest
Ural region
Western Siberia
3 p.m.

Bakor was by nature an opportunist.

It was this trait that had made him a successful Soviet commander in the Afghanistan campaign – that and his complete disregard for the value of life. His forays against the *mujahedin* and Afghan mountain tribes were renowned for their chilling ferocity and business-like efficiency. His superiors had been dismayed when he was finally cashiered from the Army; they realized they had a need for more of his kind if they were to have any chance of success in Afghanistan.

Siberia is to the Soviet people what Texas is to Americans. Everything is bigger and stronger and greater than anywhere else in the Soviet Union. Bakor was a Siberian, and when he escaped from his army captors he led his men into terrain he knew better than most, one he was equipped to survive in.

To the east of the Ural Mountains, which are over

three thousand miles long, but only fifteen hundred metres high at the tallest point, is the taiga. These are the vast frozen forests and tundra which run south into the Urmany, the biggest bog in the world. The west Siberian gas and oil fields are found here; it is the heart of the Russian economy. Small encampments are scattered through the region, temporary homes for the workers who come here and earn three to four times the salary of fellow-workers in other regions. It is an inhospitable place, where roads cannot be laid and whole drilling-rigs eventually disappear into the bog below.

It was here, in this vast region of wealth and solitude, that Bakor made his base, the centre from which his brigands operated. Once they had made good their escape by helicopter from their army guards, they soon found that there was a wealth of booty to be plundered from the region. They had started by stealing a small hovercraft from a drilling camp, some food and clothing, and some hunting-rifles; during the raid they killed two workers who opposed them. In the following six years they had become feared amongst the drilling communities. The oil and gas managements, realizing it was futile to retaliate, urged the drillers to give the brigands whatever they demanded during further raids. The pickings had been rich; food and clothing and fuel for their helicopters and land transport were plentiful. There had even been times when Bakor's men had been entertained at the official brothels that were there for the drillers' needs. In time the *chop-chop* of the approaching brigands' helicopters, army Hind-A armed assault-craft, were accepted as part of the regular routine of a Siberian drilling camp.

As Bakor grew stronger and realized his regional power, he sent his troops into the smaller military outposts of the area. These raids, few and sporadic in their timing, resulted in the capture of modern sophisticated weapons and ammunition, often with loss of life to the soldiers who guarded the stockades.

Army and police tried to combat the brigands, but the vast and inhospitable forests and tundra made detection impossible. It was a natural and impenetrable hideout, made more difficult by the nomadic lifestyle of the bandit group. The authorities played down all publicity regarding the brigands; it was as if they didn't exist. But it was a hazard that had no solutions, no end to its violent ways and unlawful activities.

Bakor had not realized who his victims were when he kidnapped them. But, being an opportunist, he realized that they were the centre of attention and effort at the mine-shaft in the Koptiaki Forest. His men had stumbled on that incident; he had decided to kidnap the family for nothing more than a small profit.

He was surprised to find they were foreigners, British. Neither he nor his men spoke English, so communication had been limited to a series of hand-signs. While Bakor considered the matter further, his men had made the young family comfortable, giving them a tent of their own and as much food and clothing as they needed to keep themselves warm and content.

Not usually interested in news of the outside world, he nevertheless tuned in one of the shortwave radios to the Russian World Information Service. He was surprised that nothing was said about their victims; it was if they didn't exist.

Bakor's instincts, those of a fox long used to the chase, told him they were important, that their price would be high. The increase in police and officials, including the unannounced arrival of the KGB general in Sverdlovsk, was a sign that the authorities were increasing the pressure. Like all good military tacticians, Bakor understood the power of information. His sources in Sverdlovsk were excellent. He also appreciated that this affair could result in battalions of military and KGB searchers being sent in to scour the forests. But, the more he thought about it, the more he concluded that the authorities would want the family alive, at any cost. Troops and fighting would almost definitely result in their deaths; negotiation was the only way out.

He had then drafted the ransom terms. Money was their only aim. Life was good, and their position secure in the deep hiding-places of the forest. It was the only home they had, the only belonging they now understood. Money, especially foreign currency, would insulate them until such time as it was safe to move back into the normal world.

After they delivered the ransom note, they tuned in one of the helicopter radios to the required frequency and kept a listening watch. There had been some discussion about whether or not their demands would be met; after all, the Soviet government had always stated that it would never give in to terrorist demands of any kind. But, apart from a general anxiety about the scale of their demands, the brigands were in good humour and light spirits. It was a new game with new rules, a welcome break from their usual banditry and havoc that occupied them in the lonely Siberian self-exile.

After they had received the reply code-named 'Koptiaki', Bakor set about planning the transfer of the family in exchange for his five million pieces of silver.

He grinned as he looked out of his tent, at a brigand scurrying with some hot water towards the hostages' tent.

'Cut open a Russian and you find a capitalist.' He remembered the old saying, realized its truth.

Who were the hostages? What made them so important that a KGB general, a member of the Politburo, should come all the way out here to mastermind their release? His sources in Sverdlovsk had passed that piece of tattle on.

Bakor shrugged. It didn't matter. The money was all that mattered. That, and their own safety.

He went back to his task. It was time to plan the transfer.

Hotel Amerika
Sverdlovsk
4 p.m.

Vashinov stayed in the library all afternoon, waiting for his officers to report back to him. By 4 p.m. he was informed his men were all in place and ready to move as quickly as circumstances demanded.

The local KGB chief had supplied him with a secretary, she of big breasts, ruddy complexion and inviting hips. He had sat her opposite him, played the role of an important personage to impress her. It wasn't necessary; the local officer had told her that she would be expected to satisfy all his needs, but Vashinov didn't know that. The more he saw her fall under his charm, the more he believed in his own power and undoubted sex appeal. She, in turn, found him overbearing and pompous, but she was a country girl, used to the flattery of the male species.

When he finally suggested they go upstairs to his rooms to continue working in privacy, she sighed with relief. He took this as a sign of passion, a flag that reflected her desperate desire for him. She was actually relieved that things were coming to a conclusion, after which she could return to her apartment in time to change and go on to her amateur theatrical rehearsals. It was an American comedy called *How to Succeed in Business without Really Trying*, and she had a small part in it.

On their way upstairs, he left her for a short while and entered the room where Vera Kasyanova was. The young girl had got dressed and was lying on the bed when he came in without knocking. She had sprung up, surprised by his sudden and unannounced entrance.

She said nothing but watched him with a curious mixture of fear and hatred. He came towards her, put his hand out and held her chin upwards and examined her face. There was a cut under her left eye, surrounded by bruising, and another larger orchid-shaped bruise on her right cheek. He smiled, wanted her to know that her pain didn't worry him, that there was more to come. Then he turned sharply and walked out of the room, to his buxom amusement who waited impatiently in the corridor.

Myeloski watched them from the end of the corridor. He saw Vashinov put his arm round the girl's waist and lead her towards the staircase that climbed to his rooms.

He had been busy himself and had spoken to Yashkin who was due to fly out, on the president's orders, to help Myeloski lead the investigation.

The policeman had already contacted the Sverdlovsk commissar and soon realized that Vashinov had bought his loyalty. It had taken a threat by telephone from Yashkin and a personal call from the president's senior assistant to ensure that any information regarding the brigands must be immediately passed to Myeloski as well as to the KGB.

The policeman, on seeing Vashinov disappear up the stairs with the girl, went down to the restaurant. It was his fourth meal of the day. Impending crisis always stoked up his hunger and added to his ever-expanding waistline. He missed the Englishman's company, but Duncan had retired to his room, determined to catch up with his sleep and remain fresh for any further developments.

Duncan had been asleep for half an hour when the door opened and Vera came in. He came instantly awake, his eyes following her as she closed the door behind her and came over to the bed. She carried a cup of tea and put it on the table beside him, sat down next to him.

'My turn to be the waiter. Thirsty?'

He nodded and levered himself up into a sitting position, the pillows fluffed up behind him. He took the cup and sipped the tea, watching her over the rim.

'I wanted to tell you . . . about me.' She returned his look, direct and honest, as she knew she could be with him.

'Nothing to tell.'

'It's important.'

'Not to me.'

'To me.'

He said nothing; she knew he accepted her, didn't sit in judgement on her.

'I don't regret anything I've ever done. Maybe I will, one day, but you can't live always crying about the past.'

She stopped, knew that she was explaining her life to herself as much as to him. Maybe it didn't matter; maybe he was right.

'Why isn't it important?' she asked him.

'Just isn't.'

'Your eyes tell me you care.'

'The windows of a man's soul.' He smiled at her, sharing the small joke.

She thought of her life, wanted to tell him about the Moscow orphanage where she had grown up, about the caretaker who had made life easier for her because she shared his bed when she was only eleven, of her realization that sex opened doors that gave her an easier life than she could ever have expected from any other means. She thought of all those men, faceless now as then, who had enjoyed her body but never touched her soul. How could she explain that to him, tell him that she had never loved, never wanted, never felt the pain of yearning she felt in her stomach now? How could she feel like this about a man she didn't know, had only met a few times, who had seen her being beaten and disgraced by another? His kindness, his concern for her was a new experience.

Vera Kasyanova was falling in love.

'Are you married?' she heard herself ask and immediately cursed her own stupidity; it was a silly and unnecessary question.

He shook his head. 'No.'

'Why not?'

'Never wanted to.'

They sat in silence, content in each other's company. Duncan was surprised at himself. He enjoyed the peace, the calm he felt when close to her. There had been women in his life, but none who had ever captivated him as she did, none who was more than good company and good sex.

He reached forward and stroked the bruise on her right cheek. 'Seems to be getting better.' She reacted sharply, his touch like an electric shock across her face. He thought he had hurt her. 'I'm sorry.'

She took his hand, held his fingers as she pulled his hand to her face, held it against the bruised cheek.

Then they made love.

It was gentle, a loving that neither had known before. He came four times and never lost his hardness. It surprised her; she had only known that once before in all her years, in a Moscow hotel room with a forgotten Vietnamese diplomat. Duncan was also surprised, it was the first and only time it was ever to happen to him.

Afterwards, when they had finished, they lay together, wrapped in each other's body and silently content in their togetherness.

One day she would tell him about her past. If he ever wanted to know. But she realized he was right. It really wasn't that important.

The instructions for the transfer of the hostages came through just before the buxom KGB secretary arrived late for her rehearsals.

They were delivered, in a handwritten note, to a post office near the Club Panther. The building was closed for the night, but the note, sealed in an envelope, was posted through the door by one of Bakor's men who had been dropped at the edge of the city by truck and who then caught a bus into the centre. The envelope had been a problem; it was not the sort of equipment normally carried by the brigands. One of the men had made it out of folding another sheet of paper before gluing the corners down to seal the note.

After it had been posted through the door, he returned to the city outskirts on a stolen motorcycle and met his companions so that they could return to the brigand rendezvous-point some four hours away.

Before returning to his comrades, the messenger had called into a small drinking club and rung the police headquarters on the wall pay-phone. He told them to pass a message on to the police commissar that there was a letter of some urgency waiting for him at the post office near the industrial centre. He told the policeman on duty that the message must be passed on immediately as a matter of life and death and that the commissar must be told that the caller was code-named 'Koptiaki'.

Fifteen minutes later, before the messenger had left the city limits, four uniformed policemen arrived at the post office. The postmaster was on his way, having been hurriedly rung and told to present himself at his place of work. But the police squad were under specific orders and did not have time to wait for the postmaster. Their senior officer, using his gun-butt, smashed the

312

glass-paned door down and broke into the letter-tray that lay behind it. There were some twenty letters there, and he took them all. He returned to the central police headquarters and left behind one hapless officer to explain to the postmaster why they had had no alternative but to break down the door.

The police commissar had rung Vashinov immediately he had received the message code-named 'Koptiaki'. He also decided not to contact Myeloski directly, but to ask Vashinov to pass the message on to the Moscow policeman. In this way he felt that he had carried out his duty in a diplomatic fashion and would thus avoid being involved in any conflict there might be between the KGB and the Moscow police.

Vashinov got to the police station ten minutes after the letters were delivered. The commissar decided not to open them, but to wait until the KGB general arrived.

When he did, he took the letters into a small private room on his own and looked through them. The home-made envelope caught his eye first, and he carefully tore it open. He sat back and read the contents. It was a clever plan, but one which his men would handle with the efficiency he expected of them.

He pocketed the note, thanked the commissar for his excellent work and said he wouldn't be needing the police any longer, and returned to the Hotel Amerika.

When he arrived there he called his two senior officers together and made the final arrangements for the next day.

Marshka's dacha
Outside Moscow
8 p.m. (Moscow time)

Vashinov rang Marshka with the information on the transfer two hours after he had received the envelope.

313

When he had finished his report, and omitted nothing, Marshka asked him when the note had been delivered. He made no further comment when Vashinov said it was some two hours earlier. The general, realizing his mistake, then apologized to the old man and said that he had spent the time arranging for the delivery of the ransom money and also organizing his troops for the transfer.

Marshka said nothing, told Vashinov to contact the president and hung up.

Hotel Amerika
Sverdlovsk
12 p.m.

Vashinov knew he had lost Marshka's confidence; maybe he had never had it. But this was the general's chance, his opportunity to rid himself of the old man's collar and finally build his own power-base. Even though he agreed with the president about the return of a constitutional monarchy, there were many other aspects of his regime that he saw as destructive policies.

As a member of the Politburo, Vashinov was expected to show a united front to all outsiders. But as the head of the KGB his instincts and duties were to be secretive, to protect the past and still be the guardian of the Soviet Union against all enemies, both from within and without its borders. The trouble was that these days it was difficult to define who exactly her enemies were.

Glasnost, the politics of open discussion, was particularly difficult for the KGB. Vashinov remembered the shame and ridicule the department had felt when the most senior officers of the service had been interviewed on a television forum. They had said there were no secret files on Soviet citizens, no terror-camps and no 'James Bond' agents. It was all lies, but it was the only

314

way they could show that the KGB was no secret organization.

Vashinov had been well schooled in the language of the KGB. He understood, more than most, that the breakdown of law and order would eventually lead to anarchy and the cessation of Soviet society. The last thing anyone wanted was another revolution. The president was going too far, was allowing the train to run away without anyone in control on the footplate.

It was time to put the brakes on, time to slow down *perestroika* and allow the Soviet Union space in which to find her own freedom. The grandson of a peasant, Vashinov understood that the Soviet Union was peopled by the descendants of peasants who wanted and needed to be told what to do. His training didn't allow him to know better. He couldn't see that the people were changing, that the Soviet Union was moving into the modern world. He had come to hate the free elections, the loss of respect for the Communist Party, and the confusion that came with what passed as freedom.

To Vashinov there was no difference between martial law and a well-ordered disciplined society. To him, freedom had become the freedom to starve, the freedom to lose what their forefathers had fought and died for. Freedom was cheap, only a word that now devalued what the greatness of the Soviet Union and her past had once come to represent.

But then, unlike the president and Marshka, the general was not a man of vision.

He called one of his officers and sent for Myeloski and Duncan. The policeman was down in the bar, halfway through a large sandwich – Amerikan Sandwich as the house speciality was known – and said that he would find Duncan and bring him up.

While he waited, Vashinov was connected through to the Kremlin and spoke to the president. He informed him of the latest development and said that he would

315

now wait for instructions. He added that in his view some effort should now be made to meet the kidnappers' demands. He went on to say that it could be kept covert and that funds could be instantly drawn from one of the KGB's secret operational accounts in Switzerland or Bermuda. The brigands were unlikely to tell the press, or anyone else for that matter, that they had been paid. If any were to go abroad, then the KGB would hunt them down and silence them. He sensed the chill that passed through the president as he said that. His conclusion was equally chilling. After the transfer and safe passage of the hostages, he would unleash troops that were already in the area and kill the brigands. Even if most of them escaped, it would appear that the KGB had saved the family and no one had given in to terrorists' demands.

'The hostages would know,' said the president.

'Only what the brigands told them. We would simply deny it. We have little alternative, Comrade President. If we don't respond, they will kill the hostages anyway.'

'These outlaws have managed to evade our troops for many years. Why do you think we could capture them now?'

'Because we've had other problems and no major campaign has been launched against them. If it was to be our priority, with all our resources concentrated on that matter, then they wouldn't stand a chance.'

'I hear your words. I will take further advice. Until then, do nothing.'

'As you wish. But I need to get some helicopters into the air. If the brigands send out a broadcast message, we need to know.'

'You have permission for that.'

The president rang off. Vashinov was pleased. What he didn't tell the president was that each helicopter would be already carrying teams of his best, most highly trained combat troops.

Myeloski found Duncan alone in his room.

Vera had left him reluctantly, her body still in pain and needing rest. He had sent down for some food, and the couple had eaten together, relaxed in each other's company. During their meal, Vera had told Duncan about her relationship with Vashinov, how he had taken her under his wing and, in his strange fashion, looked after and protected her. Until she had seen Duncan at the Savoy Hotel, until she had felt those first pangs of yearning, there had been no reason to break the relationship.

When Duncan asked her what Vashinov was doing in Sverdlovsk, what was the true reason for his visit, she said she knew little. All he had told her was that he was there to resolve the kidnapping and, in his words, 'bring the whole damn mess under control, the way it should have been a long time ago'. She went on to say that he was ever critical, and sometimes dismissive of the president and his 'weak and cowardly ways'.

After she left, he thought about Vashinov. As a member of the Politburo he was a powerful figure, as the head of the KGB even more so. Duncan's instinct told him that danger was near, that if he wasn't watchful on all fronts, then his efforts would be doomed to failure.

He was pleased when Myeloski told him where they were going. At least he would be able to see Vashinov's eyes, see the man, determine the enemy.

Vashinov kept them waiting while he finished his call to the president. When they finally entered the sitting-room, hastily prepared by the hotel staff, Vashinov was in the armchair by the window. He signalled the two of them to sit, which they did, close together on the small sofa facing Vashinov.

'We have received the exchange details from the brigands.' Vashinov held up the note.

'May I see it, Comrade General?' Myeloski asked.

'No need. I'll tell you the details.' Vashinov asserted

317

his authority. He had only called them up so that when they reported to their various superiors, the general could not be accused of withholding information. 'The exchange is to be made tomorrow. No time or location has yet been indicated, except that it will take place in the morning, between nine and eleven. The location will be in the area north of the Trans-Siberian Railway, bordered by Sverdlovsk, Serov, Tiumen and Ural.' Serov and Ural were small towns to the north.

'That's an enormous area,' blurted out Myeloski.

'Sixty thousand square kilometres. Three hundred by two hundred.'

'All forests and tundra.' Myeloski said that to Duncan. He turned back to Vashinov. 'There has to be more.'

'Of course.' Vashinov was bored, his game growing tiresome. 'We are to wait for a ground-to-air signal on the frequency they used before. One three three decimal seven seven. We are to have one helicopter in the air at that time, flying in a random pattern within that area. As soon as they are satisfied that there is no back-up, they will give the pilot instructions as to where to land. He will then leave the money, in a secure bag, in that specified location. He will then take off and fly in the direction they tell him to. Once clear, and once they are satisfied that they have the money, they will give him instructions as to where the family is. They will already have the royals in a safe place, protected from the elements, with plenty of food and clothing. Our pilot will then fly there, pick them up and bring them to safety.'

'Shit, that's impossible.' Myeloski's frustration exploded. He didn't care if Vashinov was a member of the Politburo.

'That is the only way they—'

Duncan cut across him. 'There's no guarantee that the family will be freed.'

'I know that. But our communication with the bandits is only one-way.'

318

'No, it's not. We can contact them on that frequency. Tell them it's not on, that the swap has to take place at the same time. Money for hostages.'

'Too risky. The decision has already been made.'

'Then, we must go in the helicopter.' Myeloski came back into the conversation.

'Not possible.'

'It's my investigation, Comrade General.'

'Not any more. As of now it's a KGB operation. No more investigations. Just results.' Vashinov stood up, the appointment concluded.

The two men left the room; there had been little point in arguing any further. They kept their silence in the corridor, not wanting the guards to hear them. They returned to Duncan's room, where they sat in further silence, each man alone in his own thoughts.

'I must ring Moscow.' Myeloski broke the silence.

'They can't help. He's right. He's got the equipment and the resources. We've got nothing.'

'It's too fucking risky.'

'Too late to change the plan now.'

Myeloski rounded on the Englishman, angry with his compliance. 'So you'll leave it to them, when we've come this far.'

'Didn't say that. All I said was that ringing Moscow is not going to help.'

'And . . . ?'

'We need to be in the air. At the same time as the helicopter.'

Myeloski laughed. 'Vashinov is not going to give us a helicopter. Or are you going to steal one again?'

'It worked last time. Anyway, you've got your authority from Moscow. Just use it again, if we have to.'

'And when we're up there, then what?'

'I don't know. But at least we'll be up there, at least we could be in a position to do something. We'll be listening out on the same frequency. We'll know what's happening at the same time as them. Any better ideas?'

The policeman shook his head. 'You're crazier than I am.'

There was a soft knock on the door, but before Duncan could answer it Vera had opened it and come in. She stopped, surprised to see Myeloski there.

He stood up, equally surprised. Then he saw the look that passed between Duncan and the girl, saw their closeness. 'I'll go, then.'

'We'll leave at five. Airport by six.' Duncan looked at his watch.

'I'll be ready.' Myeloski smiled at Vera, bemused by the situation, and left the room.

'Sorry.' She came towards him, apologized for her indiscretion.

'Don't be. You all right?'

She smiled; he put his arms round her.

'What're you doing at the airport?'

'Plane-spotting. Didn't I tell you I was a spy, after all your military secrets?'

She stepped back, stung by his joke. 'You still don't trust me, do you?'

'It's best you don't know what's happening. Then nobody can force it out of you. Can they?'

She shook her head, remembered how he had found her and came into his arms again.

When they finally went to sleep, Vera Kasyanova slept as deeply as she ever had, slept in the crook of his arm as he lay watching the street-lights flickering on the ceiling, as he wondered about the coming day and his final opportunity to rescue Victor and the rest of the family.

Vashinov, tired but sexually aroused, went looking for Vera Kasyanova. When he found she wasn't in her room, he stormed the corridors, demanding to know where she was. One of the guards finally informed him that he had seen her slip into the Englishman's room.

He contained himself, knew it would be a mistake to burst in on them, to show his weakness at a time when he was to make his move for supreme power. He sent his car to fetch the luckless secretary who had long since returned home from her rehearsals. When she arrived, she entered the room to find him already in bed with a young man whose uniform lay crumpled on the bedroom floor.

She smiled; suddenly there was an excitement in the air. She had never made love to two men before. As she climbed into bed between them, she thought of the rehearsals and how well they had gone, of the men who had watched her from the auditorium and admired her, wanted her. So, too, was it here, in this bed; she would also have an audience, would give of her best in her performance.

Tonight was indeed going to be a night to remember.

Sverdlovsk Airport
6.30 a.m.

Dawn came with the fog; the twin runways were closed owing to the poor visibility. Passengers milled around the small terminal, all waiting for the weather to improve so that they could continue their various journeys.

Myeloski left the Lada at the far end of the muddied carpark, hidden between two large lorries. He didn't want the KGB to know they were there; it was always possible that they had his registration number and would report any movements to Vashinov.

Myeloski had knocked quietly on Duncan's door earlier that morning, as they had arranged. The girl was gone, and Duncan was already dressed, waiting to go. The policeman made no comment about Vera; he could discuss that later on. He was more concerned about how they would leave the hotel; walking out of the lobby and

321

into the street would alert the KGB immediately.

But Duncan had already made his plans. The first rule of the SAS when you walked into a building was find an alternative way out. Escape routes saved lives. He led Myeloski down the corridor and to the small storage-room at the end. When they had closed the door, Duncan moved to the window and, taking out his knife, prised the window open. It had not been opened for years, the frame had been painted over many times. He heard Myeloski stumble and curse in the darkness behind him and waited for him to compose himself.

When he had loosened the window-frame, he put his knife away and carefully slid the sash window up. He was pleased to see that the sash cord held, that he did not need to prop the window up. When it was fully open, he softly called Myeloski to him. The policeman came to the window, looked down at the darkened unlit alleyway at the side of the hotel, out into the swirling fog. He listened; there were no sounds from the alley below.

'How do we get down there?' Myeloski's question was anxious; it was over thirty-five feet to the hard slabbed surface below.

Duncan pointed to a small ledge which ran under the window and towards the back of the hotel. It was about twelve inches wide.

'You're joking!'

But Duncan was gone into the darkness, through the window and out on to the ledge. He waited for Myeloski and held his hand out to help the portly policeman through the window. Myeloski knew he had little choice; he plucked up his courage and squeezed himself, with Duncan's assistance, through the tight opening.

Eventually, after what seemed forever, he stood on the ledge, his rounded paunch pressed into the outside wall, his back hanging over the ledge some thirty-five feet above the alley. The Englishman moved away cat-like into the darkness.

The policeman followed, edging along slowly. He left the safety of the window, knew he would crash to the ground below.

Then Duncan vanished. Myeloski realized he was on his own, started to panic. Where had the bloody Englishman gone?

Then his hand touched an iron frame, rusty and gnarled in its age. He felt further and realized it was a side to a ladder. He pulled himself along, hugged the ladder for safety.

'Where've you been?' Duncan's mocking voice floated up from below.

Myeloski looked down and saw the Englishman grinning up at him. It was a fire-escape, and Duncan had known it was there all along, had not told Myeloski of it, had made him believe that he would have to traverse the whole side of the building on the ledge.

'English bastard!' he cursed softly. The British had a strange sense of humour.

Duncan tugged at his leg, a signal to follow him down the ladder.

When he reached the last rung, Duncan had already checked the street and come back to Myeloski.

'OK. There's no one about. I hope you brought the keys.'

'Bastard!' Myeloski cursed again. Duncan grinned back, then motioned the policeman to follow him to the car.

The drive to the airport was uneventful, but tortuously slow in the fog.

While the two hunters drove to the airport, the KGB units at Irbit readied themselves.

The four Havok helicopters were fully fuelled and armed. They carried heavy-calibre guns in the undernose turret and sixteen anti-tank guided missiles. In addition to rocket-packs slung under the short stubby wings, the Havok could also carry up to twenty combat troops.

At 5 a.m., four hours before the appointed time, the helicopters took off and flew at tree-top level to predetermined locations within the specified area. Once there, they put down and waited. Those in the forest locations simply kept the trees as their natural cover, the two aircraft in the tundra pulled camouflage-nets over them and stayed hidden from any potential observers in the sky. In this pattern, no part of the large exchange-area was more than fifteen minutes away from the 200-mile-per-hour aircraft.

The large Hook helicopter waited at the Irbit base. It was to be the designated aircraft with the ransom money and the one which would pick up the royal family. It was also to carry fifty further combat troops, not part of the agreement with Bakor.

Vashinov had tired of his sexual game with the young soldier and the plump secretary. The soldier had been overawed by his superior and had made love in a fashion akin to painting by numbers. Obviously inexperienced, he had done precisely as he was bidden. The secretary had certainly improved on her afternoon performance and seemed more lively, but without Vera it wasn't the same. He had tossed them out of his bed at three in the morning, then tried to sleep, but to no avail.

Vera stayed in his mind; the recollection of her body helped keep him awake. After fitfully snoozing for the next two hours, he had decided to go and see her. The thoughts that crossed his mind of her liaison with the Englishman caused him to be jealous; it was not an emotion with which he was comfortable.

Some fifteen minutes after Myeloski and Duncan left, Vashinov knocked on Vera's door. He heard her call out and he entered the room. She had obviously been asleep. She tried to wake up fast when she saw who it was, and sat up and pulled the bedclothes round her naked body. The general was relieved to see the

Englishman wasn't there. He had half-expected him to be.

'You better now?' His manner was gruff, and she sensed he felt ill at ease. But she had known him a long time, knew what had really driven him there.

She nodded, pulled the blanket closer to her.

He laughed. 'Shy, eh? Not like you.' He came over and roughly pulled the blanket from her, exposing her nakedness. It was the only way he knew to behave. He looked at her, didn't see the bruises, only the alluring form and shadows of her body.

Then he took off his robe and climbed on to the bed with her. She lay there, silent but enduring as he filled her with his lust and heat. Finally, when he had finished, he lay still on top of her. She had not moved, not taken part in his moment. He sensed the disgust, saw her lying there, the tears soft in her eyes. He rolled over, grabbed his robe and put it on. He felt embarrassed in his nakedness, the ridiculous embarrassment of after-sex going through him.

'You're a bitch. Just a whore. Remember that. That's what you'll always be.'

He reached over as he shouted, grabbed her hair in his rage and frustration, dragged her from the bed. She kept her silence, knowing that any strong reaction from her would only enrage him further. He stood over her; she curled up to protect herself from his kicks. He let go of her hair, stepped back, watched her get up and crawl back into the bed and cover herself once again. She saw the hurt and hatred in his eyes.

'That fucking Englishman. Does he know what you really are? Does he, tart?' He saw she was hurting, had started to sob quietly. 'Cry all you want, bitch. When I've finished today, there won't be much of him left. Him or anyone else, including his precious little family. Then you'll have to run back to me, won't you? Well, you'll have to crawl on your hands and knees. On your fucking hands and knees.' He picked up a glass vase that stood on the chest of drawers and threw it at her in his rage. It hit her on the leg, hurt her as she yelped, although the blankets cushioned most of its sharpness.

He turned and stormed out of the room, slamming the door behind him. She sat there, shaking in her fear, knowing that he meant great harm to Duncan. She suddenly swung her legs out of the bed and started to get dressed.

Sverdlovsk Airport
8 a.m.

The fog was still thick on the ground, the sun overhead desperately trying to burn through. Duncan, after searching the apron and the hangars, found no helicopters. There were a few aircraft, mostly civilian airliners, including the president's Yak-40 which Vashinov had arrived in. He noticed the AN-2, the radial-engined biplane he and Myeloski had arrived from Tobolsk in, still parked at the far end of the ramp, away from the main terminal.

He returned to the terminal, where the crowds had built up as travellers waited for the weather to clear. Myeloski had said it was easiest to get lost in a mass of people, and they both acted as passengers waiting for a flight.

He found the policeman at the side of the packed terminal, near the phone-booths. He was surprised to see Vera with him.

'What're *you* doing here?' he asked her when he got to them.

'I had to see you.'

'Look, I—'

Myeloski interrupted him. 'Listen to what she's got to say.'

326

Duncan stopped, waiting for her to speak.

'Vashinov came to see me after you'd gone.' He looked into her troubled eyes, was frightened to ask what had taken place. She saw his concern. 'It was all right. Nothing happened.' She could tell he knew that she had lied. 'He got angry. Shouted. Said that it didn't matter anyway, that there wouldn't be much left of you or the family.'

'He said that?'

'Yes.'

Myeloski interrupted. 'I told you they were up to no good.'

'Did he say anything else?' Duncan asked Vera.

She shook her head.

'Why? What's he get out of it?'

'We can find that out later. Did you find a helicopter?' Myeloski's question was urgent.

'No, something else. Come on, let's go.'

'I'm coming with you.' Vera's statement stopped them both. Duncan turned and looked at Myeloski, who grinned.

'Let's just go,' he said.

Duncan turned and left the terminal by the side-door, went through the ramp gate and towards the AN-2.

Myeloski stopped when he saw it. 'You've got to be joking.'

'It's no helicopter, but it's the next-best thing. It'll fly as slow as fifty miles an hour, and I can land it on a sixpence. At least we're up in the air, at least we'll hear the transfer instructions at the same time as everyone else.'

Myeloski nodded sheepishly, his fear of flying once more coming to the fore. They walked to the big biplane, its old-fashioned shape looming larger than it actually was in the greyness of the fog.

Duncan turned the handle of the cabin door; it twisted open, and he stepped into the interior of the plane. He reached up into the bulkhead, up to where he knew there was a light-switch, and knocked it on.

The interior was flooded with the harsh brightness of a floodlight which was suspended from the ceiling by a solitary wire. As he turned to help Vera and Myeloski in, a man came out of the cabin, half-asleep, rubbing his eyes. It was the pilot, the same one they had flown with before.

'Hi!' said a smiling Duncan.

'Shit!' said the pilot, recognizing Duncan. 'Not again!'

''Fraid so.'

Vera was already in the plane, and Duncan pulled Myeloski up. The policeman smiled at the pilot, who turned away in despair.

'Just like old times,' Myeloski joked nervously.

Duncan closed the door behind Myeloski and came up to the pilot. 'Are you fuelled up?' he asked the pilot.

The pilot didn't bother lying. He knew Duncan would check the gauges. 'Full fuel. But nothing's moving in this weather.'

'We just want to get up. We'll worry about getting down later. Any cloud above?' Duncan, like all pilots, knew that fog was never more than three hundred feet high; the weather above it was usually bright and sunny. If that were the case, then the fog would eventually burn off as the temperature rose.

The pilot nodded. 'It's clear.'

'Good. Then it'll burn off. Do you know, I still don't know your name.'

'Yakov.'

'Hi, Yakov. I'm Duncan. And that's Ahmed and Vera.'

'I suppose she's police as well,' Yakov said, casting an appraising and approving eye over Vera.

'No. KGB.'

'You're joking?' He saw that Duncan wasn't and he whistled through his teeth. 'So what's up this time?'

328

And Duncan told him, in brief detail, the object of their journey. When he had finished, he watched for Yakov's reaction. It was as he had hoped. Although he didn't give a damn about politics, the pilot had a strong sense of adventure. He laughed, slapped Duncan on the back.

'OK. It'll be good sport. A long shot but, if any plane can do it, this one can. Mind you, we won't be able to get away that quickly. This is an old bird; it won't outrun the helicopters.'

'We'll worry about that when it happens. Got any maps?'

Yakov turned and leant into the cockpit, produced some half-million-scale terrain maps. 'This is what I use.'

Duncan took the maps and spread them on the floor. 'Where the hell do we start?'

'There's an old training-camp at Irbit,' commented Yakov. 'Only a few caretakers there, but the sort of place the KGB have kept going over the years. Their people could be there. The brigands will know that, too.'

Myeloski leant over the pilot's shoulder, looked down on the map, as Yakov pointed to Irbit.

Yakov continued. 'The brigands are part of the community up here. They've passed me a couple of times, showing off with their fancy flying. They'll stay near the deep forest tree-line. Up in that area, north of Tavda. That's where they'll feel safe. Like the back of their hands, that's how well they know the area.'

'How well do *you* know it?' Myeloski asked.

'Better than the back of my hand. There're deep cuts all the way through the forests up there, wide enough for helicopters to fly along, like great roads through the birch trees. It's where the pipe-lines run. If you don't know the area, then they'll never be followed, however many aircraft the KGB have.'

'Are you convinced they'll go there?'

'No. But that's where I'd go. If I was them.'

'OK. Let's wind her up. No point hanging round here,' said Duncan.

Duncan and Yakov climbed into the front seats as Myeloski and Vera strapped themselves into the rear. Yakov looked out of the window, saw that there was no one nearby, and fired up the big Shvetsov radial engine. It roared into life, flames belching from its multi-exhausts as it built up power. When he had completed his checks, Yakov turned the plane under half-throttle and then taxied out into the fog-laden taxiways. It was slow work, with both Yakov and Duncan keeping a careful watch on the white taxi markings that led to the runway. Duncan imagined the frantic activity in the tower as the air-traffic controllers tried to contact the plane, but their radios were switched off; no one could reach them.

Just before they reached the nearest of the parallel runways, they saw a white flare explode above the runway, a warning for them to stop. They ignored it, checked their instruments and then applied full power.

The Shvetsov roared, and the AN-2 started its groundroll. Although Yakov knew the airport well, all he could do was hold the stick steady and hope the plane didn't wander off the runway. Just before they got to take-off speed, Duncan saw a vehicle parked across the runway; there were two men on the running-board, waving at the plane to stop. As the plane got closer the two men jumped and ran away from the vehicle. Yakov pulled back on the stick, and the big biplane shuddered into the air, its wheels passing inches over the vehicle.

'Fucking idiots!' screamed Yakov, then burst out laughing. Duncan turned to look at the two passengers behind him. Vera watched him intently and smiled at him. Myeloski had his eyes closed and was lost in his own private prayer.

In Moscow the watcher saw the blip that was Myeloski

330

suddenly leaving the town of Sverdlovsk. He called his superior and started to track the policeman. At the same time he dialled into the satellite and attempted to pick up a picture of whatever vehicle Myeloski was travelling in. It would take time, up to half an hour, but at least he had a strong signal.

His supervisor contacted the president's assistant, who went and awoke the president. The president asked to be kept informed and then rang Marshka.

'I don't know all that's going on, but we mustn't let this get out, Uncle. Vashinov mustn't know,' he said.

Ten minutes later, a written note was waiting to be picked up by a KGB despatch-rider at the satellite-tracking centre. But before the message could be collected a police officer took the envelope and confronted the watch supervisor who had written it and left it for delivery to the KGB. The watch supervisor confessed he had been passing on information to the KGB. He was then asked to write a false report saying that Myeloski was still reported to be in Sverdlovsk. After this note was substituted for the original one, the watch supervisor was escorted to police headquarters where he was to spend the next few hours.

The phone rang beside the president, and he picked it up. 'Nothing will get out, little reindeer. May God be with the policeman and the Englishman.'

The AN-2 broke out above the fog and into the bright sunlight at two hundred and fifty feet. It turned north-east and thundered along at a steady 115 miles per hour. It would take nearly ninety minutes to reach the northern forest tree-line.

Duncan applied full cruise power while Yakov pored over the maps stretched across his knees.

'When we get to the tree-line, we'll follow it on the chance that we see some activity.' Yakov hoped he had been right, that the brigands would operate in the north of the area and had not decided to do something foolhardy. He hoped the old bird could stand up to it. If things got rough, she was no match for a modern armed combat-gunship. He knew the reputation of the brigands better than most. Taking prisoners was not one of their trademarks.

Ivan Bakor led the Oldenburgs towards the lead Hind-A helicopter. It was a misty morning; the strands of cobweb-like wet moisture hung in the trees above him. He marvelled at their good humour; and, considering their recent ordeal, they looked well. Behind him, his men were breaking camp; this was not a place they would come back to. They had already determined their next base, over a thousand kilometres to the east.

Bakor's plan was simple. He would fly the two helicopters side by side to a sheltered clearing some hundred kilometres to the south of their present camp, just at the base of the forest tree-line.

Once there, they would leave the family in a shelter they had already prepared, with food and other provisions. In case there were any wolves or bears, he had arranged to leave a hunting-rifle, some dynamite and some flares. Once he had dropped the hostages, the two helicopters would fly east to a point near the camp at Irbit. He was pleased with his choice. His scouts had already given a full report on the four Havok helicopters that were supposedly hidden in the forest. Irbit was the last place they expected him to go.

North of Irbit he would call on the hostage frequency of 133.77 and ask that the money be dropped ten kilometres north of the camp. When the money was dropped, and the ransom helicopter had moved away, one of his Hind-A choppers would move in quickly and take the money. Once they had checked that the carrier had not been booby-trapped, they would fly east at full speed in formation. He knew the confusion this would cause. Were they to be followed by the Havok aircraft, or should they stay hidden until the hostage pick-up point was transmitted? It would be a nightmare for the KGB commander.

Fifteen minutes later, as they neared the tree-line, they would transmit the hostage-area co-ordinates and then split up, disappearing into the forest to meet up some thousand kilometres to the east.

It was a simple plan, and stood every chance of success.

But, just as Bakor had fallen prey to good fortune, so the hand of coincidence was about to be played.

As the two Hind-A helicopters lifted off from their old camp, an old Antonov AN-2 chugged north, flying no more than two hundred and fifty feet above the ground, too low to be picked up by ground radar.

All three aircraft headed for the northern forest tree-line.

Vashinov had worked himself up into a fury. He strode backwards and forwards in the Hotel Amerika library, shouting and cursing everyone in earshot.

He had just been told that a plane, an old AN-2, had taken off in the fog at Sverdlovsk airport without air-traffic permission. He remembered that Duncan was a pilot and immediately asked that the Englishman be brought down to see him. After a thorough search, they found that Duncan and Myeloski were nowhere to be found. The general had then rushed up to Vera's room, but she had gone as well.

He stormed downstairs, had the guards on the hotel entrance questioned. No one had seen them go, not through any of the normal entrances. Finally, one of his officers reported that their car was also gone. He told them to check the airport and, yes, within ten minutes it was found parked well away from the terminal, in the lorry-park.

333

So they were in the air. And they would hear the bandits' transmission. He cleared the room and then called his senior commander at Irbit. He told him what had occurred.

'The plan goes ahead.' Vashinov was in too deep now to stop. 'When the transmission is made, send not one, but two Havok aircraft to the hostage pick-up point. One is to proceed as planned, the other is to hold back. An AN-2 transporter—'

'A biplane?' interrupted his commander.

'Yes, a fucking biplane. It'll arrive there; of that I am sure. Destroy it, knock it out of the sky. Make sure they're all dead before it even hits the ground.'

He put down the phone which linked directly to Irbit. Apart from anything else, it would finally get rid of that tart Vera and her beloved Englishman.

Then he remembered the message he had received from Moscow. There had been no mention of Myeloski leaving Sverdlovsk; surely the satellite would have picked that up. The message quite clearly stated that the policeman was still in the city. He picked it up, reread the copy that had been faxed to him. Dammit, he had been deliberately misled. The time of the report was the giveaway; Myeloski would have been in the air for twenty minutes by then.

It was Marshka. He was the only other person who knew of the watcher, apart from the president. Maybe they had come together; maybe at this exact moment they were plotting his downfall.

He grinned. It was too late now. Any disaster that befell the Oldenburg party would be blamed on them. He, Vashinov, would appear as the only man who had tried to save the situation. His two enemies were far away; Moscow had become their prison.

The watcher caught sight of the AN-2 after one hour. He had tracked the area on the satellite camera, magnifying the radio image a thousand times, following their slow progress across the sky. When he was certain it was them, he called his supervisor. The two of them then monitored the flight of the biplane, the supervisor keeping in constant touch by telephone with the Kremlin. He also decided not to allow a shift-change. The next few hours were crucial; he wanted his best men on duty, however tired they were.

At the same time, a second watcher tuned a second camera from the same satellite on to the area ahead of the AN-2's apparent flight-path. It was the first time the stand-by camera had been tested, and it was being asked to play an impossible role. It was searching for any sign of movement that could be recognized as a helicopter moving across the terrain. It really was trying to find a very small needle in a very big haystack.

In Houston, another watcher yawned over his screen. The signal from Duncan's credit card was still stationary. The watcher decided that the Englishman was either very tired or dead. He looked up at the clock on the wall. It would soon be time to change his watch and go home.

Without his information from the Moscow satellite centre, Vashinov realized that he was reacting blind. He had a choice; either put up one or more Havok helicopters or sit tight. He decided not to take the risk. If the helicopters frightened away the brigands, any further action would be dependent on them contacting the authorities again. And this time, as he well knew, Marshka would take charge and block out Vashinov.

He would have to wait for the brigands to contact him on the airways frequency. It would be up to the helicopter crews to react as quickly as possible, to inflict the maximum damage as planned.

The larger Hook helicopter had been in the air for nearly an hour, waiting for the transmission. They would have to make their move soon, unless they had an alternative game-plan, a strategy that he had somehow missed.

He turned and looked at the radio set that had been rigged up for him, a relay set that was tuned to the 133.77 frequency that would spurt out the words when the brigands made contact.

'Come on. Damn. Come on.'

The set remained silent. There was still plenty of time to go.

The Kremlin
Moscow
5 a.m. (Moscow time)

In Moscow, the president had cancelled all his appointments for that day. He had sat in his office, waiting for news, but the time passed too slowly. It was only 5 a.m., but he had come in early to wait at his desk.

As he waited, he thought of what Marshka had told him, of the Beria Archives. It was something he would have to face, sooner rather than later.

He called his assistant and arranged for the chief librarian and archivist of the Kremlin to be called in. The archivist lived only a few blocks from the Kremlin, and he presented himself to the president's office within half an hour.

The president smiled; he saw the sleep in the man's eyes, the wisps of hair that floated across his forehead that had not been combed properly. He apologized for waking him so early, then explained what he wanted. The archivist was surprised at his request. No one in his thirty years in the Archives had asked to be taken to the Stalin Room. He explained that the door had two locks, the key to one of which he had in his office.

Before he could continue, to say that he did not know

336

where the other key was, the president interrupted him. 'I have the other.' Marshka had given it to him at their previous meeting.

The archivist led the president across the middle of the Kremlin to the enormous Arsenal building. It was where Duncan had first been brought, where he met Yashkin and where Myeloski told him in detail about the kidnapping.

The two men walked down the long government-officed corridors to the north side, where the Arsenal tower was. Although the majority of government literature was stored elsewhere, it was in this smaller, more secure area that information of a highly classified nature was kept. The great secrets of the years, an Aladdin's cave of information, would have been a historian's dreams come true.

The Archive, one of the Kremlin's great secrets, consisted of a series of sealed rooms, all with two locks on their individual doors. The archivist always had one key and kept those keys locked in a safe. The second key was maintained elsewhere, sometimes with the KGB, sometimes with the senior officials of government departments. He was quite sure that many of the keys had disappeared over the years, their functions forgotten. But the rooms were off-limits; their secrets remained closed. In addition to the two keys, one also needed the written authority of either the most senior minister of that department or, as in the case of the Stalin Room, the president or general secretary himself.

This time there was no signed authority, but the archivist was not going to argue that point with his visitor.

He took the president into his office and went to the big wall-safe at the side. He clicked the correct combination and swung the door open. The president watched him search through the documents and keys until he found the correct one. He carefully took it out and then closed the safe again.

He led the president out into the corridor and down the stairs at the end. They climbed down the stone steps, their shoes ringing in the confines of the narrow stairwell. They reached the basements, forgotten rooms that had once been dungeons. The president felt the shudder of the cold dead air suddenly circulated by the movement of the two men and the opening of the large doors that guarded the area. At the side he saw rat poison.

'We clean this area about once a month,' the archivist answered his unasked question. 'There are no rodents here; we can't afford that, not with all these papers and objects here.'

He reached one of the doors that led off the cellar, put his key in and turned the lock. It opened easily. He held out his hand for the other key, and the president passed it to him. The second lock opened just as easily. He passed the key back to the president and then swung the door open, reached in and switched on the light, an old single bulb that hung from the ceiling.

'That's a relief. Sometimes the lights don't work, and we have to get a new bulb.' He stepped aside to let the president in. After he had entered, the archivist started to follow him in, but the president held up his hand. The archivist, knowing it was against the rules, decided once again not to argue. He went back into the corridor and heard the door into the Stalin Room close behind him.

The president looked round the lead-lined room; it was a square, about ten metres by five. There was a small desk in the middle with two wooden chairs. Along the walls there were wooden cabinets arranged. He walked up to them and saw that they were in date order. He felt the foreboding of history; here were all the secrets of those terrible Stalin years, of the purges and massacres and the orders that spelt death for millions of

338

Russians. He thought of the other rooms down here, each with their similar and sometimes terrible secrets.

But he was here for a purpose, not to revel in the secret and guilty history of his predecessors. He smiled; this is where *glasnost* would remain buried.

He went to the cabinet Marshka had told him about and opened it, saw the rows of numbered drawers, this time identified alphabetically. He pulled open the one marked 'B', saw the various files in their buff metal cases with hinged flaps. Most were marked 'Beria', but he looked for the one with 'Beria-Tsar' stamped across it. When he found it he took it to the table, sat down and pulled out the contents.

There were some photographs and a written document some four pages long. He started to read; his heart sank as he absorbed the contents. If only he had known all this before he set out on his course to return a constitutional monarchy to the Soviet Union.

11

LANDING THE CATCH

Soviet Airspace
Western Siberia
10.15 a.m.

The Hind-As, flying a few feet above tree-top level,
broke out into the clearing which had been selected as
the drop-off point.

The lead helicopter, with Bakor and the hostages
aboard, hovered over the clearing while the second
gunship circled to check for any intruders. They were
operating on radio silence, so the second helicopter,
having checked the area, returned and the pilot visually
signalled an 'all clear' to the lead ship.

The Hind-A dropped down into the clearing and
landed.

Four armed brigands jumped out before the ship had
touched down and took up guard positions at the corners
of the clearing, crouching low into the undergrowth as
they did so. When each man had signalled that all was
clear, Bakor came out of the helicopter and signalled the
family to follow. Another brigand helped with the

youngest child, who was now crying, frightened by the noise.

The family, led by Bakor, kept bent forward, keeping clear of the overhead rotors which were still turning, and moved away from the helicopter. When clear, Bakor showed them the protection hide that had been prepared, while one of his men quickly erected another tent for their cover. The family was warmly dressed, so there would be little chance of the morning chill affecting them.

Then Bakor held out his hand to Victor Oldenburg. Victor shook his head and turned away, put his arm round his wife and helped her prepare for the well-being of the children.

Bakor shrugged, then turned and ran to the helicopter, calling his men as he did so. He stayed by the door as they climbed in, then shouted at Victor, loudly above the sound of the revolving blades. Bakor then brandished the guns and ammunition he was leaving for their protection, laid them on the ground and climbed into the aircraft.

Before the door was closed, the Hind-A had lifted up and tilted forward to join its sister ship. The two aircraft then swung south, flew for a quarter of a mile to clear the tree-line and then dropped to the flat permafrost no more than ten feet above the ground. In this formation, they flew south towards the Irbit camp, a good half-hour away.

On the ground, still in the forest, the family had no idea of what to expect. Victor picked up the rifles that had been left and the box of flares. He decided not to use the flares, but to wait until the helicopters were well clear of him. The terrain was flat and if he fired the flares, which went no higher than eighty feet as they were ground flares designed to frighten away animals, they could still be seen some twenty miles away. The trees, some topping eighty feet, would block out the flares anyway. He decided to wait, to help the family settle down under cover, and then climb one of the trees and let the flares off into the sky.

The Antonov AN-2 landed in the scrub, near a small copse of birch trees, when Yakov saw the giant Hook helicopter circling to the south. He knew it was a military aircraft, and they didn't want to be seen. They waited there, the engine now silenced in case there were any ground troops nearby.

Myeloski said he wanted to relieve himself, his stomach was in turmoil after the low-level flight, and Duncan climbed through the back and opened the door for him. Myeloski clambered out and went into the copse to carry out his duties.

'Want to get out for a minute?' the Englishman asked Vera. He knew they would be there for a little time while they waited for the Hook to move away.

She climbed out of the plane with him, enjoying the chill of the fresh air in her lungs after the bumpy ride in the old plane. The two of them walked round to the other side of the copse and looked out towards the spot where they knew the large helicopter was circling. Duncan could just make it out in the haze, flying at some two hundred feet, and he pointed it out to Vera. They watched the big helicopter circling until they heard Myeloski stumble out of the undergrowth and come towards them.

'What did we come down for?' he asked, peering in the direction they were looking.

'Big KGB helicopter. Can you see it?' Duncan showed the policeman where it was.

'You sure they didn't see us?'

'I don't think so. Otherwise they'd have come after us.'

Within five minutes the Hook had disappeared. Duncan led them back to the plane.

Vera heard it first. She stopped, grabbed Duncan's arm to listen. The noise became clearer; it was the pulsating *woosh-woosh* of a helicopter rotor, not too close, but recognizable in the distance. Duncan pulled the two of them into the copse, away from the AN-2.

He saw the first Hind-A gunship, no more than four hundred metres away, just above the ground and travelling at over 150 knots. It was heading south, towards where the Hook had been. Within seconds, its sister ship came into view, tracking the aircraft in front.

The two helicopters never saw the AN-2; it was shielded by the copse. Within a minute, the two aircraft had disappeared; only the sound of their disappearing rotors remained.

Duncan grabbed Vera's arm and rushed to the AN-2. He pushed her and Myeloski in, climbed in and shut the door. He went up to the cockpit.

'Did you see them?' he asked Yakov.

'No, just heard them. Where did they come from?'

'Almost directly north.'

'Give them a couple of minutes, then we'll take off. Try to follow them.'

'How far to the tree-line?'

'Ten minutes. Maybe a little more. Why?'

'They may already have dropped the hostages. It's ten o'clock. They've only got until eleven to complete the mission.'

Myeloski interrupted from the back. 'That's a big chance. What if they haven't dropped them?'

'We'll never catch them anyway; they're moving at nearly twice our speed. And if we go up higher, so we can see them, then there's a good chance they'll see us, too. They'll leave the hostages somewhere under cover and well away from the ransom pick-up point. I reckon they've already dropped them.' Duncan couldn't explain his instinct, an instinct honed over years of fighting terrorists.

Myeloski nodded. He knew it was the only way.

'Let's get going,' ordered Duncan. 'North, to the tree-line.'

'They'll see us.'

'Not if we keep down to twenty feet.'

'In this bird? You're fucking joking.'

'I'll do it if you don't. I think time's running out.'

Yakov shook his head, then switched on the magnetos and cranked the big radial engine over. As soon as it fired, Duncan leant forward and released the brakes, applied the throttle, and the plane shuddered as it tried to lift out of the deep tyre-ruts it had caused in the permafrost, and then rolled free.

The AN-2 taxied to the north side of the copse, keeping the trees between it and the disappearing helicopters, and then picked up speed as full power was applied and finally lifted into the air six hundred feet later.

Although the first watcher saw the AN-2 stop on his screen, then lift off again, it was the second operator, on the satellite stand-by camera, who saw the flash of the Hind-As.

They were too quick for him to receive a clear picture, but he knew that there had been some activity down there, something fast-moving near the AN-2.

He reset the camera and enlarged its viewing footprint. Although he wouldn't get an accurate picture of the type of aircraft, at least he would determine its speed and direction. As he waited for the spaceborne radio camera to refocus, as he waited for the computer in the air-conditioned room below to re-evaluate the signals sent down from the satellite, he called to the supervisor who was sitting with his colleague at the next radar-table tracking the AN-2.

'Something on the screen,' he said. 'Fast-moving, southbound.'

*   *   *

344

The big Hook transporter continued to circle to the south, not aware of the Hind-As that had been moving rapidly towards it some twenty kilometres to the north.

Bakor realized he was getting too close to the Hook, that if he was seen now it would certainly jeopardize the transfer operation. Neither did he want to turn east or west as any sideways movement would be easier to spot from the high-flying transporter. He told the pilot to set the helicopter down. They would have to wait until the route was clear again.

The two aircraft settled into the tundra and stopped, their rotors still turning.

Bakor and some of his men climbed out. In the distance they could just make out the big helicopter circling in the sky. Bakor knew he couldn't break radio silence, call up the helicopter on 133.77 and tell it to move away to the west. That would only tell the authorities that they were positioned near where he intended to make the drop. They might also trace the radio transmitter; God only knew what level of sophistication their equipment had reached.

He looked at his watch for the umpteenth time in the last few minutes; it was the sign of a nervous man. Things were running late, and he didn't want to go past thc dcadline.

The AN-2 reached the tree-line as Bakor brought his gunships to ground. It had been a bumpy ride, flying no more than a few feet off the deck. Duncan had left the controls to Yakov and was impressed with the bush pilot's high level of skill. The old plane was an extension of the pilot's soul. He had flown at full power, the throttle fully forward pressed against the firewall, the big Shvetsov radial screaming its protest. They had narrowly missed some of the small birch trees that tried to survive in the terrain, thin trees that sprang out of low ground-mist as they rushed towards them.

In the back, Myeloski had shut his eyes again; the onrushing ground outside the small windows had been too much for him. Vera, oblivious to what was going on around her, saw only the Englishman, knew how important this operation was for him, sensed his anxiety, sensed his urgency.

'East or west?' Yakov asked, as they saw the tree-line approach. He was leaving the decision to Duncan.

'East for twenty miles, then turn around and we'll work the western section.'

'We'll have to climb. They could be inside the tree-line. I'm taking her up to two hundred feet above the trees, keep about half a mile in.'

'OK,' Duncan agreed; it was probable that the brigand helicopters had dropped into a clearing deeper in the forest. He didn't know if another helicopter had been left with the family, to stay with them until the ransom money had been picked up. Myeloski had said the brigand group were rumoured to have two gunships, and he had certainly seen two fly past earlier on. But it was time to take risks, time to stand out from the crowd.

The old biplane lifted up from the tundra floor and climbed at a slow rate until it was over the trees, then turned east to begin its search.

At quarter past ten, Vashinov knew that time was beginning to run against him. He had followed the brigands' instructions exactly; that is, unless they had found out about the troops and Havok gunships that were hidden on the ground. There were only forty-five minutes to go before the deadline was over. He had expected them to make their move earlier.

Normally a man who bided his time, Vashinov knew that he would have to force events if his plan were to work. He had to find the royal family, had to get to them before anyone in Moscow knew about it.

There was a knock on the library door, and his assistant came in.

'There's a Moscow policeman arrived at the airport. He asked for you and for transport to your headquarters,' his man reported. 'An Inspector Leonid Igorevich Yashkin, head of the Moscow Bureau. He says he's got special instructions from the Kremlin. He's here to monitor progress.'

'Is he still at the airport?'

'Yes, Comrade General.'

'Then, arrange immediate transport. And make sure he doesn't get here for at least fifty minutes.'

The assistant left the room to carry out his orders. So they were hauling in the leash, making sure he didn't overstep the mark.

Like Bakor, he looked at his watch for the umpteenth time; his nervousness made him sweat under the collar.

He would give it a little more time. Then he would unleash his own hounds of hell.

The watchers in Moscow had lost contact with both the AN-2 and the Hind-A helicopters.

The AN-2 could not be seen as it merged into the trees below it. The watcher reprogrammed his camera for a bigger footprint; he would identify the biplane through its movement patterns, just as his colleague had tried to do earlier on with the fast-moving helicopters.

The second watcher, once he had brought the bigger footprint up on his screen, saw nothing. He looked down on an area some fifteen kilometres by twelve kilometres and, with the aid of his supervisor, had also tracked the adjoining areas. There was no contact, no movement, only the track of the Hook transporter circling to the south.

'I can open a bigger footprint,' said the operator.

'No. They can't have moved that fast to go out of your range. Not unless they were jets; and there're no

347

military operations today. They've all been cancelled.'

'Then, they've landed.'

'Probably. It looks like it's the drop-off point.'

'That close to the Hook? I don't think so.' The operator's logic was unassailable.

The supervisor considered. There was the chance they had not seen the huge helicopter circling to the south, but that was unlikely. The only other reason, if the movements his operator saw were the hostage aircraft, was that the Hook had unknowingly forced them down because they didn't want to be identified.

'Keep the big print on your screen,' he ordered. 'If they're down there, then they'll have to surface.' He went to a phone at the side of the room and dialled the number in the Kremlin. He also sweated; talking to the president made him uncomfortable.

Deep in the cellars of the Kremlin's Arsenal, the chief librarian and archivist hurried from his office down the stairs and to the Stalin Room.

He listened at the door before he knocked, heard no movement, got no answer. After a moment, he tried again, rapped harder on the door. He heard the president's muffled voice through the thick door bid him enter. He pushed it open and saw the president, still sitting at the table, his face ashen. In front of him, on the table, the documents he had been reading were spread out.

'There's an urgent call from your office, Comrade President,' the archivist informed him in a hushed and tentative voice.

The president looked up, not seeming to recognize him at first. Then he nodded, looked down at the documents and scooped them back into their metal container. He stood up and walked back to the cabinet, filed the container under the 'B' index and closed the cabinet door.

'Has anyone ever been in here, seen this file?'

'Not in my time. Not in nearly thirty years.'

'Are you certain?'

'As much as I can be, Comrade President. When I heard you were coming, I checked the index-book to see when the file was last opened. Everything must be signed for, you see. There are no signatures, no records of anyone opening the file. And, as you know, a librarian must be present when the file is opened. No one could have done that without it being reported.'

'I was left on my own.'

'But you are the president.'

'Someone else, of equal importance, could also have been so treated.' He recalled that Marshka had known. How many others had shared the hideous secret?

The archivist had no answer for that. 'The telephone call. They said it was urgent.'

The president nodded and led the archivist out of the room. When they had locked the door, the president pocketed his key and turned to the archivist. 'No one is to go near that file without my personal authority. In fact, no one is even to go in that room. Is that clear?'

'Absolutely, Comrade President.'

As he left the vast cellar, with the solid old wooden doors leading into the individual rooms, the president thought of all the other terrible secrets that were locked away down here, the awful misdemeanours and tragedies that were born of power and greed and self-interest.

It was a dark place, this locked-away conscience of Russia, this place that would always remain beyond the eyes and knowledge of the rest of the world.

Upstairs, he took the call in the archivist's office. It was the radar supervisor, reporting back to him. He listened carefully before speaking. 'Keep watch. Miss nothing. I shall be back in my office very soon. Report immediately something happens.'

He put down the receiver and left the Arsenal, left to

go and sit and wait for this awful crisis finally to come to an end.

It was Myeloski who saw the clearing first, saw people running, waving.

He had been told by Duncan to look out of his side, to look for any movement or any other sign of the hostages. The tree-tops, to him only a few feet below the plane, were needles of doom waiting for the plane to fly into them. But, if they were as close as he imagined, then it was his duty to disregard his fears and help in the search. As he looked out, his stomach rumbled, his juices begging for food. It was a sure sign of nervousness, of impending disaster.

The clearing he saw, about three hundred yards to the right, seemed empty at first. But just as it moved out of his vision he thought he saw someone running into the clearing. He looked harder, then seemed to see someone else before the clearing disappeared in the foreground of tree-tops.

He wasn't sure, but couldn't afford to take any chances. He called Duncan, shouting loudly as he did. The Englishman quickly came into the fuselage of the plane, next to Myeloski.

The policeman pointed out of the window, backwards and to the right. 'I think I saw something. Some movement. In a big clearing over there.' He jabbed his finger in the direction he indicated.

Duncan climbed back into the cockpit and told Yakov to bank sharply right and do a 180-degree turn. The pilot did as ordered; the plane swiftly turned towards the clearing.

They had been flying very slowly, at no more than 65 miles per hour, and once Yakov had completed the turn they searched the area in front of the swirling propeller.

Yakov, the most accustomed to the terrain, saw the clearing first. As he swung a few degrees to his left, he

350

also saw people, two of them, small sticks in the distance. Before he could yell, Duncan had also seen them, pointed excitedly at them.

'There!' he shouted.

Yakov swung the plane low, kept his flaps down and poured on the power. He was near a stall speed and did not want to crash into the forest. He brought the speed back to 55 miles per hour by pulling the nose up and dropping his undercarriage. In this attitude he dropped towards the clearing, below the height of the trees.

At forty feet above the ground, as the biplane seemed to hang in the air above the clearing, Duncan recognized Victor and Anna.

'That's them! Let's get down there!' The exhilaration in his voice spurred them all on.

Yakov pulled up the undercarriage to get rid of any drag, and the plane started to climb, clear of the trees and away from the family. Once above the trees, he circled to the left and prepared for an approach. It would be tight. The undercarriage was released, and the plane, in a landing configuration, once more descended to the clearing. But, just as they pased over the tree-tops, Yakov flicked the undercarriage lever and pushed the throttles forward. The AN-2 climbed once again, once more over the trees.

'What's the matter?' shouted Duncan over the roar of the Shvetsov engine.

'We'll get down OK, but it's too short. We'll never take off; she doesn't climb that fast.'

Duncan didn't argue. He knew Yakov was a good pilot, was right not to take an unnecessary risk. 'OK. Stick her down near the tree-line. I'll go in and get them out on foot.'

Yakov turned the plane south, flew the half-mile to the tree-line and landed the AN-2 at the edge of the forest.

Duncan was the first out, slipping on the permafrost as

he turned to help Myeloski and Vera step from the plane. Yakov had parked under the shelter of some trees; they could not be seen from the air.

'I'll go in alone. I can move faster. You stay here. I'll be back within half an hour.'

He turned and started to run, run as he was trained to, into the semi-darkness of the birch-tree forest and towards the hostages that he had come across Europe to save.

It took Duncan six minutes to cover the half-mile that led to the clearing. When he saw the open space through the birch trees, he dropped down, pulling the Coonan Magnum from his shoulder holster. There was no visible movement, so he circled the clearing; if it was a trap, they would expect him from the south. When he was northside of the open area, he came closer to the edge of the forest, crouching in the undergrowth so as not to be seen.

He saw nothing for a while, then a small movement to his right caught his eye. He watched, and made out the shape of a hide, saw a rifle-barrel pointing out. He kept position, waiting to see who the gunman was. Then, after nearly three more minutes, he heard a baby cry, saw the top of the hide move.

He knew it was Oldenburg. And he was sure that there was no one else around the clearing. He mustn't surprise them; they wouldn't know it was him, could react in a hostile manner.

'Victor!' he shouted.

There was no response from the hide.

'It's Mark.' Still no response. 'I'm to your left. On the edge of the forest. I'm going to walk into the open. If it's an ambush, stay where you are. If not, come out of the hide and we'll get out of here.'

He watched the hide, saw the gun-barrel move slowly in his direction. He hoped it was Victor, but he had no choice; he knew he had to move fast.

352

He stood up in the undergrowth, the Magnum still in his hand, cocked in case he needed it. He came forward into the opening and walked slowly towards the hide, the rifle now following his movement. He grew more cautious, sensed it was an ambush, otherwise Victor would have shown himself. The steel of the Magnum was a comfort in his hand; his finger covered the trigger, firmed up on it.

As the hide-cover was sharply lifted, Duncan dropped to his knee, lifted the Magnum up to bear on the hide. But Victor Oldenburg stepped out, his face still anxious, but a bullish grin of relief spread across it.

Duncan came up and sprinted towards them, shouldering his gun as he went. They met, arms wrapped round each other in the embrace of friends who have great affection for each other.

'You're late,' said Victor Oldenburg.

'Trust you to get lost,' came the quick reply. 'Come on. They may come back.' Duncan saw Anna and the children still in the hide. The two men turned and helped the others out. Duncan held the youngest to him and led them all into the forest.

Oldenburg, carrying the youngest daughter, called out to him: 'Where are we? Still in Russia?'

Duncan suddenly realized the horror of what the family had been through. They had not even known where they were, had been kept in the dark since they were first kidnapped. It was a long story, but it would have to wait.

'Yes. Come on, we have to get out of here,' he answered. Then he led the family through the undergrowth towards the escape-plane.

In Moscow the watchers had lost total contact with both the Hind-As and the AN-2.

The supervisor, in constant communication with the president, decided to leave things as they were. He was convinced the aircraft concerned had landed. At some stage, he knew, they would have to move again, would have to break their cover. The only link they had was the steady flash of Myeloski's transmitter on the screen.

He told the watchers to stay glued to their sets. They were his two best men. If anything of size moved in the areas covered, they would know.

Vashinov's patience was flagging. With only twenty minutes left to the deadline, it was time to stir the pot.

In life he had learnt that when things could turn against you it was sometimes wiser to stoke up the action, get things moving and, with luck, cause others to make the mistakes.

He spoke into the phone that connected him to the unit leader at Irbit.

'Get the Havoks up. Search the area. And hit them hard if you find them. Blow the bastards out of the sky.'

He looked at his watch again. It would all be over, one way or another, by the time the Moscow policeman arrived.

He wondered why the president hadn't contacted him. He knew Marshka would have planned a move, would now be plotting against him. But it was too late. One way or another, Vashinov was about to ensure that the ransom would never be paid, that the kidnap would be successful and that the men in Moscow would carry the blame.

The Havoks, on receiving their orders on a coded transmitter, broke cover and lifted off from their hideouts.

One of them was only twelve kilometres from the brigands. Its camouflage cover was hauled up, and the big rotors swung as the turbines fired up. Three minutes later it lifted into the air and started a sweep-search to the east.

Bakor's lead pilot was the first to see it as it flew at two hundred feet above the surface. He called Bakor, who followed it through his binoculars. He knew of the Havok combat-ship, knew it could outrun and outgun his own.

'Bastards!' he shouted to no one in particular. 'They've bloody double-crossed us.'

He followed the trail of the Havok until it was far enough south-east not to see them at their low altitude.

'OK. Let's get back, get those bloody hostages and move into the forest.' He watched as the pilot allowed the rotor to pick up speed. 'And I don't want to be more than five metres above the ground. Make this the tightest mission you've ever flown.'

The Hind-As lifted into the air and turned north, flying just above the tundra, back to the tree-line.

They saw the AN-2 through the birch trees when they were only a hundred yards from the forest's edge. He had already warned the family of the danger they were in, that the big biplane was their only escape-route.

Yakov was the first to see them; he raised the other two to go and help while he prepared the plane for a quick departure.

Myeloski and Vera went towards the hurrying group, but Duncan waved them back to the plane. They stood by the door as the group reached them; they quickly helped lift the children into the fuselage. Anna followed the children in, then Vera and Victor.

The giant radial engine spluttered into life, the backwash hitting Myeloski and Duncan.

'See anything?' Duncan shouted at the policeman, who shook his head.

'Are they all right?'

'Fine. Let's get out of here.'

Duncan pushed Myeloski into the plane and followed him in as the aircraft started to move off. He closed the door, then checked that all the passengers were safe.

Anna sat in one of the seats, holding the baby and the little girl. Vera sat in the only other seat, holding the other girl to her. Victor Oldenburg and Myeloski held on to the struts of the fuselage frame, bracing themselves for the take-off.

Duncan pulled himself forward into the cockpit, slid into the right-hand seat. As Yakov taxied away from the tree-line and lined up for a take-off, the Englishman scoured the horizon for any approaching aircraft.

The biplane bumped along on the permafrost surface as it picked up speed and lifted into the air.

'Where now?' Yakov shouted over the loud sound of the radial to Duncan.

'North and west. Any trouble's going to come from the south.'

Yakov turned the plane west and lifted it over the forest, kept it at some hundred feet above the trees. With his precious cargo on board, there was no way that Yakov wanted to risk hitting a downdraught that would force them to crash in the forest.

The watcher on the first screen shouted as he saw the movement generated by the AN-2. 'They're on the move. They're moving.'

His excitement was lost on the supervisor, who sat at the second screen, watching the explosion of movement that had been picked up by the stand-by satellite camera. In addition to the Hook helicopter, still circling to the south, there had been three movement-tracks, two of them side by side moving to the north, a third moving very fast to the east.

The supervisor, realizing that he would have to follow either one of the two separate sets of movement-tracks before they went off his screen, ordered the operator to switch to a bigger footprint. While they waited for the computer to realign the satellite lens he went over to the first watcher's screen.

'It's them all right,' his operator said. The blip that was Myeloski pinpointed the movement track of the AN-2. 'They're going north-west. Do you want me to close-up on them?'

'No.' Although their tracks were on different screens, he knew that the fast-moving north-bound pair of aircraft were heading directly for the slower-moving biplane. He needed to keep the larger view, to know if and when the AN-2 would be discovered.

'I've got them on the big picture,' the second operator shouted across to him. He went back to the stand-by screen, now covering an area of seventy kilometres by sixty. The tracks were not visible now; the aircraft appeared as single blips as they would on any air-traffic control system. As the two men watched, another blip, as fast-moving as the east-bound aircraft, appeared on the right-hand side of the screen. It was moving west, running parallel and to the south of the east-bound aircraft. Although they couldn't identify it, it was a second Havok combat helicopter, also searching for the kidnappers.

What the two men, both highly experienced military radar operators, did recognize was a traditional search-pattern used by the Army and the KGB.

'They're all coming out to play,' said the supervisor, reaching for the phone. He shouted across to the first watcher as he dialled: 'How long before they get to the AN-2?'

'About ten minutes.'

The phone in the president's office was answered, and the supervisor made his report. The president asked for his assumptions, and he gave them.

'The AN-2 is too slow to outrun them, Comrade President. There's a chance that they may not see the biplane, but I wouldn't count on it.'

The president told him to continue reporting and put down the phone.

It was time to call his own professionals into the game.

The Hind-As reached the tree-line six minutes later, helped along by the southerly wind that had now built up, that had blown away the final curtains of mist and left a clear, sunlit, cloudless day.

The lead gunship climbed over the trees and towards the clearing, followed by its sister ship. When they reached the clearing one minute later, Bakor's helicopter landed but the second aircraft stayed above the trees, watching for any surprise intruders.

Bakor and some of his men, fully armed, raced out of the helicopter and to the hide. They were wary in case Oldenburg opened fire, but Bakor was convinced he would not risk his family if they were caught in a crossfire.

The hide was empty, the cover thrown back. He told his men to search the forest's edge, to find their tracks. As he searched the hide, he saw that the flares and rounds of ammunition were still there; they would have gone if the family had struck off to find their own way out of the forest.

He knew they had been rescued before one of his men called, from the southern end of the clearing, shouting that he had found tracks moving south.

He ran back to the helicopter, ordering his men to follow. As they climbed aboard, the helicopter swung up, dipped its nose as it turned and rose from the clearing.

Bakor ordered his pilot to fly south to the tree-line, and to climb higher so that the could see any other traffic. The pilot applied full torque, and the twin Isotov turbo-shafted engines screamed as the helicopter went straight up and into the sun, straight up to its hovering height of nearly eight thousand feet. The second helicopter followed.

As the Hind-A circled, the occupants searched the

horizon for a contact. They saw nothing; Bakor had no alternative but to use the radio.

They had two frequencies selected on the boxes, one permanently on 133.77, the other on a non-standard frequency of 123.45. This was the frequency to be used for contact between the brigands' two aircraft.

'Follow the tree-line to the south-west. We're going north-west. Radio contact only if sighted.' The radio went dead; Bakor had no idea who else was listening.

They never heard the radio call, but they picked up the blips of unidentified aircraft above one thousand feet at the air-traffic centre in Sverdlovsk. The KGB officer, told to watch and monitor the control room, immediately called his unit commander at Irbit.

After the commander had spoken to Vashinov, the two most northerly Havok combat helicopters were despatched by coded transmitter to the north-west, to intercept and identify the unknown aircraft.

They turned north and flew at maximum speed to investigate.

The change of direction was also communicated to the president as the satellite camera picked up their signal and relayed it to Moscow. He knew the slow biplane needed to know that they were being chased, that the fast-closing helicopters were all probably combat-armed and had hostile intentions. He couldn't tell if the hostages were on board, but it was obviously the centre of everyone else's attention.

His alternate game-plan had already been instigated. He had to warn the hostage group. He picked up the phone and called his assistant.

Two minutes later, the Sverdlovsk air-traffic centre broadcast the following message on frequency 133.77.

'Calling Myeloski. Myeloski. Four aircraft with possible hostile intentions heading towards and overtaking you, south-east of your track. Believed to be fast-moving helicopters, armed. Suggest you take avoiding action. Do not respond. Listen out this frequency.'

The loudspeaker in the AN-2 cockpit crackled out the message. Yakov and Duncan both looked out of the left windows and saw nothing.

'Down. Get lower,' Duncan shouted at Yakov. But there were only trees below, their tops a hundred feet below them. Yakov pushed the nose down, the biplane picked up speed as it downhilled to the tree-tops and then levelled out, only a few feet above the sharp-topped trees.

As the message was broadcast, Bakor looked behind him, now aware that the Havoks were on his tail, although he could not see them.

'Heading north-west,' he ordered the pilot, taking the reciprocal track to that which had just broadcast his position. Then he saw the glint and reflection of the sun off its tilted wings as the AN-2 dived for the trees. 'There!' he pointed as he shouted. 'About fifteen kilometres, eleven o'clock. Take her down, fast. Get under radar cover.'

The two Hind-As dived for the tree-tops, increasing their speed as they closed in on the distant, but slow-moving biplane.

The Havoks, coming from the south, had no contact with the brigands' aircraft. But their officer in the control tower dutifully reported all that was visible on the air-traffic area screen. Within a minute the position of the Hind-As was passed on to the Havoks by the Irbit command centre through the scrambled decoder. They turned left fifteen degrees, were now fourteen minutes behind the targets.

In the biplane, Yakov concentrated on his low flying while the others looked out of the left-hand side of the plane towards the south-east.

'We could land,' Yakov told Duncan. 'Turn south to

the tree-line and put down. If Air Traffic know we're here, know we're in trouble, there must be some help on its way.'

'No. They'd catch us before we cleared the trees.'

Then he saw the valley to the right, a long needle-like clearing between the trees that must have been one of the routes that loggers had used in the past. At the bottom of the shallow valley there was a river, thin and silvery as it wriggled up the clearing.

'Follow the river, down, under the tree-level.'

Yakov looked down, saw the thin valley with the trees no more than a hundred and twenty feet across. His wingspan was only forty feet; he would have no more than a wing's length on each side for safety. If he veered off course any more than that, the trees would rip his wings off, bring the biplane crashing to the forest floor.

He let out a loud yell, like a paratrooper about to jump off a plane, released his tension and then pulled the throttle back, got the speed back to 55 miles per hour. He was only just above his stall level. Then he lowered the nose gently and flew the plane down into the narrow tree-lined valley, to forty feet above the ground, over forty feet below the tops of the passing birch trees.

Myeloski, not knowing what was happening, suddenly saw the trees out of his window, thought they were crashing, closed his eyes and braced himself against the fuselage for the impact. When nothing happened, he opened his eyes again, saw that they were flying through the forest.

The Hind-As saw the biplane's manoeuvre from five kilometres away, saw the plane disappear into the forest. The two helicopters were now at tree-top level, and Bakor thought the plane had crashed into the trees. He started to curse, his plan blown up on the forest floor. But as they approached the area where he had seen the plane go down they found no wreckage, just a thin winding valley between the trees.

'Fucking hell!' he cried. 'That's what you call flying.'
He shook his head in admiration. 'Keep your speed up.
We'll catch them in the next two minutes.'

'Then what?' the pilot asked.

'Force them down. Don't blast them. They're our
passport to the future.'

'What about the Havoks?'

'If we force them down before they get here, they'll
never find us on the forest floor. We're all out of radar
range now. We're on *our* turf; we play by *our* rules.'

The radar controllers in Sverdlovsk had lost contact with
everyone except the two high-flying Havok gunships.
The KGB officer who stood behind them had no further
information to pass on to Irbit. He saw the Havoks start
to fan out to fly a search-pattern. He knew then that
they hadn't found the other aircraft. On the bottom of
the screen, south of the Havoks, two further targets
appeared. It was the other KGB gunships flying north
to help their comrades in the search. But they were
out of the game; they were too far away to have any
impact.

'What the hell's that?' The air-traffic supervisor
suddenly jumped out of his seat and leant over the area
screen. Two more blips had appeared, just over two
hundred and fifty kilometres to the north, fast-moving
and heading for what could only be called combat zone.

The KGB officer didn't wait for any further information; he was already dialling his commander at Irbit.

In Moscow the watcher spoke into a headset microphone.

'All targets now converging. They've found our man.'
As he spoke he saw the three blips that represented the
AN-2 and the chasing helicopters merge into one.

'Roger,' crackled the answering voice, stone hard and
emotionless in its reply.

362

*　　*　　*

The pilot of the leading Hind-A saw the biplane first, pointed it out to Bakor. It was below them, slow-flying in the tree-lined valley.

'Bloody bucket ships,' swore Bakor. Then he spoke into the radio on the 123.45 frequency, told the other pilot to go down and trail the biplane.

As the second helicopter complied with his order, Bakor kept the lead ship just above and behind the AN-2, far enough away not to be seen. When his second helicopter had dropped into the valley and shadowed the biplane, Bakor instructed his pilot to overfly the plane, to show themselves.

The noise of the Hind-A passing overhead was the first warning those on board the biplane had that they were discovered.

Yakov leant forward, knew the helicopter would soon come into view. Duncan saw it at the same time; the fast-moving gunship passed in front of them, slowed down and hovered some fifty feet above. The downdraught caused the biplane to stagger; Yakov applied more power to keep it steady, to avoid being flipped into the trees that ran alongside the wingtips.

After nearly a minute of this, the Hind-A raced ahead and disappeared. Yakov and Duncan looked at each other. They knew it wasn't over yet. They flew on, unaware of the helicopter that trailed them some three hundred metres behind.

As they turned the slow valley bend to the left, they saw where the helicopter had gone. It was ahead of them, about half a mile, facing them and hovering at their height.

'Shit!' yelled Yakov. 'He's trying to force us down, to land.' His hand instinctively started to pull the throttle back, to push the plane down to land.

But Duncan overrode him, put his hand over Yakov's fist and pushed the power-stick forward.

'What're you—?' Yakov tried to pull the throttle back, but was no match for Duncan's iron grip.

'Keep it going. He wants us alive.'

The biplane flew on towards the hovering plane; as it got closer the sound of the radial engine filled the valley, as if shouting out its warning of death to the suspended helicopter.

'He's not going to move. Fuck you!' But Duncan's hand held Yakov firm, the plane screamed towards the helicopter, its nose in a high low-speed configuration. The helicopter disappeared from their view, blocked out by the giant rounded engine cowling of the AN-2.

Yakov waited for the crash, for the tearing shrieks of metal on metal, of the two heavy aircraft colliding in the sky.

The biplane flew on, its path unhindered by the helicopter.

'What happened? Where are they?' Yakov fought to keep control of the plane, fought to keep it steady and away from the trees.

'Bastards dropped underneath us,' shouted Duncan. 'Didn't have time to go up.'

'You're fucking crazy!' the Russian pilot replied. 'Crazy bloody Englishman.' Then he laughed and knew there was worse to come.

Bakor had shouted at his pilot to dive, not believing that the biplane would continue on its suicidal course. Whoever was flying it had nerves of steel; he would have taken them all out rather than surrender.

'Stay down!' he ordered, not wanting to lift up into the chase Hind-A. When that had passed overhead, he told the pilot to take the aircraft up, to overfly the biplane once again.

'Here he comes again,' said Yakov as Bakor's gunship hove into view, once more above and ahead of them. Once again the downdraught rocked the plane; this time it was harder to keep the plane on a steady course. The gunship got lower, the wash from its rotors stronger. It was more difficult to fly the biplane; most pilots other than Yakov would have crashed into the trees by now.

'What now? Fly up and crash into him?'

Duncan smiled, appreciated Yakov's humour. At least it meant the pilot was keeping his nerve.

'I think they're going to try to bump us,' Duncan replied as the helicopter got closer, slipped behind slightly to avoid the swirling propeller of the biplane.

As if to answer him, the helicopter dropped a few feet and hit the AN-2, caused it to shudder. Duncan swung round, saw the fear of those who were helpless in the back. As he turned forward, the helicopter jarred them again, forcing the left wing to dip. But Yakov, with instant reaction, had straightened the ailerons, levelled the plane out, but not before there was a crash and a small section of the lower wing hit an outstretched tree branch and tore nearly a foot of it away. Duncan looked out, saw the trailing wreckage of the wing. But the bird still flew; a monoplane would have crashed out of the sky with that much damage.

'Made in Russia. They don't make them like this any more.' Yakov's laughter filled the cockpit. He had the plane under control again.

'Take them this time.' Duncan looked at the pilot as he spoke. Yakov understood, the excitement of battle now coursing through his veins. He applied more power and waited for the helicopter.

A minute later it happened. The plane started to rock its wings again as the downwash of the nearing helicopter rotors had their effect.

Then came the crash, but this time the helicopter kept its position, pushing down on the biplane.

Yakov applied full power and, as the giant propeller bit into the air and the plane surged forward, he pulled the control-stick back, lifted the AN-2 up into a sharp climb and took the helicopter with it.

In the Hind-A, the pilot, realizing what was happening, applied full torque and tried to pull clear, but it was to no avail. The fast-climbing plane roared upwards, knocking the helicopter over on to its side.

Duncan looked out, saw the gunship flip on to its back and crash into the trees. As its fuel-tanks exploded, a ball of fire engulfed the trees that were crushed under its fall.

The biplane levelled off a hundred feet above the trees and settled into a steady course. Unknown to its pilots and passengers, the second Hind-A, which had seen all that took place, lifted up into the clear sky behind them. The pilot, having seen the destruction of his commander and comrades, flicked the toggle on his column and prepared to fire his four-barrelled Gatling-type 12.7-millimetre machine-gun at the biplane, prepared to take his revenge for his fallen friends and blow the AN-2 out of the sky. The pilot followed the biplane, made sure of his aim before pressing the button. So intent was he on the kill that he never saw the Mig fighter streaking towards him.

The first Mikoyan Mig-31, code-named Foxhound, fired its air-to-air Aphid missile, at a range of only a thousand metres, straight at the Hind-A. The missile, released from its underwing mount, streaked its message of death at the gunship and exploded just below the spinning rotor-mount and sheared the fuselage from its only method of flight. As the rotors spun helplessly into the air, the fuselage fell to the forest, and disintegrated in the trees like its sister ship only a few moments before. Its debris and the remains of its occupants slithered to the forest floor.

The second Foxhound, two miles behind the first, saw there were no available targets and peeled to the left, following his leader back to their base some five hundred miles to the north. The two 1,500-miles-per-hour planes climbed rapidly to fifty-five thousand feet, the low-level run having consumed their fuel at a remarkably thirsty rate.

'Mission complete.' The lead pilot called his radar controller over the radio, when he had settled into his high-level cruise two minutes later, having climbed at over fifty thousand feet a minute. 'Returning to base.'

The two Havoks saw the flames of the explosions in the distance, saw them clearly in the sunlight.

The lead gunship turned towards the flames, the second craft taking up a formation position behind him. They flew on, their instructions clear. They were to destroy any craft in the area; no one was to escape.

In the Sverdlovsk control-room, the KGB officer watched the fast moving blips that told him high-speed jet fighters had approached the area and were now departing to the north, their mission apparently complete. He still had an open line to Irbit, and he reported the facts as he saw them to his commander. Then he saw the blip of a slow-moving aircraft appear on the screen; the AN-2 had climbed above a thousand feet and was now in radar contact. He saw the two Havok gunships racing towards the biplane. They had obviously made contact. When he finished telling the commander, the line went dead. He hung up his receiver and went back to watch the screen.

The Irbit base commander contacted Vashinov and gave him his report. The KGB general listened quietly; he knew there was no point in shouting, in losing his control.

When the commander had finished, Vashinov knew he had no choice. His orders were simple. 'You know what to do. Don't let me down this time.'

The watchers in Moscow saw the Havoks closing in on the biplane.

The supervisor was on the phone. 'The Migs are returning to their base, Comrade President. They will not be able to return to the area in time. The other aircraft are KGB Havok helicopters. I have confirmation of that from the air-traffic centre in Sverdlovsk. There is a KGB officer with them, monitoring progress.' He listened for a moment before continuing. 'No, I do not know if their intentions are hostile. They are only minutes away. I will report as soon as I have confirmation of their actions.'

He put down the phone and went back to the screen, looked down, over the watcher's shoulder. The picture on the screen was now on the close-up footprint. He saw the satellite picture of the slow-moving biplane, now heading south-west, back to Sverdlovsk.

It was a crazy game, he thought. They didn't even know if the family was on board. A game of assumptions, played with life and death as the only conclusion.

It all depended on the Havoks. A few minutes more would determine if their intentions were friendly.

As the biplane flew steadily towards Sverdlovsk, those in the rear laughed and were joyous because of their escape.

They had known nothing of the incidents behind them, had not seen the Mig Foxhound shoot down the second Hind-A, had not even been aware of its existence. They had heard an explosion, but had presumed it to be a secondary blast from Bakor's downed gunship.

Duncan turned to his left, saw the shadow of the Havok blot out the sun as it steadied alongside, its grey-black fuselage and hung armaments menacing. As he turned to Yakov, he saw the second Havok, on the left-hand side of the plane, take up a similar position to the first.

The two men in the cockpit looked at each other. Was this the start of another play? In the back, as Myeloski,

Vera and the family became aware of their escorts, a silence descended, fear once more became the currency.

'Comrades, we are here to escort you to Sverdlovsk.'

The voice, speaking in Russian, crackled over the loudspeaker. Duncan heard Myeloski clap his hands in joy, turned and saw Vera's face relax with relief, saw her smile break out as she caught his eye. Victor and Anna watched him anxiously. They had not understood the transmission.

'Will you confirm you have the hostages on board?'

Yakov turned to Duncan for his response; the Englishman nodded, it was too late to deny anything. If they were to be knocked out of the sky, then the helicopters would do it, whatever their reply. At least, on this 133.77 frequency, others would know that the family had been rescued. He heard Yakov confirm that the family were on board.

He turned back to Oldenburg; his mission had been a success.

'We're going home.'

The biplane followed its escort back to Sverdlovsk; the Havoks flew slightly ahead, their instructions from the base commander quite clear.

Make sure you get them back. Forget your other orders. They never were. Just get them safely home.

In Houston, the watcher decided things were not as they should be. He picked up the phone and called his supervisor.

'Got a problem. That Englishman in Russia, he ain't moved for nearly twelve hours. Either he's dead, or he's gone and dumped that transmitter on us. I don't know what's going on, but maybe we should do something about it.'

In Moscow, the screens went blank, the watchers put on their hats and coats and went home.

Above them, the stand-by satellite camera had been stood down; the other, now on its biggest footprint, scanned the weather patterns for transmission to the weather stations below. It showed cloud movements, rainfall and even a small tornado that was building up off the Soviet Union's eastern seaboard, just off the city of Magadan.

The technicians at the National Weather Bureau were elated; they had been trying to trace the fault for days. As soon as the transmissions were picked up, they called the television stations.

That night viewers of Soviet television would see the satellite pictures broadcast after the news, as part of the weather programme.

They had missed the satellite pictures, many phone calls and letters of complaint had been received; they would be pleased to know that normal service was being resumed.

'Trouble with satellites,' said the weather announcer to his audience that night, 'is that they always break down when you need them most.'

12

LANDED

Hotel Amerika
Sverdlovsk
2 p.m.

Yashkin had arrived at the Hotel Amerika ten minutes after the AN-2 was picked up by the Havok gunships. It was then 11.30 a.m., half an hour after the brigands' final deadline.

He was taken to the library, where an exuberant Vashinov gave him a warm greeting, wrapped his arms round him in a traditional Russian welcome, and told him the hostages were safe, were on their way back.

'Now, what is so important that the president has sent you personally to pass on his message to me?' Vashinov smiled as he spoke, watched the little turd squirm.

Yashkin saw the arrogance in the general's eyes, saw him mocking him. With the family safe, his instructions were unnecessary. They had been to take command of the operation, to commandeer all the KGB forces under the president's banner and to make sure that the president, by phone from Moscow, could control the operation. It had been the fog that delayed his arrival.

'It was a message of support,' he lied, 'to let you know that the president was behind you.'

'He could have told me that on the phone.' Vashinov's dismissive answer mocked Yashkin, and the policeman saw the open grin on the man's face.

'He also felt, with Captain Myeloski out in the field, that any help of a police nature would benefit the operation. I was here to advise where necessary, Comrade General.'

'Well, it wasn't necessary. And when I see the president, I shall tell him of your support.'

Vashinov called his assistant into the room and told him to look after the policeman, make sure he had anything he wanted. The interview was obviously at an end. It was a curt dismissal, and Yashkin had no alternative but to withdraw.

The second floor of the hotel had been prepared for the family, and the president's plane made ready to take them back to Moscow.

Vashinov had then driven to the airport to meet the Oldenburgs. He had introduced himself, congratulated Victor on his grasp of the Russian language, and then travelled back to the Hotel Amerika with the family in the Zil limousine. When they arrived, he had taken them up to their rooms and made sure they were comfortable. A direct telephone line had already been prepared so that Oldenburg could phone abroad. Vashinov left the family. If any calls were made, he would soon have a transcript of the conversation. Some habits never died.

He had been concerned about Vera and grew even more anxious when he saw her with the Englishman. But he had shown a warm front, embraced them all and congratulated them on a job well done. The Englishman's firm gaze rattled him; he knew he would have to deal with that situation before Duncan turned on him. The matter was further exacerbated by Vera, who clung to the Englishman's side – something Duncan never attempted to discourage.

While these social activities were taking place, the camp at Irbit was rapidly evacuated, the troops and their equipment airlifted out in the Hook transporters. By the time the hostages had arrived at the hotel, anyone visiting the former KGB training-base would have found it deserted, save for the few caretakers who lived and worked there.

The children had been bathed, fed and put to bed when Duncan went up to see the family. He sat with Victor and Anna. They were eating, getting used to the simple culinary offerings of the Hotel Amerika. He took them through the recent events, from their capture up to their rescue. When he had finished, as they drank their tea, the couple were silent, absorbing what he had told them.

Victor Oldenburg was the first to speak. 'Is George Leeming all right?'

'Fine. He and the interpreter are back in Moscow, at the British embassy.'

'And the press don't know why we're here?'

'They don't even know you were kidnapped. The Russians can still keep the lid on things when they have to.'

'I'm sorry I couldn't tell you.'

'No matter.'

'It does matter. Anna wanted to. She said you had a right to know, especially after all we'd been through in the Falklands.'

Duncan shrugged. 'It's past now. The plan now is to get you back to Moscow, when you're ready to travel, and then, after meeting the president, fly you all back together to the UK.'

Anna, exhausted after her ordeal, soon excused herself and retired. When she had gone, Victor turned to his old friend, his eyes probing.

'What didn't you tell me in front of her?'

Duncan decided not to share his deepest thoughts with Victor. 'Not a lot.'

'Who were the people who kidnapped us first? I saw them being killed, Mark. We all did. Just gunned down in front of us. Who on earth were they?'

'I don't know,' he lied. 'Truthfully.'

He saw Victor didn't believe him, but their trust ran deeper than most. He sat in silence, his lie a wall between them.

'We've known each other a long time. I trust you as I know you trust me. I accept there is a reason for you not telling me what you know or believe to be the truth. I'm prepared to leave well alone, to wait until you feel you can tell me.'

Duncan said nothing; it was best left that way. He changed the subject, decided to tell him about Myeloski, how the policeman had been the prime mover in following the trail, in finding the kidnapped family. He said he would be grateful if Victor could meet Myeloski, spend a little time privately with him after he had rested.

'No. Let me meet him now. It's the least I can do,' replied Oldenburg. He had not spoken to the policeman after they had landed, had not had time to thank him or the pilot as he would have wished to do.

A KGB aide was despatched to find the policeman; Duncan correctly guessed that he would be in the restaurant downstairs. They chatted generally as they waited.

Myeloski knocked on the door some five minutes later and entered the room. Yakov the pilot was with him, standing in the background, and Duncan beckoned him also to enter.

The four of them spent the next half-hour discussing the events of the past few days. It was surprising how quickly events had moved. It was a relaxing time, and Duncan could see Victor Oldenburg winding down, coming back from his terrible ordeal.

374

Outside the doors to the rooms, six armed policemen were on duty. This time there would be no mistake.

Vera, left on her own, went quietly to her room to wait for Duncan. There was a KGB officer outside her door; he had been told to find her and take her to Vashinov.

She followed behind him, trying to control the fear and trepidation she felt, knowing that she would be the butt of his fury. She had considered ignoring the officer and waiting for Duncan, but that would have been futile; this was Vashinov's kingdom, these were his soldiers.

The officer opened a door into Vashinov's living-area and let her in, closing the door behind her. She stood there, knowing he would soon come to see her.

The general, not realizing that Vera was in the adjoining room, the one used for private meetings, waited on the phone for the president. The call had only just come through; he listened as he heard the clicks as the operator put him through.

'Comrade General?' The president came on; the formal greeting warned him that all was not well.

'Yes, Comrade President.' Vashinov kept his response formal.

'Are things well there?'

'Yes. The family is settled; they are to fly back tomorrow morning. In your personal jet.' He knew that would irritate the president; it was always referred to as the Politburo transport, never as his personal plane.

The president ignored the barb. 'I have spoken to Grigory Marshka.' Vashinov said nothing, waited for him to continue. 'He has told me of the arrangement between the two of you.'

Vashinov realized the president was guarded, that he feared the line might be bugged. 'Arrangement?' he asked.

'We both know what I'm talking about,' came the quick reply.

'I can only presume to understand.' Of course he understood. Marshka had told the president of the plot, the old man's idea in the first place. At least they couldn't prove that he had set out to destroy the hostages and then blame the two of them for it.

'Grigory Mikhailovich is to make a statement on your respective actions at a specially convened Politburo meeting to be held an hour from now.'

Vashinov could see that they were moving fast, cutting him out whilst he was stuck in this awful hotel. 'As a member of the Politburo, shouldn't I be given the opportunity to be present, especially as it would seem to concern me more than others?'

'I was hoping to announce your resignation at the meeting.'

The words exploded softly. Vashinov paused before replying. 'And Marshka?'

'His has already been accepted by me personally. It will also be announced.'

'After his statement?'

'After his statement.'

'Will he also tell them of the Beria Archives?' Vashinov heard the gasp at the other end, knew his words had struck home, that the president knew of the Archives. Vashinov had learnt that and many other secrets of the Stalin Room when he had threatened a librarian many years ago with the death of his son as a subversive element. Marshka was not the only member of the Politburo who understood that knowledge was power. 'If he is to make a statement, then he should reveal all. If he does not, then I will. A public statement by me would cause the press some small excitement.' He grinned; it would blow their minds more likely.

'What archives?' The president played for time, tried to think through the situation.

'We both know what I'm talking about. I am nearer

the secret than you are. Now may be the time to seek out history, really to spread the message of *glasnost*.'

'Enough. Say no more.'

'Is Grigory Mikhailovich still to make his statement?'

'I shall come back to you.'

'No time. Make up your mind now, or I shall arrange my press conference.'

There was a long silence, broken only by his shallow breathing, before the president answered. 'We will hold back on any statement until you have returned and we can discuss the matter more fully.'

'Thank you, Comrade President. I shall arrange my own transport and return after the family.'

He hung up on his leader; it was Vashinov who terminated the discussion. He grinned. He knew that the president would be ringing Marshka, would be turning to the old man. He had already ordered one of the Havok helicopters to remain at Sverdlovsk airport; he would travel back in one of his own KGB aircraft. The others were all on their way home, back to their Moscow base.

He turned and went back into the lounge, stopped, startled by Vera's presence. He had not expected anyone to be there. He came into the room, towards her.

'How long have you been here?' he asked angrily.

'I only just . . . I was told to come in.'

He lashed out at her, hit her across her face, knocking her to the floor. She put her hand up to protect herself, but he walked away, into the middle of the room.

'Get up.'

She pushed herself up and came slowly towards him.

'Where's your English bastard?'

'Downstairs.'

'With his bloody Romanovs. No time for you now, eh? Not fucking good enough. We all know where a whore's place is.'

She didn't answer. She knew what he said could well be true. But her growing love and need for Duncan

377

submerged her fears. Hope always answered the unanswered questions.

'And what happens when he's gone back to that shitty little island of his? When all you have left is me? Eh? What happens then, whore?'

He saw that his words had little effect on her. But he would wait his time. He had brought her up here for his pleasure, but the mood wasn't on him; she irritated him with her whining ways. He would deal with her later, when he had the time.

'Get out. Go back to your Englishman.' She turned towards the door, to leave the room. 'Remember, I haven't finished with you. Soon, when all this is over, you'll have me to answer to. Just us, precious. Just you and me.'

She went through the door and fled to her room. She knew all about Vashinov's ways; this time she would be lucky to escape with her life once Duncan had gone.

Yashkin was waiting for Myeloski when he returned to the lobby; it was the first real chance they had had to speak since the triumphant return of the kidnap group.

They went to Myeloski's room where Yashkin was given a full report by his subordinate.

He grew more concerned as Myeloski, now not hampered by a possible bugged telephone, went through his recent travels in greater detail. When he had concluded, Yashkin asked the obvious question.

'Are you sure it was the KGB?'

'Yes.'

'Why would they be involved?'

'No idea. The answer's in Moscow.'

'In the Kremlin? No.' The disbelief in Yashkin's voice was genuine.

'All I know is that it was a highly organized operation, carried out on a large scale. It may have been covert, but it involved a lot of people.'

'The girl, was she a KGB plant?' Yashkin referred to Vera.

'I don't know.' He remembered the bruises Vashinov had inflicted on her, had heard the story of the House of Ipatyev from Duncan. 'Probably not.'

'And she heard Vashinov say that he would kill the hostages?'

'That is how she understood it.'

'What the hell's going on, Ahmed Alekseevich?'

'You tell *me*. You're in touch with the bigwigs.'

Yashkin shook his head, had no answer for Myeloski.

He decided to confront Vashinov. It was the only way he could further his investigation. He didn't mention that to Myeloski. After all, his orders had been to report directly to the president. Despite his doubt, Yashkin's sense of duty overcame all.

Marshka's dacha
Outside Moscow
2 p.m.

The president's telephone-call had unsettled the old man; he had no idea that Vashinov knew of the Beria Archives.

'Where now, Uncle?' he had been asked. He couldn't answer and begged time to consider.

He looked out of the window, out at the late summer. It had always been a time he loved, when the colours of autumn started to change the face of the countryside, when nature flaunted its face at all around. For all the revolutions, for all the wars, for all the weapons, for all the industrial might, nature dismissed it all and just went about her business as she had for millions of years.

He had lived at the pretty wooden-roofed dacha for over thirty years; it was a small one by Politburo

379

standards, but one that had never attracted any envy, and it had been part of his instinct for survival.

He also knew that he was past the autumn of his own life. He knew he could not survive much longer; even the president couldn't save him now. He would be the forgotten man, another ghost of the past, joining Stalin and Beria and Trotsky and all the others. Even Lenin. He wondered if there was a God, if there was a spirit.

He chuckled. Lenin would have got a shock when he came face to face with his Maker. How would he have talked his way out of that one?

He held up his hands, turned them in front of his face and looked at their aged and gnarled shape.

Well, Father, see the hands of a murderer. Not quite Stalin or Beria, but still deep in the blood of thousands who were killed in the revolution. Did I really do these things in the name of Mother Russia, really for a new fair society? Or was it simply for my own survival? I have done things in my life you would not believe me capable of. Maybe you saw it, from up there, maybe all you really felt was shame that I was your son.

I must dip my hands again, Father. But this time it is not for survival. This time it is to help make your Russia whole once again.

He swivelled in his wheelchair and went to the phone. When his assistant had connected him to the KGB headquarters in Dzerzhinsky Square, he issued his orders.

There were still many who obeyed him, feared him and the files that he had carefully nurtured over the years.

The power of the man still lived on.

The Oldenburgs were all asleep, and Vashinov was frustrated. He hated waiting for the game to continue. Vera kept crossing his mind; he needed relief, needed sex.

He once again sent down for her, told the guard to bring her up whoever she was with.

She had been with Duncan, had sat with him in her small hotel room and listened to him speak of England and his family and of Russia. She said little, only wanted to hear his voice, understand the man through his words. She had not told him of the overheard conversation in Vashinov's rooms and did not want him to know she had been there.

The guard had come and insisted that she accompany him to the general's quarters. Duncan had urged her to stay, but she knew she had little choice, said there was nothing to fear and that she would return soon.

'I'll be OK,' she said, trying to ease the concern and distress she saw in his face. 'Nothing'll happen.' She hated the untruth, but knew why she had been summoned.

Vashinov was in his dressing-gown, waiting for her, pacing impatiently up and down the room.

He gave her a drink, Japanese Scotch with lemonade; it was a drink she had always liked. She sat in the small armchair, waiting for his next move, waiting for him to assert his sexuality. As he walked in front of her, he told her how sorry he was, how much she mattered to him, how they could start again.

She didn't believe him, knew that his words were designed to soften her up, make her warm to him. He saw she hadn't touched her drink, urged her to finish it as he brought the bottle to her. He stood in front of her, laughed, then pulled open his robe. She saw his hardness, saw him reach down with his free hand and stroke it. It grew thicker as he stretched the skin; he moved his body and tensed his thighs as he masturbated in front of her. When it was at its biggest, when he felt he might come over her face, he thrust it towards her, towards her lips.

There was a knock on the door.

He stepped back, angry at the interruption. 'Who is it?' he shouted.

'Colonel Yashkin,' came the muted reply.

'I'll call you later.'

'I have to see you now.'

Vashinov growled his annoyance; the man was over-stepping the mark. He closed his robe and told Vera to go into the next room, handing her the bottle to take with her. When she had left he answered the door, let Yashkin in. The policeman was surprised to see him in a robe this early in the evening.

'It'd better be important,' Vashinov growled, letting the robe fall open so that the policeman could see the size of his erection.

'It is, Comrade General,' Yashkin answered, fighting to keep his eyes on the general's face and ignore the hugeness of the man that was so openly displayed.

'Come in, then.' Vashinov led Yashkin into the room, beckoned him to sit in the chair Vera had just vacated.

'Well?'

'There are disturbing elements emerging about this morning's rescue-attempts. I have been instructed by the president to bring them to your attention.' Yashkin lied, but was safe in the knowledge that he had the Kremlin's authority to investigate the matter further.

'What disturbing elements?'

'That the KGB were under instructions to seek and destroy the hostages after the ransom-exchange had been made.'

Vashinov's hardness between his legs disappeared, something not unnoticed by the policeman. 'Under whose instructions?' asked Vashinov, protectively pulling the robe around his body.

'I was hoping you would help me resolve that.'

'Sounds pretty wild to me. Even in this age of rumours.'

'I believe there was a KGB unit based at Irbit.' He had discovered that while he was mixing with some of the KGB administrative officers in the bar, local officers who had been drafted in to help keep order at the hotel, not trained to keep their mouths shut as well as their Moscow counterparts. He had also heard that combat troops were stationed at the base. But that was all he had picked up; his policeman's instincts had now taken over.

'Irbit used to be one of our training-camps. Now closed. I think we keep a small staff there. Do you always overstep your authority? KGB matters should not concern you.'

'I was told by the president to leave no stone unturned.'

'Does he know of your suspicions? Have you spoken to him?'

That was when Yashkin make his first mistake. 'No, Comrade General.'

'Or anyone else?'

'No.' That was his second and last mistake.

Vashinov grinned; it unsettled the policeman. 'What else do you suspect?'

'That the base had combat troops stationed there.'

'Absolutely true.'

Yashkin stopped, surprised at the man's frankness.

Vashinov continued, enjoying his moment. 'It was my intention to destroy the brigands. I could only do that with my own troops. You see that, don't you?'

'Yes.' Yashkin was pleased. So that was the line he was going to take.

'You believe it, of course?'

'Yes, Comrade General.'

'Then, you're a fool.' Vashinov laughed; the policeman was stung by the remark. He saw the glint in Vashinov's eyes, saw the boastful mockery and decided to keep quiet. 'You are right, Colonel. There was a plot. To kill the hostages. Do you know why?'

'No.' Yashkin looked round the room; he realized he was in danger.

'Then, I shall tell you.' As Vashinov spoke, he walked to his tunic that hung over the back of a chair, leant over and took out an automatic revolver. He pointed it at Yashkin, smiled chillingly as he did. 'I would stay seated, Colonel. If you move, I shall have no hesitation in despatching you to meet your ancestors.'

He came and sat opposite Yashkin, his legs splayed as he straddled a chair, his robe falling open and displaying his nakedness once again, the revolver now carelessly held and swinging, barrel pointed down, in his right hand.

'Our brave leader and some of his cronies have led Russia a merry dance. We have lost our direction, have seen the Eastern Bloc crumble, have even allowed Germany to be reunified. You'd think we would have learnt our lesson. I mean, they tried to invade us twice in the last eighty years. What's to stop them doing it again? In this stupid quest for freedom and democracy, all we have to look forward to is chaos and despair. The old ways may have been harsh, but at least they fed the people.'

'All social change causes pain. Even the revolution did that.'

'A philosopher as well as a policeman.' Vashinov was in no mood for an open discussion; his sarcasm kept Yashkin silent.

'The death of the hostages would have been blamed on the brigands. It would have created a sensation;

people would have accused the president of causing their deaths by his crazy scheme. In the turmoil, in our national shame, a new order would have arisen. In time, when we had quelled the strikes and the riots and all the nationalists, the Soviet Union would have been great – as it should always be. Yes, we were going to kill the hostages. Your bloody policeman and his little English friend put paid to that, didn't they?'

'That's what Sta—' Yashkin stopped, regretted his interruption.

'Go on.'

'It was nothing, Comrade General.'

'That's what Stalin was doing. Did I finish it correctly?'

Yashkin nodded. Vashinov burst into laughter.

'Your president is no different from Stalin. He also has secrets that are terrible in their knowledge. Let me tell you about one of them. About the Beria Archives. You know who Beria was, of course.'

Yashkin nodded. All Russians knew of Stalin's infamous chief of secret police, the High Executioner who became Minister of the Interior and a member of the Politburo.

'Did you ever hear of Vyshinsky?' continued Vashinov.

Yashkin shook his head; it was not a name he was familiar with.

'Stalin's chief prosecutor. The courtroom lawyer, Beria's lapdog, who sentenced millions through his courts to be executed by the secret police. Nearly thirty million Russians died in the purges, in just ten years. Old Joe Stalin made Hitler look like a social worker, eh? He was a funny chap. Worked till four in the morning. So all the senior officials did the same, to impress him. Trouble was they had to be in again by nine, while he, the wily old fox, slept till twelve.' Vashinov laughed at his own joke, then turned his head and looked directly at Yashkin; the hawk watched its prey.

'So, Mr Policeman, what has old Beria, long since forgotten, executed by a bullet to the head, what's he got to do with the predicament we now find ourselves in?

'During the investigations, when Beria's courts were here, in Siberia – the famous "enemies of the people" trials – Vyshinsky stumbled on a half-mad peasant farmer. This kulak, from a region west of here, told them the amazing story.

'That his father had been a Bolshevik, not a Russian but an Austro-German. He had fucked this kulak's mother, and as soon as she was pregnant shot back to Moscow where he was never heard of again. But he had been one of the guards at the house where the tsar and his family were executed. In his short liaison with the kulak's mother, he had told her of the murders, told her secrets he had sworn never to tell.

'All that terrible knowledge. It must have haunted the simple peasant woman, pregnant, in fear for her life for the secrets she knew. No wonder her son was born half-mad. When he was old enough, she told him what she knew; and he, not knowing the enormity of his information, simply told everyone. But no one believed him; he was mad anyway. After his mother died, he worked on farms, travelled from town to town, one of life's victims.

'But the secret police took him seriously; in those days of suspicion and intrigue, everything was taken seriously. Vyshinsky's report was sent to Beria. Beria himself came to Sverdlovsk and personally interrogated the kulak. You know what he found? That somehow, in the terrible ravages of time, in the aftermath of the revolution, the truth of the murders had been locked away, never to be revealed to anyone. It was an awful situation, one that could never be disclosed. The legacy of the Romanovs lived on.

'Beria returned to Moscow and told Stalin. They decided that the truth must remain as rumour, that what they had found must be left to fester and rot where it was. The world was mad enough without letting the inmates out of the asylum.

'The kulak was killed, immediately executed as an enemy of the people, the village he was born in destroyed; over six hundred villagers were also tried and murdered, then buried in mass graves. It caused no alarm; communities were being wiped out every day in the thirties and forties.

'So the secret was kept, all the papers of the investigation taken back to Moscow and buried in the confidential vaults of the Kremlin. You'd think they would've destroyed the documents, eh? No, not us Russians. Save everything, file it away – the disease of the civil service. And there you have it. The Beria Archives.'

Yashkin realized Vashinov had finished and would say no more. 'What did the kulak say? What did they find that was so terrible?'

'You're a policeman. That's up to you to find out.'

Vashinov suddenly stood up, bored with the game. 'Time for you to go, little poodle. Back to your master.'

Yashkin stood up nervously; the big man intimidated him. As he turned and walked to the door, he heard Vashinov's words behind him.

'It's frustrating, when a policeman has all the clues, knows he's on to the biggest case of his career, and won't be able to do anything about it.'

It was the last thing he ever heard. Yashkin half-turned, not knowing what Vashinov meant. But the steel butt of the automatic revolver crushed his skull, smashed into the bone, split his head open. He fell to the ground, blindly and helplessly reaching out towards Vashinov. But Yashkin was a frail man and he was dead before he finally slumped on the floor next to Vashinov's feet.

The general knelt down and wiped his gun-handle clean on the dead man's clothes, wiped off the blood and flesh and splinters of bone. As he stood up, he heard Vera gasp behind him; she had come to look into the room, had heard the loud grunt from the policeman as he died.

'Shut up.' Vashinov's voice, deadly in its effect, stunned her into silence. She stepped back, out of sight. She remembered when he had killed before, only a few months earlier, when in the heat of sex he had strangled a boy prostitute as he ejaculated over his chest.

She heard Vashinov go to the phone, heard him order one of his trusted officers upstairs. A few moments later there was a knock on the door, and Vashinov let his subordinate into the room.

'I want him taken away. Destroy the body, bury it in the tundra.' She heard Vashinov deliver his orders and knew they would be obeyed instantly. 'If anyone asks, he has not been seen. He left the hotel half an hour ago. Get one of our Moscow guards to verify it. Is the base at Irbit clear?'

'Yes, Comrade General.'

'And the helicopters?'

'All returned to Moscow. Apart from the one waiting at the airport for you.'

She heard nothing for a moment, and then Vashinov appeared, the officer by his side.

'Take her to her room. Under arrest. No one is to see her. No one, unless you have my express authority.'

He stood back as the officer came forward, took her roughly by the arm.

Vashinov grinned. 'The end of the road, Princess. Time to say good night.'

13

GOING HOME

Hotel Amerika
Sverdlovsk
6 a.m.

He had sat up all night, sat on the end of his bed catnapping, deep in his own thoughts. There had been the short nightmares, more ugly dreams than nightmares. The family were safe, but the tension continued. In the past, when he had completed a successful mission, he had had the ability to switch off immediately, to return and live a normal life. This time it was different, the danger not passed.

But it was a different danger, not for others, but for him. He knew he must act soon, must not let the moment pass. It was what he wanted, a time to take stock and search for a future.

He had not waited for Vera after she had been summoned to see Vashinov, but had sought out Myeloski. The policeman and Yakov had been in the bar, with Morrison. They were regaling him with the story of the forest rescue when Duncan joined them.

They had all been drinking heavily, and they sat and chatted exuberantly at a corner table by the window, away from the local police and KGB officers.

Myeloski noticed Duncan's still mood, but he didn't question him about it, presumed it was his reaction to the aftermath of the rescue. They had both lived at a frantic pace, both undergone pressures that were not part of everyday life. Except that wasn't so in the Englishman's case. Myeloski recalled Duncan's background; he had been in his element. As Yakov went on about the merits of the AN-2 and how it had continued to fly with part of its lower wing torn away, Myeloski watched the Englishman, nodding and smiling, but not really taking part in the chatter, his beer untouched by his side. Duncan caught the policeman looking at him, smiling warmly in his direction. But the eyes told all. Duncan was worried.

The only time Duncan spoke was to Morrison. Yakov and Myeloski had gone to the toilet. They saw Duncan huddled with Morrison when they returned, and there was a conspiratorial attitude in the way the two had their heads inclined. They had broken apart when the others reached the table and had not mentioned their conversation.

Myeloski was also concerned about Yashkin. His superior officer had disappeared, gone walkabout without informing him. He presumed that it was on orders from Moscow, that Yashkin had his own duties to execute.

They had all stayed there till nearly midnight, with the exception of Duncan, who twice left the group to go elsewhere. Each time he returned, the look of concern had increased; whatever was troubling him had not been resolved.

Duncan had, in fact, gone to see if Vera had returned to her room. The first time his knock was unanswered, he knew she was still with Vashinov but could take no

390

further action. His first responsibility was to the Olden-burgs, and there was nothing he would do to jeopardize that. Arguing with the KGB over jealous loves was not what he had been sent out here to do.

His second visit had a more sinister result. There were two armed guards outside her bedroom, both KGB and both with Kalashnikovs strapped over their shoulders. He had advanced down the corridor, tried to knock on the door, when one of the guards barred his way with the gun.

'I just want to see her.'

The guard shook his head. 'Not without the general's permission.'

'Vera!' Duncan stood his ground, shouted through the door.

The second guard stepped forward, positioned himself beside Duncan. The Englishman felt the machine-gun's muzzle in his side. 'Are you all right, Vera?' he called again and felt the barrel pushed harder into his side.

'I'm OK.' Vera's voice, muffled, answered him through the door.

'Satisfied? Now fuck off,' said the first guard.

Duncan turned sharply and walked down the corridor, down the stairs and back to the bar. He knew a death sentence hung over Vera's head.

The small group broke up at midnight. Yakov and Morrison, now three sheets to the wind, were going on to the Club Panther. Myeloski, who had looked forward to a night out, decided he would stay in the hotel; the Englishman could need his support later on. He was also concerned that Yashkin had not returned. Although Yashkin was his superior officer, they were good friends, and the older man had helped Myeloski over the traumas of a broken marriage.

Duncan had gone to his room, having first checked Vera's floor and seen the same two guards were on duty. They had laughed at him; one had barked like a dog, signifying that he was after a bitch on heat. Myeloski had followed him up, after checking at the desk to see if Yashkin had returned, and knocked on his door. Duncan had answered it, but not opened it fully, not wanting the policeman to come in.

'Everything all right?' asked Myeloski.

'Fine.'

'So you're off tomorrow? With your people.'

'At seven. The embassy has sent two senior officials down. They should be arriving in the next hour. *The* official escort.' He emphasized the 'the', laughed at his joke. 'Now the difficult bit's over, that's when the worms come out to play.'

'And Vera?'

'Back to her duties.'

'I'm sorry.'

'These things happen.'

Before Duncan had finished his sentence, Myeloski's intuition told him that the thing wasn't over. The Englishman was about to take matters into his own hands, and there was nothing the policeman could do about it.

'See you in the morning,' he said.

'Good night, Ahmed Alekseevich.'

Myeloski nodded and turned to go.

'Listen . . .' Duncan spoke softly to catch Myeloski's attention.

The policeman swung back, saw the look of warmth and friendship on Duncan's face.

'All the help . . . it was fantastic. We all owe you a great deal. Especially me. I just wanted you to know that. Whatever else, I hope it made us friends.' The two men were still; they understood he spoke for both of them.

Duncan closed the door, and Myeloski went to his bed. He knew it was the girl, but there was nothing he could do to help. Crazy fucking Englishman. Crazy fucking Vashinov. Crazy fucking world.

Duncan catnapped through the night, rested without falling into a deep sleep in case there was any further trouble.

Now, after his troublesome night, he was ready to pull his life into shape. He looked at his watch, swung his legs off the bed and went to wake up the family.

When he had left them with their breakfast, sorting out the children, he went down to the lobby. The two officials from the Moscow embassy were there, having had no more than two hours' sleep since they left the capital. He introduced himself and confirmed that the arrangements were complete. They would leave the hotel at seven, drive to the airport and return to Moscow in the president's jet.

'I shall find my own way back,' he announced to the surprised diplomats.

'You're supposed to be returning with us,' one of them replied.

'I can't. I'm a serving officer in the SAS. I spend most of my time operating under cover in Northern Ireland. The last thing I want is to go public. My instructions are to find my own way back, away from the official party.'

The diplomats believed his lie. Duncan added that he would bring the family down by seven, then returned upstairs to help Victor and Anna prepare for the journey.

Vashinov was there to greet them when they descended the steps into the lobby at seven o'clock. He introduced them to the British diplomats and then led them to the big Zil parked outside.

Duncan stayed back; he had already said his goodbyes to the family in their rooms, had explained why he was not travelling with them. Victor Oldenburg had taken his hand, held it warmly and thanked him; then, because he was his friend, had embraced him. It was a warm moment, one they would both remember.

'See you in London.'

Duncan hadn't replied, had simply nodded and then led the family downstairs.

Myeloski waited by the Zil. He would also be returning to Moscow later. He was surprised that Morrison had not appeared; the Club Panther owner was not the sort who would miss a big occasion like this. He was also deeply worried about Yashkin, who was still missing. When the Oldenburgs had reached the car, they had made a special point of approaching Myeloski and Yakov. The two of them had shaken hands with the couple and said their goodbyes in the street.

It was an impressive scene in an already crowded street. A large formation of official cars and police motorcycle outriders waited to escort the party to the airport. Passers-by, many on their way to work, stopped to gawp at the proceedings. In a short time, a sizeable crowd of a few hundred, curious in their intent, packed the pavements and surrounded the official party. Myeloski looked round and saw that Duncan was also missing. Where had the Englishman got to now?

Duncan had reached the third floor before the family and their escort had even crossed the pavement to the Zil.

As he had hoped, the two guards were at the end of the corridor, attracted by the activity and commotion from the street below. They had opened the window and were craning to get a better view. Duncan came up behind them, the big Coonan Magnum in his hand.

'OK, comrades. Back in you come.'

The two guards had swung round, tried to get their heads back into the building, but had clashed with each other. When they finally were clear of the window, it was too late to react. The barrel of the Coonan Magnum looked deadly. Without any further instructions, they both dropped their Kalashnikovs to the carpeted floor.

Duncan pointed at one of them, told him to pick up the guns, to hold them by the barrel end with the butts

394

pointing downwards. He then came behind them and pushed them forward, towards Vera's room.

'Knock!' he ordered one of the guards. Vera answered the door, amazed by what she saw. Duncan pushed the two guards in and closed the door behind them. He told the guard to drop the machine-guns on the floor and then told them both to kneel, facing each other, with their arms behind them.

As they bowed their heads, he brought the gun-butt down on the back of one guard's neck. As he fell forward, the other guard rose swiftly, and Duncan hit him across his chin, knocking him to the floor, next to his unconscious partner.

He saw Vera recoil, didn't know she had witnessed the death of Yashkin in a similar manner. 'Don't worry. They'll just wake up with a bad headache.'

'Why?'

'Because I'm not leaving without you. We'll go to Moscow together.'

'I can't.'

'If you stay, you're dead.'

'He won't let me go.'

'When I get you back to Moscow, to the embassy, we'll—'

She came forward, put her finger on his lips to silence him. 'He won't let go because . . . because I saw him kill a man last night.'

'What man?'

'A policeman.' As she spoke, Duncan remembered Myeloski's concern; it must have been Yashkin. 'He killed him with his own hands, just smashed his head in.'

She started to cry, and he put his arm round her.

'Then, we tell the authorities what you saw.'

'They won't believe me. Against him. The head of the KGB. Don't you realize? We'd never get the chance.'

'We got this far. For all his power.'

'I don't want you in danger. Be safe. Go home.'

He laughed. 'Danger. Bread and butter.'

He never gave her a chance to answer, just turned to the unconscious guards, bound their hands and legs with strips of the bedsheets, then gagged them loosely in such a way that they could still breathe in their unconscious state.

He put his hand to her shoulder and propelled her forward, out of the room. He locked the door behind them. They had no more than ten mintues before the guards came round, possibly twenty before they were discovered.

The excitement from the street continued. The sounds of street-bustle were muted as they floated through the open window at the end of the corridor. It meant that the motorcade had not moved off yet. He held her hand and led her to the far side of the corridor, opened a glass-panelled service-door and took her through. Duncan had already worked out his escape-route that morning, when he had gone up to help the royal family prepare. They descended the service-stairs at the back of the building and finally stopped at a solid wooden door which led into a windowless corridor between the kitchen and the restaurant.

They went into the kitchen; it was as deserted as the rest of the hotel. As they walked towards the rear exit, an old man stood up; he had been rummaging in one of the cupboards. Duncan saw his torn overalls, the flash of fear on his face, saw the loaf of black bread sticking out of the top pocket. He smiled, shook his head and walked to the exit. The old man, probably a tramp, was stocking up while the kitchen staff were outside, joining in the excitement of the royal departure.

Morrison's Datsun 240Z was parked across the road, its long snout sticking out of a side-alley.

As they crossed the street Morrison got out to greet them, waiting for them by the car door.

'Where's the car?' asked Duncan.

Morrison magnanimously indicated the Datsun, his hand sweeping back.

'But that's yours.' Duncan had expected a Lada or one of the other Russian-built vehicles.

'This'll outrun anything on the road. Maybe not in England, but here no problem.' He held up some documents. 'All that you need if you're stopped. Including a permit to travel in the west Siberian region.'

'Forged?'

'Of course.' Morrison laughed at Duncan's joke. 'By the same printer who produces the real ones. There's also a map. Go east. On Route 333.'

Duncan took the documents, held his hand out warmly to Morrison, who smiled and clasped his hand.

'Why?' asked Duncan

'Because that's how they do it in the movies. And if I keep you alive, then maybe you'll go home and get me that guitar you promised. You remember the guitar?'

'Of course.'

'A Fender?'

'A Fender. Only the best.'

Duncan climbed into the driver's seat, kept the map on his lap and threw the other documents on the rear seat as Vera got in the passenger side.

Morrison spoke to him through the open window. 'You're a salesman for the Japanese Suntory whisky company. Say that you're visiting all the clubs in the region to drum up business. All the necessary documents are in the back. Use your passport, say you're an Englishman working over here for them. It may not work, but it'll slow them down. I'm sorry, but it's all I could do in the time.'

'That's great.'

'Some food in the back, sandwiches and snacks from the club. A few bottles of whisky. Your samples. Don't drink it; it'll be good for bribes. And a full tank, with two five-gallon containers behind you. The less you have contact with people, the better. One final thing. In four hours, I shall report the car as stolen. That way I'm covered. By then, if you're lucky, you should be more than three hundred kilometres from Sverdlovsk. When they start to look for the car outside the city limits, another day could've gone by. You better go. You know the first bit of the route.'

'Thanks. The car . . . I appreciate that.'

'I needed a new one anyway. Be lucky, Mark. Both of you.' He stepped back, held his arms out. 'To love, to the memory of Jim Morrison, to wherever it leads you, and to a happy ending.'

'You're just a fucking romantic.'

Morrison laughed and waved them away.

Duncan turned the key, and the engine burst into life. He heard the roar of the perfectly tuned engine, remembered it from the night they had first gone to the House of Ipatyev. He gave Morrison one final smile, then slipped her into gear and pulled out into the road, turning right to avoid the small crowd that was still waiting for the motorcade to leave.

He looked in his rearview mirror. Morrison was already gone, the road deserted apart from one or two parked cars.

Myeloski saw Morrison coming through the hotel lobby and out on to the front steps. The motorcade, after a seemingly interminable wait, was now starting to move, the police outriders clearing a way through the crowd with their sirens in full peal. Myeloski pushed his way to the steps, to Morrison.

'Where've you been?' he asked the club-owner.

'Trying to get here. I've had to leave my car a few streets back.' Morrison was shouting to be heard above the cacophony of cheering crowds and wailing sirens. 'Shit, I didn't want to miss it. I wanted to see the Englishman again, before he left. Is he with them?'

'No.'

'What do you mean, no?'

'He didn't go with them.'

'Where is he?'

'I don't know. Just that he didn't go.'

'Secret service types. Live by their own rules.' He winked at Myeloski. 'Let's get a drink. Maybe he's in there.'

He turned and walked back into the hotel. Myeloski took one last look at the now fast-moving and disappearing motorcade, then followed Morrison in. He knew Duncan had started his action. Maybe after a meal and a drink things would fall into place once again and he could work out what the Englishman was up to.

Duncan drove past the House of Ipatyev as he left the city boundary. It was a painful memory for Vera, and she angled her head away from the house and looked straight ahead. The guards in front of the walled building saw the Datsun, admired its sleek racing shape as it sped past. The tinted windows blocked any of them from getting a good view of the occupants.

Past the House of Ipatyev and on the road to the north-east, they sat in silence, comfortable and safe in each other's company. Duncan smiled, remembered the scene at the end of *The Graduate*. It had been about two young lovers, one a social dropout, the other a girl who had been hurt by him but still loved him. At the end, when he has stopped her from marrying another, they catch a bus and go off together on their journey into the future. They sit together at the back of the bus, she in her wedding dress, he in casual clothes. They don't look at each other, neither speaks, both wonder about the future and what it holds for them. But in their silence there is a certainty that they both have what they want, a love sprung from nowhere and a future, however uncertain, together.

As Duncan drove, he watched her from the corner of his eye. She had that same certainty, that same sense of acceptance of her future that the actress Katherine Ross had on her face at the end of the film. Life, as they say, is just like the movies.

He followed the road, the map spread on his lap. Five kilometres out of Sverdlovsk he came to a fork in the road. The main highway, three-lane and wide, continued on to the right, signposted to Chelyabinsk and Omsk. But his decision was already made. He swung left on to the smaller road; he could see its thin two-lane tarmac ribbon leading into the forests in the distance.

The signpost read Bogdanovich and Tiumen.

'This is not the road to Moscow,' she said.

'Change of plan,' he replied.

He had, by chance and by design, come this far. There had to be a reason; he couldn't let it go when he was so near.

We're coming home, Grandfather Denknetzeyan; we're finally coming home.

Sverdlovsk Airport
9 a.m.

The Yakovlev Yak-40 climbed out of Sverdlovsk, its three Ivenchko Al-25 turbofans trailing power and sound behind it, its nose tilted up in an eight-degree climb-path as it sliced through the air at two thousand vertical feet a minute.

On the ramp, an agitated Vashinov watched the president's jet nose into the clouds, carrying the family back to Vnukovo-2, the private VIP airport outside Moscow. Although he wanted to return immediately to the Hotel Amerika, he knew he must stay there, looking skyward as if the Romanov bastard could still see him, wave as enthusiastically as any Politburo member would be expected to.

His assistant had caught him just before he had walked

through the glass door with the family towards the ramp and the aircraft parked there.

'The girl's gone,' he had whispered. 'And the Englishman.'

Vashinov felt the rage rising within him, a flush reddening his neck and his cheeks. He smiled, smiled when he wanted to shout and demand results.

'Any idea where?'

'No, Comrade General.'

'Where were the guards? On fucking holiday?' He tried to control himself, but knew he was losing the battle. His expletive was picked up by one of the British diplomats, who turned angrily towards him. Vashinov smiled back, apologetic, realized the man understood Russian.

'He knocked them out. One still hasn't come round. Then tied and gagged them.'

Vashinov turned away from the group, turned his back on them. He knew the Englishman was good; he should have taken more precautions. 'When?'

'While we were leaving the hotel.'

'Clever.'

'I've put out a description. Of them both.'

'Love's fucking folly,' Vashinov muttered to himself.

'Comrade General?'

'Nothing. Get back to the hotel. I want everyone on it. I'll come there when this lot's over. What about the policeman?'

'Myeloski?'

Vashinov nodded.

'He was in the bar at the hotel, eating and knocking back beer,' the assistant replied. 'Kept asking if anyone had seen his boss.'

'A pig, drinking at this time of the morning. If he was with us, I'd soon sort—' Vashinov stopped sharply; he smiled, the idea was so simple. 'Put out the order. If they're seen, shoot on sight. Shoot to kill.'

'He's English. It'll be difficult to explain away.'

'He's also very dangerous. He shouldn't have killed that policeman.'

The assistant looked up sharply. Vashinov grinned back, raised his eyebrows in a mocking gesture.

'Discover the body. By the time I get back. Somewhere in the hotel.'

He turned back to the royal group, who had now moved through the glass door and on to the ramp. Without looking back, he strode after them. Two minutes later, his face beaming with the satisfied smile of a man who has done his job well, he turned back to look for his assistant. He was relieved to see the man had gone.

The Kremlin
Moscow
9 a.m. (Moscow time)

The president was about to leave for Vnukovo-2 Airport when Vashinov's call came through.

As he sat at his desk, his overcoat on but unbuttoned, his hat on the table in front of him, Vashinov's words sent a chill through him that had nothing to do with the weather.

'It is my sad duty to report the death of Leonid Igorevich Yashkin, your chief of police in Moscow. His body was found in the cellars of the Hotel Amerika half an hour ago by the local police. He was buried under half a ton of coal. It is only a small storeroom; he would not have been found for weeks if we hadn't been searching the building anyway.'

'Why was the building being searched?'

'One of my operatives, a girl, Vera Kasyanova, was suspected of being in league with the brigands. She was under arrest, awaiting interrogation. While the

Oldenburgs were leaving the hotel, while all our attention was on escorting them safely to the airport, someone attacked the guards outside the girl's door, held them with a gun and then knocked them unconscious, almost killed them, and helped the girl escape. After the men were discovered, the building was searched for their assailant. It was during this that the body of Colonel Yashkin was found.'

The president was silent. The damn thing wasn't over yet. And poor Yashkin. Poor Leonid Igorevich. He had served him well, always been a good faithful friend and servant of the State. But what had he found, what secrets had he uncovered that caused his death?

'There is more, Comrade President.' Vashinov's voice broke his thoughts.

'More?'

'The girl was in the next-door room when I last spoke to you. Unknown to me at the time, I might add. She heard our conversation. She heard my reference to the Beria Archives, to the Romanovs.'

'She must be found. Have you any idea where she is? Or who she was with?'

'The assailant was identified. By the guards who were attacked.'

The president was impatient. 'And?'

'It was the Englishman.'

'Englishman?'

'The one who was sent over to help with the investigations.'

'Why? Why should he attack your guards?' His voice was disbelieving.

'A matter of love. Even your other policeman, Myeloski, will tell you that.'

'He's a trained professional. One of their best. It seems unlikely that . . .' The president stopped, not wanting to show his instinctive mistrust.

403

'I can only report what has happened, Comrade President.'

'And you think he killed Leonid Yashkin?'

'Or *she* did. And *he's* protecting her. I have no idea. Not until we find them.'

'Your men are looking for them?'

'Yes. Also the local police. We can keep it quiet for now. If you're not satisfied, we can always call in the Spetsnaz.' Vashinov knew the president wouldn't want that; the Spetsnaz were the Soviet special-purpose forces, the death-and-glory boys who were the last to be called in.

'Capture them alive.'

'Of course. But he is armed. If he resists, then my men, or the police, will have no alternative but to defend themselves. You should also remember that he may know of the Beria Archives.'

'I am aware of that.'

The door opened, and his secretary came in, he knew to tell him that his car was ready to take him to the airport. He held up his hand to him, signalled him to be silent.

'Alive. I want them alive. Keep me informed.'

He put the receiver down and stood up, picked up his hat. He would have liked to ring Marshka, but there was no time. He wished he had those portable telephones they all had in the West.

'Make sure there is an office and a phone for me at the airport. And, if Vashinov calls back, find where he is so I can contact him.'

Club Panther
Sverdlovsk
1 p.m.

Myeloski heard the awful news from Vashinov's assistant.

He had responded calmly, showed no emotion, wanted only to listen.

He courteously thanked the assistant, said he was horrified by the news and would be in his room if he was needed. He said he needed time to think, that he would contact Moscow for further instructions.

When he returned to his room, the fat policeman calmly locked the door, then sat on the bed and openly wept for the death of his dearest and noblest friend. Leonid Yashkin had been his mentor, his father and his partner. To lose one such person was tragic, to lose all three devastating.

Twenty minutes later, when he had washed the emotion from his body, when the last sobs had racked him, when he had beaten his chest for the last time, Ahmed Myeloski calmly decided to avenge Yashkin's death. He would use all his powers of perception, all the years of experience to trace his friend's killers.

He had thought about what the assistant told him, examined the facts clinically from every angle. It was unlikely that Duncan had murdered Yashkin, not unless the policeman had threatened the Oldenburgs. And there was no motive for that. Yashkin had never been a schemer, a power player. He was a good policeman who sometimes overstepped the mark, but always for the right motives.

Myeloski knew that Duncan was enraptured with the girl, but not enough to kill. In self-defence, yes, but not in such a cold-blooded way.

His conclusion was simple. It all revolved round Vashinov. He sat there, running through the events of the last few days, looking for a starting-point. If he was to outwit the KGB general, then he needed a lead that no one else had.

That was when he recalled the night before; that was when he remembered Morrison.

He left the Hotel Amerika and drove to the Club

405

Panther. He saw that he was being followed, but decided not to try to lose his 'tail'. He wanted them to trust him, think he was a simple touch. That would make it easier when he needed to get away from the KGB.

The Club Panther was crowded, the afternoon drinkers out in full force after their morning shift. Myeloski asked for Morrison at reception, then went and sat at an empty table, waited for the sixties-style club-owner to join him. While he waited, he ordered a beer. The KGB team walked in two minutes later, saw him and went to the bar. On the stage, a stripper peeled her clothes off and staged her routine to an audience who were more intent on catching up with their drinking.

Morrison came through the door at the back, his Cuban-heeled boots flashing below his wide bell-bottomed tartan trousers. He wore a green satin Cossack-collared shirt and a John Lennon peaked cap. He came directly to Myeloski's table, pulled up a chair and joined him.

'You've got company.' Morrison referred to the KGB men.

'I know.' A waiter came up with a beer for Myeloski on a tray. He waited for payment, but Morrison waved him away.

'You been a bad boy?' He laughed, then saw no reaction from the policeman. 'Serious, eh? Well, join the club. I just learnt someone's stolen my car. I reported it, and you know what the police said? "Come down to the station, fill in a report and give us a description." By the time I can get there, they could be in Moscow, even New York.'

'They?'

'Whoever nicked it.' Morrison refused to be drawn. 'Duncan turn up?'

'I was hoping you could answer that.'

'He's not been here.'

'What were you two talking about last night? When Yakov and I left to go to the toilet?'

'Can't remember. Nothing important.'

'Someone killed my boss last night.'

'The one who went missing?'

'Yes.'

'Shit. I'm sorry, Ahmed Alekseevich. I'm sorry it happened.'

'The KGB say it was Duncan.'

'What do you say?'

'That they want me to believe that.'

'Then, he's been set up?'

'Whatever. He looks guilty as hell if he's on the run. Come on, don't play around with me. What did you talk about last night?'

'Said he wanted to get away. Said the girl was in danger. Someone was beating up on her. Told me he wanted to take her home.' Morrison stopped, not wanting to commit himself further.

'Home? Where the fuck's that?'

'Search me. He needed a car.'

'Pity yours was stolen.'

'Isn't it?'

'He'll need help.'

'Is that why you brought your friends?' Morrison cocked his head towards the KGB.

'Our friends are here because they don't trust me, either.'

'I don't know where he is.'

'He must have given you some idea.'

'Nothing. Just said the girl had been beaten up and then arrested, locked in her room, an armed guard outside her door. Said he wanted to help her.'

'What sort of help?'

'Maps, that sort of thing. To get away, I suppose.'

'And he's taken your car?'

'I never said that.'

'Trust me.'

Morrison shook his head. 'Me, I don't trust anyone.'

407

'Especially the police.'

'You said it.'

'You're stupid. I can help him.'

'Just wanted a car, that's all.'

'Your car.'

'So you keep telling me. Look, I haven't even seen him since last night.' Morrison lied; Myeloski could tell.

There was little point in continuing. He looked over to the KGB; if he stayed there any longer, they would become suspicious of Morrison. God knows what they would do to get the right answers out of him. He'd seen the results of their style of interrogation before. He drained his glass and stood up. Then, for the benefit of the KGB, gave Morrison a warm farewell hug, kissed him on both cheeks. It was as if they were close friends, nothing more. Morrison, realizing what the policeman was doing, returned his embrace.

'If he needs help, call me,' Myeloski whispered in Morrison's ear.

The two men stood back from each other; across the room the KGB team prepared to leave.

'Why do you believe Duncan didn't kill your friend?'

'Because he's a soldier, not a murderer.'

But, if not Duncan, then who? Vera? Was the Englishman protecting the girl? Somewhere there was an answer, and it was up to him to find out.

The two KGB operatives followed Myeloski out of the Club Panther, out of the din of the steelworkers who didn't give a damn who lived and who died as they knocked back another beer before returning to the heat and disease of industrial Sverdlovsk.

It had been a clear run. They had passed very little traffic – the odd passenger-car, mostly farm or forestry trucks, the usual convoy of dump trucks that seem to fill Soviet roads. They had even seen a Pepsi-Cola lorry going in the opposite direction, very fifties in its style and colouring.

The road was good by Russian standards, good because it had only recently been resurfaced. That was the problem out here: the extremes of weather meant that railway tracks were always being ripped up and replaced, roads were always being tarmacked.

The terrain had changed little, sloping gently downwards to the east, away from the Ural Mountains. The journey had been interspaced with small pine and birch forests which gave way to flat agricultural land, with shallow lakes that were scattered along the route. Because of the gentle fall of the ground, the lakes were still, there were no rushing rivers.

Duncan had driven at a steady 45 miles per hour, not wanting to draw attention to the car by doing excessive speeds. They saw no police, no helicopters that might have been watching from above the tree-tops or hovering along the road as it wound through the farmlands.

They had stopped once, pulled into one of the small forests and driven along a narrow soggy cart-track to a small clearing.

Duncan had parked the car on the edge of the clearing, under the trees, so that they could not be seen from the air. After eating the snacks provided by Morrison, they had left the red Datsun and walked deeper into the forest, Vera's arm linked through Duncan's. She was starting to relax now, beginning to feel more at ease. He never asked about Vashinov, why she had been arrested; presumed it was because the general wanted her for himself.

'I need to tell you what happened last night.'

He shrugged. He knew the death of the policeman had upset her, but hadn't wanted to pursue the matter while she was still in a state of shock.

'I didn't go to see Vashinov,' she snapped, mistaking his silence for accusation.

Vera walked away from him and sat under a tree, perched up on a root. He came to her, leant against the tree, saw she was irritated.

'I'm sorry, I didn't mean—'

'Everyone always thinks the worst. I need to talk. About last night.'

'OK.'

She sighed, shook her head, took a deep breath, and then told him about the horrors of the night before. As she spoke, she watched his face for a reaction, saw the alarm when she told him the way the policeman had died.

'I should've told you before.'

'Probably. But it makes no difference.' He understood the state of shock she must have been in, how little he had helped her because of his dirty expectancy. The professional in him also realized that the authorities would be after them sooner than he expected, especially if someone linked them with the dead policeman. Their disappearance would look more than suspicious. And if they got to Morrison, told him about the murdered Yashkin, then there was a good chance he would tell them about the car. At least he hadn't told Morrison where he was going, where his destination lay.

'Come on,' he said to Vera, reaching out and helping her up. 'Time to get going. Tell me the rest in the car.'

He led her back through the forest to the car, then got back on to the main road as quickly as he could. He kept the speed at forty-five, desperate to go faster, yet unable to in case it drew further attention to them. He thought of Myeloski, recalled that Yashkin had been a close friend as well as his superior. The policeman would have been frantic to apprehend the fugitives, would want to know why Duncan had disappeared. If anyone could trace them, it would be the crazy policeman.

As they settled down to the journey once again, he told Vera to continue, to try to remember the dialogue, to recall what was said. He saw it was painful for her; the memory of what happened shocked her. With his free hand, he reached out and encircled her fingers, squeezing gently as he tried to reassure her. He felt her squeeze back, but as she spoke her voice dropped to a whisper as she recalled the brutality she had witnessed, now so distant from the safe cocoon of the travelling car.

But she was also KGB-trained. The years with Vashinov, the years of winkling pillow secrets out of diplomats and other influential visitors, had taught her to remember every detail, every last word that she was told.

He said nothing as he drove, never interrupted her. He had been at debriefing sessions before, knew the secret was in listening, keeping the flow going. When she faltered, he pressed her hand, gave her strength to continue. He was impressed by her level of recall, realized that she was simply following her training, missing nothing. She was the complete professional.

The truth was confusing. What were the Beria Archives? What did they contain that was so devastating that it resulted in the callous murder of a senior policeman? What was the hidden game in which he was unwittingly involved? And, most of all, how far up the ladder did it reach? It could go beyond Moscow, even all the way back to London and Downing Street.

That was when he realized they were on their own, there was no safety-net this time. The only way to resolve it was to go on, to play the game and get to the end.

As he held Vera's hand tightly in his, he saw the newly built church steeple and rooftops of the small town in the distance.

He knew it was Talica. At last, journey's end.

Vnukovo-2 Airport
Moscow

The president had been in the VIP lounge for ten minutes at Vnukovo-2 Airport when the Oldenburgs' plane touched down.

He stood at the large plate-glass window and watched the small jet taxi off the runway and towards the terminal. There was a narrow blue carpet that ran from the terminal entrance to where the plane would eventually come to a stop. Someone had suggested a red carpet, but the president had vetoed it, feeling that such an obvious welcome would be too extravagant at this stage.

To his left he saw a gaggle of airport workers, no doubt intrigued by the impending arrival of unknown VIPs. Above them, on the roof of the terminal, were the police marksmen. This time, he had decided, they would take no chances.

Vasily stood beside him, preening himself for the presentation. He was a sucker for pomp and ceremony, especially when it involved him. The president smiled, envying the British their honour system, whereby enemies and friends could have their egos massaged by the offering of a knighthood or a peerage. It would be an ideal way to buy off the likes of Vasily; bribery with no corruption was an honourable way out of the lion's den.

Outside the room, in the narrow corridor that led to the tarmac, George Leeming also watched the small jet taxi in. Beside him stood the other British policeman, Sergeant Williams, and the interpreter, Louise Taylor. Leeming felt naked; the reassuring weight of the handgun he normally carried was missing. His gun had been taken by the kidnappers, and the British embassy had refused him another. But the Oldenburgs were still his responsibility, and it was his intention to take up his charge once again.

The plane bounced on its front wheels as it came to a stop. The main door opened, and the landing-steps were pushed up to the entrance.

Victor Oldenburg was the first to appear.

As soon as the president saw him, he led the small welcoming party out of the VIP room, along the corridor where Leeming stood, and out on to the tarmac. By the time he reached the blue carpet, the family were descending the steps.

With the natural instinct of a 'people's politician', the president broke from the official reception-party and strode out to the bottom of the steps, meeting Victor Oldenburg as he stepped on to Moscow tarmac.

He embraced him warmly. It was a shame there was no waiting press, he thought. One of the great pictures, the camera apertures freezing the moment when the president of the Soviet Socialist Republic first met the man who would be king, grand duke of all Russia, Victor Oldenburg-Romanov.

Marshka's dacha
Outside Moscow

Marshka waited until he knew they were safe in the Kremlin.

He thought of the phone-call from the president, made from the airport just before the family had landed.

Vashinov's fate was sealed. He had already organized that. The Englishman was of more immediate concern. His disappearance from Sverdlovsk was worrying. Vashinov had told the president that the girl had overheard the conversation regarding the Beria Archives. If she and the Englishman were together, then he could only presume that Duncan also knew of the secret.

The Englishman was a trained soldier, probably a top agent. His instinct would be to seek out and identify any such rumour. It would be a powerful card for the West to hold in any future negotiations. The girl, a prostitute, would believe his lies, would help him unwittingly solve the mystery. He, too, would have to be stopped.

He recalled his conversation with Vashinov, remembered that Duncan was of Russian descent, his family name was Denknetzeyan. The family name was of Siberian origin; they had been White Russians.

He picked up the phone and called for his assistant.

When the man presented himself, Marshka told him to search the computer files for anything to do with the Denknetzeyans.

Two hours later, when he had the information, he asked his assistant to find Moscow police captain Ahmed Alekseevich Myeloski. He was expected to be in Sverdlovsk, probably still staying at the Hotel Amerika.

If the policeman was that good, then it was time for Marshka to help him use his skills to find the Englishman, time to save the situation before it got out of hand once again.

Talica
Western Siberia

The small travellers' lodge was the last building on the east side of the town.

Like most small towns and villages in Siberia, little had changed since the days of the revolution. The buildings were as they had been, now adapted to a communal way of life.

The red Datsun sports-car was stared at as it drove

slowly down the main street, a confused mixture of dwelling-houses and run-down shops. It was a close community, and it didn't take the unusual sports-car to tell the inhabitants that there were strangers in town. The few people in the street watched silently. They were used to keeping their own counsel after centuries of domination. In their hearts, they were still peasants; the revolution had simply brought them different masters.

Duncan kept the car moving, not wanting to draw too much attention, realizing that this was probably the first time many of them would have seen such a distinctive car. He was relieved to see no police, no uniformed officials who might show more than a passing interest.

The small 'Holiday Inn' illumination, garish in its yellow neon light, blinked at them from the roof of the squat brownstone building as they turned the corner. Duncan smiled wryly as he saw the familiar welcoming sign that was known the world over.

He nudged Vera, pointed at the hotel and parked in front of the entrance.

The uniformed policeman watched them from his desk as they entered the small hall that was the reception-area. Behind him, through the arched opening, there was the glint of a steel door that opened on to a small prison cell.

The building doubled as both local hotel and police station. That was why it was built of stone and not of wood like the other structures in Talica.

Duncan took Vera's arm, so as to keep her moving forward, not to falter in her step.

He smiled at the policeman. 'Is this a hotel or not?'

'It is.' The policeman said no more, watched the couple suspiciously.

'Good. And that's one of the rooms?' Duncan joked, pointing at the small cell.

'Where're you from?'

'England. We need some rooms. You have rooms?'

415

The policeman shrugged and rose from the table. He crossed the room and opened the door on the opposite side.

'Maya!' he shouted through the doorway, into the dark of the house.

'What is it?' a woman's voice answered, muffled by the walls that separated them.

'Visitors. For the hotel.'

The woman's voice grumbled in the distance as he closed the door and went back to his desk. 'My wife's in charge of the hotel. She is coming.'

'Thank you.'

'This is a long way from England.'

'A very long way.' Duncan silently thanked Morrison, thanked him for the identity he had provided. He reached forward and offered his hand to the policeman, who had no alternative but to take it. Duncan shook hands vigorously, as he imagined a salesman would.

'I'm a salesman for the Suntory whisky company. From Japan. We're thinking of exporting more of our products to Russia. I'm here to explore the market.'

'You speak good Russian.'

'In England we learn languages in college. I chose Russian. It has proved fortunate.'

'This is your wife?'

'No. She is an interpreter.' He realized his mistake as he spoke.

'Why do you need an interpreter? With your Russian.'

Duncan shrugged. 'Ask your Ministry of Commerce. It was their suggestion.'

The policeman wasn't convinced: he looked hard at the two of them. 'Your papers?'

As they reached for their documents, the policeman's wife entered the room behind them. The uniformed officer took Duncan's passport first and leafed through it. Seemingly satisfied, he handed it back.

'Your visa?'

416

Duncan reached in his pocket and took out the sheaf of papers that Morrison had given him. He watched the policeman study the forgeries. At last, grudgingly, he seemed satisfied, passed them back.

The officer took Vera's identity-card and looked at it. Duncan saw it startle him, saw him raise his eyebrows. He looked up at Vera, then quietly passed the card back.

'They want rooms,' he announced to his wife. Then he went back to the magazine he had been reading.

The couple turned to the woman, her peasant hard-working heritage obvious from the lines on her face and the cracks in her skin.

'One room?' she asked.

'No. Two, please,' Duncan answered.

She pushed the registration-book forward; it was a simple school exercise-pad.

'Cash or credit card?'

'Cash.'

She was pleased. She still didn't understand how the credit card machine worked. Duncan remembered the transmitter card he had left behind in Sverdlovsk. Well, it was time to pay his own way. The Americans would by now have realized that he had gone underground. He wondered what Woodward, the MI5 man, would make of that.

When they had filled in the register, she led them into that part of the house which was the hotel. Duncan turned to the policeman before he followed her.

'I have some whisky in the car. I'll get you some later.'

The policeman smiled for the first time. 'Good. I like whisky. Even Japanese.' His laughter followed Duncan up the stairs.

'What did you show him?' he asked Vera, in English so that the old woman wouldn't understand.

'My KGB identity-card.'

He laughed. 'In for a penny, in for a pound. Sorry, a rouble.'

The joke went over her head. He smiled, enjoying her innocence.

'Have you bags?' the policeman's wife asked.

'In the car. We'll get them later.'

They followed her to the small rooms which were next to each other on the first floor. Duncan entered the second and waited for the old woman to go back down the stairs before joining Vera. As he waited he looked out of the window, out on to the flatland forest which disappeared to the horizon.

He expected to feel something, an emotion of homecoming, of belonging.

As he stared into the horizon, his eyes searching for Destayala and the home of his ancestors, he felt only emptiness. It was a strange brooding landscape, unfamiliar and hostile.

Suddenly he regretted coming, regretted being there.

As the void grew inside him he heard Vera's soft knock on the door.

He still had some way to go. The journey had to reach a conclusion, and his instinct and training, he knew, would force him through all the way to the end.

Whatever else, he had to follow through to journey's end.

He went to the door and let her in.

Sverdlovsk Police Station
Sverdlovsk
Western Siberia

Myeloski, having drawn a blank with Morrison as to Duncan's whereabouts, turned to what he was best at. Detection.

The first rule of good police work is that if you can't go forward, then go back. There's always something missed along the way.

418

The search of the Hotel Amerika had yielded nothing. Duncan's and Vera's rooms were bare of clues, already cleaned and ready for the next occupants by the time he got there.

He desperately wanted to search Vashinov's suite: his instinct told him that. He climbed the stairs to the general's rooms, but found two KGB officers guarding the corridor. He would have to wait until Vashinov left the hotel to return to Moscow before making progress there.

He realized that could take time, that Vashinov would wait until matters had been cleared up in Sverdlovsk. He would certainly be in no hurry to leave, not if he was directly involved in any of the antics that had recently taken place. And of that involvement Myeloski had little doubt.

His deliberations led him back to Igor Mischnev, the retired steelworker Duncan had gone to see with Morrison. He remembered that Duncan had been excited by the visit, but the discovery of the brigands' ransom note had removed any need to pursue that avenue. Myeloski decided that it was as good a starting-point as any.

He called Morrison and arranged to meet him at the block of flats where Mischnev lived. Then, after grabbing three Dunkin DoNuts from the shop on the corner, he drove to the Home for Retired Steelworkers on the far side of town.

Morrison had arrived as Myeloski drew up at the entrance. The policeman, with white sugar around his lips and chin from eating doughnuts as he drove, saw that Morrison leant on the bonnet of a black Moskvich. That meant that the red Datsun had not been returned, that Duncan was still out on the road and well away from Sverdlovsk.

'Why do you want to see him?' asked Morrison.

'When all doors are closed, you try anything.'

'Enjoy the doughnuts?' Morrison noticed the sugar around Myeloski's lips.

'Who're you? Sherlock Holmes?'

They caught the lift to the eighth floor and rang Mischnev's doorbell. The old man, surprised but pleased to see Morrison, let them into his small flat.

Morrison introduced Myeloski as a journalist from Moscow, a colleague of Duncan's.

'The foreigner,' said the old man, turning to Myeloski. 'I liked him. Why do you want to see me?'

'Your story, about the tsar not being killed, was—'

'The tsar *was* killed. I said the boy Alexis and his sister Anastasia were allowed to live.'

'Of course. I meant the members of his family.'

'So why do you want to hear it all again? Don't you trust your friend?' he asked mischievously.

'Of course I do. But it's all so incredible. I thought he might have missed something.'

'You don't have the look of a reporter about you.'

'I can't help how I look.'

'I suppose that comes from snooping around people's lives, eh? Which bit do you want to know?'

'All of it. All that your father overhead in the Hotel Amerika.'

The old man shrugged, then once more went through the tale he had told Duncan. It was as Myeloski had heard it from the Englishman; there was nothing new.

'Is that all?' the policeman asked Mischnev when he had finished.

'That's all,' the old man replied.

Myeloski knew he was lying.

'It's an unusual story. Of course, there have been many rumours about what happened to the Romanovs.'

'I didn't ask you to believe it.'

'My friend's life may be in danger.'

'Why?'

'Because there are those who would harm him.'

'Because of what I told him?'

'Possibly.'

'You speak in riddles.'

'Then, tell me the truth.'

The old man smiled, shook his head. 'You're no reporter.'

'No. I'm a policeman.'

'I have nothing to say to policemen.'

'Why not?'

'Because I want to live to a hundred.'

'Those days are past, Comrade Mischnev. Nobody's going to drag you away to jail just to silence you. All I want to do is save my friend. And Morrison's friend.'

The old man turned back to Morrison for confirmation. The club-owner nodded. Mischnev angled back to Myeloski.

'Good friends,' continued Myeloski. 'We've all been through a lot together. Now he needs us. I don't know whether or not you can help. But I'm stuck in a deep hole and I can't find my way out. Tell me what you know. It could save his life.'

The old man considered before answering. 'My father heard they were to be taken to a madhouse. Somewhere north of Tiumen. In the country, away from the big towns.'

'Why there?'

'Why not? Who's going to believe them, that they're Romanovs?' Mischnev cackled with laughter. 'Not when the person next to them is shouting he's Ivan the Terrible.'

'And you don't know where?'

'No. Except it was no more than a day's journey away.'

'Why?'

'Because the Jew and Voikov were back in Sverdlovsk two days later. And they weren't going to leave the

Romanovs running free around the countryside, were they?'

'Unless they handed them over to somone else. Someone who took responsibility for the Romanovs.'

'Who knows? But in those days of the revolution nothing was ever that planned. I think if they took them anywhere, then it was within a day's travel of here.'

Myeloski got little more out of the old man and left with Morrison soon afterwards.

'If Duncan contacts you, you must call me,' Myeloski said to Morrison when they were back on the pavement.

The club-owner nodded, but it didn't convince the policeman that he would adhere to his wishes. He got into the Lada and drove to the police station.

At the station he asked for maps of the region and, armed with these, he took over a small interview-room. He spread the maps and pored over them, but found nothing that was of help. A day's journey in those days could have been anything up to a hundred kilometres. There was little of note on the charts, only small towns and villages of little importance. It was an area of simple farming, peat-cutting and logging. There was no sign of any asylums or major hospitals.

He left the room to ask one of the local policemen when the desk sergeant called him over.

'There's a call for you. Moscow. You can take it at my desk.'

Myeloski shook his head. He didn't want to be overheard. 'Put it through to the office I was in,' he said.

He walked back into the small room and waited for the phone to ring. When it did he picked up the receiver.

'Myeloski,' he said.

'Captain Myeloski?' a voice that the policeman didn't recognize asked.

'Yes. Who is this?'

'My name is Grigory Marshka. Do you know who I am?'

Myeloski was startled. Everyone knew who Marshka was. 'Yes, comrade,' he answered.

'We are both responsible to the same authority. The highest. Do you understand?'

'I do.' Myeloski presumed Marshka meant the president.

'We must find the Englishman as soon as possible. I may be able to help you in that matter. But, before I do, remember that there are many who would harm him if they were to get to him first. Whatever I tell you is for your information only. Is that clear?'

'Yes, comrade.'

'Good. The Englishman could be on his way to Moscow. We already have people waiting at the British embassy and watching the roads into the capital. But I don't think he's coming here. He is of Russian origin. His family name is Denknetzeyan. They come from the Talica region, to the west of Tiumen.'

Hotel Amerika
Sverdlovsk
Western Siberia

General Vashinov sat at the table naked, the small Sony tape-recorder whirring in front of him.

Behind him, on the bed, the buxom secretary waited, irritated that he had left her to answer the door and take the tape-recorder from his assistant. She was late for the theatre and wanted to finish this performance to go on to her next.

Vashinov grinned as he listened to the soft voice that filled the room.

'But I don't think he's coming here. He is of Russian origin. His family name is Denknetzeyan. They come from the Talica region, to the west of Tiumen.'

As he listened, Vashinov clapped his hands in delight.

There was more mileage left in the game. This time there would be no mistakes.

This time the general would do the job himself.

Thirteen kilometres south of Talica
Western Siberia

The red sports-car bounced along the road that ran to the deserted logging-camp, the main highway over three kilometres behind them.

The forest undergrowth had spread across the pitted roadway, its roots ripping through the tarmac mercilessly.

It was a bright night, the moon low and clear in a cloudless sky. Duncan drove on his sidelights, not wanting to be seen by any low-flying aircraft that might be on the lookout for the car. He was a man unaccustomed to taking unnecessary risks; he knew it was only a matter of time before they came looking for him, before they traced him to Talica.

Finding out about Destayala had been easy. He grinned as he remembered. Myeloski would have approved of the policework.

He and Vera had gone down to the restaurant bar for a meal and to pick up any gossip. The rooms were heaving with life. In addition to being the local hotel and gaol, the Holiday Inn was also the social centre of the town. As evening descended, the local peat-cutters, farmworkers and loggers descended on the building as it was the only place of entertainment in Talica.

The local police officer, on seeing them enter the bar, waved them over to his table. As they joined him they saw he was already well into one of the sample bottles of Japanese whisky.

'Drink?' he shouted above the noise of the crowd. When they nodded, he called for two vodkas from the barman.

'If you want to eat, tell my wife. She'll put you to the front of the queue. Otherwise you'll be here all night.'

'Thanks,' replied Duncan, not showing his annoyance at the policeman's obvious lustful appraisal of Vera. 'This could be a good place for whisky sales.'

'If it's cheap enough, they'll drink anything. Even Japanese cat's piss.' The policeman laughed heartily at his own joke, leaning over and stroking Vera's arm as he did so. Before he could go farther, his wife called him over to the restaurant. She was used to his lechery and knew when to intervene. He cursed her as he left the table, the whisky-bottle tucked firmly under his arm.

'Let's go to the bar,' Duncan said, rising from the table and leading her to the counter. The barman had their drinks, and Duncan paid for them. At the far end of the bar was a group of older men. Duncan deduced they were collective farmworkers from their attire. He took Vera's arm and guided her towards them.

Joining in their conversation was easy. They were interested in strangers; Talica was not a town that had many. They spoke of the town, answered the innocuous questions that Vera and Duncan asked. Then they asked him about England, about the rest of Europe.

'I have a friend back home. His family came from Russia. Tiumen, I think. His name's Denknetzeyan.' It was time to move forward. He watched their faces for a reaction as he spoke.

Nobody answered.

'White Russian,' he went on. 'Had an estate somewhere near Tiumen. Doesn't ring a bell, does it?'

'What if it does?' one of them asked.

'Just thought he'd like to know.'

'I heard you're a whisky-peddler,' one of the others said.

Duncan laughed, then turned to Vera.

'Get a bottle for our friends from the car, will you?' He handed her the Datsun keys as he spoke.

'One bottle?' asked the worker.

'Two bottles. Didn't I say that?'

The farmworkers laughed at his joke, the greed apparent in their eyes.

Twenty minutes later they were on their way to Destayala, the farm estate that Grandfather Denknetzeyan had left all those years ago.

They had left the main Talica-to-Tiumen highway ten kilometres to the east of the town. They followed the rutted disused road northwards, deep into the forest and towards the old logging camp. They were to look for the entrance to the estate before they reached the lumber works.

Vera saw it first; the prettily shaped villa that stood arched in the trees with the moon hanging low to its left.

'There!' she indicated, touching his arm. 'Through the trees.'

Duncan braked, and the car slithered to a stop on the moss-covered highway. He looked to where she pointed and saw the silhouetted shadow of the house that stood there.

Anxious to get on, he snicked into first gear and drove the car forward until he found an opening in the tree-lined avenue that had once been the gateway to the villa. He swung the wheel, and the car slid through the grass and on towards the house.

They stopped near the front entrance to the building.

It was as the old men in the bar had told them. Deserted, forlorn, a forgotten victim of the past. It had fallen into disrepair when the peasantry, without the experience or initiative to administer the building, had left it to the forest and the harsh Siberian winters.

Vera was first out of the car. Duncan sensed her excitement, knew that she had got caught up in his search, in his quest for the past.

'It must have been beautiful,' she said, linking her arm

426

through his. He said nothing. He couldn't explain the emptiness he felt inside. There were still no answers, no reasons for him being there.

He looked up at the old villa. The front door had long since been boarded up, the birch planks nailed across the entrance themselves now rotting. The windows were just oblong holes in the walls, their frames rotted, the panes of glass shattered and long gone. Inside the house they could see most of the ceilings had collapsed, that the moonlight sprayed down through a roof where sections had caved in over the decades.

He led her to the side of the house. Where the small east wing joined the house, the outside wall had fallen down. The masonry now lay in a pile of rubble across the path.

'Wait here,' he said, scrambling across the fallen debris and into the house. The room he entered was large, had obviously been one of the main reception-areas. The ceiling had held, but the large door into what was the hallway had rotted down to its hinges. As he looked round the room he heard Vera clambering over the debris, the masonry sliding under her feet. He turned and helped her into the room.

They went into the hall, saw the hole in the roof where the atrium had been. He realized that the roof had held after all these years, that the only opening was where the glass dome had fallen in.

He led her to the rear of the house, to where he imagined the kitchens would be.

The stone-slabbed floor, the open fire-grate of the room they entered proved that they were in the service-area. It was here that Grandfather Denknetzeyan would have first seen his sister Katya and the maid Esmereldi.

They picked their way over the debris of the fallen years, went to the boarded-up door that was at the back of the room. He forced the door open, its hinges long since rusted up. When it was wide enough to let a man

427

pass, he slipped through the narrow entrance, the girl following him.

She saw him reach into his coat pocket and take out the torch he had brought from the car. She saw the steps leading down into the cellars as he switched it on, the sharp light leading them down the stairs. She followed him down, her right hand on his shoulder for guidance.

The room to his left was the scullery. Duncan knew it was where his grandfather had first hidden when he came into the house.

They continued on down, deeper into the blackness.

There were three rooms in the ice-cold basement. Two of them were bare and had obviously been coldroom storage-areas.

The third, a smaller room, still had its door intact.

He pushed it open and shone the torch in.

It was a room that had stood still in time, had been too far away from the rest of the house to be looted or lived in.

The small chest of drawers had rotted, the wooden chair tilted on one side, its leg snapped off.

Against the wall there was a rusted iron bed-frame, its mattress shredded and fallen to the floor between the springs after it had been gnawed at by the rats and other rodents who were the room's only visitors.

Duncan knew that this was where Katya had been raped, where his great-grandfather had been so brutally murdered all those years ago.

This was where Grandfather Denknetzeyan must have stood and listened to the tale of horror his young sister had told him.

He remembered the old man, remembered their closeness, remembered how lost he had felt at his funeral.

Then he finally cried for his lost grandfather.

Vera put her arms round his back, held Duncan as he sobbed for all that was lost, for everything that he believed he would never find.

Myeloski had returned immediately to the hotel, bringing the sheaf of maps with him. The police had been loath to let them go, but he had insisted, grown ugly in his demands. The desk sergeant had shrugged his shoulders; it wasn't his lot to argue with senior officers from Moscow.

On the way back, Myeloski had attempted to contact Morrison from a call-box. Most of them had been vandalized, but he eventually found one near the hotel. Morrison was out, uncontactable. He didn't want Morrison to ring him at the hotel, in case the phone-call was bugged. He needed one more shot at the club-owner, one more attempt to find out if he knew where Duncan had gone.

The last thing he wanted was to be off on a wild-goose chase to some small Siberian town when Morrison could possibly furnish the answers.

But they were waiting for him as he walked up the steps of the Hotel Amerika.

'General Vashinov would like to see you, Comrade Captain,' said the KGB officer who stopped him at the entrance.

Myeloski was taken up to the general's suite where he was kept waiting for nearly twenty minutes. He could hear Vashinov in the next room, heard his muffled voice giving out orders. But the sounds were too garbled for him to determine what was said.

Eventually the door swung open. Vashinov entered, and behind him Myeloski saw a group of KGB officers. It had obviously been a high-powered meeting.

'Good news, Captain,' boomed Vashinov. 'We think we've traced our man. And the slut he's with.'

'Great.' Myeloski's smile hid the fear that engulfed him. 'Where, Comrade General?'

'Out in the country. To the east.'

That was where Talica lay. 'Where exactly?' continued Myeloski.

'I'll have the precise details later. In the meantime I want you to rest up. It's going to be a hard day tomorrow. We're leaving early in the morning. At six. You'd better come with me in my helicopter.'

The policeman realized Vashinov was trapping him in the hotel. And he was taking him along to keep him out of mischief.

The policeman rose to leave the room. 'I shall get some rest, Comrade General. Thank you.'

'That's what we're here for. To work together. We'll get that English bastard, you know. My instinct tells me it was he who killed Comrade Yashkin. We'll find him and tear the truth from him.'

Myeloski knew then that Duncan was dead if they found him first. He nodded and went to the door.

'By the way,' Vashinov's voice stopped him. 'I've ordered a guard to be placed on your door. This Englishman's a trained killer. Let's not take any chances. One dead policeman's enough as far as I'm concerned.'

'Thank you, Comrade General. For your concern.'

Vashinov beamed at the fat policeman as he let himself out. Then he threw back his head and laughed. He still hadn't decided whether to kill the Englishman or Vera first.

Myeloski was escorted by an armed KGB officer to his room. When he had shut his door, he heard the scrape of a chair being pulled up as the guard settled down on his watch.

He knew he couldn't ring Marshka or the president. He needed time to think. He switched on the television set in the corner. It was an old episode of 'Dallas', the American soap opera that had taken the Soviet Union by storm. He watched the screen, the image meaningless to him as he pondered the situation.

He picked up the phone and asked for a number. When the operator gave it to him, he dialled and waited for it to be answered.

'Talica police,' said a sleepy voice. 'Do you know what fucking time it is?'

'I would like to speak to the officer in charge.'

'Who wants him?' came the wary reply.

'Captain Ahmed Alekseevich Myeloski, Moscow Police.'

There was a pause at the other end, a sharp intake of breath.

'I suppose it's about this Denknetzeyan character. This Englishman.' The voice on the phone confirmed the worst to Myeloski.

'Of course,' said Myeloski.

'I've already told your people. He went out with the girl about ten o'clock. They've not come back.'

'How do you know if you're asleep?'

'Because the front door's locked. It's after midnight, you know.'

'Where did they go?'

'I already told you. I don't know. But they were asking about an old villa to the north of here. I don't know why. The bloody place fell down years ago. It's just a ruin now.'

'OK. Thanks.'

'See you in the morning,' came the exasperated reply.

Myeloski put down the phone.

The net was closing round Duncan. And there was nothing Myeloski could do about it.

The fields west of Destayala
Talica
Western Siberia

They had followed the path through the forest, the

overgrown walkway that led away from the back of the house.

Vera knew that Duncan wanted to leave the loneliness of the house, that his search had not ended.

They walked quietly between the trees, their way lit by the bright moon. She had linked her arm through his, hugged him as they made their way. They were in no hurry; he knew the danger, if it came, would not be there until the morning.

'Wouldn't it be something if we could rebuild it the way it was?' she said.

Her words were of hope, a glimmer of ambition in the despair that he felt. To give life to the past. He remembered Victor Oldenburg's words, so long ago, on that hillside in Gloucestershire. 'All those generations of hardship, suffering, happiness, the whole business of living. Kill the line and you kill all that they went through.' That's it, Victor; I'm beginning to understand now.

'Wouldn't it? Wouldn't it just?' he replied, his excitement building.

'You can see it was once a fine house.'

'I wonder who has title to it now. The State?'

'Probably. Why?'

He laughed. 'Imagine if I bought it off them. Back into the family.'

She went quiet; he sensed her distance.

'What's wrong?'

'Nothing.'

'Come on, what's up?'

She shook her head, not wanting to share her secrets. He respected her privacy. She would tell him if she wanted to.

They found the chapel as he had hoped. On the edge of the forest, just before the ground started to rise up to the low ridged hill.

It was smaller than he had imagined, the wooden dome silhouetted against the night-line.

They approached it carefully, not expecting to find anyone there, but not prepared to take any chances.

When they were close, Duncan saw that the chapel had not fallen into ruin; its windows were intact, its doors whole.

The chapel was still a place of worship, a place that had stood against the ravages of communism since the revolution all those years ago. The villagers must have protected their religion over the years in this distant and forgotten wood.

They looked through the windows, saw the simple altar and a few wooden seats that had been there for centuries. It was an enchanting place, somewhere to come to rest in a troubled world.

He led her away from the chapel, to the small cleared area by the side. It was a simple graveyard, with many of the headstones broken and laid flat on the ground. But the graveyard was well tended; it had not been allowed to succumb to the ravages of nature.

On most of the headstones, the inscriptions read 'Denknetzeyan'.

The dates went back over centuries.

He found his great-grandparents' graves, side by side as Grandfather Denknetzeyan had said. There were two simple headstones, and he reached out and touched them both, felt the stone warm under his touch.

'Over here,' Vera called softly.

He went over to where she knelt before another simple headstone. She looked up at him as he shone the torch to identify the inscription more clearly.

'Ekaterina (Katya) Nikolaevna Denknetzeyan. 1901–1974.'

So Katya had come home to Destayala.

And Duncan realized she had only been sixteen years old when she had been raped and locked away as a servant by the soldiers in the old villa.

It was also the first time, in all his years as a battle-hardened warrior and trained soldier, that he fully understood the horror of war, the unnecessary brutality of violence.

He stood and put his arm round Vera and led her away from the small graveyard.

At last he understood why he had come here.

It wasn't to find Destayala or the spirit of his past.

He had simply followed his instinct.

It was to find himself.

They went back to the chapel. While Vera watched, he expertly forced the lock with his knife and gained entry into the chapel. When he had taken her in, he told her to wait whilst he returned to the car for some coats and some food.

He ran back to the car, started it and drove it deep into the forest so it couldn't be seen easily. After covering it with fallen branches, he returned to the chapel.

Like all Russian churches, there were no pews, no seating in the central worship-area. There were a few scattered wooden seats around the wall and Vera had fallen asleep on one of them. She was startled when he gently shook her awake and gave her a folded coat to rest her head on.

'I want to sleep with you,' she said. 'Not on my own.'

'These seats are a bit narrow,' he joked.

'Then, we'll sleep on the floor,' she said, swinging her legs round and standing up.

They made a bed on the floor, behind the altar, of coats and a blanket he found in the car. They both undressed and, after wrapping the clothes round their naked bodies for warmth, held each other closely.

'Why did you come back here?' she asked, her head buried in his shoulder.

'Somebody had to,' he replied.

Then they felt the stirrings for each other, felt the

434

warmth of need and love, felt the desire for sex that often comes with over-tiredness and exhaustion.

They made love gently, slowly moving with each other, not wanting to rush or for the moment to end. He felt big inside her, knew it was the yearning that produced that feeling.

As they made love, he lying on top of her, trapping her under him, their eyes never wavered from each other. They watched their own love in each other's eyes. Her hands played with the hair on the back of his neck; it was something she liked doing with him. It gave her security, increased her ardour for him.

Then, after a long time, when they could hold their love for each other no longer, they came together in the silence of that small chapel.

They lay together, he still inside her.

'Do you remember when we were walking and you asked me what was wrong?' she asked him.

He nodded, watching her as he held her.

'You said you'd buy the villa back from the State, rebuild it.'

'It was only a thought.'

'To you. But you already have a home. Somewhere you live, somewhere to go to. I don't have such a place. Just a KGB apartment, till they take it away. When I am no more use to them.'

'It'll be different now.'

'How? After this, when they come, nothing will change. Not against them.'

'It'll change.'

'I want it to. I want your hope. But how do I believe it? We come from different worlds. You have money, importance. Even your family won't accept me.'

'Nothing to do with them. This is where it all starts.'

'In bed, yes. Then we're the same. But out there, to the rest of the world, we don't belong together.'

'Rubbish!'

'No. Your family, they're grand people. There's no place for a whore in your world.'

And he laughed. He remembered the people he had killed, the companies his father had destroyed, the workers who had been laid off in the name of profits for the bank, the families broken up and made homeless for business expediency.

'Compared to my lot, you're a bloody saint,' he said. Then he thought of his small mews house, tucked away in the safety and sophistication of London, away from these forbidding and remote Siberian forests and permafrost. He thought of his Bentley, the old lady tucked away in her garage, waiting for him to turn the ignition and take her out on the roads she was built for. It was his home, yet it was empty. When he was there, he gave it life. But it had always been empty, a place he could run to, a haven from his other existence. People made homes. Vera and he, they were people. It didn't matter where; that they were together was all that was important.

'Tell me about your people,' she asked. 'You know my world. I know nothing of yours.'

He spoke of his family, of the division he felt between himself and the rest of them. He was warmer about the house, even told her about the Bentley and how the delivery-men left the papers and milk for him in the boot. He smiled; it was one of the idiosyncrasies of his life he enjoyed.

She laughed when he told her, then asked about his other life, the one he shielded from everyone.

He shook his head; the nightmares were for him only. 'It's not important. Destayala is important.'

'Why?'

'Because we all need hope. And that's where it starts. Where my roots are.'

'But you're English.'

'And always will be. But I need to do something with

436

my life. Something positive. Something that lasts. To rebuild Destayala, to learn to live with you, that's a good start.'

'Vashinov won't allow that.'

He knew the dangers more than she did. 'Tomorrow we'll work our way back to Moscow. Once we're there, once we're in the British embassy, then we'll be out of his reach. We came here because we had nowhere else to go. Now we have each other, we can go anywhere we want. Live here, in London; go where we want. Trust me.'

They fell asleep together. It was a deep sleep. It was a good sleep.

Five hours later, at eight in the morning, Duncan came awake fast.

In the distance he heard someone whistling.

Vera lay asleep in the crook of his arm, and he eased away from her, trying not to wake her. But the movement startled her, dragged her out of a deep sleep.

'Keep still!' he warned, holding his finger to his lips.

He went to one of the windows and looked out. It was a bright summer day, the morning sun harsh in a cloudless sky. Coming over the hill was a man, dressed in a black robe, enjoying the morning freshness as he strolled towards the chapel.

'Get dressed. Visitors,' he urged.

They hurriedly put their clothes on and cleared up the debris of their night together. Vera folded the blanket and their coats neatly as Duncan went to open the door.

He stepped out into the sunlight as the robed man came to the chapel. The man stopped, surprised to see someone come out of the chapel. He was a young man, no more than thirty, with a deep black beard and a shock of red hair.

Duncan realized he was a priest.

He also knew it could be a trap. He searched the

437

horizon for any other intruders. He saw nothing, but knew he must remain alert.

'Hello,' said the priest.

'Good morning,' he replied. 'Is this your chapel?'

'God's chapel,' came the gently mocking answer. 'One that is in my charge, yes.'

'It's very lovely.'

'You're not from this area?'

'No. From England.' Duncan saw the priest look over his shoulder, knew that Vera had come out behind him. 'We came to see the old house. It was very late. Then we looked for the graveyard.' He saw the look of surprise on the priest's face. 'We found the chapel, and because it was very late and getting cold we spent the night here.'

The priest saw that the door had been forced, walked past Duncan to look at it.

'I'm sorry. I'll pay for any damage.'

The priest turned and faced him. 'What's so interesting about the graveyard?'

'My English name is Duncan. My family name is Denknetzeyan.'

The priest smiled. 'So you came to find your roots.'

'Yes.'

The priest put out his hand in a welcoming manner. Duncan took it and shook hands. He introduced the priest to Vera, explained that she was Russian and to be his fiancée.

'I'm surprised to see the chapel still standing. Especially after the state of the house,' said Duncan.

'It was too far away, too isolated for the authorities to check up on it. It became a shrine, a safe haven at the time of the purges and the attacks on our religion.'

'Grandfather would have liked that,' Duncan said softly.

'Grandfather?'

'My grandfather. Ilya Denknetzeyan. His sister is buried in the graveyard.'

'Ekaterina Nikolaevna.'

Duncan nodded.

'A remarkable woman,' the priest went on. 'She came back here after the revolution. The house was falling apart, this chapel deserted and left to rot. She worked hard, made it a place of worship once again. One by one, the local people came here to worship. The old priest from Talica took the services. He used to come up here on horseback. I swear he was over a hundred when he died.'

'And Katya?'

'Tuberculosis. About twenty years ago. She was a saint, was always ready to help those more unfortunate than herself.'

'Where did she live?'

'In the house. In a small room in the cellars.'

Duncan remembered the room. So that's where she had spent most of her life, in the darkened room where she most felt her shame.

'The villagers looked after her, brought her food and clothing. And, apart from helping them, she cleaned the church, tended the family graves. After her death we vowed to maintain the little graveyard. Since *perestroika* the congregation have gone back to the big churches in the towns. But some of us still come here, to our secret little chapel. You don't let something like this go. Not when you might need it again.'

'That's good.'

'Why?'

'Because things should live on.' He recalled Victor's words, all those months ago on the Gloucestershire hillside. He suddenly understood his friend's quest for the past, his need for family.

He welcomed himself back to the world.

The priest smiled. 'This place is your heritage. Maybe that's why you came back. To put it right. But, before that, you must tell me why you are both running from the police?'

Duncan and Vera looked at one another, then back at the priest.

'Not us,' said Duncan.

'An Englishman and a Russian girl. That's who my friend the policeman in Talica says everyone is looking for. Now, how many Englishmen and pretty young women do you think there are around here?'

'Did he say why they were looking for us?' asked Vera, pushing past Duncan towards the priest.

'For killing a policeman. In Sverdlovsk.'

'They're lying.'

The priest looked into her eyes; she saw he believed her.

'I'm not a believer, Father,' she continued. 'I have never needed . . . what you call God. Only myself. I'm all I could trust. Some people would call me bad. But this. Murder. Killing. We haven't killed anyone. But they are after us. And they will probably kill us. I would like to sit and talk to someone. In the last few days I have started to . . . Life is very different from what it was a week ago. Can I talk to you?'

'Of course.' The priest signalled them to enter the chapel, then followed them in. Duncan held back, sat at the rear on an usher's stool as the priest and Vera went to the small altar. Vera knelt on the floor, and the priest stood before her, next to the window.

Duncan listened to her voice, realized she was unknowingly in a confessional. As she spoke, he realized that it was also for him to hear; it was her way of telling him of the terrible things she believed she had done, of the life she was part of until only a few days ago.

He listened to her talk of a childhood without a home or parents, of her prostitution and her recruitment into the KGB, of the vilification of her body and soul at the hand of Vashinov and the others who abused her. The more she spoke, the more he realized how much he had fallen in love with her. It was her vulnerability that held

440

him, her innocence in a world of depravity. At times her voice dropped; he had to strain to listen. It was the moments she was most ashamed of.

He was so engrossed in her words that he never saw the men moving through the forest towards the chapel from the direction of Destayala.

He never saw the sniper with his long-barrelled rifle rest it against the trunk of a tree to steady his aim.

Duncan leant forward to listen, heard the words 'a new life, a new hope'.

The first bullet shattered the glass as it exploded in the priest's head, killing him instantly.

The second bullet took out Vera as she leapt to her feet, horrified by the blood and fleshy mess of the murdered priest.

Duncan hit the ground hard, the Coonan Magnum already out in his hand. He heard shouts in the distance, heard someone laugh. But his concern was only for Vera, even though he knew from the way she had jerked and then fallen that she was already dead.

He rolled along the floor to where she lay, her arm twisted behind her back, her neck sliced by the sniper's bullet. He reached out and touched her leg, squeezed it, felt her lifelessness as the tears came.

His instinct and training took over as he heard the voices get louder.

He rolled towards the window at the back and lay still near the door. He pushed himself up so that he could see without being seen. There was a group of four soldiers approaching; their hats signified they were KGB. The sniper led them, relaxed and walking in the open towards the chapel.

They had only expected two people. Nobody had known the priest would be there. He now saw others in the distance, still partially hidden in the trees, attracted by the sound of the rifle-fire. Some of them moved into the clearing, out from the shelter of the trees.

He saw Vashinov with the second group.

Myeloski was to his right, frantically signalling and shouting at the general. Duncan couldn't hear what he said.

He crawled to the door and went out on to the wooden platform, the building shielding him from the small group who approached.

Duncan stood up and waited for them to come round the corner.

His first bullet took out the sniper. The soldier's mouth dropped as he realized there was still someone alive, but the bullet went into his open mouth and blew the back of his head out before he could turn to run.

The other three, panicked and confused by the loud explosions of the Coonan Magnum gunfire, never even pointed their Kalashnikovs before Duncan had fired five more shots into them.

He leapt forward to pick up three of the automatic weapons from the fallen soldiers as those in the forest opened fire.

Their reactions were too late. Scooping up the weapons, he turned and ran up the hill towards the trees, keeping the chapel between himself and the pursuers. He was over the brow of the hill before the others had even reached the chapel.

And Duncan ran, deeper into the forest, deeper into the safety of the undergrowth. He ran as he was trained to, pushing himself harder as the pain started to burn into his chest. He knew they wouldn't catch him, not unless they were Spetsnaz troops, which he doubted.

When he was deep in the forest, when he couldn't hear them blindly crashing through the undergrowth after him, he calmly set about preparing the battleground from where he would exact a most terrible revenge.

He had become a soldier again. He was in his element, and all thoughts of the terrible deeds that had just transpired were driven from his mind.

The killing machine was about to be switched on.

Marshka's dacha
Outside Moscow

The old man knew of the deaths within the hour.

He listened on the phone, the line from Talica crackling as he heard the grave news.

'The policeman, Myeloski. Was he party to the killings?'

'He was there,' came the reply.

'His reaction?'

'He tried to stop them, but it was too late. It all happened so quickly.'

'Vashinov?'

'It was he who unleashed the attack force.'

'When will you fulfil your mission?'

'When I have my men about me. It is too dangerous at present.'

'Move as soon as you can.'

'And the Englishman?'

'He is of no importance any more. Only as a means to an end. Have they any idea where he is now?'

'No, sir. But they are sending teams in to flush him out.'

'Don't fail me.'

'I won't, Comrade Marshka. I, too, have my reason for exacting a satisfactory conclusion to this matter.'

Marshka put the phone down.

Although he hadn't told him, he knew what that reason was. He trusted his man; after all, they both wanted the same thing.

He hoped the Englishman was as good as his reputation. He would have to keep his pursuers at bay whilst Marshka's people readied themselves.

The longer the chase, the better the chance of success.

The secrets of the Beria Archives would finally be safe.

The forest north of Destayala
Talica
Western Siberia

Duncan smoothed the leaves over the last of the four hides he had hurriedly built when he heard a low warning whistle about a hundred metres behind him.

The whistle, a call of recognition between the pursuers, told him that they had moved faster than he had expected. But it didn't matter now; he had prepared well and laid his plans. He also knew the hunters were not used to guerrilla tactics. You never whistled. It was too high-pitched and carried farther than other warnings.

The four hides were scattered over five hundred metres; two of them had Kalashnikov automatics standing by in them. He carried the third rifle as well as his handgun, now fully loaded with a spare clip. Weapons were no problem; he would simply take them off his victims as he ambushed them.

Aware that the first group was not far behind, he slipped into the hide, the automatic rifle beside him, his Coonan Magnum in his hand.

He had deliberately wiped all memory of Vera from his mind as he could not function at his best if he thought of her. He was immersed in his task. He knew the agony of grief would live with him for the rest of his life, but now was not its moment.

He smiled wryly; it was ironic that he was playing the Russian Defence. Draw the enemy farther into trouble, stretch their lines of communication, isolate them from each other.

He settled down to let the first group pass him.

It didn't take long. In their inexperience they were

impatient to catch up with him. There were five in the group, spread out over two hundred metres. From his vantage-point, deep in his hide, he could either see or hear all of them.

He let them pass and waited for the second team.

They followed fifteen minutes later, noisier than the first. They didn't expect trouble, believing those in the earlier group would encounter Duncan first. Their line was scattered, their cover minimal. They were impatient to catch up with the action.

The soldier Duncan chose to hit first was the one who at that moment lagged behind to relieve himself only a few metres from the hide.

He was obviously desperate, his relief obvious from the animal grunts he made as he urinated against a tree. Just as he was about to finish, when his mind was at its most relaxed, Duncan struck.

He came out of the hide fast and silent, his long-bladed knife already held forward and pointed at the soldier.

The Russian spun round, his hands still round his penis, as Duncan came up behind him and drove the knife through the back of his neck.

A fountain of blood and urine sprayed up as the soldier fell back, his kidneys still working although he was dead by the time he hit the ground.

One minute later, the dead officer was buried in the hide where Duncan had lain. His weapons, which included two hand-grenades and another Kalashnikov, were stripped from him and taken to be safely stored in the next hide, some eighty metres away.

Duncan, now concealed in the second shelter, waited for the next group.

Before they arrived, one of the dead soldier's comrades came back looking for him. Duncan watched him as he called his name and stumbled through the undergrowth looking for his friend.

When he came near the second hide, his automatic now in the firing position but with the safety-catch on, Duncan waited for him to pass.

Before the soldier was aware of anything, Duncan was out of his hole, the knife pushed up through the soldier's chest, puncturing his left lung and straight into his heart. As the man fell dead, Duncan put his arms round his waist and picked him up in a fireman's lift. He ran with him for some hundred and fifty metres in the direction that the second group had gone, well away from the line of hides. Satisfied that he had moved far enough away, he laid him on his stomach, in an open area where he could easily be found. He then took his extra ammunition-clips and two more hand-grenades. He pulled the pin on one of the grenades and wedged it under the dead soldier. The weight of the soldier kept the detonator in place. He had already placed two more grenades, their pins still intact, in the dead man's pockets, next to where the live grenade was now primed.

He turned and ran back to his second hide where he once again took up his position.

Within five minutes the third wave of soldiers came along. It was the largest group by far, consisting of six KGB officers and three policemen. One of them was the local officer from Talica called out to help in the search. When they had passed, Duncan slithered out of his shelter and backtracked to the first hide.

The Talica policeman found the corpse, shouted out the alarm. The others hurriedly took cover, searched the trees and undergrowth for any sign of warning movement. Then they started to shout to one another, trying to determine what had happened.

Duncan watched them, unseen in his position. He saw one of the KGB officers move towards the corpse, get to within five metres of the body. Satisfied that there was no immediate danger, he signalled the others forward and waited for them. A small group formed around the lifeless soldier.

Duncan was surprised by their amateur actions but realized that they were local officers who had never been trained in basic warfare. He wanted to call out, warn them of their stupidity. But the weapons they carried made them his enemy; there would be no mercy if he was caught now.

He watched the inevitable happen.

One of the KGB officers moved forward and turned the dead soldier over so that he could identify him.

The hand-grenade rolled over, its spring popping out as it was detonated. The group of men recoiled as they realized that a booby trap had been sprung. The body turned halfway on to its back, the two other grenades now also visible.

As they turned to run, Duncan opened fire from the hide, spraying them with the Kalashnikov from eighty metres away.

The group panicked, some started to shoot blindly in his direction, others fell to the ground to take cover.

The first grenade blew four seconds after it had been detonated. The force of the explosion ripped through the other two grenades, detonating them simultaneously.

The explosion either killed or disabled five of the group, including the policeman from Talica. Later on the investigating officers would find his hip flask intact, half-full of Japanese whisky.

As Duncan continued to shoot, the second group, on hearing the explosion and burst of fire, raced back to support their comrades under attack. Duncan slipped his now empty Kalashnikov into the first hide and moved under cover to the farthest hide on the left. He slid into it and positioned himself so he could watch their movements.

It took time for them to organize themselves, and the soldiers panicked; firing easily gave away their positions.

He saw them spread out and moved towards the position from which he had opened up on them.

It was a time to watch. They were not his real targets.

Back at the chapel, Vashinov stood at the door and looked in the direction the shootings and explosions had come from. Behind him, Myeloski sat down, still mortified by the sight of the dead priest and Vera.

'They think they've got him pinned down, General,' one of the local KGB officers shouted, holding up the radio which was their contact with the men in the forest.

'What's happened? Ask them, for fuck's sake!' Vashinov screamed back.

The officer spoke into the radio, then ran towards Vashinov. 'He opened fire on them. Hit a lot of them. But they know where he was shooting from. They're circling the area.'

'Kill him! Don't take chances. Just kill the bastard.'

The officer repeated the order into the transmitter. 'They want more men, sir.'

'Then, get up there. You,' he said pointing to the radio operator, 'stay here. I need to be in contact.'

He watched as the remainder of the soldiers started to move up the hill. 'And be fucking careful. Don't walk into another ambush,' he shouted after the disappearing men.

He turned and looked at Myeloski.

'We'll see the end of this little game soon.' The general came into the chapel, closing the door behind him. He looked at the two bodies, now covered in blankets. 'What do you think the priest was doing here?'

'I don't know.'

'This chapel. That graveyard outside. Well maintained, eh? I wonder why. Do you think he knew the priest?'

'Maybe. Except he'd never been here before.'

'He's a Denknetzeyan. And this is his family home.

They've probably been paying the priest for years to look after this lot. Even holy men are open to a bit of bribery, you know.'

Myeloski's silence irritated Vashinóv. He saw it as insolence.

'You're the policeman. You're going to have to make a report directly to the president.' Vashinov deliberately kept Marshka's name out of it, didn't want Myeloski to know that he had bugged his telephone-call. 'You must tell him about the priest.'

'Maybe he did know him. Or maybe he just happened to be here.'

'Why?'

'Because it's a church.'

'Everyone prays these days. You don't have to sneak all the way up here to do it. And this isn't a real church, just a relic from the past. That policeman from Talica, he identified the priest. Said he served a number of churches in the region.'

'Then, why was he here?'

'Doesn't it spark your policeman's curiosity?'

Myeloski knew he was being needled. But he didn't want to rise to it, sensed that he wasn't yet out of danger. 'It'll come out in time.'

'Even a little spark.'

'Let's catch the Englishman first. He'll have the answers.'

'Not if he's dead.'

'They might take him alive.'

Vashinov laughed. 'After he's killed half my men?'

Myeloski didn't reply. Vashinov walked to the front of the chapel and kicked the blanket that covered Vera off her face. He looked down at her head, almost severed from her body. Her eyes were still open, the shock of seeing the dead priest still contorting her lips back as she had been killed.

'She was the best,' the general said wistfully.

Myeloski looked away, not able to behold the scene before him.

'If you don't know about the priest, then tell me why she was here.'

'I have no idea.'

'You spent time with her and the Englishman. They must have said something.'

'Nothing.'

'They killed your boss.'

Myeloski stood up, his fat frame shaking with emotion. But he still maintained his silence.

'There must've been a reason. They must've said something, given some clue.' Vashinov came back to Myeloski, stood before him flaunting his power, his hands defiantly resting on his hips. 'Tell me. What do you know of the Beria Archives?'

Myeloski stared ahead, puzzled by the question.

'I mean, the Denknetzeyans were White Russians. Committed to the Romanovs. Determined to bring about the downfall of the Republics. And they had the money to do it. After all, they're rich bankers. And he was here with the Oldenburgs. It smells a bit, don't you think?'

The Beria Archives. What were the Beria Archives? And what did they have to do with the Romanovs? Myeloski said nothing as his mind raced frantically, trying to find a thread in Vashinov's muddled words.

'I think the Englishman meant us all great harm. The girl was just stupid, a diversion. He used her, used her devotion to him. But this priest, there must be others like him. Others paid by foreign money to build up a network of agitators to bring back the Romanovs. I think your boss, Yashkin, stumbled on the truth. That's why they killed him.'

Vashinov turned away, triumphant in his untruth. The baiting torment of Myeloski had unwittingly solved his problem. He would, through his trusted KGB operatives, lay clues that would reveal an underground conspiracy to bring back the Romanovs. He would reveal the president for the weak fool he was and put the whole affair down to Western money, Western influence and Western greed.

Myeloski saw the opening, saw where this had all come from.

'Baikolovo. That's where the real answer is.' He regretted the words before he had finished saying them. The look on Vashinov's face as he spun round told him that he had just signed his own death-warrant.

'So you do know.'

'Only rumours. I hear only rumours.'

'A little knowledge is, indeed, a very dangerous thing. Just like your boss. Thought he knew all the answers. Knew nothing in the end.' Vashinov grinned. In the distance they heard the rapid fire of gunshots. 'Looks like they've found your Englishman.'

He went to the door and opened it. 'What's happened?' he asked the radio operator, who was listening to a report on his radio set.

'They've got him. He's gone down into a hole in the ground. They're working round him, surrounding him. They're going in with grenades and automatics,' the officer yelled, his voice high with excitement.

Vashinov turned to Myeloski, his grin triumphant.

'Nearly there, my friend,' he said, his harsh voice chilling the fat policeman. 'All will soon be over.'

Vashinov came back into the chapel, closing the door behind him. In the distance the rate of gunfire increased as his men closed in for the kill.

By spreading themselves over a wide area, the KGB trackers had stumbled on one of the five hides.

Realizing that their quarry had gone to ground, they had organized themselves more thoroughly as they pushed back through the undergrowth.

451

They found his hiding-place ten minutes later.

A policeman had seen the barrel of a Kalashnikov with its round muzzle barely inches out of a hide. He had signalled the others, and the officers had slowly worked their way round until they surrounded the ground shelter. This time they were more careful, alert and ready for any possible booby traps. They had even switched off their radio communicators so that there would be no unnecessary sound to give themselves away.

The senior KGB officer, he who had led the first group past Duncan, opened fire first, his Kalashnikov ripping bullets into the hide. Next to him the radio operator hurriedly reported their discovery to those waiting at the chapel.

The rest followed immediately, a vicious crossfire of lead tearing into the body that lay hidden there. One of the soldiers threw a grenade which exploded yards short of the shelter, throwing up dirt and rotten undergrowth. A policeman, unused to his weapon, thought he saw a man stand up. The policeman raised his line of fire, and the bullet struck a KGB officer on the opposite side. As he fell, his companions thought that the Englishman had stood up and was retaliating, so they, too, raised their line of fire.

The crossfire knocked out three others, before someone realized what was happening and screamed for them to stop shooting.

When silence had come back to the forest, when they realized that the man in the shelter was dead, the senior KGB officer came forward to see the damage they had done.

That's when he saw the body wasn't that of the Englishman, but of a dead KGB officer.

The Kalashnikov that was strapped to the dead man's arm told him that they had been set up.

He yelled a warning, and those that had not been hit by their own men dived for cover.

They lay hidden behind trees in silence before the senior officer told them to spread out once again.

But they knew the Englishman had gone. Otherwise he would have taken them out when they discovered the decoy.

The senior officer reached over and took the radio from its operator, dead after having been hit in the chest by the crossfire.

He switched it on and spoke quietly into it, wanting further instructions.

In the distance he heard men running through the undergrowth. It was the reinforcements Vashinov had sent up.

Through the closed door Vashinov heard the radio crackling its excited message. He listened for his operator to reply, but there was only silence.

Impatient to know what had taken place, he turned away from Myeloski and opened the door.

The operator lay on the wooden steps, a thin red line across his neck where his throat had been cut. The blood spread down across his collar and soaked into the front of his shirt as Vashinov watched.

The radio was in Duncan's hand. In the other was a Kalashnikov with its black muzzle pointing straight at Vashinov.

The commander in the forest asked for further instructions over the radio.

'Keep moving forward. Follow him. Every available man.' Duncan spoke into the radio before putting it down.

He came forward, pushing Vashinov back into the chapel with the barrel of his gun. Behind the general, Duncan saw Myeloski, his eyes open, incredulous at the sudden turn of events. Vashinov moved back until he was level with the policeman.

As Duncan came into the chapel, he saw the two

bodies lying there. He saw Vera's uncovered face, saw the look of terror frozen on her features. He half-turned towards her, the emotion washing over him.

In that moment of lost concentration, Vashinov moved.

He spun behind Myeloski, grabbed him round the neck as he drew his pistol from its holster. He held the gun to the policeman's head, was shielded from Duncan's weapon by the fat man.

'Stand off,' he said.

Duncan brought the automatic to bear on the two of them, but he knew Myeloski was dead if he continued.

'Put it down.'

Duncan shook his head, kept the gun pointed at the two of them.

'Then, it's a trade. His fat life for mine.'

'No.'

'There's no choice. Move to the side, then let me pass. When I'm outside I'll take him towards the forest. When I'm there, safe, I'll let him go.'

'No.'

'He's your friend. You're pulling the trigger.'

Vashinov pushed Myeloski towards the door, forcing Duncan to go backwards. In this strange formation they left the chapel and came out into the open. Duncan swung round so that his back was to the wall. He moved closer to them, his gun-barrel only inches from Vashinov's head. He saw Vashinov tighten his grip on the trigger; knew that if he shot the general the muscle spasm in Vashinov's hand would fire the gun into Myeloski's head.

'Stand back!' ordered Vashinov.

Myeloski's eyes were rolling with panic, but he kept his teeth clenched tight.

Vashinov grinned and then walked backwards with Myeloski. He knew Duncan wouldn't want to break from the cover of the chapel. The distance between them increased as Duncan stayed with his back to the wall.

It was at that moment that Myeloski fainted, his body heavy and limp in Vashinov's hold.

Behind Vashinov, Duncan saw one of the KGB officers returning to the chapel. When he saw what was taking place, he opened fire, shooting towards Duncan.

Duncan rolled towards the open door, firing at the officer some sixty metres away. Vashinov, now encumbered with Myeloski's dead weight, let the policeman fall and sprinted towards the forest, firing at Duncan as he did. Duncan's Kalashnikov jammed at the precise moment and he pulled out the Coonan Magnum, but Vashinov was zig-zagging out of range. He pulled out one of the hand-grenades he had left, flicked the pin and threw it towards the soldier who was firing. The grenade exploded, and a piece of shrapnel hit him in the leg, bringing him down.

Myeloski was coming round, and Duncan shouted at him: 'Come on. Come on.'

The policeman heaved himself up and ran towards the chapel. Duncan grabbed his arm and pulled him into the chapel. Vashinov was nearly up to the trees by now.

'Let's get out of here. Can you run?'

Myeloski nodded. Duncan told him to run back to the house, down to Destayala.

As the policeman ran away from the chapel, Duncan went in and knelt by Vera. He closed her eyes, then her mouth. He kissed her gently, stroked her cheek. He never saw the ugly wound, only her beauty as he had known her. Then he covered her face with the blanket, turned and left her in peace in that small chapel.

He caught up with Myeloski, now panting heavily, near the villa. He led him into the trees to where the red Datsun had been hidden.

When they were both in, after he had pulled off the branches with which he had hidden the Datsun, he started the engine and gunned the red sports-car past the house and down the driveway. Through the trees he saw Vashinov's helicopter parked in a clearing and saw men running towards them.

But they were clear, and he sped down the path and back on to the road that led to Talica.

'Don't go into Talica,' warned Myeloski. Duncan applied the brake and skidded the car off the road and under the trees. 'He'll have his men there. And they're on a shoot-to-kill order.'

'Even if I'm with *you*?'

'You've just saved my life, Marko Markovich. If you think I'm your passport to freedom, forget it.'

'Still stuck together, eh?'

Myeloski nodded. 'I'm sorry about Vera.'

'Yeah. Well. We've got to get to Sverdlovsk. Work our way back to Moscow.'

'No. They'll be watching for us. We've no chance against the KGB. Let's go north.'

'Why north?'

'To a small town. Baikolovo.'

'What the hell for?'

'Turn around and take the road to Tiumen. After a few kilometres from here you'll find a road to the north, to Troitskiy. Take it. Have you a map here?'

'In the back,' replied Duncan. He spun the car back on the road and accelerated sharply away from Talica. As he drove he watched the policeman rummage in the back of the small car for the road-map Morrison had supplied. He knew Myeloski would tell him in time and he trusted the policeman's instincts when it came to turning half-rumours into cold facts.

Four kilometres later they reached the left turn that led to Troitskiy. As Duncan swung into the turn, he heard the clatter of a helicopter in the distance. It had to be one of the KGB gunships. He put his foot down, pushed the car until the speedometer needle swung over 180 kilometers per hour and tucked in under the tree overhang, with two wheels in the dirt and two on the road.

The sound of the helicopter faded above the roar of the engine as it pulled away towards Talica. Myeloski, his head banging on the rear of the roof, turned back to the front, a map clutched in his hand.

'Can't you bloody drive straight,' he snarled, 'or aren't our Russian roads good enough for you?'

As he looked out of the front windscreen, he saw the road unwinding rapidly in front of him. Only then did he realize the speed they were doing. It was too much for Myeloski and he looked down, frantically studying the map that he had opened on his lap.

'It's about forty kilometres from here,' he shouted, not looking up from his endeavours. 'Turn right at Troitskiy and you'll pick up the road soon afterwards.'

The paint-faded signpost to Troitskiy came up a few moments later, and Duncan slowed the car down as he entered the town. It was as Talica, small and provincial. The streets were empty as they drove through. Once out of the centre the car built up speed again as they hurtled along the country road.

As Myeloski had predicted, the road to Baikolovo came up almost immediately, and Duncan turned north towards their destination.

'Why we going there?'

Myeloski, without looking up, told Duncan of his visit to the old steelworker, Igor Mischnev. As he spoke, his voice trembled as his body was bumped vigorously by the speeding car. He told him of the conversation, of the old man's confession that he knew where the Romanovs could have been taken.

'Why didn't he tell me?'

Myeloski snorted, then tapped his nose. 'You only have a nose for trouble, not for sniffing things out.'

'It's saved you a couple of times. So why Baikolovo?'

'After I finished with the old man I went back to the

457

police station. Went through the old maps of the region, through the criminal records, found out where the asylums were. I knew they had to be within a day's travel. I found only one that dated back to the revolution.'

'Baikolovo.'

'You'll make a detective yet. Yes. Just outside the town.'

The terrain had gradually begun to change as they roared along, the narrow road breaking out of the forest and on to the flatland of the permafrost, deeply scarred by the peat-cutters as they toiled for their sparse rewards.

'Why did you run? Why didn't you go back to Moscow with your people?' Myeloski asked his companion.

'He was going to kill Vera. I couldn't leave her there.'

'Why?'

'She saw him kill Yashkin.'

Duncan heard Myeloski swear under his breath, the truth sucking the breath out of him. He said nothing until the policeman had composed himself.

'What happened?'

Duncan repeated the terrible saga that Vera had told him, omitting only the details of Yashkin's horrible death at the hands of Vashinov.

'It's hard to believe that Allah is always merciful,' was Myeloski's only comment when Duncan had finished. 'But we must. It's the only fucking way to hang on. The story they put out was that either you or the girl had killed him. Why didn't you take the girl with you? Back to Moscow with your people?'

'I told you. She was in her room. Under guard. I wouldn't have got her out of the front door.'

'What the hell are we doing here? What the hell are we going to find?'

'I've no idea.'

'Probably find Lenin, Stalin and the whole fucking Romanov family locked away up here.'

As they sped along, Myeloski reached in his pocket for a cigarette, which he eventually lit, having first devoured a Hershey bar which he found squashed in his coat pocket. As the small car filled with the pungent smoke of the policeman's cigarette, Duncan heard the distant sound of a helicopter. Out in the open, he knew that he would easily be spotted on the empty road. He jammed on the brakes, and the car slid off the road and on to the soft shoulder.

They searched the sky to the west until they saw the glinting blades of the Havok gunship as it sped northwards. It seemed not to be looking for them, seemed to have a different purpose as it raced along at only a few hundred feet above the ground. When it was clear of them, Duncan drove back on to the road and continued on towards Baikolovo.

They saw the building before they saw the town.

It was an old square stone building that lay well back from the road. A high wall with an iron-railing top surrounded it. The small windows and starkness of the place told them it was what they were looking for.

The sign at the entrance simply confirmed their instinct: 'BAIKOLOVO SOVIET ASYLUM FOR THE INSANE.'

As the car swung through the old metal gates and on to the narrow shale driveway, they saw the Havok gunship settled on the patchy grass that constituted part of the garden. The house was nearly two hundred metres away, and Duncan saw the faces of people in the distance, peering out through the small barred windows. They had obviously been attracted by the landing helicopter, not an everyday sight at this forsaken place.

Duncan braked the car viciously to a full stop, then climbed out, grabbing a Kalashnikov from the rear. Myeloski followed him. There was nothing else he could do.

By the helicopter, two KGB combat officers stood

near their machine. Neither was obviously armed. A third sat in the cockpit of the Havok. Duncan presumed him to be the pilot.

Vashinov leant against one of the few silver birch trees scattered throughout the garden. Those in the house couldn't see him; the gunship obstructed their view of the KGB general.

'What's he up to now?' asked a vexed Myeloski.

'Have you got that gun of yours?'

'Yes.'

'You're probably going to have to use it.' As Duncan warned Myeloski, he searched the wall for any further KGB men. The place was singularly deserted. 'If you hear a shot, get down fast. They could have a sniper up at the house.'

He moved forward carefully, his gun cocked and ready to fire.

As they got nearer the small group, none of the KGB officers made any move to alarm them.

'He's tied to the fucking tree.' Myeloski was first to realize that Vashinov had his arms bound behind him. A wire hawser was attached round his ankles and snaked along the ground to where it was secured to the helicopter undercarriage.

They stopped about twenty metres from the group, Duncan's machine-gun now pointing directly at the senior KGB officer by the gunship.

'Journey's end, my friend. You won't need that.' The senior officer came towards them, his hands held high to signify he was unarmed.

Duncan stood his ground, the barrel of his weapon never wavering from the officer's chest.

'What's this, then?' shouted Myeloski. 'What tricks are you people up to now?'

The KGB man stopped. 'No tricks. Just changing the rules.'

'Why?'

'Because that's the way it is. The result is all that concerns you. Not the cause.'

'Shoot him, Englishman. Don't bloody think they're not after you as well,' Vashinov shouted over to them.

'He's got a point,' said Duncan, moving closer to the officer, his gun now only inches from his chest.

'You're not that important. You can just go home when all this is over. Both of you.'

'How do we know that?'

The officer laughed. 'Trust in *glasnost*,' he replied, turning his back on Duncan and walking towards the bound Vashinov.

'Kill him now,' pleaded the general. 'I'm your only chance to get back alive.'

'You don't remember me, do you?' the officer asked Vashinov when he had reached him.

'I'll remember you when I sign your execution order.'

'Not even a twinge of memory. That's a pity. Dying without knowing why you're dying.' He turned to the second officer by the Havok and signalled him over.

When his subordinate reached him, he held out his hand. The second officer gave him a rusty metal implement, machete-like in its shape. It was an old peat-cutting tool. He turned back to the general.

'I come from this region, you know. This is what they used to cut the peat. My father worked the cuttings. East of here, near Irbit. He wanted more for me, didn't want me to be a peat-cutter like him. So he got me into the KGB, back there in the old camp at Irbit. All he wanted was for me to have a better life.' As he spoke, he swung the tool menacingly in front of Vashinov.

'What's that to do with me?'

'I'll tell you what it's got to do with you. Because I was good, because I fitted in and was conscientious, they transferred me to Moscow. I was nineteen years old and proud of what I had achieved. Then you came along. I remember the first time I saw you. You were a colonel then. The rising star. You impressed me. And I thought I impressed you. Only you didn't want a good officer. All you wanted was another fresh arse to bugger, another boy to beat up. You still don't remember, do you? And when you'd had enough you just wrote me off. Sent me back to Irbit. Well, I didn't forget you. I wear these epaulettes because I earned them. How many boys did you destroy, Vashinov?'

'You're fucking mad.' Vashinov turned and shouted at Duncan. 'If he harms me, you'll never get out of Russia alive. Shoot him and I'll protect you. I swear it.'

The officer turned and looked at Duncan, waited for his answer. After a moment, the Englishman lowered his Kalashnikov to the ground. The officer turned back to Vashinov.

'It's time, General. Any last requests?'

'Be a realist. You have ambition. Use it.'

'No final requests, sir?' The officer's simple question told Vashinov that he was a dead man.

'Fuck you!' Then Vashinov laughed. 'But, then, I already did. Arsehole.'

'Why? Why did you do all that?'

'That, my little cunt, is for me to know and you never to find out.'

Vashinov's laughter grew louder, his body convulsed with the irony of it all. And he remembered his mother, and his own desperate youth, and hated her. Before he died, he blamed her for all he had become.

And his booming laughter turned into a piercing scream as the officer drove the rusted blunt machete into his groin, splitting him open from his balls to his belly button.

Vashinov's head and chest slumped, his waist remained firm, wedged into the tree by the peat-cutter.

Myeloski turned away and was sick as the officer freed the cutter from the tree, wiggling it loose as the blood poured down and stained the tree.

Duncan, realizing their danger now that Vashinov was

dead, pointed the gun at the officer who turned to face them.

'Cut him loose,' the officer ordered his number two, then signalled the pilot to start up the turbine.

As the blades slowly started to wind up, he came to Duncan.

'You don't need that,' he said, indicating the gun. 'You're both free to go.'

'Why're you here? In this place?' asked Duncan, the gun still held steady and level.

'Because this is where he said you would come. And where I was ordered to wait for him.'

'By Moscow?'

The officer shrugged. His orders were not the Englishman's business.

'And the Beria Archives?' Duncan asked.

'What's that? I've done what I had to do.' The officer looked down at the still retching Myeloski. 'Get your friend out of here. He needs your help.'

The officer turned away and went to the gunship.

Duncan helped Myeloski up and led him to the car. When they had reached the red Datsun, they turned to see the Havok lift into the air, the steel hawser still connected to its undercarriage. As they watched, the helicopter turned westwards and tracked through the gate and across the permafrost, no more than twenty feet above the ground.

Vashinov's body was dragged behind, bumping along the hard ground as it was towed at high speed into the distance. Duncan knew that the body would be disintegrated within fifteen minutes, that there would be no trace left of Vashinov, no evidence that he had ever existed. Before anyone ever managed to search the area, the wolves and other wild animals of the area would have devoured whatever was strewn over the wide area the helicopter would now cover.

When Myeloski had finally stopped retching he helped

him into the car, then walked round and climbed in the driver's seat.

'You OK?' he asked an ashen-faced Myeloski, who nodded.

'There was no need for all that.'

'Fair justice. Live by the penis, die by the penis.'

'You have an awful sense of humour.'

'Yeah? Tell that to Vera. And Yashkin.'

Duncan put the car into gear and drove up towards the peering faces and the barred windows of the Baikolovo Soviet Asylum for the Insane.

Myeloski said nothing. He knew that, for all its violence, justice had finally been served.

Marshka's dacha
Outside Moscow

'Irbit on the line, sir,' said the assistant, handing the receiver to Marshka.

The old man took the phone and waited for his man to leave the room before he spoke.

'Is it done?' he asked.

'The plan was executed as requested, sir.'

'Good.'

'The Englishman and policeman were there.'

'How are they now?'

'In good health. Probably on their way back to Moscow. Do you wish to have a full report?'

'No need. All is best forgotten.'

'And the files?'

'Any record of duties carried out by you or your two companions in the past will be destroyed immediately.'

'They'll be relieved to know that.'

'How is the family?'

'Well, sir. I look forward to seeing them on my return to Moscow.'

'No doubt they are as eager to see you as you are them.'

He clicked the phone down and then buzzed for his assistant.

'Call the president's office,' he said when the man answered. 'Say it is a matter of urgency that I see him immediately.'

When the assistant had left the room, Marshka wheeled himself over to the window and looked out on the pleasant garden that surrounded the house. He had always enjoyed it and now he missed the walks he used to take around the grounds.

He sighed at the inevitability of the future.

He would miss it all.

Baikolovo Soviet Asylum for the Insane
Baikolovo
Western Siberia

Myeloski stared out of the upstairs window, down at the small crowd who had congregated round the red Datsun that was parked there.

A mixture of inmates and guards, it was probably the first time any of them had seen such a car with its fiery sports look. He saw that some of the inmates kept their distance, frightened by the car as if expecting it suddenly to roar into life and charge them, hurt them. One of the older women, in a faded floral-print smock, kept darting through the crowd and prodding the car, then running away and hiding behind the others.

They may seem mad to us, he thought, but they're as sane as anybody in the security of their own worlds.

Duncan sat on a bench behind him, lost in his own thoughts. Myeloski wanted to reach out to him, but knew he couldn't touch him.

They waited for the asylum director, not knowing what they would find or what to expect.

They had driven up to the building, watched by the confused and excited faces at the windows. No one had come to greet them as they climbed out of the car, and Myeloski had walked up to the large thick wooden door and rung the bell.

A male nurse had opened it, keeping it slightly ajar, not wanting to allow Myeloski in. It was to be expected. It was a secret place lost in its own past and its own being.

It was not a place for outsiders, whoever they might be.

'I want to see whoever's in charge,' said Myeloski weakly, still not fully recovered from his ordeal of only a few minutes earlier.

'The director is busy,' came the quick defensive reply. 'Why do you want to see him?'

'Police business. It's an urgent and confidential matter.' Myeloski produced his warrant-card and showed it to the nurse.

The man nodded, then started to close the door, but Myeloski put his foot against it, jammed it open.

'You must wait here,' said the alarmed nurse. 'I will tell the director.'

And he shoved harder on the door, forcing Myeloski to retreat backwards. The door thudded shut with a heavy force as Duncan came up alongside him.

Five minutes later the door was opened once again by the nurse. 'Come with me,' he snapped.

The two of them followed him into the dim gloominess of the asylum, a building little changed since it had been built over a hundred and fifty years earlier. The nurse led them down the high-ceilinged hall and towards the staircase at the end. All the doors were thick and had heavy bolts on them.

As they climbed the narrow stairs, frightened faces

466

appeared at the landings, faces that became nervous forms which scuttled away as Duncan and Myeloski approached them.

A small group of five inmates was clustered at the bottom of the steps that led to the second landing. The nurse roughly pushed past them and entered a small office that looked out on to the front courtyard.

As Duncan and Myeloski tried to follow him, a young overweight woman in the group suddenly tore her smock off and threw herself at Myeloski, laughing as she rubbed her naked fleshy body all over him. The others all joined in, jostling the policeman as he fought to get past.

The nurse came out into the hall and fought his way through to Myeloski, brutally pushing the group aside. He pulled the girl from Myeloski, deliberately squeezing her heavy breasts in his hands, making her yelp with pain. He threw her to the ground, cruelly laughing as he did, treating her as if she was his property to be dealt with as he wished.

Duncan moved quickly to protect her, but Myeloski stopped him. He led the Englishman into the room, through the babble as the inmates ran for the stairs and for the safety of the building's recesses.

'Wait here,' said the grinning nurse, closing the door and leaving them alone in the small office.

Twenty minutes later, as Myeloski stared out of the window at the group round the red Datsun, the door opened and the director of the asylum, a weasel of a man in a grey suit, walked in.

'Why do you want to see me?' he asked curtly, going to his desk and sitting down. 'What official business does a policeman want with me?'

'We're trying to trace long-lost relatives of someone who was killed in Moscow. We believe they could be here.' Myeloski's lie flowed easily from his tongue, causing Duncan to look up sharply at the policeman.

'A letter would suffice. Why take the trouble to come all the way out here?'

'That doesn't concern you, Comrade Director.' The hard bullying edge had returned to Myeloski's voice.

'Was the helicopter that landed earlier also none of my concern?'

'Yes.' Myeloski glanced at Duncan, not knowing what the director had seen. 'It was here to help us in our search.'

'For what?'

'For the suspected perpetrators of a serious crime in Moscow. We believe that someone may be coming here with the intention of harming one or more of your inmates.'

'Why?'

'That is not for discussion at this stage.'

'I see. Then, who are you here to protect?'

'That also is confidential.'

'Bugger your confidences. I don't care what you do outside, but in here it's my responsibility.'

'All I want is to see your records.'

'Only with proper authorization.'

Myeloski took his warrant-card from his pocket and held it in front of the director. The weasel-faced man glanced at it, then shook his head.

'That only proves you're a policeman. Nothing else.'

'I can have this place crawling with police within the hour. And the KGB. It's a joint operation. That was their helicopter. Do you really want me to do all that?'

The director was not a man easily intimidated. 'If you want. All I ask for is proper authority,' he answered the red-faced Myeloski.

'How far back do your records go?' Duncan's cool voice cut through the tension.

They both turned and looked at him.

'The people we're looking for are very old,' he continued, rising from his chair and coming over to the director's desk. As his coat swung open, the butt of the Coonan Magnum in its holster was conspicuously visible. 'I can assure you we mean them no harm. We are here to protect. To that end we have the same motive. It would be unfair to them for you to doubt us.'

The director watched the eyes of the man who spoke. He was used to reading personalities, understanding temperaments. Unlike the fat policeman, whom he knew was simply a bully with no real resources, the other was a person of substance. He was not a man who would accept refusal easily, would use any means to achieve his conclusions. The quiet glint of the pistol-handle simply confirmed the director's view.

'Our records were only started properly in the nineteen fifties. Until then, asylums weren't hospitals, but simply places where you threw those who didn't fit. How old are the people you're looking for?'

'In their nineties.'

'There can't be that many old people here. Not that old.' Myeloski tried to take the initiative again.

'We have over four hundred inmates here. Many of them – probably as many as thirty – are in their later life. This is not a pleasant place. In many cases, we have no idea where they came from, or what was wrong with them. Many were locked in here because they were an embarrassment. Over the decades, even those who pleaded that they weren't insane were locked away in little rooms until they became so. It was a terrible place. My predecessor came here in the sixties and worked wonders to improve things. In my time, in the last eight years, I have tried to follow his example. It's difficult; we have few resources. But we do our best with what we have. If I appear guarded, then it is because I simply want to protect my patients. That's why I ask for proper authority.'

'I understand that,' replied Duncan. 'But we have to progress. You can see I'm a foreigner.' The director nodded. 'I'm English. I was sent over here to find some people who were kidnapped. Those people, English but of Russian origin, were related to the Romanovs.' Duncan saw the director's eyes suddenly sharpen, knew that he was on the right track. 'Although that mission was successful, it's opened another doorway. If the rumours that have surfaced are taken seriously, then someone here could be in great danger.'

'And what is that rumour?'

'That not all the Romanovs were killed. That some were brought to this place and left to rot and die.'

'Impossible. I would know.'

'Not if you haven't records. We're talking about seventy years ago,' Myeloski snorted.

'Impossible to conceal.'

'Even if they were brought here and locked away, never to be seen again? Who would believe them, here in this place?'

'It would have been known.'

'Are there any patients who have claimed to be Romanovs?' Duncan's quiet question was explosive.

The director rose from his desk and went to the window. He looked down at the group which was still fascinated by the red car.

He turned back and faced the two men. He knew they would bring more if they weren't satisfied.

'Come with me,' he said.

Then he led them out of his office and into the darkened corridor.

The president's office
The Kremlin
Moscow

The eyes of the boy were the eyes of the father.

'Hello, Uncle.'

'Comrade President.'

'So it's to be an official meeting.'

'At times like this, yes, it's best to be formal.'

The president closed the door and pushed the wheelchair towards the desk.

'Take me to the window,' said Marshka. 'I want to look down on the cathedrals.'

The president pushed the old man past the desk and to the window.

'Bring your chair next to mine. Enjoy this with me.'

The president turned his chair away from the desk and sat. The two men looked out on the crispness of the late afternoon, watched the *apparatchiks* and the tourists mingling in the sunshine below.

'Would you like me to order a samovar of tea, Uncle?'

'No. Afternoon tea is for old men. Not for us, little reindeer.' He reached over and touched the president's hand, held it in his own. 'All those people. Faceless. But each has a story, each has love and tears and money problems. And every one of those scurrying nameless people down there thinks that his problem is the most important on earth. Isn't it amazing how we all feel painful emotion, yet rarely understand that those next to us can feel just as deeply?'

'Isn't that the strength of man's survival?'

'Can a ruler ever understand his subjects? Can he do his best for them because he believes he suffers with them? I used to think so. But I was wrong. To find that out after all these years. It's a terrible waste of life.'

'You did everything because you believed in it.'

'Arrogance. Nothing more. Camouflaged as strength and humility.'

'It's not over yet. The Soviet people will realize that their future is in unity. They can keep their nationalism, their religion, their local laws. But to have a tsar as their symbol of unity. It can work, Uncle.'

'Time will tell.' The old man chuckled. 'My father

471

believed it would make Russia whole again. I followed his dream. I should have had my own.'

'You did what you believed in. It's what you always taught me.'

'I did what was good for me. That's why I survived. Stalin, Khrushchev, Brezhnev. I outlasted them all. Because I did what was good for me. Were they the honest men, little reindeer? Or me? At least you knew where you stood with them.'

'Where now, Uncle?'

'You were right. We should have left it to the people. Not tried to influence them as I did with my little tricks. Hmph,' he snorted loudly, as though dismissing himself. 'No place for tricksters like me any more.'

'I need your support.'

'You don't. You're your father's son. You can stand alone.'

'I want to change the Politburo. We don't need the KGB on it any longer.'

'Or me.'

The president didn't answer for a moment. His voice was more determined when he finally spoke. 'You must have a hero's retirement. That will be—'

'No.' Marshka interrupted and released his grip on the president's hand. 'I am the villain. Act accordingly. Strip me of my honours, tell the truth of what took place. If the truth doesn't come out now, then it will only come back to haunt you. Too many people know of my involvement in the kidnappings. There is no alternative. It was a mad scheme anyway. That's what comes from years of plotting and bending the rules. Reality and madness – it all becomes one. You must distance yourself from me.'

'I can't do that,' said the president. 'You're my family.'

Marshka smiled. He looked at his protégé's face and remembered the time in Leningrad with the dead

German officer. He knew then that it would be all right. Duty would come first.

The eyes of the son were truly the eyes of the father.

In the gardens
Baikolovo Soviet Asylum for the Insane
Baikolovo
Western Siberia

The graveyard had grown over the years, starting from a small plot by the kitchen gardens and spreading away from the house towards the southern perimeter.

The older parts were overgrown, owing to the shortage of land and the high death rate of the inmates. Many of the graves had been used more than once; it didn't matter because nobody mourned the asylum's dead. In those far-off days before the turn of the century, it was an embarrassment forgotten, a humiliation discarded.

The newer graves were well tended, and there were two inmates weeding the area as the director led Myeloski and Duncan through the plots.

'Over the years, there must have been more than five hundred people buried here,' the director explained. 'It's easier now; most of the bodies are cremated.'

They left the tidy shale path and walked into the long grass, towards the old section of the cemetery with its broken headstones and forgotten past.

He stopped at the end of a row of graves, between two marble headstones that stood out from the rest because of their polished faces.

No names marked the stones, only simply printed numbers. There were no dates of birth and death, no inscriptions.

'Who are they?' asked Myeloski, kneeling between the graves.

473

'I'm not sure. But each year we get an anonymous donation from Moscow to keep them clean.'

'I presume they were inmates.'

'They were. A man and a woman who were brought here many years ago, well before any records were kept. They said they were brother and sister. The man was sickly and apparently died in 1938, just before war broke out.'

'And the woman?'

'Five years ago. She was well into her eighties.'

'Why show us these graves?' asked Duncan.

'Because she called herself Anastasia. She used to speak of her brother often, used to call for him, didn't accept that he had died. His name was Alexis.'

'The tsarevich.' As Myeloski spoke, he felt the hairs stand up on the back of his neck.

'Possibly. Who knows?'

'How did they come to be here?'

'As I said, it was before we had any proper records. She didn't say much, even during the times I spent with her. She was withdrawn, frightened to speak of her past. She may not even have remembered where she came from. But, if I pushed her too hard, she would break down, cry out for her brother. Then she would go into herself again, only repeating the words, "Mustn't tell. Papa will be angry. Save Alexis."'

'Are you sure no one knew where they came from?'

'I'd tell you if I did. When the records were started, there was a short case-history of each patient. Hers showed that she was kept in a solitary cell for extremely violent patients ever since she arrived. I don't know when that was, except that it was well before the war. Her brother shared the next-door cell. They were pretty basic in those days. Bare wooden floors, a horsehair mattress and a bucket for ablutions. It wouldn't have been unusual for them to have gone for weeks without seeing anyone. Nobody understood the mind then; they were simply locked away.'

'Was she dangerous?'

'No. Really a gentle creature, almost childlike in her actions. I was surprised that she had been classified as dangerous. We tried to move her out into the general wards, but she always wanted to go back to her little cell. We put a decent bed in there, and also a chair and a table. But she continued to sit in a corner near the window, on the cold floor. The only thing she ever did was knit.'

'Knit?'

'That's right. She once responded to treatment when she saw a female nurse knitting some children's clothing. She begged for the wool and needles. We were worried, in case she attacked someone with them. But we decided to let her try. She took to it straight away; it was obviously something she had once been good at. In the end we left her with the needles on her own. She never tried to harm anyone, just sat and knitted. Shawls and scarves. That's all she ever made. I never found out any more.'

'There would have been a guard on her, if she had really been the Grand Duchess Anastasia.'

'No need. If she'd been brought in secretly, locked away as a violent patient, nobody would have believed her anyway. And as the years passed, and staff changed, she would just have been another mad woman with an unknown background. We also have two Napoleons, one Peter the Great and Five Yuri Gagarins.'

The director took them back to the red Datsun, through the crowd of inmates that still surrounded the car, and saw them off.

They had stopped at the gate, turned to take one last look at the building.

'What do you think?' Duncan asked Myeloski.

The policeman shrugged. 'Doesn't matter, does it? Just another rumour now. I'm starving. I've got to eat.'

'Some things never change.'

'I like my food. Got to like something. Are you coming back to Moscow?'

'I want to stay here. In Talica. I'd like to rebuild Destayala.'

'For Vera?'

'For me. For my grandfather. For what I never was. For what I want to be.'

'Good enough reason.'

'It's enough for me. I'm going to bury Vera near Katya. It'll give more meaning to the place for me. Or do you think your Immigration people will throw me out?'

'Not until you've returned Morrison's car.'

'I owe him a guitar.'

'A guitar?'

Duncan laughed. 'Yes. A guitar.'

'So that's what the car cost you. Anyway, when they cut through you, they'll find it's all Russian. No, they won't throw you out.'

'And you?'

'I'll die a Moscow policeman. It's all I know, all that I am. I wouldn't know how to be anything else. I hope I can come up here and spend my holidays with you.'

'Just bring a bag of cement and a shovel.'

The policeman laughed. 'I envy you, Marko Markovich.'

'Why?'

'Because you've got a dream.'

The director of the institute stood and watched the red Datsun spurt forward and swing out of the gate on the road back to Talica.

He turned and looked up at a turreted window, high on the roof-line of the big building. The window, like all the others in the asylum, was barred with a heavy iron grille.

He pondered for a moment, then shrugged and walked into the building. He still had a day's work to get through.

*　　*　　*

The old woman also watched the red car disappear down the road. It was of no real interest to her. Any more than the helicopter had been or the death of the strange shouting man who had been tied to the tree.

She was fortunate. She could see more than most from her barred room at the top of the building.

The excitement ran through her as she looked down. The shawl she was knitting was almost finished.

She was pleased with her handiwork and smiled to herself as she concentrated on finishing the task in hand.

And she hummed softly the tune that had remained in her memory for all these years.

> Ring-a-ring o' roses,
> A pocket full of posies,
> A-tishoo! A-tishoo!
> We all fall down.

THE END

BLOWBACK
by Denis Kilcommons

'IF IT IS A BLOWBACK, WHO'S RESPONSIBLE
FOR THE HITS? THE CIA? THE CHINESE? OR
THE KGB?'

The roll of film on the dead man's body set off alarm
bells in M16. What was the Home Secretary's daughter
doing in Vienna, and in the arms of one of Europe's
most wanted terrorists? Can the scandal be stopped
before it goes too far?

Damage limitation or, as he calls it, cleaning up other
people's messes, is one of Lacey's specialities. So
debriefing Sara Mathieson and dealing with her lover
seems pretty routine. That is, until Sara is killed in SIS
custody and her death is linked to a series of assassin-
ations in Europe. Then Lacey knows it isn't routine. It's
something big: something that doesn't square with the
Rules of the Game. Someone, somewhere is playing
dirty. But is it the Wicked Witch of the East? Or of the
West?

Set in the uncertain new world of East-West relations,
BLOWBACK is a high-speed thriller of almost unbear-
able tension combined with an ingenious plot which
saves its final nerve-jangling secret to the end. Following the promise of the award-winning THE DARK
APOSTLE it confirms Denis Kilcommons as one of
today's masters of the thriller genre.

0 552 13656 9

THE NEGOTIATOR
by Frederick Forsyth

The kidnapping of a young man on a country road in Oxfordshire is but the first brutal step in a ruthless campaign to force the President of the United States out of office. If it succeeds, he will be psychologically and emotionally destroyed. Only one man can stop it – Quinn, the world's foremost Negotiator, who must bargain for the life of an innocent man, unaware that ransom was never the kidnapper's real objective . . .

THE NEGOTIATOR unfolds with the spellbinding excitement, unceasing surprise and riveting detail that are the hallmarks of Frederick Forsyth, the master storyteller.

'Confirms Frederick Forsyth's position as one of the world's best thriller writers'
Wall Street Journal

'Intricately plotted, fast moving and full of surprises'
Evening Standard

0 552 13475 9

A SELECTED LIST OF FINE TITLES
AVAILABLE FROM CORGI BOOKS

THE PRICES SHOWN BELOW WERE CORRECT AT THE TIME OF GOING TO PRESS.
HOWEVER TRANSWORLD PUBLISHERS RESERVE THE RIGHT TO SHOW NEW RETAIL
PRICES ON COVERS WHICH MAY DIFFER FROM THOSE PREVIOUSLY ADVERTISED
IN THE TEXT OR ELSEWHERE.

☐	12504	0	**THE SMOKE**	*Tom Barling* £3.99
☐	13253	5	**SMOKE DRAGON**	*Tom Barling* £3.99
☐	13081	8	**CROW'S PARLIAMENT**	*Jack Curtis* £2.95
☐	13082	6	**GLORY**	*Jack Curtis* £3.99
☐	12550	4	**LIE DOWN WITH LIONS**	*Ken Follett* £3.99
☐	12610	1	**ON WINGS OF EAGLES**	*Ken Follett* £4.99
☐	12180	0	**THE MAN FROM ST PETERSBURG**	*Ken Follett* £3.99
☐	11810	9	**THE KEY TO REBECCA**	*Ken Follett* £3.99
☐	09121	9	**THE DAY OF THE JACKAL**	*Frederick Forsyth* £3.99
☐	11500	2	**THE DEVIL'S ALTERNATIVE**	*Frederick Forsyth* £4.99
☐	10050	1	**THE DOGS OF WAR**	*Frederick Forsyth* £3.99
☐	12569	5	**THE FOURTH PROTOCOL**	*Frederick Forsyth* £4.99
☐	13475	9	**THE NEGOTIATOR**	*Frederick Forsyth* £4.99
☐	12140	1	**NO COMEBACKS**	*Frederick Forsyth* £3.99
☐	09436	6	**THE ODESSA FILE**	*Frederick Forsyth* £3.99
☐	10244	X	**THE SHEPHERD**	*Frederick Forsyth* £2.99
☐	13654	4	**BLOWBACK**	*Denis Kilcommons* £3.99
☐	13477	5	**SERPENT'S TOOTH**	*Denis Kilcommons* £3.99
☐	12662	4	**GAIJIN**	*Marc Olden* £2.99
☐	12357	9	**GIRI**	*Marc Olden* £3.99
☐	12800	7	**ONI**	*Marc Olden* £3.50
☐	13214	4	**TE**	*Marc Olden* £3.99

*All Corgi/Bantam Books are available at your bookshop or newsagent, or can be ordered from the
following address:*

Corgi/Bantam Books,
Cash Sales Department,
P.O. Box 11, Falmouth, Cornwall TR10 9EN

UK and B.F.P.O. customers please send a cheque or postal order (no currency) and allow £1.00
for postage and packing for the first book plus 50p for the second book and 30p for each
additional book to a maximum charge of £3.00 (7 books plus).

Overseas customers, including Eire, please allow £2.00 for postage and packing for the first book
plus £1.00 for the second book and 50p for each subsequent title ordered.

NAME (Block Letters) ....

ADDRESS ....

....